Unveiling Magic
School of Magic Survival 2

CHLOE GARNER

Cover design by Melody Simmons

Published by A Horse Called Alpha

ISBN: 9798510265934

CONTENTS

The New Normal

Valerie sucked on a tooth as she looked around the room.

Dr. Finn had painted a lot of it, the furniture, the walls, the ceiling, the floor, with a savannah theme, and a lot of the desks and chairs were upside down with thickets of grass and plants tied to the legs.

She had to give it to him, he was creative about it.

He was also standing behind her with a stopwatch.

That beeped on the minutes.

Man, oh, man how she hated that stopwatch.

She didn't know where the baton was hidden, or even what it would look like, precisely. It could have been painted brown and hidden in with some of the grass, or taped to the underside of a lab table.

Or he could have cast an invisibility spell on it and hung it from the ceiling, for all she knew.

Was invisibility possible?

The fact that Valerie didn't know it *was* possible didn't mean it wasn't.

She took a step forward, feeling out the tension of the magic in the room around her. She had come to understand that some magic users had a gift for figuring out casts by touch - by physical sensation of some kind - but Valerie was not that kind.

She wasn't going to know what the magic was that she was experiencing until she was well through a cast to dismantle it, or at least redirect it, and even then sometimes she didn't ever really work it out. She just got to the point that her magic and the magic there in the room kind of meshed or melded or whatever, and she could move on.

The stopwatch beeped.

"Could you just turn it off for once?" Valerie asked, though something in the room jangled in a way that warned her she shouldn't *keep* talking. There was magic in there tied up in sound.

She looked over her shoulder at Dr. Finn, who smiled broadly without showing his teeth. His ears shifted up when he did that, and it made her want to grab him by them.

The man wasn't that much older than she was. Most of the other teachers were from her mom's generation, but he was only twenty-three or twenty-four, she forgot, and she had no idea what business he had calling himself 'Doctor'.

Though.

That was how Lady Harrington had introduced him, and Valerie hadn't ever found grounds to argue it, other than that he had a baby face and it needed to be pinched, and a person with a doctorate should be serious and wear glasses.

He did wear glasses.

Valerie turned her attention back to the room, taking a bag off of her back and kneeling gingerly, taking out a blue powder that seemed about right and sprinkling it on the floor.

There.

Yup.

There where it turned into bright blue fire? She shouldn't go over there. She took out a piece of fish-smelling string and wrapped it around her hand once, then slapped the floor where the dust had enflamed, and there was a whistling like air coming out of a huge balloon. It only lasted a moment, but the jangling of the sound-triggered cast told her that she was still treading awfully close to the line, and she needed to get to that one quickly before she accidentally set it off.

The day she had spent without eyebrows had been the opposite of fun.

She moved forward, cast by cast, fighting off magic with magic, a bag of ingredients that Dr. Finn had seemed to have selected from out of Mr. Tannis' room at random.

Some days, the practicum room was a puzzle. If she was clever about it, there was a right way and a wrong way to go, and if she went the right way, it was relatively straightforward to find the baton. Some days, it was a death march, disabling one cast after another, searching every inch of the room before she tracked down the baton.

It was grueling and demeaning, but…

But.

She was doing magic.

She wasn't sitting in the library reading about it.

And as she continued to work at her progress, she had to secretly admit that she was having the time of her life.

Because she was actually *good* at this.

Yes.

The eyebrow thing.

And sometimes they'd put away dinner by the time she got down there, and she had to go eat the cold boxed dinner that Sasha had crated up for her.

And no one else had to do anything *remotely* like this. Valerie understood that the seniors had to go through a challenge course as a team, at the end of the year, but nothing so maniacal as what Dr. Finn would set up on a thrice-a-week basis for her to work through.

He was a natural.

Lady Harrington had hired him over the winter break, and he'd shown up at her last class of the day, the first day of second semester and informed her that she had a special elective.

None of the teachers trusted her with magic implements, yet, outside of Mrs. Reynolds and Mr. Tannis, so the fact that he put a bag into her hands and told her to go nuts? She'd loved it.

And she still *did*.

It was just so *meticulous*, and at the same time, it wasn't like she was working off of knowledge that actually lived in her *head*. It was like she was using someone else's knowledge that poured through a hole in her brain like sand through an hourglass. Just a trickle at a time, and barely enough to do the next thing.

Dr. Finn had told her frequently that as she practiced, it would get easier and she would be able to work faster, but it didn't feel that way.

It felt like she was crawling on the floor through a dusting of blue powder, trying not to put her head up high enough to get her hair scorched off by the random shots of flame emanating from… over there, somewhere.

She'd get to it as soon as she could, but there was something up here ahead of her that was going to melt her shoes to the floor if she wasn't careful, and it really didn't matter that Lady Harrington had set her up with an account that was linked to her mother's account, Valerie didn't feel like buying new shoes.

Again.

Six weeks into the second semester, and the damage from Mr. Finn's practicum was taking a toll on everything about her.

She was gonna get better.

Yeah, right.

They were just dragging her down the path to learn what she had to by encouraging her that someday it wouldn't be this hard.

Everyone just practiced and learned.

Every time Valerie put her hands on magic, something blew up.

At least this way, it was Dr. Finn's fault.

She took the lighter out of the bag and lit the cord of grass tied to a desk leg, feeling something unstable nearby that she needed to address soon, but she was hoping it would be so simple as to find the baton the first place she looked.

The room did *not* have adequate fire suppression, so a rather large wad of dry burning grass did nothing but make the top half of the room smoky.

There was no baton, but there was a new problem.

The smoke had interacted with several of the spells and had put one of them onto a timer that Valerie could feel ticking down. Whatever it was that it was designed to do, she had maybe a couple of minutes to find it and shut it down.

She checked the desk leg once more, just to be sure the baton wasn't there.

It wasn't.

There was a sound of something large and mechanical sort of... *crunching*... just out of sight behind a cabinet. She needed to go see what that was, too, but the floor had... invisible strings tying it to the ceiling that she had to make it through first.

No telling what it *actually* was, but that was how it felt to her.

She went digging through her bag once more.

The stopwatch beeped.

Valerie was halfway through mauling her dinner when someone knocked on the door.

Valerie frowned at Sasha, and her roommate got up to answer it, stepping out of the way to reveal Ethan Trent.

Things had been cool between them ever since Valerie's birthday party. He'd admitted he'd been spying on her for his dad, and she'd thought that she could forgive him for it, but then her lifelong best friend had *also* been spying on her, and a whole bunch of *other* people had turned up to try to kill her and her mom - who had *also, also* been lying to her about everything - and Valerie was just fed up with it.

She got the sense that Ethan got it, even though he still looked over every time she walked into a room.

She'd liked him.

A lot.

But she'd loved Hanson, and, well, *her mom*, so that didn't help much.

"Mrs. Young asked me to come get you," Ethan said, and Valerie looked down at her dinner.

"I'm busy," she said.

Mrs. Young was the receptionist in the front office, and not someone that Valerie held in high esteem, though the woman did think the world of Sasha.

"Can Sasha go?" Valerie asked as the thought flashed through her head.

"You need to come," Ethan said. "Really."

Valerie grumped down at her dinner, then stood up and put her shoes on, walking out the dorm room door and into the hallway still carrying her food.

He glanced at it, but didn't say anything.

"How was your session with Dr. Finn today?" Ethan asked.

"You keeping track of which days I'm up there?" Valerie pushed back.

"No. But we all heard the explosion and no teachers went running by, so it had to be you."

That was valid, actually.

"It was fine," Valerie said.

She'd found the baton, so yay for her, but she was going to need a new pair of jeans, since the ones she'd been wearing were now lime green.

The man had the *worst* sense of humor.

They walked toward the office, and Ethan glanced over at her several times like he had something he wanted to say, but Valerie didn't want to hear it, and she never gave him the window to talk to her.

Finally, as they approached the door, he turned his back toward the office and put his hands out to her as though to physically stop her.

She didn't quite walk into them, and she didn't quite walk *around* him, but she considered both.

"Look," he said. "I know I messed up. I'm a jerk and I've always been a jerk, and then I really liked *not* being a jerk because of how it made you look at me, and I should have told you a lot earlier…"

"You think everything is about you," Valerie interrupted. He didn't, actually. He'd mostly been nice to her when no one else would have. But it was an insult that would land, and she knew it. "I'm just done with trusting *anyone*. Everyone lies to me, and, you know?, in the middle of that you aren't someone I can count on, either, so… I don't want your apology. It isn't about you. I'm just retrenching back with the people I can *actually* trust."

"You mean Sasha," Ethan said. She shrugged.

There was Mr. Jamison, too, but she wasn't going to point it out, because it didn't matter. The outside war between factions of magic users had taken another big turn with two mass civilian casualty events, and Mr. Jamison was basically working full-time for the war effort and *then* teaching classes. Valerie hadn't seen him but once since the break.

"Not my fault that *everyone* lies to me," she said.

"Okay," he said quickly. "You just… You need other friends. Sasha is great, but you *need* other friends in the community. You're out on your own, and I don't think you see it."

"So I *need* you," Valerie said, pursing her lips hard. He sighed.

"I didn't mean it that way," he said. "Look. I... I wanted to warn you before you walk in there. I mean, I *want* to talk to you, and I never get to, but I really wanted to warn you..."

Valerie dipped her chin toward her chest.

"Yes?"

"It's Hanson."

She squinted at him.

"It's what?" she asked, bolting around him and into the office.

Yes.

Yes, indeed.

There sitting on one of the couches, all six-foot-two and two hundred pounds of him, was her ex-best-friend-in-the-world, Hanson Cox.

"Hi, Val," he said meekly, and she shook her head.

"What on earth are you doing here?" she asked.

"Mr. Cox is here seeking asylum," Lady Harrington said, coming out of her office. "And I've just received my confirmation from the Council that we're going to give it to him."

"Why?" Valerie demanded. "He doesn't know any magic. He's got a mom out there and a dad. Isn't it *their* job to take care of him?"

"I went home and no one was there," Hanson said. "I've been staying with friends at school for months, and the police are looking for them, now, but... Something happened to them, and it was because I came here that weekend. I'm worried."

"I'm afraid that I have to tell you, young man," Lady Harrington said. "The Council knows exactly where your parents are. Your mother was called up into work while you were here, and she was forced to leave without notice. They thought that your father would come home to care for you, but his situation got more complicated, too, and there was no one to reach out to you without endangering you further. It was safest for everyone if you remained a civilian, by perception, if an orphaned one."

Hanson licked his lips.

"They're alive, though?" he asked. Lady Harrington nodded.

"Yes, and your mother sends her regrets."

Valerie wondered what, exactly Martha Cox *had* said, because certainly 'regrets' didn't cover it.

For a moment, Valerie wanted to sit down next to Hanson and hug him; the *wretched* few months he had to have gone through, thinking that his parents were likely dead... Dealing with police and the school...

"What have you told your informal guardians about where you are now?" Lady Harrington asked.

"That I had some family up north that I could find, if I just went," Hanson said. "They didn't like it, but they let me go."

"You should contact them and let them know that you arrived safely," Lady Harrington said. "You can use the phone in my office."

Hanson glanced over at Valerie and swallowed hard, again words that he wanted to say, but she shook her head.

She didn't want to hear them.

She looked at Ethan as Hanson followed Lady Harrington to her office. Ethan was standing against the door, whether because it had simply been convenient or because he was intentionally blocking her exit, she wasn't sure.

"I don't know why I'm here," Valerie said.

"I thought you two were friends," Mrs. Young said from her desk. "He was your only visitor."

Not technically true, but whatever.

"I don't want to see him," Valerie said.

"Would have thought you'd be more sympathetic," Mrs. Young said. "Seeing as you're his only friend in the world, and it's just the way it was when you first got here."

Hanson was massively popular. Girls didn't generally want to *date* him, because he wasn't *sexy*, the way the guys the girls were chasing after were, but he was friends with *everyone*.

The idea of him being along in the world was laughable.

And then tragic.

Ethan jerked his head toward the hallway and opened the door. Valerie went out, considering for just a moment the option of just going straight back to her room, but she waited for Ethan while he closed the door.

He opened his mouth and closed it once. Frowned.

"What's going on with you?" he asked.

"Hanson's mom had him spying on me for my entire life," Valerie said. "And I found out the weekend he came here."

Ethan paused, nodding slowly.

"I get that you're mad at him," he said.

"No," she answered. "You don't."

"I do," he said. "Every single one of the kids that I sit with every single day at lunch is telling their parents everything that we talk about, everything that we do, who sits with who, who talks to who and about what… Shack might be my best friend. I think he is. And our parents work together. They're on the same side, not just of the war, but of the politics, too, but I *know* that he goes home and tells his mom everything that I say, and I know that he sends her a letter twice a month with the potential political alliances within the Council brats. Maybe it won't be this way forever, I don't know. But the first year, as everyone is figuring it out, especially *us*, when there are so many of us who are going to be headed for power after graduation? Everyone spies on everyone, and nothing is secret. That's my whole life. So maybe I don't get why you're *angry*, but I get where you are."

"How can you stand it?" Valerie asked. "Not having any friends?"

"I've never had any friends," Ethan said. "Just friendly political acquaintances. You're spoiled, having had real friends out there in the real world. Sasha's brothers, too. They aren't interested in power; they're just going to school for the education and then they're going to head off and do something lucrative and interesting. They've got great friends, I hear. But I don't get friends. I had one for like a minute, but between me and my life, it died pretty fast."

She looked away.

"I said I would keep your secrets," Ethan said. "So where everyone on the Council *knows* that your mom was here, my dad didn't hear it from me. I'll tell him that Hanson is here, but I'm not going to tell him why you two aren't friends. I'm going to keep my promise to you. He can't even *tell* his mom stuff, now, because they aren't going to tell him where she is…"

"Do you know?" Valerie asked abruptly, and he shook his head.

"I just know the kinds of jobs that people get called up for on that kind of warning," he told her.

Valerie shook her head.

"I... I don't even know who he is," she said.

"I bet you do," Ethan answered. "I'd give quite a lot for a real friend. Especially in the middle of everything now."

She considered, then nodded, sighing.

"I hear you. And I miss him. But I *busted* him. He didn't even *tell* me. He was going to go home and..." She shrugged. "Tell her everything."

"How did you find out?" Ethan asked.

"Mr. Benson recognized his mom. His dad, actually."

Ethan frowned.

"Then why did they call her up? Having an insider on you is about as valuable as anything else. You think she's a fighter?"

Valerie shrugged.

"I don't know. I don't know her, either, apparently."

Ethan sighed and nodded.

"Everyone wants to know how to get a line on you," he said. "If you're as good as everyone seems to think... and I'm not saying *I* don't think you are, just..." Valerie nodded, releasing him to keep on. "Anyway, if you're that good, everyone is going to want you on their side."

"I messed up Dr. Finn's practicum tonight," she said. "I got so many parts of it wrong..."

"No one else could *do* what you're doing," Ethan said. "That I do know. I know about how they train naturals, usually at an upperclass level because they're doing classwork with the rest of us for underclass, but... They've got you doing upperclass natural work and... If Lady Harrington thinks it's worth it, you're *good*. And everyone wants you to like them and trust them and align with them."

"Including you?" Valerie asked.

He shrugged.

"Either you trust me or you don't, Valerie," he said. "I can understand why you wouldn't. But I like you a lot and... You need friends. You need to know who you *do* trust, because eventually someone is going to get in close and you want to know whose advice you can trust."

"Everyone has an agenda for me," Valerie said.

"You're right," Ethan said. "Cost of being good. But you know what? Looks from here like that guy in there… He may be the one with the least agenda of all of us."

He pointed his thumb over at the office, and Valerie looked. Hanson was sitting in the chair again, his back to her.

She sighed.

"Why are you rooting for him?" she asked.

"Because he's a good guy and he deserves it," Ethan said. "And because I'm hoping if you can forgive him, maybe you can work your way up to forgiving me."

He gave her a little smile, playful, then ducked his head.

Valerie looked over at Hanson again.

"They'll keep him here?" she asked, and Ethan nodded.

"Sounds like."

"Then I've got some time," she said. "I'll think about it."

"Don't leave him too long, if you're going to forgive him. This place is brutal when you don't have friends."

"Allies," Valerie corrected, and Ethan shrugged.

"Same thing, when you get past the trust thing."

She nodded.

"Tell me about it."

Her class with Mrs. Reynolds wasn't until right before lunch, now, and Sasha was in it with her. Today, Valerie sat in the back in order to have a little more space to whisper and pass notes with Sasha - not that you *had* an awful lot of room in a class of twelve, nor with Mrs. Reynolds teaching it.

I really want to sit with him. Sasha's most recent note to her said. Valerie looked at it for a moment, then turned it over, raising her eyebrows to try to force herself to listen as Mrs. Reynolds looked at her.

They'd talked late into the night, the night before, but Sasha was still deeply torn in her sense of loyalty to Valerie versus her interest in seeing Hanson as soon as possible.

The girl was deeply smitten, and at any other point in Valerie's life, she would have been charmed by how fitting the match was.

It still felt like Hanson was a stranger, though.

She'd known him her entire life, yes, but if he'd been capable of *being* something that completely different than the person she'd thought she'd known, what else was it possible was true about him?

Anything.

Just about anything.

He was someone completely different from her best friend, and in *becoming* that different person, he'd eradicated the guy she'd always known.

Hanson was gone.

She'd grieved him for weeks without understanding that that's what it was until Christmas break, when she'd had the dorm to herself and a lot of time to think about things other than magic.

Like her parents.

And Hanson.

Then do it, Valerie finally wrote back when Mrs. Reynolds moved her attention on to someone else.

The woman knew.

Valerie knew it.

Mrs. Reynolds knew that Valerie knew.

And still.

Hanson Cox was *in the building*, and Valerie didn't feel like there was any way she was going to focus on a lecture. Not today. Not anyone's lecture.

I can't. Not if it's going to hurt your feelings.

Valerie looked over at her and gave her a dour look.

"I'm not that fragile," she whispered.

I know you wouldn't do it to hurt me. And it's possible he's still a really good guy. I just can't look at him.

Then maybe I shouldn't be hanging out with him, Sasha said.

He is hands down the best guy at this school, Valerie answered, tucking Sasha's reply under her text book and pulling her eyes wide at Mrs. Reynolds again.

Plants.

And stuff.

The difference between herbs and vegetables.

Strange that that would matter more in a magic class than her biology class had ever considered.

Mrs. Reynolds was a good teacher. Valerie's favorite. She was strict with her rules, but she loved her plants and she went out of her way to make sure that Valerie got a shot at understanding what was going on, rather than just assuming she would catch up if she was able.

Valerie usually put in her best effort for Mrs. Reynolds' class.

But.

Today.

Hanson.

This was the only place that he could think of to come to for safety.

Or.

Was he lying?

She'd thought about it a little, last night, that maybe his mom sent him here to spy on Valerie full time, like he had before, with hopes that getting him close where Valerie couldn't just avoid him would mean that the two of them would pick up where they left off.

It was ingenious, actually. A perfect cover, since his mom appeared to actually have been missing. Maybe she'd stayed just long enough to tell him how to make his asylum request, then vanished.

Either way.

Either way, Valerie had to either trust him or not.

Ethan was right about that.

She couldn't keep him out at arm's length and ignore it anymore.

If she trusted him, she had to *trust* him. Believe that he hadn't wanted to do it, that he'd gone along because that was just how it had always been, and that he wouldn't go back and do it again, if he said he wouldn't.

Had he said he wouldn't?

She'd been too preoccupied with sending him away to really pay attention to what he'd said, that weekend.

If he *did* say that he wouldn't…

It would be just like Ethan, and she hadn't forgiven or trusted him, either.

"Miss Blake, Miss Mills, would you stay after to talk to me for a minute?" Mrs. Reynolds asked.

There it was. Well and truly busted. Valerie sneaked a look at Sasha's final note as the bell rang - *It doesn't matter. I'm your friend first.* - then she tucked it into her book and put the book into her backpack, going to stand at the front of the classroom next to Sasha.

Sasha Mills was *not* used to being reprimanded by authority figures.

"I need to know what's going on with you two," Mrs. Reynolds said, sitting down behind her desk. "You're two of my best students, and it's not like you to fail to pay attention for an entire class, much less disrupt it."

Valerie glanced at Sasha, then turned forward again.

"My friend, Hanson, is back," she said. "His mom disappeared and he came to the school looking for someplace safe to stay until she comes back again."

"Is that...?" Mrs. Reynolds asked, then frowned. "I'd heard that we had someone show up last night, but I didn't get the details. I thought he was a civilian."

"He's a liar," Valerie answered. "Beyond that, I don't think there's a lot I can tell you about him."

"Oh," Mrs. Reynolds said slowly, then dropped her head. "*Oh.*"

Valerie tried not to interpret what Mrs. Reynolds thought she'd figured out. It didn't matter.

"She's upset," Sasha said quickly. "And Hanson and I... we were starting to be friends, when he was here before, and I don't know what to do, whether I should hang out with him or not..."

Sasha fell silent as she figured out that that was not the important part of the conversation just now.

"Do you know who his contact was?" Mrs. Reynolds asked.

"His mom," Valerie said. "After that, all I know is that she went here. Could be she went dark. No way of telling."

"Lady Harrington took him in?" Mrs. Reynolds asked, and Valerie shrugged.

"Hasn't kicked me out, yet, either."

The corner of Mrs. Reynolds' mouth went up and she closed her eyes.

"It's a *clue*, Valerie. Take it. Lady Harrington wouldn't take him without a reference."

Martha Cox had been called up by the Council. That was what they'd said, right?

It meant that she was likely *reporting* to the council, spying on Valerie as a route to spy on Susan.

Was it better if your friends were spying on you, rather than your enemies?

"Don't let it happen again," Mrs. Reynolds said. "I'm going to let it slide today, because I think that you aren't likely to have civilians turning up looking for magic protection again this semester, but don't let it become a habit."

Valerie nodded, grabbing Sasha's elbow as the girl failed to notice their cue to leave, and they walked down the hallway toward the cafeteria.

"Maybe I shouldn't sit with him," Sasha said. "I mean, he did lie to you, and he's been spying on you all this time. Maybe it's not that I'm worried about being a bad friend as that I'm worried that he's not the kind of guy I should want to be with at all, anyway."

Valerie looked over at her.

"You think too much," she told her friend. "No. I mean." She sighed. "I get it. Maybe you're right, even. Girls dating guys that they *know* are bad people is… I hate seeing it. I mean, you just want to grab them by the throat and shake them, sometimes. All the signs are there. He's going to cheat on her, he's going to hurt her, he's going to ignore her, whatever, and she just goes after him because… Whatever. You know? She just won't give up on him."

Sasha waited, then nodded.

"But…?"

Valerie smiled, licking her lips.

"Right, but. But, it isn't wrong for you to give him a chance to prove that that's not who he is. You aren't going to offend me by talking to him. Just… stay alert. If you get the faintest glimmer of an idea that he's just using you, bail. You know?"

"And *that* wouldn't be stupid?" Sasha asked. Valerie shrugged.

"Most dating is stupid, on its face. You don't do anything. I mean, it's not like we're actually going to *date*, since none of us can leave this place. You just kind of moon over each other for a while and make a point of paying exclusive attention to each other and then... I don't know, you get in a fight or you get over it, and you both move on. Most dating has no point at all other than to be fun. If you aren't having fun, if you aren't going where you want to go, get out. I'm not going to say a word about it. I want you to be happy. But don't worry about it being *stupid* until you're ignoring clear warning signs and people are telling you that you're making a mistake."

Sasha stopped walking and turned to face Valerie.

"So you don't think that going to sit with him at lunch would be a mistake?"

Valerie would have tipped her head back and laughed if Sasha had been even an iota less sincere in asking.

"It's a chair," Valerie said. "It's only a chair."

"But you *hate* him," Sasha said, setting off walking again. "How could I?"

Valerie stopped walking, turning her attention from Sasha to the floor for a moment, feeling through all of the years of play and talk and laughter...

"I feel betrayed," she finally said. "Like I never even knew him. I don't trust myself to see who he actually is, because I'm so... angry at losing what he was. Maybe I want to use you to get to know him, because you don't have any of that. Maybe you can prove that he really is what I thought he was, and it was a bad situation he couldn't get out of."

"You would trust me with that?" Sasha asked quietly.

Valerie paused, wondering if she really trusted Sasha's judgment with people that much, then she nodded.

"I do."

Sasha hugged her unexpectedly, and Valerie hugged her back, then lifted her head as she heard Hanson's voice over the background noise reaching them from out of the cafeteria.

"Oh, yeah? I'll take that bet, but I'll double it."

There was laughter, and the level of conversation went up.

Sasha looked at Valerie with alarm, and Valerie shook her head.

"Hanson comes from a family of yellers. That's his conversational voice."

"What's going on?" Sasha asked, and Valerie shrugged.

"Hanson seems to be doing just fine," she answered, continuing on toward the cafeteria.

Hanson was at the central table with the Council brats.

Ann, Patrick, and Milton seemed to be put out that he was permitted there, but Hanson and Shack were facing down over trays of food, still shouting at each other, and Ethan had his elbows on the table, watching with a wide grin.

"Eating contest?" Valerie asked, sitting down next to Ethan. He looked over at her with surprise and she shrugged. "I'm not staying. Just trying to make sure everyone survives the day."

He nodded.

"Eating contest."

She sighed.

"The cafeteria folk aren't going to know what hit them, if Shack is competitive at all."

"He do this often?" Ethan asked, and Valerie nodded.

"Have they talked stakes?" she asked.

"I think it's just bragging rights," Ethan said.

"No, Hanson always has something in mind for these," she said. "Even if it's just something he can trot out a bunch in the future."

"If I win, I want your dorm room," Hanson said.

Valerie glanced at Ethan.

"Who is Shack's roommate?" she asked.

"Me," Ethan said softly.

"Told you there'd be stakes," Valerie said.

"Fine, then if I win, you've gotta show up every morning to spot me for workouts," Shack answered. Hanson grinned.

"Done."

He gave Sasha a quick look and winked, then noticed Valerie and froze. She shook her head.

"Go beat him," she said. "We'll be awkward later."

He looked at her for one more breath, then flashed a grin and darted over to the food line with Shack.

"You think he's got this?" Ethan asked.

"I do," Valerie breathed, watching as Sasha neatly sat in the chair next to Hanson's.

Valerie had no intention of coming *back* here once she got her food, but she'd sit in front of an empty table to watch the contest before she left.

Didn't know who she'd sit with instead, actually, but she'd work that out later.

"You know what he's like to live with?" Ethan asked.

"He shouts in his sleep," Valerie answered, unable to contain the smile. They'd stopped having sleepovers when they hit puberty, but she'd heard the stories from away games, how he woke his roommates up in the middle of the night shouting about absurd, unexplainable things.

Get the duck! Get the duck! It went that way!

"Awesome," Ethan said.

Valerie looked at him seriously for a moment.

"You'd take care of him, right?" she asked.

"Why? Does he need it?" Ethan countered.

"The dorms have been attacked in the last three months," she said. "Having good strong wards up…"

He nodded.

"Of course."

"He doesn't deserve how they're going to treat him," Valerie said quietly, and Ethan looked around.

"Actually, he's got a lot of fans, just now," he said. "He's a fun guy, and… I don't know. He's not here for classes. He's just here for protection."

"You think that's it?" Valerie asked, and Ethan grinned.

"You want me to tell you that everyone is intimidated by your natural talent?" he asked.

"Not right now," she said. "But I want you to believe it."

He wove his fingers under his chin and nodded.

"Oh, I do."

She shook her head and watched as Hanson and Shack came back with their trays.

"Four minutes?" Hanson asked. Shack nodded, grinning wide. "Four minutes."

Valerie raised an eyebrow at Sasha, who returned a dour look.

No, this was not how she'd envisioned this going.

The two boys counted it down and started eating.

This part was rather unremarkable, and Valerie had seen it any number of times before, so she went to get her own lunch, instead, filling a tray as far as she cared to and then scanning the room for other plausible places to go.

She actually had the beginnings of relationships with a few of the girls, at this point. Something about saving them from demons had raised her credibility, though a number of them actively blamed her for the whole thing, which meant the various cliques all had at least one girl in them who hated Valerie.

She had to be clever about her choice, here.

The rest of the room was very engaged with the contest, and teachers had started coming in from the hallway to see what the unusual commotion was about - usually lunches were a well-discipline event at the School of Magic Survival - but no one interfered as Hanson and Shack devoured the food in front of them.

By some boy-code, they would both know who won, when it was over, though Valerie just saw two messy trays typically. She had about a minute left before it was all over and everyone would go back to their original conversations.

There.

Rebecca and Ginger. They didn't mind her. She went to sit down next to Rebecca, glancing once over her shoulder again as Hanson put his arms in the air and Shack threw himself back from the table. It had been close. When Hanson destroyed someone, he didn't celebrate that much.

"Oh, my gosh, I'll never understand," Rebecca was saying.

"Gross," Ginger agreed without turning away.

"Who is he, anyway?" Rebecca asked.

"He's actually a friend of mine from back home," Valerie said. "He's staying here for protection, because his parents are both busy."

"Thought your back home was all civilian," Rebecca said, and Valerie shrugged.

"There was one magic-using family there," she said, jerking her head toward Hanson. "Anyway, have you guys looked at the essay that we're doing for Mr. Hardy?"

She successfully turned the conversation, mostly listening as Rebecca and Ginger went on from there. She looked back once as Hanson and Shack were talking and finishing their meals, and she caught Ethan watching her. He looked pointedly at the empty chair next to him, and she shook her head, laughing with Rebecca at something Ginger had said.

She hadn't forgiven them. Not either of them.

But maybe she'd taken the first step.

That was something only time could tell.

Sasha was on cloud nine that night as she came in from walking with Hanson. Valerie was working on her essay and had a book on rock properties that she'd borrowed from the library and was attempting to memorize. Her library privileges were hard-won and deeply appreciated.

"So?" Valerie asked without looking over.

"He's been through so much, Val," Sasha said, throwing herself onto her bed and putting her arms under her head.

Only Hanson called her Val. And her mom.

"I imagine he has," Valerie said. "I actually believe his mom left."

"Don't be like that," Sasha said. "Please? If he's a stranger, can he just be a stranger?"

"Nope," Valerie said, turning the page in her book and writing down another list of things she needed to know from the section headings.

It was a well-organized book. Kept everything in lists, rather than wandering down roads of history and cross-related stuff.

"He wasn't sure he could even get back here," Sasha said. "He stayed in the city for all this time because he thought he was completely friendless."

"Hanson is never friendless," Valerie answered, then put down her pen and spun in her chair slowly to look at Sasha. The look in the girl's eyes was nothing short of dreamy.

Valerie couldn't help but smile.

"He knew you were going to be angry when he got back. He still wants to be your friend, though."

Of course he did.

He hadn't lost anything from their relationship, and he might still be able to cash in on it. That proximity to her.

Everyone wanted to use her to get to her mom, and then her mom had seemed to think that Valerie had value unto herself.

What, Valerie couldn't begin to imagine, but... The fact that *everyone* who had wanted to get to be friends with her seemed to have an ulterior motive at this point seemed to support it.

Except Sasha.

Valerie narrowed her eyes at the girl - not for the first time - wondering if it wasn't possible that Sasha was just the most clever and deceptive of them all, but Sasha just stared at the ceiling with a dopey smile.

There was simply nothing deceptive about her.

"I didn't ever want to see him again," Valerie said, and Sasha looked over at her, concerned. Valerie shrugged. "I can't believe he would do that to me. And his mom. For all those years, the two of them, lying to me every time they even *spoke* to me."

"He couldn't have lied about everything," Sasha said. "You were friends for forever. You had to have known almost everything about him."

"Apparently not," Valerie said.

"He's moved in with Ethan, now," Sasha said.

"They actually let him?" Valerie asked. "I wasn't sure if they would.

"Apparently Franky Frank is a lot different from Mrs. Gold," Sasha told her. "As long as no one is *immediately* in danger of dying, he doesn't care what they do."

Valerie raised her eyebrows and Sasha nodded.

"Shack is talking about building a third bunk in there and all three of them cramming in."

"Oh, the smell," Valerie said. "Ethan's going to end up having to move out, just to survive."

Sasha smiled, covering her face with her hands.

"I'm so happy," she said.

There was no way the girl was going to keep her guard up against Hanson. He really was that nice a guy, at least the way he put it on.

Valerie missed the idea of him, and there was a deep-gut pang of grief.

"We talked about everything," Sasha went on. "He's going to teach me about sports, and I'm going to teach him magic…"

"Hold up," Valerie said. "He doesn't know any magic. I thought that was the point. It kept him safe."

"Maybe from demons," Sasha answered. "But if his parents are connected to the Council - and it really does sound like they are, to me - then I think that he's got as much to fear from the Superiors as the rest of us do."

Valerie frowned, considering this.

She'd been genuinely concerned about him, there for a moment. That was instructive, though she was too ill-feeling to figure out why or how.

She'd *just* been settling in, when he'd turned up and blown it all up, and she was *just* getting used to what her life was *again*, when he turned up once more and blew it all up. And suddenly Sasha was madly in love and Ethan was the one being reasonable.

What.

Just.

What?

"Do you think I shouldn't?" Sasha asked, pressing Valerie after a moment's pause.

"No," Valerie answered. "That's not it. You know better than I do. It's just… he's still a civilian, in my head. The idea of him being a magic user…"

Sasha rolled onto her side and frowned.

"He may have known what magic *was*, and you didn't, but he's basically no better off than you were when you first got here, and he doesn't have the advantages of being a natural, the way you do. He's going to be so far behind, and I doubt he works as hard as you have to catch up because… Well, I've never *known* someone who works as hard at school as me, other than you."

Valerie nodded.

"He's really smart," she said.

"I know," Sasha gushed.

Valerie tipped her head back, groaning a laugh.

"You're *awful*," she said. "I wasn't this bad, was I?"

"When?" Sasha asked, sitting up.

"With Ethan," Valerie said.

"You were in love with Ethan?" Sasha asked.

Valerie jerked mentally to a halt and stared at Sasha.

"You're in love with Hanson?" she countered.

"What?" Sasha asked. "Yes. Maybe. I don't know. I… Were you in love with Ethan?"

Valerie shook her head.

"No." It was more tart than she'd *absolutely* meant it to be, but it was exactly right all the same. "Not even close. I just really liked him, and he kissed me the one time and…"

"He *kissed* you and you didn't tell me?" Sasha asked.

Had that gotten past her?

"I thought I did," Valerie said. "Maybe *you* forgot."

"Would I forget?" Sasha asked.

"I don't know. My mom turned up and we locked everyone in their rooms and then there were dead people upstairs. I barely remember anything from that night."

Sasha frowned, then nodded slowly.

"You make a good point."

"Of course I do," Valerie said. "Now you need to slow this train down and think about it. You're talking about the guy who pretended to be my best friend my *entire* life and then turned out to have been a spy. I get that you like him and you probably trust him completely and whatever, but you *can't* go falling in love with him in two days."

"Well," Sasha said slowly, then flipped onto her back and grinned at the ceiling again. "He makes me so happy."

Valerie shook her head and spun back to her book, unhurried.

She wanted to warn Sasha not to let him break her heart the way he'd done to Valerie, but... Way, way, *way* down, underneath how badly she wanted to never see him again, she trusted and believed that what he'd done was something that had rooted from his mom - not him - and that he would never hurt her friend intentionally.

Glancing back at Sasha once more, she stood, going to get her shower kit and her towel. Sasha took almost no note of her as she left, going past the bathroom at the end of the hallway and up the stairs to the boys' rooms. Before ten, she was allowed to be *in* the hallway, but not in the rooms.

She knocked on Ethan's door, and Shack answered.

"Oh," he said. "Valerie." He paused. "Um. Who are you here to see?"

"Hanson," she said. He looked at the towel over her shoulder, and she raised an eyebrow.

"I could hardly come up here and threaten him if Sasha knew that was what I was about to do, now can I?"

Shack frowned, humored, and turned. Hanson was already coming to the door. Ethan peeked around the corner, curious, but gave her half a smile and retreated back around the wall again.

"Hey, Val," Hanson said, starting to pull the door closed behind him. Valerie stuck her foot out so that it couldn't pivot, and she lifted her chin.

"We can be friends again," she said. "You, me, *all* of us. But on one condition."

"Anything," Hanson said.

"You hurt her, I will break with *all* of you so hard and you will never see me or hear from me again. Is that clear? You tell me now if you don't mean it, if it doesn't mean to you what it does to her, and I'll break it to her gently and you can still try to earn forgiveness. But if you let it go on and you hurt her? I will make sure I never lay eye on *any one* of you again."

"Hey," Shack called. "How did I get caught up in this?"

"You were here," Valerie answered, without taking her eyes off Hanson.

"Fair enough," Shack grumped cheerfully enough.

"I can't promise that," Hanson said quietly. "I…" He swallowed. "She's so sweet, Val."

"She is," Valerie answered.

"I can't promise that it's going to end well. You know that."

She nodded.

That voice. So familiar to her.

"I know. I'm not asking you to marry her. If it ends and she's sad, that's fine. If you two end up not working, that's fine. But you lie to her, you cheat on her, you abandon her? If you *do* something to hurt her, now, in the past, or in the future… I mean it. I can deal with it, for me, but I *won't* deal with it for her. You understand?"

He looked her in the eye, his expression level, sincere.

She would have called it entirely transparent, except for everything.

"Yes."

She nodded, then tipped onto one foot for a moment to look around him.

"You two have any suspicion he's lying to me, speak now or forever hold your peace," she said.

"Would you take candy-covered unicorn boy *with* you?" Ethan called. "Please? He's getting a bit disgusting for our taste."

Hanson looked off to the side, and Valerie tried to smother a smile.

"I'm going to the library after my shower," she said. "If you need an escape destination, you're welcome to join me."

Shack lunged for a desk, shoving books into a backpack.

"Sold," he announced, then straightened, grinning. "Don't know the half of it, I'm sure, but they deserve another chance. You're too awesome to just let it go like that."

"You're too good for these guys," Valerie answered, then reached up to touch Hanson's face. It was strange, for her, but it felt right, and he crushed her in a hug.

"I missed you," he said.

"I missed you," she answered. "And it isn't all fixed. I still don't feel like I *know* you."

"I know," he said. "I wanted to tell you... I don't even remember how long I've wanted to tell you. I just... Would you have even believed me?"

She paused at this, as he let her go, then she shook her head.

"No. But you should have, anyway. At least when you came here, and you *knew* that I knew."

He nodded.

"I know. It was deciding between you and my mom..."

She frowned hard. She'd never thought of it like that.

"I have big problems with your mom, now," she said, and he nodded.

"You and me both."

That was a gut-punch. He and his mom had been so close...

She shook her head.

"I'm going to go shower and then study. We'll talk."

"All I could ask for," Hanson said. "I really do like her."

"Fair warning," Valerie said. "She's thinking that she might be in love with you."

He pressed his lips, just a flicker of a motion, and something about the way his hairline eased... and the way the guys in the room held their breaths...

"Oh, for crying out loud," Valerie said loudly. "You do, too."

He looked to the side without turning his head, and Valerie shook her head.

"I wash my hands of both of you. I have rocks to study."

"Rocks!" Ethan called from inside the room, and Valerie grinned.

"I'll be at the library in fifteen minutes," she called back.

"See you there."

Her hair was wet when she dropped her stuff back off in the room.

Before very long at all, Sasha was going to find out that she'd made up with Hanson and Ethan, but it wasn't going to be right now.

"I'm going to the library," she said. "Been sitting here too long."

"Should go for a walk," Sasha told her. "It's beautiful outside."

"It's *dark* outside," Valerie answered, smiling. "You want to get something to eat after that?"

The cafeteria put out desserts after nine on Thursdays, if you were one of the first ones to get there.

"I'll be there when they put them out," Sasha said. "Get two."

Valerie smiled.

"Thanks."

Valerie took her stuff and walked to the library, finding Ethan at one table and Shack at another. Ethan had tactically spread all of his books out across the table to fill up the whole space; he stood, without looking up, and picked up one of them to reference something, then frowned and picked up another, flipping pages through it as he sat again, clearing the spot across from him.

"Slick," Valerie said, sitting down.

"Means so much, coming from you," he answered without looking up. She wasn't sure what to make of it, then the corner of his mouth came up and he turned.

And there.

Just like the first time.

Without her permission or agreement.

There.

That quease in her stomach and the way her toes felt hot.

That was why she'd liked him from the beginning.

Yes, she could *see* it now. The bad boy in there, defying authority and disengaging from the things that adults told him were important.

But.

There was also an earnestness to it, an *interest* in it, that look.

She licked her lips and looked away, getting her rock book out of her backpack while she waited for the goosebumps on her arms to pass.

He was still watching her when she sat up again, though without quite the same intensity.

"Am I forgiven, too, then?" he asked, and she looked up to meet his eyes once more.

27

Drew a breath.

That caught.

She laughed, unable to meet him with seriousness.

Leaned over the table so that Shack was at least *unlikely* to hear.

"You know that kiss was too good for me to just completely walk away," she breathed, and he grinned.

"Right?"

She sat back against her chair again, then pulled her feet up onto the next chair over, situating her book on her knees and her paper on the desk next to her.

"And now, I actually *am* going to study rocks," she said. "Unbelievable."

"And things can go back to normal," Ethan answered.

Valerie flicked a glance at him.

"Normal?" she asked. "What's normal? I'm still at a school studying *magic*, my mom is still off being a special forces ninja assassin, and someone let in a bunch of demons to try to kill me."

She paused.

Paused *hard*, in point of fact.

"Someone *let in* a bunch of demons to try to kill me," she said after a moment.

"You don't know that they were here *specifically* for you," Ethan said, then dipped his chin. "Do you?"

She swallowed.

She *wanted* to trust him.

Wanted to trust *someone* that completely.

She hadn't even tried to explain it to Sasha - not really.

"I think they were," she said after a moment, not quite there yet.

They'd left when her father had turned up and rescued her. Gotten her *out* of there. It meant they were after her.

She *knew* that.

But how could she convince him without mentioning her father?

"I hope they weren't," he answered. "They could have just been here to cause trouble, or they could have been here for anyone else… I mean, they *killed* Yasmine. Maybe that was why they were here. Something about her dad and the Council."

Valerie shook her head.

"Either way, someone *let them in*. Mrs. Gold told me when I got here that the defenses here had stood for a hundred years, and yet they've broken down *twice* since I've been here."

"Twice?" Ethan asked.

Shoot.

That had been a secret, too.

She was exploding with all of these secrets and just bumping into her threatened to reveal them.

She leaned out across the table again.

"Are you willing to risk violating curfew?" she asked.

He checked his watch.

On a school night, they were supposed to be in the building by ten and in their rooms by midnight. Mrs. Gold had some nefarious way of checking on the beds, but not on whether or not they were in the building.

"What's up?" he asked. She stood and he went over to hit Shack in the shoulder with the back of his hand.

"Cover for us," he said, and Shack shrugged without looking up.

"No worries."

Ethan nodded and started for the library doors.

Just like that, he'd walk out with her, no context needed.

Was she too untrusting, or was it just his disregard for the rules, anyway?

Probably the second one.

She followed, going to the front doors of the school and out into the darkening night.

It was a bit overcast, this night, and the lawn was crispy underfoot. There was a sharp, cold breeze, and Valerie wished for a moment that she'd gone back to get her coat. Her wet hair was going to be the death of her.

"Warmer down in the trees," Ethan said, reaching over and taking her hand. He spoke a few words and his skin went warm against hers. She tucked her arm in underneath his and let her head down onto his shoulder.

Just so easy.

Just like that.

They walked quickly down to the tree line, then Valerie tucked in against one of the big oaks, sitting down in the remaining leaf litter while Ethan kicked a gap in the leaves in front of her and put his hands down over the bare ground.

More words, and a soft blue flame came up from the ground, billowing larger as he worked on it, and putting off a powerful heat. It wasn't *hot*, it just drove away the cold like it hadn't been there.

"I can't do that," Valerie said after a moment. "I don't know how."

"Funny thing is, I bet you *would* know how, if it was that or freeze to death," Ethan said, coming to sit next to her. "Hoping the blue is dim enough that they can't see it from school."

She nodded, settling.

"So," she said softly. "There's so much."

"So much what?" he asked.

"I don't know who to trust," she said. "I'm certain that someone put the cast in the hall by the girls' dorms because they were letting in the demons, and I'm certain that they did it so that the demons could come and kill me. I just don't know who did it, and why, specifically. And if I don't know why, I don't know... I don't know why they *wouldn't* try again."

"Are you afraid?" he asked, and she shifted to sit nearer to him.

She wasn't afraid, but it was just so... She wanted an ally, and she wanted that ally to be *him*.

"No," she said. "Not for me. Maybe I should be, but I'm not. I'm afraid for everyone else."

"How are you so certain?" Ethan asked. "Did someone say something to you?"

She watched the blue flame dance.

"You promised to keep my secrets," she said. "That you won't tell your dad or anyone."

"I did," he answered.

"My dad told me," she said. "Actually, he told me that when he got me out of there, they would leave, because I was the one that they came for."

"Your dad was at the school that night?" Ethan asked, twisting to look at her. She sat up and nodded, knowing that he could only just see her in the dim light of the magic fire.

"Yeah."

"And no one saw him?" Ethan asked.

"He kind of has this thing with *time* and stuff," Valerie said. "He never really explained it, so I didn't understand it."

"When did you leave?" Ethan asked. Valerie shifted to sit back against the tree, now her arms low across her chest.

"That night," she said. "We left and he drove… all night, more or less, I think… I slept most of it. And then we were at this house and… He told me a lot of things that I haven't figured out yet, who I believe. Mostly him, actually, which is… weird. But his story makes a lot more sense."

"*When?*" Ethan asked. "I talked to you that *morning.*"

"I know," Valerie said. "And I remember that. I don't really remember what we talked about, because I was dazed from the fight, but I do remember that you were there and that I was really *glad* you were there, because you felt safe."

"I'm confused again," Ethan said.

"I know, imagine how I feel," Valerie answered.

She couldn't see his face well at all, but she didn't need to to imagine his expression.

It would have been her expression, as well, hearing this story.

"You just said…" he started, and she nodded.

"That I was far, far away at a house. Yes. And I was here with you at breakfast. Both of those."

"That's not possible," Ethan said.

"I really wish I could agree with you, because then all of this would make a lot more sense."

"Valerie, you need to talk to someone about this."

"I did," she told him. "Mr. Jamison. He knew that my dad was there, too, because he found the magic my dad used to lock my dorm room door closed to keep the girls in there safe while we left."

"*You* held the door closed," he said. "Sasha *saw* you."

"I know," Valerie said. "And *I remember.* They warned me that it would be weird, but it really wasn't enough to prepare me for it.

31

I *think* I was actually in both places, and I have no idea how. I really don't."

"You *told* Mr. Jamison, and… he didn't think that was weird?" Ethan asked.

"No," Valerie said. "He knew that my dad could do that, and he also knew it was going to suck. And it did. I'm just… I'm not saying I'm *over* it or that I've recovered or figured it out or anything… Just that I manage not to think about it very often any more, and that's working for me."

"You really think that your dad was *here*," Ethan said.

"I do."

"And he took you away for a day."

"For two weeks," Valerie said. "He taught me to fight and he taught me to do magic and… It was good, actually. Training with someone who *got* me."

"Two *weeks?*" Ethan demanded.

She nodded, just watching the fire. The specter of those memories was unsettling, even this far out.

"Two weeks."

"With *your dad?*"

"Yup."

"Who's supposed to be *dead?*"

"He went quiet. No one ever confirmed he was dead," Valerie said. "My mom didn't seem that surprised, when I mentioned him."

"Valerie," Ethan said quietly. "I made a promise and I'm going to keep it, but you need to *tell* someone that."

"I did," Valerie said again. "Mr. Jamison…"

"I mean someone who *knows* things," Ethan cut in, not rudely. "I… Look, I'm sorry. I didn't… Not until kind of later… I knew your dad wasn't dead. The Council has picked up evidence of it a few times, and… He went quiet because he came from a Superior family. His parents hated civilians, and his *sister* is a *fanatic.* She's really, really high in the ranks on the Superior side. He was with the Council for a while, but then he switched *back.* He's one of them."

Valerie's kneejerk reaction was to argue with him, but she let the words settle, considering them.

"You know it's true," Ethan said after a moment.

"No. I don't," Valerie answered. "I just also know I've been wrong a few times lately, haven't I?"

He fell silent, now, giving her time to think.

She wasn't going to tell him about Gemma. That wasn't her secret to tell.

But none of it rang true. Not really. Her mom hadn't been worried about her being with her dad, nor had Mr. Jamison. Just the Council, and their contact with him had been through a handler who was a double-agent.

Of *course* the man would tell them that Grant Blake was a traitor, and that was why he'd gone quiet.

"No," she finally said. "His story makes more sense than yours."

"He *did* come from a Superior family," Ethan said. "Did you know that? Did he tell you?"

"No," Valerie said, though it would have explained how deeply Lady Harrington disapproved of him. The woman was a purist unto herself.

"And that doesn't bother you?" Ethan asked.

"No," Valerie said again. "It doesn't. It doesn't *matter*. I told my *mom* that I spent time with him, and she never even blinked."

"Did she know he was *alive*?" Ethan asked.

"I don't know," Valerie said.

"Maybe it was shock," Ethan said. "And hope. She bailed on the magic world a *long* time ago. The Council only figured out what happened to your dad maybe ten years ago. A long time after she took you and disappeared. Maybe she had no idea what happened, and she just assumed he was still... You know, *good*."

"Mr. Jamison found his magic on the door, right where I saw him put it," Valerie said.

"Maybe he was the one who let the demons *in*," Ethan said. "So he could come in and rescue you from them."

Had Mr. Jamison been *specific* about the door being where he'd found the magic? Valerie couldn't remember. She *thought* that's what he'd said...

"There are spies on the Council," Valerie said. "People who are taking information back to the Superiors. Though... My dad

said that our understanding of how their politics work is really…
bad."

"Oh?" Ethan asked. "He talked about them?"

"A lot," Valerie said.

"He's *one* of them," Ethan said, exasperated.

"He isn't," Valerie answered, more certain as she thought more
about it. "But they aren't *fighting* so that they can kill people. They're
trying to take away people's magic so that only *they* get to be magic,
and that process keeps killing people by accident."

Ethan was silent for a long moment.

"That actually explains some things I've wondered about my
whole life," he said slowly.

"But it's a *secret*," Valerie said. "If you tell anyone that, they're
going to know that someone from their side is talking to our side
and they'll figure out who and…"

"I get it," Ethan said after a moment. "It's the same way my
dad is with secrets on the Council. They have people working for
them getting that kind of information, too, you know."

Valerie nodded, skeptical, but willing to be supportive if it
helped him give her more benefit of the doubt.

"I'm risking peoples' lives, telling you any of this," Valerie said.
"If they find out my dad is alive, some things are going to… They're
going to figure out some stuff that's going to get good people killed.
He told me that very specifically."

"Or he could want you to keep his contact with you secret so
that he can work on turning you," Ethan countered, simply being
faithful to his opening perspective. He wasn't as passionate as he
had been at first.

"Or that," she allowed.

"Wow," he said after a moment.

"Yeah. It's been killing me, not having anyone know."

"I bet. You remember being in two different places at the same
time?"

"The memories came to me after I got back, but it was like I
never left. I could remember everything that happened, during that
time, and *still* remember everything that happened with my dad. It
was awful."

He put his arm out, and she shifted to lean against him again.

"That's not all, though," she said after a minute.

"How could that *not* be all?" he asked.

"The night that you... The night that my mom came."

"The night of your birthday party," Ethan said, and she nodded.

"There were people after her," Valerie said. "They found her, because she came to see me, and they attacked the school. That's why we locked everyone in. And we went up to Mr. Tannis' room and she fought them. She killed them all... and I helped her."

He breathed for several moments.

"Did you actually kill anyone?" he asked.

"No," she said. "But I built casts that did, and I cast at a pair of them with magic that *could* have killed them, if they hadn't been warded."

"It matters, that you haven't killed someone," Ethan said.

"Why?" Valerie answered. He pressed his cheek against her hair and shook his head.

"Not to anyone," he said. "I just... I know that it's different. If you didn't *actually* do it, then it's different."

"How do you know?" Valerie asked.

There was a very, very long pause.

"Because I have," he said, his voice low.

There was a thud that Valerie felt through the ground, and the sound of breaking glass up at the top of the hill.

Valerie was on her feet and Ethan was extinguishing the fire as the first voices reacted. It wasn't loud, but Valerie could hear people yelling and the sounds of a fight. Things breaking and slamming into walls.

"Go or stay?" Ethan asked, next to her again.

"Go," she said, insulted.

"If they're looking for you..." Ethan said.

"I won't live with myself if I hide down here and they kill Sasha, looking for me," Valerie said.

"Fair enough," Ethan answered. "Are you ready?"

She shook her hands out, looking up at the sky and wishing for a moon.

"Ready as I'm gonna be."

Nothing is Safe

By the time they hit the front doors, students were already pouring out, and Ethan and Valerie had to struggle to get through the doors.

"What's going on?" she asked a girl she recognized.

"They're…" the girl said, then she was running again.

Valerie shouldered her way through and made it to the far wall, standing against the office glass as Ethan put an arm out toward her.

"Come on," he said. "I haven't seen Sasha or Hanson yet."

Valerie grabbed his hand and ran down the hallway with him, pausing at the wall where the hallway turned. There was a corner, there, before the dorm hallway started, and they stood with their backs against the wall, listening to voices Valerie didn't understand.

"Demontongue," Ethan whispered. "I don't understand much, but I think they're trying to get your door open."

"We have to stop them," Valerie whispered back.

"You ever fought a demon?" he asked, then looked up as the ceiling shuddered. "They're upstairs, too."

"Where is Mrs. Gold?" Valerie asked. Last time this had happened, the woman had been right in the thick of it. Valerie hated to think that the woman hadn't made it, this time. "I swear, if she's dead, I'm just going to give myself up."

"Don't you dare," Ethan said. "They want you as leverage against your mom, because she's saving even more lives than you can imagine. You have to stay safe so she can do her job."

"How is this safe?" Valerie hissed, and they both went silent for a moment as the voice changed to English.

"Do it."

She looked at Ethan and he shook his head.

There was a flurry of magic energy from around the corner, and as Ethan stepped forward, Valerie put her arm out, pressing him back against the wall again.

She breathed slowly, feeling the potency of the cast.

It was drawing energy from *everywhere*. The floors, the walls, the ceiling, patterns, colors, everything.

And she knew - she just *knew* - that if she tripped one of those connections, it was going to go off, and while it was most certainly going to kill Sasha, it stood a very good chance of killing her and Ethan, too.

"Be still," she mouthed.

They listened for a full minute longer - a minute that felt like an eternity - then she put her face flat against the wall.

More thumps and dust drifting down from the ceiling, and shouting.

Footsteps.

On the stairs.

There was a tendril of magic attached to the stairway door.

She could *tell*.

"Valerie," a voice said.

Her eyes flew open.

"Dr. Finn," she said. "What are you doing here?"

"Probably the same thing that you're doing," he said. "But better. I knew this is where I needed to be, but I'm not standing there waiting for someone to blow up the whole building."

"What now?" Ethan asked.

"Valerie Blake, you need to get to work," Dr. Finn said.

"I can't move," she said.

"You can *speak*," he answered.

She turned her head to look at him, standing there in the hallway coming from the same direction she and Ethan had.

"If for no other reason than that it's very traumatic to watch a friend get exploded, I'd recommend you remove some of the triggers from where they are actually attached *to* him," Dr. Finn said.

"There are too many," Valerie said.

"It's called a spider bomb for a reason," Dr. Finn said.

"Spider bomb," Ethan echoed, breathless.

He knew what that was.

"They're coming down the stairs," Valerie said.

"And there are presumably girls in their rooms who are going to get curious and open their doors," Dr. Finn said. "So we need to move quickly."

"You're going to help me?" Valerie asked.

"You think I'm going to stand here and beep a stopwatch at you?" he answered. "Quickly, now."

Valerie nodded, forcing herself to focus.

She'd been training for this.

She needed to get to the stairwell door, and then down the hallway. She had to remove every thread of the net of magic that the demon had cast, and then... Well, and then she was going to let Dr. Finn or *someone else* disarm the bomb, because her jeans were *still* neon green.

"I thought they wanted her alive," Ethan said. Valerie looked at him, exasperated.

"I don't know if you know, but the type of magic that we do requires intense focus," Dr. Finn said, his mind somewhere else.

"Oh, sorry," Ethan said.

"Don't move," Valerie said, closing her eyes and breathing.

She could feel where it was attached to Ethan, the tension of the bit of magic stretching across her body.

But.

She could also feel how easy it would be to pluck.

All she had to do was get direct focus on it and pull along the thread...

Focus proved elusive as she stewed in the awareness of what would go wrong if she pulled the wrong direction, even slightly.

"You can do this," Ethan murmured, and she nodded, letting the magic form in her head.

It wasn't... cohesive or mannerly or even *real*, the way the magic formed, but it had been working for her in her tests with Dr. Finn, and when she let it be, the words came to her, slipping through her lips like reciting poetry. The tendril went tight and she almost choked, but she managed to go on. With no more force than that, the tendril broke free and retreated around the corner like an elastic.

"That one's gone," she whispered. "But you still shouldn't move. There are a hundred more."

A thousand more, if you went around the corner, or looked up, but...

One more.

Dr. Finn was moving more quickly than she was, but he had use of his hands, and he had stuff in his pockets that he was using.

She just had her voice for now.

She targeted more tendrils, plucking them one by one. The feet were on the landing of the stairwell and she hadn't moved yet.

Focusing harder, she sensed out the tendril attached to the door, routing her magic around and through all of the others.

If the bomb went off, the people in the stairwell might make it, so long as the door hadn't opened yet.

Right?

Now or never.

She got hold of it and let her magic ease, not a second to waste, but trying not to rush, either.

Rushing was what had gotten her jeans.

The bolt on the door pulled and she tensed her magic, pulling the tendril free in the same moment that the door opened.

"Stop there," Dr. Finn said. "If you take one step through that door, every person in this building will die."

Valerie had never heard him use that voice before, but everyone froze.

Everyone.

"Please let the door close and don't let anyone try to open it," Dr. Finn said. "Yes, you. Is anyone upstairs in immediate need of medical help?"

"I don't know," the kid said. Valerie didn't know him by his voice.

"Close the door," Dr. Finn said. "Stop anyone. It's quite simple."

The door swung closed.

"Well done, Valerie," Dr. Finn said without changing his posture at all. "I didn't have line of sight on it."

"I can't do this," Valerie answered.

"You can and you must," Dr. Finn said, tearing through more and more of the tendrils.

The entire hallway behind her, the entire line of doors... Any one of them could set off the bomb.

"You can do this," Ethan said again, and she nodded.

"Okay. Yes. Okay."

One at a time.

Just one at a time.

She would have preferred to lock the doors the way she had with her mom, but she was too focused on clearing out the bomb triggers.

One by one, Ethan knocked on each of the doors, as fast as she could get him to them, and he let the girls inside know that they needed to stay in.

Mrs. Gold didn't answer her door, but there wasn't anyone in the hallway.

Maybe they'd gotten lucky, though it didn't explain the sounds Valerie had heard.

"Ethan?" Sasha asked as they got to Valerie's door. "Is that you?"

"It is," he said. "Are you okay?"

"What happened?" Sasha asked. "Is Valerie with you?"

"Someone attacked again," Ethan said. "There's a bomb out here, but Valerie is working on dismantling it. You just need to stay inside, okay? If anyone comes out, they could set it off."

There was a long silence.

"What happened upstairs?" Sasha asked finally.

"We don't know yet," Ethan answered.

Valerie licked her lips, continuing to work, then she frowned.

"I've got stuff in there I could use," she said.

"What stuff?" Ethan asked.

"My whole kit," Valerie said. "Sasha, open the door."

Valerie checked the door quickly as Sasha turned the knob and began to open it, but she was certain she'd cleared it before she'd let Ethan knock on it.

Sasha looked around quickly, but every one of the triggers was invisible; only the bomb there in the middle of the hallway was physically present, though Valerie knew that even that didn't *have* to be. Magic was capable of creating enough destruction all on its own.

"I need my stuff," Valerie said.

"I can help you," Sasha answered.

"If you come out here, he has to stay in," Valerie said. "I can't keep track of both of you."

"Nope," Ethan said.

"Can I go upstairs and check on everyone?" Sasha asked.

"No moving around until I clear it," Dr. Finn said.

"Or me," Lady Harrington said from the top of the hallway. "Is that what I think it is?"

"Spider bomb," Dr. Finn said, his mind still elsewhere. "Cast by a big-time demon."

"I can turn it off if you can get all of the triggers reeled in," Lady Harrington said.

"Approaching halfway done," Dr. Finn said. The man was a machine. Valerie had stopped detaching triggers the moment Sasha had started speaking.

Sasha left the door and came back with a zippered leather bag of stuff, handing it gingerly to Ethan.

He nodded, then Sasha looked at Valerie once more, as though hoping she would change her mind, but Valerie shook her head.

"As soon as we know anything," Valerie said, and Sasha took a deep breath and closed the door again.

Step by step, Valerie talked Ethan through to getting to her, then step by step back to the wall.

She unzipped the bag, her fingers itching, and she smiled.

Yes.

She needed to be slow and methodical, especially compared to Dr. Finn, because she was prone to making mistakes where he wasn't.

But the things she could do with that bag at this point.

Yes.

They were amazing.

Valerie sat down at the end of the hallway, her palms over her eyes.

She was exhausted, and she had no idea what time it was.

Ethan was sitting next to her, but he seemed to know better than to touch her.

They'd gone into Mrs. Gold's room and found her unconscious, but alive. The nurse, a woman named Mrs. Adams, had come and was working on her. Whispers had gone around that if it had happened to anyone else, they would have been dead.

News from upstairs was worse.

A lot of the guys had gotten out, but the rooms right where the demons had originally appeared had gotten… Well, Mr. Tannis was upstairs helping to get the bodies ready to take out.

Some of them had put up a good fight, and Franky Frank was already in the infirmary with serious injuries, but they said that he, at least, would recover.

No one would say who had died.

"You did it," Ethan said finally.

"People died because of me," Valerie answered.

Ethan looked over at her, but he didn't have words.

"You asked why they'd kill her, if they wanted to use her as leverage," Dr. Finn said. Valerie hadn't noticed him, but apparently he was leaning against the wall there at the end of the hallway not far from where she sat.

"I did," Ethan said slowly.

"It's because she's the only person the bomb wouldn't have killed. I'm not sure if it would have gotten me, honestly, because I'm like a roach. I'd survive nuclear holocaust. But. It was designed as a *trap* for her. If the bomb had gone off, every remaining trigger would have launched itself at her, so long as she was in range, and it would have held her until the demons had come back to collect her, which wouldn't have been long, presumably."

"Are you always this weird?" Ethan asked.

It had to have been partially because the man looked like he was their age, but it was also the exhaustion talking. Valerie almost laughed, as tired and upset as she was.

"Yes," Dr. Finn said. "Though I'm not sure that I'm the weird one."

"You two need to get to bed," Lady Harrington said, coming to stand in front of them. "The bomb is disabled and we will dispose of it before tomorrow. Mrs. Gold is going to make a full recovery, and most of the teachers are out in the woods trying to round up the students who got out. We'll have an assembly in the morning in the cafeteria, where we will discuss what happened."

"Lady Harrington," Valerie said, standing. "Please. What happened upstairs?"

"I will tell you when the time comes, once everyone is assembled."

"I think she deserves it," Ethan said. "She saved all of us tonight."

Lady Harrington paused, considering this for a moment, then dipped her head.

"I am very sorry to inform you that Patrick Rose and Conrad Smith were killed tonight," she said quietly. "We don't know if Kit Memer will survive the night or not, but we've done everything for him that we can."

Valerie looked over at Ethan, who had closed his eyes.

"Both of them," he said.

"I'm sorry," Valerie answered him, and he nodded.

"I… I don't know what to think. There were seven of us and none of us knew which five it was…"

"You're talking about the curse," Valerie said, shifting to look at him. He nodded.

"I mean, I never *really* believed it, but… It was supposed to be five of us who were the dark power who were supposed to take on leadership of the Council…"

Valerie blinked.

She'd never really put it together like that.

"You thought that the cursed ones were supposed to lead the Council?" she asked.

He nodded.

"The five cursed had a special power that would be able to break the Superiors."

"And you just assumed that that would involve the Council?" she asked.

"Obviously we would be *leading* the Council by then," he said, frowning.

"Yasmine, Patrick, and Conrad," Valerie said softly. He nodded.

"There are only four of us left."

"And me," Valerie said, her voice very soft.

He looked over at her.

"Why you?"

"My mom was there when Lan died," Valerie said. "She told me. She said I was part of it. I think. Maybe I misunderstood, but I *thought* that was what she was telling me."

"But neither of your parents were on the Council," he said.

"They both hand handlers reporting to the Council," Valerie said. "I don't know. I just… I'm pretty sure that I'm the last one of the five."

He put his head back against the wall and breathed for a moment.

"I don't want you to be dark-touched like the rest of us. I can live with it, but…"

"Why does it even matter?" Valerie asked. "If we can win the war, who cares what style of magic we use?"

"Because…" he started, then shook his head, smiling with a drainedness that he hadn't had before. "You don't even know. You've never had anyone look at you and think you were less because you weren't solid light magic. That's so strange."

"Miss Blake and Mister Trent, I have given you all the leeway I intend to. Please see yourselves to bed," Lady Harrington said, and Ethan stood up, offering Valerie a hand.

"You did really good, tonight," he said.

"So did you," she answered, and he gave her a sideways smile.

"I don't know what Shack did with your books, but if he has them, we'll get them to you before class in the morning."

"You know what my first class is?" Valerie asked, and he smiled.

"Of course I do. Just because I haven't been walking you doesn't mean I don't pay attention."

She nodded, closing her eyes and finding that they didn't want to open again.

"I need sleep," she said.

"Class is going to start early," he observed.

She nodded.

"Too early."

Way too early.

Valerie checked the library on her way to the cafeteria, but Shack appeared to have packed up her stuff and taken it with him when he'd left that night. She didn't stop in the cafeteria long on her way to her magical first aid class, where she found Ethan leaning against the wall holding her backpack.

"Hanson's worried about both of you," he said as Valerie slung her backpack up onto her back and shoved half a muffin into her mouth.

Breakfast.

"Well, Sasha can take care of herself, and I'm apparently the one who has to save everyone, so tell him to stuff it, and that if anyone's allowed to be worried, it's us about him."

Ethan grinned.

"Shack is planning on building a bunk bed over top of his old bed," he said. "He refuses to move out."

Valerie didn't blame him.

"He lost the bet, fair and square," she said, anyway, and Ethan nodded.

"I don't know where we're going to put all of our stuff, when this is done."

She let the humor slide from her face for a moment.

"Are you okay?' she asked. He shrugged.

"Shack is taking it pretty hard," he said. "Wouldn't admit it, but he and Conrad go back a long way, and… He's just a nice guy, you know? Thinks everyone is his best friend."

Valerie nodded.

"He is," she said. "I wish I could have done more."

"You defused a bomb," he said. "That's good enough for me."

"But they were here *for* me," she said. "And… that's three people, now, Ethan. I don't know how much more of this I can *live* with."

"It isn't your fault," Ethan said darkly. "I've been thinking about it, and you're right - someone is letting them in on purpose. Demons shouldn't be able to just come and go as they please, in here. The warding is way too strong. The first time, I was worried that between the two of us both sneaking to the library, we'd done something that had damaged the warding and let them in, but this time? We were outside, and we hadn't done anything. Someone else did this on purpose."

Valerie nodded.

"We need to keep thinking on that," she said. "It could be anyone, but... It's going to keep happening, and people are going to keep *dying*, if someone doesn't do something about it."

She glanced at her watch, then shifted her backpack again, still frowning. Ethan kissed her cheek quickly and brushed past.

"Gonna be late," he said.

She nodded and went to stand in the doorway of her classroom, watching him until he went around the corner, then going to sit in the back of the class.

Mr. Turner was sitting behind his desk, working on something that Valerie suspected had nothing to do with instruction.

He glanced up when the bell rang, but didn't stand.

"We have an assembly in the cafeteria five minutes after the start of class," he said. "Don't get out any of your things; plan on taking everything with you when we go."

Valerie frowned, shifting lower in her desk.

Someone was trying to get her killed. It wasn't absolutely conclusive, but it felt inescapable. They were sending demons - and they hadn't even managed to kill one this time - and those demons were eventually going to succeed at it.

Valerie didn't know how to defend herself against them, for sure, and just hoping that her reservoir of instinctive magic was big enough... It was foolish.

She'd gone running *at* them both times, and both times it had just been a matter of luck and timing that they hadn't gotten her.

How was she not *dead* already?

Her father had rescued her the first time, and the second time, the demons had left.

Why had they left?

It was all so strange and so *surreal.* Sure, she'd been here a few months, but the idea that her life might actually be *at risk* just wasn't sinking in.

That her *mom* might be risking her life…

That her dad was *alive*…

She startled as the other students started standing up, and she got her backpack up off the floor to follow them, going to crowd into the cafeteria. She saw the guys standing against the wall, but she went to go sit with Sasha.

Lady Harrington arrived a few minutes later, walking with Mr. Benson and passing a paper back and forth between them.

The woman cleared her throat, silencing the room.

"Ladies and gentlemen," she said, handing the page back to Mr. Benson. "I know that last night was a difficult one for most of you, and that very few of us were prepared for the idea that our students and our faculty were not absolutely safe while at school. We have been reviewing the magic defenses, and have come to the conclusion that there is a flaw in them, one that we have not previously discovered, and that someone has been exploiting in order to gain access to the school. As a result, classes will be canceled and all faculty retasked to working with myself and Mr. Benson to secure the building and grounds. Students are expected to remain in their rooms with the doors locked outside of mealtimes and for biological necessities. I know that this is a disappointment to you, that you have come here to *learn*, but we cannot learn if we are not first safe. So we will address the issue of safety and then - and only then - resume classes.

"On the specific topic of last night, I know that many of you have heard that we had students who did not survive. I am very sorry to announce that Patrick Rose and Conrad Smith died last night. We have informed their parents, and they will be coming today. If you happen to see them, please remain sensitive. Everyone is struggling, but losing a child is always the hardest thing a parent can face. Kit Memer has been transferred to a more capable medical facility, and we hope he will return before the end of the semester.

"That will be all. Please return to your dorm rooms in an

orderly fashion and avoid spreading speculation and rumors. No one knows anything at this point, so anything that you hear is unlikely to have any real truth to it."

Valerie watched as the guys filed out, then she turned her attention to Sasha.

"Stuck in the room full time," she muttered, and Sasha nodded, still watching after Hanson.

"It's lucky that we're all alive," the redhead finally said. "They're doing the right thing."

"Still," Valerie said. "What do they expect us to *do*? Do you think it'll take more than a day or so? Because, if so, that's, like, prison or something. They *can't* do that, can they?"

"You're welcome to call child services and report it," Ann said, sitting down next to Valerie. "Oh, wait, that's right, you can't. We don't have cell phones. Or rights. They can do whatever they want. This is all about you, isn't it? You know it is. They're protecting you, and more of *my* friends die. They should just turn you out and let them have you. I mean, really, are you worth *three* of the Council's best and brightest?"

"Lady Harrington would never do that," Sasha said, and Ann tipped her head to the side, watching Valerie.

"Do you sleep at night, little Blake girl? Knowing that this school traded three lives for yours? And counting?"

"Where were you when it happened?" Valerie asked. "Running out the door for the woods? Or asleep in your bed? Ethan and I were running *toward* it."

"You think he likes you," Ann said. "It's so *cute*. I've known him my entire life, and I can *promise* you, he uses girls like bubble gum. When you lose your flavor he'll spit you out and go looking for a new piece."

"Ladies," Mr. Benson said. "Back to your rooms, please."

Valerie stood, nudging Sasha as the redhead bristled at Ann.

"Was he at the library?" Sasha asked as they walked. "Last night?"

"What do you mean?" Valerie answered, glancing once more to make sure Ann had reamalgamated into a group of girls behind them and wasn't following along to listen in.

"How were you and Ethan together when the attack happened?" Sasha asked. "You haven't spoken to him in months."

She hesitated at this, first because she hadn't prepared a story for why she'd been able to meet up with Ethan, nor why she'd forgiven him, but then because she'd been with Ethan during *both* attacks.

Coincidence?

Was it even possible it was anything else?

Could he have been involved?

And if he had been, to what end? She hadn't been there during the attacks *because* she'd been with him.

Could he have known and intentionally gotten her out during the attacks, then let them happen anyway?

For the first one, maybe, but... Could they have put together the second attack in the space of time it took Valerie to shower?

No.

It had to be coincidence.

Or something.

Sasha was still waiting for an answer.

"Right," Valerie said. "Sorry. Just... a lot going on, you know?"

"Yeah," Sasha said. "But... You two were together when it happened?"

Sasha was not the type to let something go.

"Yeah," Valerie said. "We talked some and... I don't want to be the one who makes it weird for you and Hanson. I still think you need to be careful and make sure that he's really the person you want to be with, but... You shouldn't *not* do it because of me."

"What's that got to do with Ethan?" Sasha asked.

"I went to talk to him and... I was ready to go on seeing him, right up until I found out about Hanson. So if I'm going to try to let things go back to normal with Hanson, I figured I could at least give Ethan a chance."

"I'm glad," Sasha said. "You were happier, there for a little bit, with him. At least you had something other than school that you were doing with your time."

Valerie nodded.

She'd missed that part, too.

They got back to the room and went in, putting away their backpacks and sitting down on their beds.

"This is seriously like prison," Valerie said after a minute. "No phones, no internet, no television? Seriously, what are we supposed to *do*?"

"Read?" Sasha suggested.

Valerie blew air through her lips.

"Who *does* that anymore?"

"I do," Sasha said, and Valerie rolled over onto her stomach to hug her pillow. She'd actually had several shelves of books back home and loved to check out stacks of them during the summer from the library, but it had been a while since she'd really found something she wanted to dive into.

"I don't have any, anyway," she said. "Nothing but books about magic."

"Well, you could borrow some of mine if you wanted, but you should probably spend the time studying, as much as you can. You still have a lot of catching up to do."

Valerie wrinkled her nose.

What was the point of making up with Ethan if she wasn't even going to *see* him?

"Can we sneak out, do you think?" Valerie asked.

"I don't think you should," Sasha answered, getting out the book she'd been reading the night before and rolling flat on her back to hold it over her head.

Valerie would have been in mortal peril, like that, because she was certain she would have fallen asleep and dropped the book on her face.

"Yeah, I don't think I should, either, but it would give me something to look forward to."

They stayed there through lunch - Valerie fell asleep for almost two hours - and then they went to sit at the cafeteria table with the much-reduced Council brats. Even adding in Hanson and Sasha, the table felt conspicuous.

Elvis came to sit down next to Ethan, and the rest of the freshmen went silent as the upperclassman started eating as though his presence was normal.

"They've locked all of us in our cottages," the older boy said by way of explanation.

"So?" Ethan asked. "What are you doing here?"

"Getting out," Elvis said. "Normally we eat there, because the food is *so* much better, but being stuck in there all morning sucks."

"Then eat with your own friends," Ethan said. "What are you doing *here*?"

Elvis looked down the table at Valerie. He was every bit as attractive as Ethan, but he had that older-boy thing going on, and she still saw *exactly* why she and Sasha had been so stunned when he'd come to talk to her on the first day of school.

It just *felt* like he didn't belong with them, with the stubble on his chin and the subtle-yet-undeniable difference in the way he was built.

And man, oh, man was he *hot*.

"You need to go," Elvis said.

And that was why Valerie still didn't even like being around him.

"Why?" Ethan asked. "Why would you say that?"

"Oh, are you two a thing again?" Elvis asked. "I hadn't heard."

"Why would it be any of your business?" Ethan asked. "It doesn't matter."

"I think it does," Elvis said, then leaned further across his tray to look at Valerie again. "You shouldn't be here. The Council has safe-houses that they could put you up in, but you're risking everyone's lives, being here."

"My mom sent me here," Valerie said, not actually believing it, but refusing to engage Elvis at all. "This is where I'll stay until Lady Harrington kicks me out."

"Lady Harrington has too much pride wrapped up in this school being a fortress," Elvis said. "She won't do what's best for the students."

"If the Council was offering, they would send the offer through Lady Harrington," Ethan said. "Not you."

"She won't say it," Elvis said. "So I am. The Council could take care of her, and the school would be safer."

"You expect us to believe that Dad got in touch with *you* to try to talk her out of staying here?" Ethan asked. "They could just as easily send someone down here."

"She won't let them in," Elvis said, picking up his tray and standing. "I'm the only one who can get close enough, since you and she stopped talking. She needs to leave, and the second she's ready to admit it, I can get a car here and get her *out* of here."

"Don't listen to him," Ethan said as Elvis stood and walked away.

"Why not?" Ann demanded. "Not only does he make sense. He's *right.*"

"I'll think about it," Valerie said. "But Lady Harrington isn't stupid, and neither is my mom. The safe-houses, whatever they are, they existed *before* I came here, and the dude who snatched me off the street would have known about them. There's a reason for me to be here, and I'm not just going to ignore it because you don't like me here."

"I *hate* you here," Ann said. "You took a slot that someone more *valuable* could have had. But what I don't like right this second is that I might *die* tomorrow and it would be your *fault.*"

"Only if she kills you," Hanson said, and Ann shot him a fiery look. He shrugged, immune. "Look, I can tell there's *stuff* going on here that I don't actually know about. I'll figure it out, eventually, but I can be ignorant for now. What I do know is that murder is only ever the fault of the guy with the gun."

"Or the one who left the door unlocked and a welcome sign posted out front," Ann answered.

"Enough," Ethan said. "She isn't leaving. The safe houses are… They'd be indoctrination tools. The Council wants her to be their tool, and she isn't going to do that."

Valerie looked over at him as the table went very, very quiet.

Every word of that was going to make it to the ears of three Council members, at least, and his father would hear it very shortly after that.

Ethan returned to his meal, unconcerned, and Valerie looked around the table.

"All right," she said, fed up. "All right, this is all *enough.* We're *literally* dying here, and you guys are all still running back to your parents playing politics. At what point are you going to decide that *we* are the ones on a team, like each other or not, and start playing like *that*?"

"I am *not* on your team," Ann said.

"I am," Shack said after just a moment, then glanced at Valerie with a quick smile and went back to his meal.

"I am, too," Hanson said. "For whatever that's worth."

"I am," Sasha said, her voice quiet. Valerie could hear the need to qualify that with some kind of self-denigrating statement, but Sasha managed not to do it.

"So am I," Ethan said, very familiar and very close. Valerie avoided looking at him because she was afraid that her goosebumps might actually be visible from across the table.

Milton cleared his throat and glanced at Ann.

"I'm going to do what my mom tells me I need to do," he said after a moment. "I think they have a lot more visibility to what's going on with the war, and I want to win this war."

Valerie couldn't say he was wrong.

But apparently Ethan could.

"We tattle on each other," Ethan said, leaning across the table. "It means that we're never actually on the same *side*. The Council is *fractured* and we all know it. As soon as they get a grip on the war, they're going to start jockeying for position for coming *out* of the war, and if you guys read the histories the way I do, they just about lost the war *twice* doing that, last time. And that was with a brand new Council that didn't have any *clue* how to be petty and power-hungry like our parents are."

"That's sedition," Milton said.

"It's pragmatic," Ethan answered. "They're going to screw it up. And it doesn't *matter* what we do, they're going to screw it up. I'm not talking about *us* fighting the war, not yet. I'm talking about *us* doing something to increase our chances of *survival* and our chances of winning, once it's our job to do it."

"The war isn't going to last that long this time," Ann said. "No matter how hard Susan Blake tries to stretch it out for her own agenda."

"What?" Valerie demanded, but Ethan put his hand out to the side, physically intervening between Valerie and Ann. "My mother would never…" Valerie went on, but Ethan interrupted her.

"We said that last time," he said. "But the Superiors were ready for us at every turn, and they killed *way* too many of our best fighters for us to even hope to have a big advantage this time."

"Should have wiped them all out," Milton muttered, and Ethan held up a finger.

"I don't want to discuss what they *should* have done last time," he said.

"We have to," Milton said. "If we plan on doing any better, next time."

"It's different," Ethan said. "Different war. Different people."

"I say we all tell our parents that we're done," Shack said. "No reporting back on each other at all."

Valerie looked around the table, and Ethan nodded.

"That's what I'm saying," he agreed.

"My dad isn't going to take that as a final answer," Ann said.

Milton watched Ethan for a long time.

"My best friend died last night," he said. "And as far as I can tell, it's her fault."

"Not her fault," Shack muttered, returning to his food.

"You expect me to side with *her* over my own father?" Milton asked.

"I'm asking you to at least tell us if you're with us or against us," Ethan answered.

"I'm not with you," Milton said. "I won't do that. The Council is trying to win a *war*."

"A war we have almost nothing to do with," Ethan said. "They're spying on us because of politics, not tactics."

Shack nodded at his pile of spaghetti, slurping it up and looking down the table at Milton.

"I'm still on their side, in the war," Shack said as he finished chewing. "But this isn't the war. Not *us*. I'll tell my mom anything she wants to know about the attacks. But not about you guys. Not anymore. Ethan's right."

"No," Milton said after another moment. "I won't do it."

"Then you need to leave," Ethan said evenly.

Valerie looked over at Ethan, feeling simultaneously like he was being over-dramatic and unkind, kicking Milton off of the lunch table, but also that he was *right*.

"All right, I'm in," Ann said. "If only because it's going to take the amount of work I have to do down by at least half."

Ethan nodded, and put his hands out on the table in front of him.

"It's settled, then. We're our own team, now."

"You know that none of us are *actually* headed for power," Ann said after a moment. "They're only looking at Light School grads for the Council."

Ethan looked at her sideways and shook his head.

"We can do whatever we want," he said. "If you want to take the Council and the rest of us agree to it… we'll take the Council."

She frowned at this, then lifted her chin.

"And what if I do?" she asked.

"We're seventeen," Valerie said. "I don't think we really need to hold a vote on it just yet."

"This is when it starts," Ann said. "And I didn't say that you got a vote. There are three of us without Milton, and I only need Shack or Ethan to say that they want to take the Council…"

"Four of us," Ethan said. "She's one of us."

"Hey, I said I was in almost first," Hanson said, but Sasha elbowed him and he coughed into his fist. Ethan ignored him and looked at Valerie.

"She's not wrong, though. We have to *know* if we want to lead the Council. Because it's got to be single-minded."

"I just want to survive and have my mom come home," Valerie said. "And I'm *sick* of people spying on me."

"You can't not want *anything*," Ann said.

"Why not?" Valerie asked. "I *don't*."

Ann shook her head, then looked at Ethan with exasperation.

"Are you going to make *me* say it?" she asked, and he twisted his mouth, turning his whole body to face Valerie.

"They aren't going to let you," he said. "You're too powerful. They all know it. Everyone does."

"What does Dr. Finn want?" Valerie asked. "I'm no more important than he is."

Ethan glanced at Ann, then shrugged.

"The council consults with him on a lot of things," he said. "And he uses that access to get favors. He runs the research group, too. They kicked out the old guy so that he could do it."

"No," Valerie said. "He's… That's not what he's like. He wouldn't trade favors or steal someone's job."

"It isn't like he's telling it," Shack said. "Dr. Finn's a good guy. He took over research because he was the best anyone had seen in twenty years, and he does work for the council so they care about his interests. It's not… The research facility has a lot of good equipment and all of the ingredients and books and stuff that they could ask for. They take care of him. But it's not about personal gain and whatever."

She shot a look at Ethan.

"Was that so hard?" she asked.

"Then you tell her," Ethan said to Shack.

Valerie raised an eyebrow and looked back across the table again.

"They're right," Shack said. "Dr. Finn knew what he wanted to do, and they were happy to let him do it, but they're all *still* trying to get him to *prefer* working with them over the others, so they can use him more frequently. They're buying him stuff and trying to keep track of what he wants and stuff… You can't just *not* be involved. They're all going to chase you around and try to get you to do what they want you to. He knew what he wanted. If you don't? They're going to try to convince you to want the same thing as them."

"I just *got* here. All I want is for them to leave me alone."

"Oh, how cute," Ann said. "That's not how it *works*. I don't care if you're on the Council or not. I don't. But if you *aren't* on the Council, I want to be the one holding your leash."

"That's why my mom ran off," Valerie said. "Isn't it? You all and your politics."

"Couldn't have helped," Shack said, lifting his head. "Looks like you're going to have some time to think about it."

Mr. Benson was coming into the cafeteria, and the room fell

silent.

"Back to your dorms please, everyone," he said. "You'll be released again for dinner."

Valerie sighed with exasperation.

"I *swear*, this is prison," she said.

"Just go along," Ethan said. "And don't let anyone convince you that you shouldn't be here. If they try to make you leave, make them take you to Lady Harrington. Okay?"

She nodded, looking around the room.

"Take care of Hanson," she said, and he nodded, taking her hand quickly and squeezing it.

"You got it."

They split at the door to the cafeteria, and Valerie walked alongside Sasha.

"You didn't have to be a part of that," she told the redhead.

"I know," Sasha answered. "It's just… I don't… I think you're important," she said finally. "I think that you're a part of *something*. And… I get why my mom avoided the Council all this time, and why she kept me away from all of it, even while my brothers were in school, but I don't think that we get the luxury of staying out of it, you know? I think that important things are going on, and that we've either got to jump in and *do* something about it or… I don't know. Maybe accept that the way things are isn't going to last, and it's only going to get worse from here."

Valerie considered this, going to unlock their door and pushing it open so Sasha could go in.

"Tell me what you know about the Superiors," she said after a moment. "And I don't mean the sort of stories you've been told *about* them and why they're so bad. I mean what you really know for certain about them and why they do what they do."

Sasha sat down at her desk and frowned.

"I don't understand the difference," she said. "They hate humans. They kill them. We try to stop them, so they kill us."

"What if I told you that that isn't true?" Valerie asked. "I mean… Why? Have you ever asked that? Why do they do it? Why do they just… *hate* humans?"

"I don't know," Sasha said. "It's in the name. Superior. They think magic users are *better* than humans."

"Okay," Valerie said. "So, okay, right. But humans make up, what, more than ninety-nine percent of the population of the world? What's the endgame here? Are they *really* planning on trying to kill ninety nine out of every hundred people on the face of the planet? And if so, why aren't they just *doing* it? I mean… I can think of a lot of faster ways to kill off people than going to shopping malls and attacking them with magic."

"That's… disturbing," Sasha said. "No, I don't know if they plan to kill *all* civilians. No one ever sat them down to tell me."

"You don't find it troubling that we're fighting a group that we don't even have an *idea* of what it is that they're trying to do?"

"Enslave and kill civilians," Sasha said. "How is that not obvious?"

"Because they *aren't*," Valerie said. "They're killing batches of people, true enough, but why not *really* go after them? How are they picking their targets? What are they *really* trying to do?"

"Does it have to make *sense*?" Sasha asked.

"*Yes*," Valerie said. "One dude? Not at all. A dude and a bunch of his minions? I mean, that happens, right? But a whole organization capable of going up against the Council and my mom and everyone else? That *can't* be just a fanatic weirdo. It has to be something that they bought into and agree with, at least to some extent."

Sasha leaned her chin on the back of her chair, frowning at Valerie.

"Why do I get the feeling that you're about to tell me that everything I believe about the world is wrong?" the girl asked.

"Because that's *exactly* what she's about to tell you," a voice said as the door opened. Valerie jerked, immediately searching for the nearest weapons, but she knew that voice.

"Dad," she said. "What are you doing here?"

"We had a slight change of plans," he said. "You need to come with me."

Valerie dropped her shoulders.

"I can't do the in-both-places thing again," she said. "That was too weird."

"No, you can't do the in-both-places thing again so soon because it would kill you," Grant Blake said.

"What's going on?" Valerie asked. "I disarmed a *bomb* last night."

"I heard something about that," Grant said. "Well done."

"Not an answer," Valerie said, and he grinned.

"Is this Ivory Mills' daughter?" he asked. "Are you anything like the healer your mom was?"

"No," Sasha answered. "But I'm here to study it. Who are you?"

"Grant Blake," he answered, putting out a hand to shake hers. "Valerie's dad."

"Oh," Sasha said. "Wow. Um."

She shook his hand and Valerie stood.

"I don't want to go with you," she said.

"I don't believe I was asking," he said, turning to look at her.

"What?" she asked. "If you take me against my will, Sasha will tell Lady Harrington, and then everyone will know you're alive."

Sasha nodded quickly, and Grant gave her something of a dark smile.

"Oh I'm not just here for you. She's coming, as well. Also, while I appreciate the quick-witted attempt at blackmail, the people who matter know that I'm alive anyway."

"It's true," Valerie said quietly. "You're one of them. They turned you."

He drew his head back.

"Who have *you* been talking to?" he asked.

She shook her head, for a moment feeling soft and alone and unprepared, then stiffening her resolve and straightening.

"It doesn't matter," she told him. "I'm not coming along without a fight."

"Your mother said you'd say that," he told her. "That without demons to drive you along behind, you'd want to stay here. You're actually happy here? That surprises me."

"I didn't say I was happy," Valerie said, and he gave her a halfway smile.

"But you did say that you'd fight me to stay, didn't you? You like it here."

"I'm not convinced you're not one of the bad guys," Valerie answered. "Why would I go with you again? So that you can stuff me in a cave and throw magic at me?"

"What are you guys talking about?" Sasha asked, getting out of her chair and coming to stand next to Valerie. "I don't... I need to tell my mom, if I'm going anywhere."

"Your mother will know what happened," Grant said, glancing at her. "Susan wouldn't let Ivory Mills believe that her daughter had been abducted."

"Is that not what this is?" Valerie asked, and he smiled gently.

"No. This is... Call it a field trip. We're going out into the great wide world for you to actually see what's out there, and for you to understand what this war is about."

Valerie glanced at Sasha and drew a breath.

"If you want to fight him, I'll fight him," she said quietly. "But I believe him."

"You do?" Sasha asked, and Valerie nodded.

"What they tell us about the war... I can't be sure if it's lying or if it's ignorance, but I don't believe it. There's a war going on, but... There's a lot about it that we don't know."

"And you would just walk out of school and... Go with him in order to figure it out?" Sasha asked. "We're safe here. Isn't that the point? Maybe the war will be over by the time we graduate and we don't even have to worry about it."

There was a note of desperation, and Valerie shook her head.

"No. The war is here. You know it and I know it. And as long as I'm here, everyone in the school is in danger. I believe that, too. I don't... Maybe it's time I left, you know? I mean... You said Mom." Valerie turned her attention back to Grant. "You know where she is?"

"She's waiting for us," he answered. "She just didn't think she could get close again without Lady Harrington knowing about it and stopping us."

"Why would Lady Harrington try to stop you?" Sasha asked.

"Because she doesn't agree with our tactics," Grant said, glancing once more at Sasha but returning his attention to Valerie.

"And because she considers students people to be protected, whereas we believe they are children who need to learn."

"You're going to take me to Mom?" Valerie asked, and Grant nodded.

"Yes."

"She knows you're alive?"

"Clearly."

"Since when?"

"I didn't ask," he said. "You can ask her yourself."

Valerie looked at Sasha and Sasha rubbed her arms.

"I can keep a secret," the redhead said. "Ask her. If you just take her, I won't tell anyone I saw you."

"No," Grant said. "It needs to be both of you."

"Why?" Valerie asked.

"Because," Grant said. "When we get back, you're going to need an ally who actually knows you aren't crazy. It's time for you to disrupt everything they believe here. Here and everywhere else under the Council. They *know*, but they keep it secret because they think that spreading the knowledge that it's *complicated* will lessen the interest in fighting, and they think they can keep the fighters from figuring it out by keeping them away from the Pure."

"The who?" Sasha asked, and he shook his head.

"She has too much to learn to just take your word for it," he said. "You see our point."

Valerie hesitated.

"She would believe me," she said after a moment.

"Yes, but would anyone else?"

Valerie licked her lips.

"They think you went dark," she said. "The Council knows you might be alive, or they *know* you're alive, but they think you switched sides."

"It used to be that would have bothered me," Grant said.

"You were born to Purists?" Valerie asked.

He drew a breath, then went to the closet, getting out bags.

"Pack," he said.

Valerie glanced at Sasha, who looked like she would go along with whatever Valerie did. Valerie started putting clothes and toiletries in the bag.

"I was born to a family that natively used dark magic," Grant said, going to lean against the wall in the short front hallway. He crossed his arms and rolled his jaw to the side. "My dad couldn't use anything but dark magic, but my mom was a mage. She could use all three like they were all the same."

"Three?" Sasha asked, and Grant sighed.

"I'll be glad to have someone *else* do this part for me, because doing it over and over again is *tiring*."

"Be nice, Dad," Valerie said.

"I am," he said. "Any rate, growing up, I was supposed to go to one of the dark schools, but I had ability with light magic, and I kind of hated my dad, so I went to Light School. Mom was supportive, because there are a lot more… legitimate opportunities when you come out of one of the light schools. The light and the dark… They never did like each other, but it just kind of happened that the theories on magic, how dangerous it is and how we should be careful about who we spread it to… Those evolved differently there than here."

"How?" Sasha asked. "Do they not think that magic is dangerous?"

"Oh, the other way, Miss Mills," Grant said. "They think that spreading it ought to stop entirely."

Sasha paused at this, but Grant went on.

"By the time we were actually looking at a war, my dad was with the Pure - still is, by the way - and so was Gemma, and my mom… She died early in the whole thing. Part of why my dad ended up so hard-line. The people at Light School, Lady Beatrice mostly, talked about kicking me out because I came from the wrong side of magic, but your mom wouldn't hear of it, and she got a bunch of other students to show up and say that they couldn't just kick me out for who my parents were… I don't think even Susan Harrington could keep me on at Light School these days, but back then the Council were… more reasonable, actually."

"Harrington," Sasha said, and Valerie glanced over at her as she zipped up her bag.

"Yeah."

"You knew?" Sasha asked, her eyebrows going up, and Valerie shrugged.

"I told you he told me a lot of stuff that no one else here had been willing to say."

"She threatened to kick you out," Sasha protested, and Valerie shrugged.

"Clearly it doesn't mean all that much to her."

"I expect it means a lot more than you think," Grant said. "Our window is closing. We need to get moving."

Sasha hung back for another moment, then she finally nodded and followed Valerie to the door.

"I can't believe I'm doing this," Sasha said, and Valerie smiled.

"It's brave."

"I'm not supposed to be *in* the war," Sasha whispered as Grant opened the door. "I'm supposed to stay in school until it's over, and then go be a healer like my mom."

"The war needs healers," Grant whispered back at her. "More than almost anywhere else."

Sasha shuddered, but Valerie went to stand next to her dad as he looked up and down the hallway.

"Ready?" he asked, and she nodded.

"Yeah."

"Let's go show you what magic is really about," he said, stepping into the hallway and letting the door fall closed behind them.

The Reunion Tour

Falsifying records wasn't exactly Susan's favorite thing to do with her time, but she was decent at it.

The apartment had been easy. Pick the right one and there weren't many people who remembered who had been there before the current occupants, so she could make a story slip through there that Grant had lived there for years, before the current flareup of conflict.

Fake a driver's license, and, presto, he'd been in New Mexico for the last two years.

Go through a newspaper's archives, plant a story about a huge fish he'd caught up in the mountains... a boat's manifest for a cruise around the world...

Grant Blake had been living the high life, enjoying his freedom from the magic community and all of their drama.

How he'd actually lived was much sadder, scrambling from one hiding spot to the next, no records of any of it, trying to make sure no one could ever prove he'd been there.

He was protecting his sister.

Anything to keep Gemma safe.

Susan felt a little bad that she'd not thought of Gemma once since Valerie had been born. Not one thought for her former best friend.

She was glad that Grant had been watching over her, keeping her safe from there in the middle of the dark Council, keeping the fight alive through the years as the Pure had been perfecting their methods.

They thought they were close.

That's what Grant said.

The small-scale tests suggested that, if they could get their hands on enough data, they might finally find a combination of magic and civilian that would make the whole thing work, and then they could learn from it and expand it...

The idea of it made Susan's blood run cold.

It was possible she would be safe from it, that the magic to take away someone's magical talents would bounce off of her because she was too strong, but she had no idea how to defend from it actively, and while the non-propagationists thought that the Pure would only use the magic on civilians who would never know what they had lost, Susan couldn't imagine that the inner council of Pures would fail to capitalize on the way to instantly win the war, too.

They would start with the schools, because they were soft targets, and then they would go after the fighters, as they found them. They would go to families who had managed to remain uninvolved but who supported the Council, and it would end at the Council itself.

She needed to get close enough to see how the magic worked to try to figure through a way of defending against it, first personally and then in a larger and larger context.

She'd been close, the one time, but instead she'd found out that Martha Cox was reporting to the Council again after a long absence and she'd put two and two together and realized that she had to warn Valerie about who Hanson really was.

These days, Susan was less and less convinced who was on the good side and who was on the bad side of the war.

Stripping magic?

Bad.

Throwing new graduates into combat without so much as telling them why they were fighting and without equipping them to defend the new Pure magics?

Also.

Bad.

Killing civilians in live trials?

Bad.

Very bad.

Spying on everyone with any modicum of power or potential?

Some days, Susan felt like the only course of action open to her was to burn the whole thing down and start over.

She'd told Grant that the thought had occurred to her, and he'd laughed. The man had actually laughed.

And he'd told her that if anyone could do it, it was her.

So.

Without any new leads on the magic they were using to strip magic power, Susan was sitting with a notebook on the dilapidated couch there against the wall in the abandoned warehouse, watching the druggies and the homeless stand around fire barrels. And she was writing nonsense, freeing her mind to concoct the magic she *would use to do just such a thing, so at least she could defend against that.*

In an hour, she would set up a cast that would drive out all the indigents, just something subtle to suggest that they didn't want to be there anymore, so that she could clean the place out of the worst of what humanity left behind in such a building, before Valerie got there.

Valerie was coming.

It had been Susan's idea, though Grant had jumped on board immediately. He didn't like her being under Lady Harrington's influence, even though Susan had pointed out repeatedly throughout their relationship that she, Susan, had survived it just fine.

They were going to know that Grant was alive, very shortly, and they were going to get the clues that said that Susan had been there, the night of the first attack, and had diverted the attack by making them think that Valerie had left the school.

With Grant alive, though, and Susan taking a doubly-active role in protecting her daughter, the threat to Valerie's life kept going up.

More, though, it had taken Susan this long to get her networks back up and going again, spending cash freely and doing the delicate work of reestablishing diplomacy with people who were skittish under the best of circumstances. She couldn't have protected Valerie, before, but now she had the means to do it for at least a few months, before things turned worse again.

And they were going to.

She didn't give herself the freedom to hope that they wouldn't.

They were going to get much, much worse, and all Susan could hope was that she could equip Valerie with the knowledge and the skills required to keep herself and the rest of the Council brats alive.

This was necessary.

And it was the best way to keep her daughter safe.

It just involved spiriting her away into a drug hole in the middle of the night.

Because that was - again - where Susan's life had landed her.

They'd switched cars three times.

Valerie had no idea why, nor did she have any idea where they were, except that if her mom had caught wind that she had been in a part of town like this - Valerie didn't care *what* her excuse had been - her mom would have grounded her for, like, her entire twenties.

Grant closed the car door and looked around quickly.

"They won't be following us yet," he said. "I think we got ahead of them this time. What you do have to watch out for are the normal humans. Don't walk like prey."

"What?" Sasha asked. "What are we doing here?"

"I'm talking specifically to you, yes," Grant said, looking over at Valerie's friend. "They're going to know that if they try to rob you, you aren't going to fight back, and that's just begging for someone to try it. Stay close, keep your head up, and remember that if you had to, you could paralyze them at a touch or turn them into a frog."

"Is that true?" Valerie asked.

"Hmm?" Grant asked. "No. But she needs to move like it."

Valerie frowned.

It was good advice.

"Are we in danger?" Sasha asked.

"When aren't we?" Grant asked, and Sasha quailed. Valerie put her arm around her friend and shook her head.

"He's like this," she said. "It's pragmatic, but it sounds really pessimistic. He fights in a magic war and has been for the last twenty years, near as matters. We're good."

Sasha nodded.

"I shouldn't have come," she whispered, and Valerie shrugged.

"No going back now."

"My mom is going to be so mad," Sasha said, and Valerie grinned.

She got to *see* her mom.

She couldn't wipe the smile off her face, in point of fact.

"We've got a little walk, here," Grant said. "I didn't want to leave the car too close, in case someone did manage to follow it."

The place smelled of chemicals and grit and… stuff Valerie couldn't place, and she wanted to cover her nose and mouth with her hand, but she knew better.

"How far?" she asked, and he glanced over.

"It doesn't get any better," he said. "You just learn to live with it and keep spare clothes to change into once you get out."

"Why are we *here*?" Sasha asked.

"There are empty spaces in the world that don't tend to be worth fighting over," Grant said. "It was this or Wyoming."

"I'm sure the people of Wyoming would disagree," Valerie said reflexively, and Grant laughed.

"There are more cattle than people in Wyoming, which is exactly the point. If you need to go be alone, you can either lose yourself in a dense crowd or you can go somewhere that no one ever *bothers* going. And that's what this is."

"It's awful," Sasha said. "Why would *anyone* be here?"

"Because they don't have a choice, mostly," Grant said. "Going to get cold out fast, tonight. Need to keep moving."

Valerie and Sasha huddled against each other for heat, speeding up to match Grant.

Eventually, he stopped and opened a door on a tall, rectangular building with rust down the sides.

"This is it," he said, letting Valerie and Sasha in first.

Valerie had been hoping for more warmth once they got inside, but it was just as cold as outside, and the stench was bordering on intolerable.

"Through that way," Grant said, and Valerie looked over her shoulder at him, skeptical that this had *actually* been her mom's plan.

"Valerie," Susan called, and Valerie's misgivings evaporated.

"Mom," she answered, dropping her arm from around Sasha and jogging into a large open space with three drum barrels in the middle of it casting all of the available light.

Susan Blake hugged her daughter fiercely, then turned to put out an arm to Sasha.

Sasha ducked under Susan's arm like a chick seeking refuge, and Susan hugged both of them.

"Well, now," she said, taking a step back from Sasha. "We haven't been introduced. I'm Susan Blake, Valerie's mom, and you must be Sasha Mills, Ivory's daughter."

"You knew my mom," Sasha said, and Susan nodded.

"She saved my life more than once," she said, and Sasha turned her face away.

"She never told me."

"Sasha, if your mom ever sat you down to tell you about all of the people she's saved in her life, you'd be old by the time she was done. She's an incredible woman."

Sasha looked at Valerie.

"They told me that you requested I be Valerie's roommate. Why?"

"Because I knew that, if there was one single thing that Ivory Mills passed on to her kids, it would be trustworthiness. She's not political if she can help it, but when she chooses a side, she sticks with it."

"She ran away from the Council," Sasha said. "Just like you did. Well, not *just* like you did, but…"

Susan paused, then pulled her mouth to the side in something resembling a smile.

"If I'd known she was looking to get out, I would have taken her with me. Though I think that quitting magic would have been harder for her than me, and that's saying something."

Sasha shook her head quickly.

"No. She wouldn't have gone, if she had to stop using magic. She goes to hospitals and casts healing magic. She wouldn't walk away from that… She told me once that she'd rather die than abandon her calling."

Susan nodded.

"That's the woman I knew, all those years ago. Well, come sit. Are you hungry?"

"There is no way I could consume food here," Valerie said. It was past dinner time, though. If it weren't for the smell, she *would* have been hungry.

"Well, sit anyway," Susan said. "It doesn't get any better, but you start to notice it less."

She sat down on a couch, and Valerie sat down next to her, unable to take her eyes off her mother's face.

"I can't believe you're here," Valerie said.

"I know," Susan said. "I can't believe *you're* here."

"Why did I have to come?" Sasha asked. "I don't understand. I *want* to do the right thing, and if it *helps*…"

"Because we didn't want you to have to deal with the Council when they start really looking hard for Valerie," Susan said. "She was their lead on me, and if Grant did his job right…"

Grant cleared his throat and Susan looked over at him with a bright, teasing smile.

"… we've just slipped that lead entirely."

"Are we not going back?" Valerie asked, seeing the alarm on Sasha's face.

"After a bit," Susan answered, putting a hand out toward Sasha. "And I've already sent your mom a sign to let her know that I have you. I… It's been a long time, but if she still thinks of me the way she did back then, she'll know that I'll keep you safe like my own daughter."

"But what are we *doing*?" Valerie asked. "Dad came in all mysterious, come with me if you want to live, but he didn't tell us *anything*. How long have you two been together? What are you planning? How do we help?"

Susan nodded, turning her head as Grant came to sit on the floor nearby. Valerie wrinkled her nose at the idea of *sitting* like that, but there was a good chance the couch wasn't actually any better.

"I want you to know," Susan said finally, still looking at Grant. "I felt like we *knew*, back then. We didn't know the people or the places or the things, not like your dad does *now*, but I felt like we knew that it was more complicated, the fight that was *actually* going on than the one we were fighting. We were young and… stupid… and it was okay to be fighting good-guys versus bad-guys, and just go at 'em. It's not like that, now… I think. I think they don't even *know* how different the reality is from the story, and… If we're going to win this, we have to be doing it for the right reasons."

"Okay," Valerie said. "Then tell us."

Susan shook her head.

"This is stuff you have to see. You have to experience it. So tomorrow you're going to Ground School."

Valerie blinked slowly.

"You say that like I should know what it is," she said.

"Oh, no," Susan said, looking past Valerie. "You shouldn't, but Miss Mills does."

"Ground School?" Sasha asked. Susan nodded, and Valerie felt Sasha sit down on the couch behind her. She turned to look at

Sasha.

"What is it?" she asked.

"School of Beginning Magic," Sasha said, swallowing and looking at Susan again. "It's the lowest of the light schools. Like, if you can't get in *anywhere*, maybe you can get in there."

"So you're telling me it's where *I* belong," Valerie said, and Sasha shook her head quickly.

"No. You're *really* good. Like, one of the best alive, I think, and Survival School... They're going to do right by you, making sure you get trained up and strong and... stuff."

"That wouldn't happen at Ground School," Susan said. "What you're seeing right there, Val. That's *shame*."

"Why?" Valerie asked. "What could she possibly be ashamed about?"

Sasha shook her head, her expression saying that she wasn't sure.

"Survivor's guilt, to start with," Susan said. "She's glad she didn't *have* to go there, and to go be confronted with all of the people who *do*... She's ashamed of how glad she is not to be there."

Valerie shrugged.

"So? I knew which colleges I wanted to apply to, and I would have been disappointed if I'd had to settle for community college. Doesn't mean there aren't people going there that that's their best choice, and good for them."

Susan gave her a soft smile and shook her head.

"That's why you have to see it," she said. "Sasha knows intuitively, because she's been threatened with Ground School her entire life, but you need to see it with your own eyes to know... To see how the two sides are both really doing the same thing."

"I have no idea what you're talking about," Valerie said, and Susan gave her a cool smile. Valerie knew that smile. That was the 'do your own homework' smile, and Valerie shook her head.

"There are a pair of offices back that way that aren't completely trashed," Susan said, getting a notebook out from under the couch and standing. "We'll be sleeping back there tonight."

"Ew," Valerie said. "We're *staying* here?"

"This is where we're safe, tonight," Susan said. "We have a lot of sneaking around to do, and I'll remind you that your dad and I are still fighting a war, so we aren't always both going to be around. You may at one point wake up and we're both gone. Whatever you do, stay put, stay quiet, and stay safe. Only move when one of us are there to tell you where to go."

"Mom," Valerie said. "You kidnapped us out of the school. For this."

"It *was* kind of like a prison," Sasha said quietly, and Valerie spun to look at her. Sasha shrugged.

"It smells bad," she said. "And I'm a little worried about cockroaches eating my eyebrows. But... it's a little bit exciting, to get to actually *see* what's going on out here, right?"

Aaand now Valerie wasn't going to sleep at all.

"What?" she asked, and Sasha ducked her head.

"I don't know. I grew up with all of these big *stories* about the old war, and... Maybe if it's only smelly and inconvenient, it isn't that bad. I'd really like to see it for myself. Isn't that what you wanted?"

"Who are you and what have you done with Sasha Mills?" Valerie asked, and Sasha grinned sheepishly again.

"I don't know. It's just... I'm out here, right? I may as well just go with it. No point moping about how much safer I'd be at school, especially since I almost died there twice in the last four months."

Valerie looked at her mother again, who pretended not to notice the conversation that had just happened.

"I set you two up in here," Susan said, opening a door. "Your father and I will be here."

She indicated the door across the hallway, and Valerie paused.

"Weird," she said, and Susan nodded.

"I know."

"Hmm?" Sasha asked, and Valerie shook her head, leading the way into the office.

"It's just strange," Valerie said after Sasha closed the door. "My mom never had a man in her room all the time I can remember, and now... she's sleeping with my dad."

"Ah."

Valerie looked around the office.

There was a small cast in the middle of the floor, not unlike the one Ethan had done to give them light and heat out in the forest the night before - had that really only been one day earlier? - and two sets of blankets.

Valerie would have preferred a sleeping bag, because then nothing could have sneaked in through the sides, but the room didn't have quite the smell as the rest of the building - it mostly smelled mildewy and dusty - and she thought she could sleep here.

"If this goes bad, I'm sorry I got you into it," Valerie said.

"I made a choice," Sasha answered. "I want... I want to know what's actually going on. As much as I don't want to get involved in the war, I do want to be one of the people who knows the truth about it. You know?"

Valerie scratched her forehead.

"Hanson just turns up and I just made up with Ethan and... this. I mean, I couldn't have even gotten a couple of *days* with them?"

She heard Sasha smile, then the girl picked up a blanket and sat down, looking up at Valerie.

"They'll still be there when we get back."

"I hope so," Valerie said morbidly, then shook her head and sat down next to Sasha. "You know how to put this thing out?"

Sasha shook her head, then glanced around the room.

"I'd rather leave it on, if it's all the same to you, anyway."

Valerie nodded, squeezing her knees against her chest, then shrugging.

"Well. We're here."

"We're here," Sasha agreed, and Valerie shook her head.

"Nothing about this is ever going to be normal again," she said.

With nothing else to work on and a mysterious load of wood arriving in the afternoon, the three boys managed to build a bunk over top of Ethan's desk. Franky Frank had been the one to deliver the lumber, and he had warned them that he wouldn't tolerate a bed over top of another bed, if he was going to be relying on teenagers to build it, and also that he would judge the quality of workmanship and it would be his sole discretion whether or not they were going to get away with it, but it was a nice bunk.

The mattress didn't exactly fit, so they filled in the gap between the mattress and the outside frame with cup-holders the entire length of the bed, and Hanson was actually kind of jealous that Shack was going to get to sleep up there.

That said, if the thing came down, he was glad that he would be neither on it nor under it.

Ethan stuck his head out into the hallway, signaling Franky Frank, who came and pulled on the bed and then got up and stood on it.

"What are all of these?" he asked, toeing the holes in the wood.

"Cupholders," Shack said cheerfully.

"Where'd you learn to build like this?" Franky Frank asked, climbing back down the ladder and looking at the way the bed was attached to the wall.

"I've done some stuff with my dad," Shack said.

"It's overkill, but it looks fine," Franky Frank said. "Get ready for dinner."

Hanson grinned as the dorm monitor left, then sat down on his own bed.

"This is gonna be awesome," he said.

"Power room," Shack muttered, climbing up into the bed and sitting down. Ethan shook his head.

"It's good that we can hang out here and put up good warding. There's a lot we need to talk about."

"Geez," Shack said. "Can't I enjoy my bed for like two minutes before you have to start with the politics again?"

"No," Ethan said. "This can't wait."

"I'm actually kind of thinking about what I need to do in order to keep up with the classes here," Hanson said.

"Mostly hopeless," Ethan answered without looking at him. "Valerie has a natural gift, and she's working harder than anyone I've ever known has, and it isn't helping. The only reason she can *do* magic is because she's a natural, and I bet everything you aren't."

"How do you know?" Hanson asked.

"Two naturals at the same time..." Shack said, shaking his head. "And her parents were Susan and Grant Blake. I've never heard of your parents."

"Apparently neither have I," Hanson said.

Ethan grinned.

"I know how to do the tests," he said. "If you want to try it and see whether or not you can even *do* magic."

"Is it possible I couldn't?" Hanson asked.

"It runs in families," Ethan said, going to a drawer and pulling out a box. He glanced up at Shack, over his head, and shuddered. "Going to take a minute to get used to *that*. Anyway, if your parents weren't both really strong in it, it's always possible that your talent is going to be minimal."

"I've never tried," Hanson said. "My mom never offered to teach me."

Shack leaned out over the edge of the bed to watch as Ethan mixed things - if the thing was going to fall, it was probably going to be now - and then Ethan handed Hanson a glass bowl with a half a cup of oil in it and a bunch of stuff floating in it.

"What do I do with that?" Hanson asked.

"You drink it," Ethan answered, going back to mixing.

"Do what now?" Hanson asked. "What's in it?"

"Do you really want to know?" Shack asked. "You're drinking it either way."

"Am I?" Hanson asked, looking at it. Shack watched, unwavering, and Hanson sighed, putting the bowl to his mouth and tipping it back.

He'd probably eaten stupider things.

Ethan straightened and handed him a cup.

"Rinse your mouth out with that," he said, watching Hanson. "How do you feel?"

"How am I supposed to feel?" Hanson asked, shifting.

"He's not a strong dark user," Shack said, and Ethan glanced up at him.

"Didn't know you knew the tests."

"Seen 'em done enough times to tell them apart," Shack said. Ethan shrugged, then held up a q-tip, waiting for Hanson to drink the salty water.

"Open," Ethan said, and Hanson went with it. Ethan swabbed the inside of his mouth, then dipped the cotton into a little vial of clear goo. The cotton turned dark green, and as Ethan swished it around, the green swirled around the cotton just a bit in the goo.

"What does that mean?" Hanson asked.

"Only fair we both do it, too," Shack said, shifting to hang his legs out over the side of the bed.

Now was when it was going to fail, for sure, if it ever would.

"I've only got enough for a couple more," Ethan said, not hesitating as he continued mixing.

"I'll get you replacements the next time they let us out to wander," Shack said. "Lottie keeps them in bulk in the lab."

Ethan finished mixing, standing up to hand another bowl to Shack. They tapped the two bowls against each other and downed them. Shack twisted his head to the side, rubbing his tongue along the roof of his mouth like the mix was bitter, but Ethan closed his eyes, taking a deep, slow breath. Shack watched him and nodded.

"Yup," he said. "Knew that, didn't I?"

"Shut up," Ethan said, opening his eyes and taking the cup out of Hanson's hand and pouring a portion of the salty water into it. He swished it through his mouth and handed the cup up to Shack as he swallowed, went to get more q-tips.

"Do me first," Shack said, taking one of them to swab his mouth and handing it back. Ethan nodded, dipping the cotton into clear goo and holding it up for Hanson to see.

The cotton turned just a shade of light green and did nothing as Ethan stirred with it.

"Trophy?" Ethan asked, handing it up.

"Thank you," Shack answered.

"What does it *mean*?" Hanson asked.

"Just wait," Shack said. Ethan shook his head and swabbed, dipping the q-tip one more time into a vial of fluid the consistency of glue.

He let go.

He didn't even have to stir.

Dark green, almost black, seeped out from the cotton, dyeing the entire vial an increasingly dark shade of green.

"Whoa," Hanson said and Ethan nodded.

"I'm the black sheep of my family. Quite literally."

"Shouldn't tell people," Shack said. "Just so you know. People around here are almost all light magic."

"So I have more magic than you?" Hanson asked. "Is that what that means?"

"Just wait," Ethan said, squatting and mixing once more. He came up with three wooden bowls, a thinner mix this time, and he handed one up to Shack. They tipped them back all at once, and Hanson sucked on the inside of his cheeks.

It had a sweetness to it, and a heat. He blinked, surprised at how subtle and significant a flavor the mix had. It wasn't that he was tasting it in his tongue. It was like he could taste it with his very blood.

"Whoa," he said, only becoming aware of the room again after a moment. Ethan and Shack were watching each other.

"Let's do it," Shack said, and Ethan nodded, holding up a needle and a lighter.

"What?" Hanson said.

"There are other ways," Shack said, holding out a finger as Ethan heated the tip of the needle to red. He dipped the needle into a cup of pinkish liquid and pressed the point of it against Shack's finger until it beaded blood. Lifting the blood on the needle itself, he put it back into the liquid, where the blood hit the surface like oil spreading across water, swirling and forming patterns.

It was really cool, actually.

Bright, bright red.

It covered the entire surface of the liquid for several more moments, then formed balls and fell through to the bottom of the glass.

Ethan handed the glass to Hanson and heated the needle again, dipping it quickly into the cup and pressing it against his own thumb. Once more, the tiny drop of blood touched the pink, but this time it hissed and boiled, turning black and scattering something like ash across the surface, sinking almost immediately.

Ethan sighed.

"Someone without any ability at all, it doesn't react. The blood just falls through," Shack said. "He has light magic; the test just hates the dark magic in his blood."

Ethan nodded, then put the lighter to the needle once more.

"You ready?" he asked.

Hanson nodded, indicating his fourth finger.

At least the needle wasn't intended to be scalding hot when it punctured him.

Even having watched Ethan do it twice before, and even knowing it wasn't a big deal, it was hard not to jerk his hand away as Ethan squeezed his finger and pushed through the skin with the needle.

Blood.

It sprung up in a bead and Ethan lifted the needle, but the blood had crawled across Hanson's skin, and Ethan twisted his mouth to the side.

"Sorry, man," he said, switching fingers and doing it again.

"Oh, come on," Hanson said, and Ethan grinned.

"It's not like I do this for a living," he said, getting the bead of blood on the needle this time and dipping it into the cup.

The patterns, the colors, weren't quite as vibrant as Shack's, but it was…

Hanson watched with awe as his very own blood shone red on the surface of the cup, swirling and twisting, almost like pictures or symbols.

He waited.

And he waited.

Almost thirty seconds later, the blood started to form the tiny balls, dropping one by one through to the glass below.

"Wow," Ethan said, watching. "Did not see that coming."

"He could have gotten through to Light School," Shack said.

"If they wouldn't let you in, they wouldn't let him in," Ethan answered. "But, yeah, he's got the power."

"Tell me what it means," Hanson said, still watching, awestruck.

"You aren't as pure as Shack," Ethan said. "Where he's got power all the way up through to one hundred percent light, you're probably, what, ninety-five?"

"Like that," Shack agreed.

"He's going to be able to do *anything* with light magic. But you? When you actually get this figured out, you're gonna be a beast to be reckoned with."

Shack nodded.

"Welcome to the team."

There was a knock on the door and Ethan hastily stashed everything under his bed, going to open it.

It was Franky Frank.

"Dinner," he said, pointing his thumb down the hallway. "Straight there, straight back."

"This is going to be *killing* Val," Hanson said. "She doesn't like being told what to do, and I've *never* seen her sit still for more than like fifteen minutes straight."

"She spends all her time in the library," Ethan said, and Hanson grinned.

"But have you *watched* her? She's got fidgeting down to an art."

Ethan frowned thoughtfully, then nodded.

"Maybe."

Hanson felt a little bad, showing Ethan up like that, but whatever. It was true. Val was going to be going *nuts*.

They were almost all the way to the cafeteria before Ann saw them and came running over. She whispered something in Ethan's ear, looking smug for a moment, then glanced at Hanson with narrowed eyes and dashed away.

Ethan stopped walking, then started up again, much faster now.

"What?" Hanson asked.

"The girls are gone," Ethan said, rounding into the cafeteria and stopping.

It was full of girls.

Like, as much as it had been at lunch, at least.

Hanson scanned for Valerie and Sasha, and then the words sunk in.

"Where are they?" he asked. Ethan shook his head.

"I haven't got a clue."

They got up before the sun, the building intolerably cold and the blankets no longer holding it off. Valerie rubbed her arms, watching as her dad packed up a backpack and pulled it up onto his shoulder.

"All right," he said. "Let's go."

Susan was sweeping the building, collecting things that looked an awful lot like trash to Valerie's eye, which she stuffed into a backpack.

Sasha looked like she might be reconsidering her resolve from the previous night, but she didn't complain.

Valerie felt like complaining just to make up for how willing Sasha was to keep her mouth shut.

"Do we get breakfast?" Valerie asked.

"Don't always get every meal, when you're out here doing this," Grant answered. "Always ought to eat like you may not get food in the next day."

"We aren't on a desert island," Susan scolded. "We can stop and get something."

Valerie looked at her dad, and he shrugged.

"Doesn't make it untrue. We have to avoid anywhere we might have people see us, and sometimes that means avoiding food."

"You had a house," Valerie said. "With a kitchen."

"Which I had to abandon because they were watching too close as I went there, and they found it," he said. "It's lucky they didn't figure out who I *was*, that morning."

"Right. How are you two together?" Valerie asked. "I thought if anyone found out that you were alive…"

"That someone important would be in an uncomfortable position?" Susan asked. "It took some work and some planning, and a couple of felony-level forgeries, but I've put together a record that ought to hold up under pretty intense scrutiny that says that your dad went to New Mexico and lived under the radar just like we did, the whole time. If anyone asks, I was the one who came and talked to you the day of the first demon attack, but you didn't leave with me."

"Okay," Valerie said slowly. "So… Are you two *together* now?"

Susan licked her lips and looked over at Grant, then shrugged.

"We weren't ever *not* together," Grant said as she started to say something. Susan looked over at him, then nodded.

"It's okay if you aren't ready for us to be a *family*," she said, licking her lips once more as she looked hard at Valerie. "And if you're angry with me for how it happened, I understand, but... There was never anyone else. For either of us."

That was...

Okay, that was both the best thing Valerie had ever heard, and deeply disturbing. There was sex in the look her dad gave her mom.

"Okay, that's... no. Just." Valerie put her hands up to block what she could see of her dad, and her mom laughed.

"Sorry."

"I'm hungry," Sasha said, and Susan nodded.

"We need to walk back out to the car and check it, and so long as no one has pinged it, we'll go get some breakfast and see if we can't get you to school on time."

"You're serious?" Valerie asked as they started toward the doors. The cold air outside hit her hard enough to take her breath away.

"What do we do?" Sasha asked. "If something happens?"

"Fight," Grant said without looking back.

"Run," Susan said, louder. "We can find you, wherever you end up."

"How?" Valerie asked.

Susan cleared her throat, and Grant sighed.

"I met an old witch, a couple of years out of school. First time I'd met a magic user who wasn't one of us."

"And by 'one of us' you mean..." Susan prompted.

He looked back, annoyed, and Susan smiled brightly.

"The magic community that we are a part of, as big as it seems..." Grant started, pausing with a tone of resignation. "It's only a fraction of the magic community that exists. We think that we are alone, but we simply have managed to avoid contact with other magic users. I think that it's denial, myself, but I don't have a good explanation for it. It's actually part of the reason that we want you to see Ground School. The hubris of both sides of this fight..."

"Jumping ahead of yourself," Susan said, teasing.

"It's the important part," Grant said. "Scrying is the least important part."

"But it was the *question*," Susan said.

"Right," Grant said. "Fine. I met a witch, and she had significant magic that I'd never seen before. She knew about our fight, and she hated it, hated seeing magic users tearing each other apart over differences that were all…"

"Grant," Susan interrupted.

He sighed again.

"She taught me some magic that the community had never seen before," Grant said. "She wanted me to use it to stop the war."

"And you did," Susan said. "You just kept it all to yourself, because you like the power of being able to do something no one else can do."

"I didn't see you volunteering to go to Light School and teach them," Grant muttered.

"They couldn't learn it, at Light School," Susan answered, and Grant laughed.

"Wait, why not?" Sasha asked. "Is it dark?"

Susan looked over, then frowned.

"You're freezing. Grant, you didn't tell them to take their jackets?"

"Field work means planning ahead. Only way to learn how to plan ahead is to fail a few times."

"Mom sent me to school to live in a dorm without a pillow," Valerie said, and Susan shot her a sharp glance that was deeply humored.

"She did what?" Grant asked.

"I…" Susan started. "Did that. I did that."

He stopped, turning around to look at Susan with exaggerated dismay, then shook his head and took off his coat, handing it to Sasha.

"Fine."

Valerie smiled.

"Why would the people at Light School not be able to learn the magic that you learned?" Sasha pressed.

"Natural selection," Grant muttered. Susan shrugged an

agreement.

"It was beginning to happen, there by the end of the war, and I can only imagine it's getting worse. It used to be that Light School and Survival School were *interests*, not aptitudes. Anymore, the admission process is so... It's more political than I would have even guessed. I'm kind of stunned that Roger managed to get Valerie in."

"They needed you that badly," Grant muttered. Susan nodded.

"They still do. Anyway, at this point, they're restricting admissions so tight and screening so hard, they only end up taking the kids with the pointiest skills. I probably wouldn't have gotten into Light School, if I'd applied today, and I know for a fact that Grant wouldn't have."

"Why not?" Sasha asked. "Your entrance exam is still part of the curriculum at Light School. Both of my brothers talk about it."

Susan rolled her eyes.

"Because I can *do* dark magic. I mean... It doesn't help anything that the Council ended up getting taken over by perfect light magic users."

"Didn't used to be that way," Grant called back. "Just so you hear her."

Susan nodded.

"Used to be, the first generation of the Council, they had a dark magic user sitting, just because they wanted the broadest skillset possible."

"Purists," Grant muttered.

"Sour grapes," Susan retorted.

"No, wait," Sasha said. "You can do dark magic?"

"Of course I can," Susan said. "How do you think I stayed alive all this time? And Grant? He's *strong* at light magic, but it's his weakest discipline."

"Wait here," Grant said, setting down his backpack and taking something out. Susan nodded, going to lean against a building that Valerie wouldn't have *touched*, before all of this.

"So why couldn't they do the witch's magic?" Sasha asked once more. "Is it dark?"

"It's natural," Susan said, taking out a knife and using it to clean out her fingernails.

Valerie couldn't believe what she was seeing.

"I don't know what that means," Sasha said.

"And that is why we're going to a Pure-sponsored school after this."

"What?" Valerie asked. "Isn't that dangerous?"

"Every minute of being my daughter is dangerous," Susan said. "Von Lauv Academy is a huge school, and I think I've got every chance of slipping you in undetected. Sometimes the safest place to be is exactly the last place they'd look for you."

"I've never heard of Von Lauv," Sasha said, and Susan shook her head, perking for a moment's interest, then shaking her head and relaxing against the wall again.

"You wouldn't have. It's been renamed since the first war, and aggregated. The Pure and the non-propagationists came together and decided that they wanted to have a small number of people making high-level decisions at schools, and to try to funnel all of the objector's kids through the same classes as the Pure kids. It's a tactic that's worked. They've got a lot of kids graduating who are sympathetic, if not to the Pure, to the non-propagationists."

"Who are the Pure?" Sasha asked, and Susan sighed.

"The crazies who are going to wipe out the entire civilian population of the globe if they aren't careful."

"You mean the Superiors," Sasha said, and Susan sighed.

"I can't believe the Council is doubling down on that propaganda. No. I don't mean the Superiors. I mean the Pure. The non-propagationists would *talk* to us, if we seemed to be willing and able to have conversations that were anything other than ultimatums and posturing."

Valerie was stunned to hear her mother talk like that. She'd only been at Survival School for a few months, but everyone walked on eggshells, trying to keep up appearances, at least, with their relationship with the Council. The Council saw all and judged all, and from the look on Sasha's face, the redhead was just as shocked.

"We're moving," Susan said, standing and wiping off her shoulder. Valerie fell into step behind her mother, there next to Sasha, and raised her eyebrows. Sasha mirrored the expression.

A car pulled up to the curb at the corner, and the three of them got in, Valerie and Sasha sliding into the back seat next to each other without a word.

They'd talked late into the night.

No one knew where Valerie and Sasha had gone, who had taken them, why no one had seen them.

"You know that they've been after her," Ethan had said, grim, after a lot of speculation. "I wasn't sure I believed her, that it was *her* specifically they were after, because maybe they were just messing with the school, or maybe they were after the Council kids who are all in this year, or maybe they had an agent who had made it into the school, and that made us an easy target. But... There wasn't even an attack. They really did come *just* for her."

"But what about Sasha?" Hanson asked. "What's she got to do with it?"

"I bet she wouldn't let them take Valerie without her," Shack said. "Chick's tough. Tougher than people give her credit for."

"Why?" Hanson asked. "Why would she *make* someone kidnap her?"

"Stuff keeps happening to Valerie," Ethan said. "And Sasha's a healer. She can't just sit back and watch it. Not if she has a choice."

Hanson sighed.

He was worried about Valerie, but there was something about her, something that had always felt so *capable*, even when he'd been standing next to her on the street so that guys wouldn't come try to push her around. She'd always known how to take care of herself, and while she had no problem letting him help, she could deal with anything when she needed to.

Sasha, though.

Sasha was soft and warm and happy, sweet in a way Valerie had never even considered. Ethan was right. Sasha was a healer. Valerie was a fighter.

Sasha had no business being out there, wherever she was, even if she *wouldn't* have forgiven herself for letting Valerie go on her own.

"Are they dead?" he'd asked, laying on his back in the dark, unable to see either of his roommates, but glad he wasn't alone all the same.

"No," Ethan had answered. "No, they can't be. I won't let them."

The next morning, all three of them had ignored the call for breakfast. Ethan had said something about wondering what Lady Harrington and Mr. Benson would say about the disappearance, but Shack didn't think they would say anything.

They didn't know anything, so they wouldn't say anything.

Finally, they got up.

Showered.

Shaved.

Sat in the room.

"Wish I could go work out," Shack said.

"Anything," Hanson agreed.

There was a knock on the door and Hanson looked over at it.

It couldn't be lunch time already.

"Ethan," a man's voice said.

Ethan sat up sharply in his bed.

"Dad," he answered, standing and going to open the door.

A man walked in, the spitting image of Elvis Trent, tall, dark-haired, and serious. He looked almost nothing like Ethan.

"What have you done in here?" he asked, looking up at Shack.

"Lost a bet," Shack answered, rolling onto his back and virtually disappearing on the upper bed.

"I need to speak with you," the man said, looking at Ethan. "We're going to Lady Harrington's office to talk privately."

"I don't know where she is, Dad," Ethan said.

The man looked over at Hanson, then shook his head.

"Not good enough," he said. "That's what I sent you here for. Come with me, now."

Ethan sighed, then gave Hanson a shrug and followed the man out into the hallway and closed the door.

"Don't hold your breath," Shack muttered from his bed.

Ethan didn't come back for almost two hours. Franky Frank

brought them food in the room when Shack and Hanson declined to go to lunch. Hanson didn't know why they were staying put, but that was what Shack did, and Hanson could follow a lead.

They ate without talking, then returned to their beds. Hanson needed a ball to bounce off of the far wall, but he didn't even have that.

It was maddening, how slow time went.

Valerie and Sasha were missing, and he had no idea where.

And there was nothing he could do about it.

Nothing.

Finally Ethan returned, going to lay down on his bed.

"What did he say?" Shack asked.

"He thinks I'm covering for her and that she ran off."

"Ran off where?" Shack asked.

"Her mom is out of communication with the Council, and her dad just turned up again."

"He isn't dead?" Hanson asked, and Ethan shook his head.

"They think that someone told her about it, and she went to go find her mom. And that she knows where to look."

"How would she know that?" Hanson asked. "And why would Sasha go with her?"

Ethan shook his head.

"I just told him I didn't know anything, because I don't." He paused. "I think they've been holding out hope that Valerie would eventually lead them back to her mom, and they've lost her... and they're desperate. I was his last hope that they could get her back."

There was another knock on the door and Ethan sighed, going to open it.

He stepped back, and Hanson leaned over, expecting Ethan's dad once more.

"Mom," Hanson said, leaping to his feet. "Mom."

"Hanson," she said, looking at Ethan and Shack. "You landed with a good crowd."

"Mom," he said. "Where have you been?"

"Come with me," she said, her voice low and even. It made him feel cold, but he got up and followed her out of the room, through the school, and to the office where Ethan's dad was sitting at a table in a conference room.

"Come sit," Martha Cox said, going to sit next to Ethan's dad.

Hanson hesitated, then took a chair across from them, feeling like this was the worst version of being called to the principal's office he'd ever seen.

"Mom," he said slowly. "Where have you been?"

She shook her head.

"That's not what we're here to talk about," she said. "I need you to tell us where Valerie Blake is."

"How would I know?" Hanson asked, his voice rising. "Mom, you *left* me."

"I had a job to do. I told you, over and over again, that you do the job you have to do. This is my job."

"You *left* me," Hanson said. "I got home and you were just *gone*."

"Once Valerie Blake knew who you were, there was no purpose leaving your mother on the sidelines anymore," Mr. Trent said. "So the Council recalled her."

"And you just left without even thinking about what would happen to me?" Hanson asked, yelling now.

"You had everything you needed," Martha answered, standing and yelling back. "You don't need me to feed and shelter you. I trained you and I raised you to be smart and strong, and you were both. You ended up exactly where you needed to be, and you're fine."

"But I could have *died*," Hanson said. "I *walked* out here, Mom. I had no idea where I was going. You *left* me."

"You need to prove that you're capable of handing it when things don't go right," Martha stormed back. "Not come whining to someone to fix it."

"I'm your *kid*."

"And I'm *proud*," she retorted.

"Mr. Cox," Mr. Trent said loudly - though not as loudly as either Martha or Hanson had been yelling. Hanson looked at the man, then reconsidered his pitch.

"Yeah," he said. "I don't know where Valerie is."

"We heard that she had made up with you the night she

disappeared," Mr. Trent said. "I think she probably told you *something*, given the timing. She didn't want to run off and leave things the way they were, so she came back to her oldest friend and told him what was going on."

Hanson tipped his head to the side.

"You've never met Valerie, have you?" he asked.

Martha gave him a dark look, and Hanson almost laughed.

And then he did laugh.

"She didn't forgive me for spying on her to you guys my entire life because she needed a friend. Yeah, she missed me and I missed her, and you guys messed that up pretty bad, but she wouldn't have done it just because she was desperate. She's so much more than that. Have you even considered that maybe the bad guys finally got her? I mean, why else would Sasha Mills be missing, too?"

"Because teenage girls take five of them just to go to the bathroom," Mr. Trent said. "They flock. This is normal. Valerie left and so Miss Mills went with her. I need to know *every word* Valerie Blake said to you before she left."

"I don't remember," Hanson said without hesitation. "But none of it was about her parents. It was about *us* and about how hard it is for her to trust *anyone* right now, for how hard the Council is working to try to spy on her. And... I had no idea. Until right now."

"Hanson," Martha said, pointing a finger at him. "That woman is the key to winning this war. I gave up my entire *life* in order to keep tabs on her for the Council, I spent my son to do the same, and now, when it matters most, I expect you to come through. This has been the reason behind everything I have ever done."

Hanson crossed his arms, looking hard at his mom.

He loved his mom.

She made him laugh until his sides hurt and she was the kind of woman he admired most for how strong and how confident she was. She'd basically raised him on her own, for as much as his dad had had to work, but it had never seemed like a burden on her.

He thought she'd been happy.

"That's sad, Mom," he finally said. "Because we had a good life before you walked away from it."

"I gave up magic for this," she said. "Because winning the war that was to come was the most important thing that I could do, and the biggest contribution I could make to that was making sure that the Council could find Susan Blake when the time came."

"And now with her daughter showing such aptitude," Mr. Trent said. "We need Valerie, too. She may be key to the survival of our way of life."

"Is everyone in your universe there for you to use them?" Hanson asked.

"Yes," Mr. Trent said, giving Hanson a very hard look. "Because my direction is the only thing between ourselves and *death*. Do not kid yourself that I'm exaggerating. I know that you don't know about us, or our war, or our methods, but the Council was forged by the first war, and we exist with the knowledge that our vigilance is the best chance we have of surviving the second."

"And if that means filling Valerie's life with spies and never letting her have a real relationship with a human being who cares about her?" Hanson asked.

"You should try being on the Council," Mr. Trent replied. "What did she say to you?"

"I think she's in danger," Hanson said. "She didn't say anything to me, and honestly if she was planning on just up and leaving, I think she would have at least hinted at it. I think that someone came and took her by force, and that they took Sasha, too, and if you think her life is important, you need to start *looking* for her, because…"

He didn't want to finish that sentence, because he didn't want to think about it.

Mr. Trent looked over at Martha and lifted his chin.

"You think you can do it?" he asked.

"I think I'm your best bet," Martha answered.

"All right," Mr. Trent said. "Take him, take whatever resources you need, and bring me Susan Blake."

"Oh, if I play my cards right, I'm going to bring you the entire Blake clan," Martha answered.

First Day?

Ground School was a brick building an hour away. Valerie no longer had any sense of where they were; she'd been in a car in the dark for too many hours between Survival School and now, and they'd gone through open country and dense city, and while she was sure she could have been watching road signs to figure it out, she instead sat in the back seat watching her parents and trying to figure out what in the world was going on with them.

Her mom was the same as she had ever been, happy and confident and very bossy, with a devious playfulness to her that Valerie had always loved. Grant was just the way that he had been, for the two weeks she'd spent with him, gruff and sarcastic and dismissive, but the two of them together…

They made sense. She could see it. She could see how her mom made her dad into a different person, really, and how he could keep up with her and could make her laugh… For the first time, Valerie realized that her mother had been *alone*, raising her, and she caught a glimpse of what life would have been like if her parents had been able to figure out how to stay together.

And it was the same and different and completely bewildering all by itself.

And then you added in magic and a war.

Valerie had doubted her father, once. Been willing to believe that he was with the Pure or the Superiors or whatever the right word was for them.

Right now?

She didn't doubt that they weren't *with* the Pure, but she was beginning to doubt that they were *with* the Council, either.

For all intents and purposes, the two of them appeared to be on their own team entirely, and…

It was so tempting to just throw herself into that, go be team Blake, go charging into the middle of the war and blow it up and be fantastically right where the two entrenched sides were completely

91

wrong.

But there was a strong possibility that both of her parents were crazy.

She couldn't overlook that.

Oh, no.

Sitting there in the back seat looking out at the school, Valerie was more and more convinced that her mother *was* crazy, and that Grant was simply crazy in love.

And that maybe Gemma was the most reasonable one of them all.

"All right, these are your papers," Susan said, turning in her seat and handing them back. "You won't have the same class list, because people would have noticed that, but you do have five classes together, and the same lunch period. Try to sit *with* other kids if you can."

"Remind me what the point of this is?" Valerie asked.

"I think you'll figure it out pretty quickly," Susan said. "But the point is for you to see how the other side lives. These are kids who didn't come from magic families, so they don't come from money. Tuition here is killing their families, and it's barely twenty percent of what they pay at Survival School. They have no preparation or training, they have very few resources. This is how kids come into magic."

"So I might actually learn something," Valerie murmured.

"Don't out yourselves," Grant warned. "The Council will be looking for you, and you don't want the teachers or the staff to figure out that you're more than you seem."

Sasha hesitated.

"I'm really bad at that, actually," she said. "I raise my hand a lot."

"Then don't," Susan said, turning in her seat. "Sit at the back of the class, don't look at the teacher - look around the room - avoid eye contact, and pretend you know nothing. Spend *one day* seeing how that feels."

Sasha looked at Valerie, and Valerie shrugged.

"I'm game. You can stay or you can go."

"I did want to look at School of Magic Fundamentals," Sasha

said slowly. "I'd read that they had different teaching techniques."

"If the point is that this is some slum school with no academic accomplishment, I'd rather pass," Valerie said. "I don't get it."

"Oh, no," Susan said. "Every kid here is working hard. As hard as you or harder. Trying to justify what their parents are spending to send them here. Trying to figure out what magic *is*. The kids that get it? They get a green light into our world, where money…"

"Money falls in your lap, if you're willing to do the right things for the right people," Grant said. "And a lot of them are even legit work."

Susan nodded.

"I've never worried about money; none of our families have ever worried about money."

"Still," Valerie said. "Do we have to go *see*?"

"The Pure think that these people should be stripped of their magic. The non-propagationists think they should be kept ignorant. The Council says that everyone has a right to their own magic, if they want it. I want you to look at the school that the Council endorses to train kids who have magic potential. Every other school under the Council is screening hard. This is the only one that a kid with no magic background can get into. The only one."

Valerie looked over at Sasha once more, and the redhead shrugged.

"I want to go," she said. "I want to see it."

Valerie nodded.

"Then let's do this."

Her first class was with Sasha. The teacher took her information and directed her to an empty seat against a wall, and Sasha to another seat somewhere in the middle of the class.

The room was huge; there were at least fifty students there, and Susan hadn't been wrong - they did appear to be working hard - but the teacher was talking about the spectrum of light and dark magic and how things fit on that scale the same way that Valerie's worst history teachers had just put everything on a timeline and told them to memorize it.

She could just imagine how it would be driving Sasha crazy, the lack of background on how the different incantations, the different ingredients, the different sequences had ties to light or dark, and how those things were influenced by the way that you implemented them.

Even Valerie knew that, and she'd been doing this for all of five months.

She took notes, her eyes crossing as she tried to keep up with the blizzard of details, and then the class was over.

"Hey, I'm Lisa," a girl said, standing and turning around to greet Valerie after the bell rang. "I can't believe they're still letting new people in."

"Just got a late acceptance," Valerie said. "I guess they got to me on the waiting list."

Lisa nodded and sighed.

"People drop out all the time. This is so *hard*."

"So can you actually do magic?" Valerie asked, and Lisa snorted, looking toward the teacher at the front desk and then back at Valerie.

"There are a few of the kids in here who can, but… No. They said the first day not to expect to be able to do anything with any of this until at least sophomore year. A bunch of my friends dropped out at the Christmas break because they decided they wanted to go back to regular school and just go to college and get a job. I mean… Yeah. Anyway. It's not a big deal."

"No," Valerie said. "That's a huge deal. After how hard it was to get in here, how could you just drop out?"

"I don't know," Lisa said. "They say half the class fails out between sophomore and junior year. Do you know that? If you can't pass the test to go on, they fail you, and then where are you, you know? No diploma, can't get in to a college, no transcript. They're getting their GED and going looking for jobs. And a lot of them were really smart, you know?"

"Wow," Valerie said. "I mean, I guess I never thought about it. I just wanted to get *in* so bad. I mean… *magic*."

Lisa shrugged.

"Congratulations," she said. "Just… I don't know. I'm thinking about it, you know? You can only sit through the light-dark lectures for so long and you miss your math classes."

Valerie shook her head.

"Never."

Lisa laughed.

"What's your next class?"

"History of Magic," Valerie said, and Lisa rolled her eyes.

"Get ready to read. They assign so many books in that class, and I bet you have to catch up on all of them. Anyway. Are you in first, second, or third lunch?"

"Second," Valerie said, and Lisa nodded.

"Me, too. Come find me, if you want. First day sucks."

"Yeah," Valerie said. "Thanks."

She caught Sasha's eye, but they were splitting up from there.

Valerie had no school supplies to speak of. Susan had given both of them a notebook and a pen, but that was it. She carried that to her next class, where she went and sat in the back and the teacher never looked at her. This class was even bigger, and no one spoke to her throughout it. The teacher spent the entire class going through slides on a projector, talking about the ancient history of magic. There was no mention of a war of any kind, no mention of the Council. Valerie once more took notes, but looking at them, they told her very little. The teacher handed her a reading list on her way out the door, and Valerie boggled at it.

Sure, she'd been reading a history of rocks not long ago, but this was dozens of books that she was supposed to have read last semester, and another two dozen for this semester.

She went on.

The incantations class was about verb conjugation and how conjugation tied itself to the outcome of a spell, but no one in the room was able to work magic yet, so everything was just in theory. Valerie added a list of conjugations to her notes.

Sasha was in her next class with her, a darkened lecture hall where they sat together and watched upperclassmen work through a complex, ritualistic spell that ultimately didn't work. The teacher came onto the stage afterwards and talked through what they had done wrong. Sasha pushed her notebook over in front of Valerie and checked off the items as the teacher identified them.

Valerie found Lisa in the crowded lunch cafeteria and sat down with her tray of very public-school quality food.

Eat like this was her last meal for a while.

It was still a good rule.

"Oh, hey," Lisa said, looking up. "How was it?"

Valerie shrugged.

"My head is spinning. I can't keep up with any of this."

Lisa gave her a sideways smile and nodded.

"It just keeps feeling like that. When you talk to some of the upperclassmen, they say that it does kind of snap into place at some point… Look, I'm sorry I was having a bad morning, this morning. I've been feeling bad ever since. It's a great school, and it's a great opportunity. I mean, how many other places do you get to learn about magic? I just… I had a bad day yesterday."

"What happened?" Valerie asked.

"She failed a test," the girl across the table said. "And she moped about it all night last night."

"Shut up," Lisa said. "I should have aced that. I studied so hard."

"You studied the wrong chapter," the girl across the table said. "How many times do I have to tell you?"

Lisa gave the girl a dark look, and she didn't return her attention to Valerie for several minutes.

"I'm Valerie," Valerie told the other girl.

"Wendy," the girl answered. "First day?"

"First day," Valerie agreed.

"Not really fair," the girl said. "There's no way for you to catch up at this point. They're just setting you up to fail."

"Well, I have to try," Valerie said. "Do you have a favorite class?"

"Zoology," Wendy said. "We get to take care of animals."

Valerie frowned.

"Why?"

"Because," Wendy said slowly. "It's the introduction to the shifter class, if you have an aptitude, and I tested that I might be able to try for shifter."

Valerie had never heard of that, not once, at Survival School.

"Oh," she said.

"Don't worry about it," Lisa said. "Wendy's been bragging that she might be able to be a shifter since like the first week of school. They'll test you for it eventually."

Valerie nodded slowly, remembering to eat everything on her tray that looked edible.

"This is all so crazy," she said, and Lisa gave her a tight little nod, then went back to talking to the girl on the other side of her.

Valerie spent the rest of her lunch period listening to girls talk about their classes and the boys, then the bell rang and she was off to her next class.

And her next.

And her next.

By the end of the day, she'd given up the pretext of taking notes, just sitting numbly through the lectures, then she stood outside, appreciating the fresh air no matter how cold it might have been. There were actually students leaving like they were going home, and Sasha walked out with a pair of girls, the three of them with their heads together.

Valerie watched the three of them walk past, then a car rolled up to the curb and honked. Sasha lifted her head, then spoke a farewell to the girls and went to get in. Valerie waited as the girls went on past, then she went and got in on the other side, throwing herself into a seat and putting her arm across her face.

"That was wretched," she said. "My head hurts and I didn't learn anything."

"They're in such a bad position," Sasha said as Grant pulled the car away from the curb. "There's no guarantee any of them will be able to actually *use* magic, and the school basically requires that they drop out of high school to come do this. Anyone with any academic strength at all is looking at throwing away a future to try to learn magic."

Valerie nodded.

"I think the girl I talked to today was ready to quit."

"They have a fifteen percent graduation rate," Susan said.

"Fifteen," Valerie said. "We watched upperclassmen try to do a cast that Sasha could do with her eyes closed, and it failed."

"They did *so many* things wrong," Sasha said. "I mean, they weren't even close enough for it to be dangerous."

Susan sighed.

"I wish I could say that's worse than I thought, but the feel I get from the graduates is that magic is kind of a cult myth, around there, and anyone who can consistently get hold of it is a big deal."

"But it isn't because of *skill*," Sasha said. "They just are *doing* it wrong."

"When you grow up in a culture of magic that thinks that it's too hard and it's all about luck, you don't realize what you're doing to sabotage yourself," Grant said. "You could tell them, and they'd do the whole thing over, get everything you told them right, get a bunch of other stuff wrong, and then use that to prove to you that you have to get lucky for it to work, anyway."

"But..." Sasha started, then crossed her arms. "I can't believe that's the best the Council can do."

"It isn't," Susan said. "But at the same time, you have to ask yourself why they think they care, anyway. Why does the Council have a mandate to teach new students who know literally nothing about magic?"

"Thanks, mom," Valerie said, and Susan looked over her shoulder at her.

"I'm sorry," she said. "It was all in hopes that you wouldn't ever have to deal with any of this."

"Your mom's point stands," Grant said. "The Pure and the non-propagationists think that teaching magic to kids who don't have it already is dangerous and wrong. The Council stuffs them in there as a token argument against that, but what are they actually doing?"

"Ruining their lives," Sasha said. "They're ruining their lives. There was a girl I was talking to, and if she could just get in at Survival School, I know she could figure it out and she could make it, but..."

"She doesn't have the knowledge to get in at any of the real schools," Susan said. "And I guarantee her family can't afford the money."

Sasha sighed, laying back against her seat and shaking her head.

"So what *should* they do? Just ignore that people want to learn about magic and pretend like it's impossible?"

"I'm not suggesting anything of the kind," Susan said. "Just that the Council is disingenuous in how they deal with the issue, while at least the Pure are direct."

"And they kill people," Valerie said. "I'd rather be on the side that cheats than the one that kills."

"And I'd say that you're right, if you have to pick a side."

"But we do," Sasha said. "There's a war. You can't just defect and argue that both of them are wrong. The Superiors are killing civilians."

"They are," Susan said. "And they're winning because they're better at magic."

"Why?" Valerie asked. "Is it because dark magic is stronger than light magic?"

"Why wasn't the school warded?" Sasha asked. "We shouldn't have been able to just walk in."

"Good question," Grant said from the driver's seat.

"It's because no one cares about it," Susan said. "Getting into Von Lauv is going to take a lot more work."

Sasha looked back at the school they could no longer see and she sighed.

"It's so sad," she said. "A whole school full of them... Some of them could probably be really good."

"The *world* is full of people with untapped magic potential," Grant said. "Telling them that doesn't improve their lives at all."

"But magic makes you rich," Valerie said, and Susan turned forward again.

"Yes, but it also makes you a target. Every single time."

"Mom, I don't want to go," Hanson said as he sat in the car with her out front of school.

"You know that I went here?" Martha asked.

"I heard," he said. "That's how Val found out about you and

99

then me."

"I bet you volunteered it," Martha said. "You hated doing it the whole time you knew what it was you were doing, and the second she gave you a window to come clean, I bet you did."

"You're supposed to teach me that lying is bad and trust is important," Hanson said.

"Neither of those are true," Martha said. "Why would I handicap you with them?"

"I want to stay with my friends," Hanson said.

"You've known them for less than a week," Martha said. "They aren't your friends. And it isn't your school. It was a sanctuary while I was doing my work for the Council, and now you're with me again."

"How do I know you aren't going to leave me again?" Hanson asked.

"You don't," Martha told him. "I may yet. It depends on what the Council needs me to do. But for now we have a job, and if we can pull this off, you can write your ticket anywhere you like."

"Or I could just stay," Hanson said, and she started the car.

"No. You couldn't. We are going, and that's the only option you have right now."

He hadn't fought with her, but he'd felt the distance to the school behind him as it grew.

"You know you've only met her a couple of times," Martha said after they'd been driving for about an hour. "Any feelings you have for her are completely untrustworthy."

"Who?" Hanson asked, and she glanced at him.

"Sasha Mills. She's probably cute. I remember Ivory was, too. But you don't know her and she doesn't know you, and you're just infatuated with her. If you want my advice, and I know you probably don't want to hear it right now, but if you want my advice, she's not a good alliance. She's not going to be involved in the war, and the Council already has friction with her mom. Ann Womack. She's a good choice."

"Have you met her?" Hanson asked.

"Obviously I haven't," Martha answered, and he nodded darkly. "She's not a good choice."

"She's connected," Martha said. "And I bet she's pretty. Isn't she?"

"She is," Hanson said. "But I don't like her. I like Sasha."

"She's a *healer*," Martha said. "Just like her mother. And she's attached at the hip to Valerie Blake. Is that what you want? Your ex-best-friend's best friend?"

"I like her," Hanson said. "And I don't want to talk about it. Where did you *go*?"

"Where they told me to," Martha answered.

"And you couldn't leave a note?"

"The minute you got caught, our cover was broken. I couldn't risk leaving a note and having someone find it."

"And you couldn't have waited a few hours, or come to pick me up at school or anything?"

"I couldn't have taken you with me," Martha said. "You did fine on your own."

"Ma," he said. "What's going on? I don't like this."

"Magic," she said. "This is the *world* of magic. It's complicated and I get that it's scary sometimes, but I think you're going to really like it once you get the hang of it. And I think you're going to thrive."

"I just want to go back to school," he said.

"And the fact that you're rooming with Ethan and Shack is a very good sign," Martha went on. "I promise, I will do my very best to put you back there when we're done, though the Council is going to have to find a special, *special* exemption for you, because you left. But. If we can track down the Blakes, we are going to have so much political capital to spend, son…"

"I don't want your political capital," Hanson said. "I don't want to go hunt down my best friend."

"Which is why I waited so many years to tell you that we were spying on her," Martha said. "You really do care about her. It's the best cover of all."

"Ma," he said loudly. She pulled the car off to the side of the road and looked at him.

"If you're looking for an apology, you aren't going to get one, son," she said. "I've always looked out for you, tried to position you to take advantage of any opportunity that came up, and I did what was best. I don't care if that's not how you see it, because it doesn't change what I did or why. Is that clear?"

"Where's Dad?" he asked.

"Out," she said, spinning the wheel to get back up onto the pavement and continuing on. "He doesn't know anything. He's been on assignment since before you went to the school the first time."

"Is he magic, too?" Hanson asked. "They said that you both went to Survival School. Showed me a picture."

"Then why are you asking me?" Martha countered. "You know he is."

"What does he *actually* do?" Hanson asked.

"Your father loves you," Martha said. "Wants to blow a giant hole in the world to make it a better place for you, so that's what he does."

Hanson stared out at the road ahead of him.

"You can't find them," he said. "If that's where Val went, you aren't going to find her mom. No one can. It's what they all say."

"I've got you to help me track Valerie, and there is no one else in the *world* better at tracking Susan Blake than me. I've devoted my entire life to observing her, and I can track her magic, so long as she's actually casting and I can get close enough."

"What will happen, when you find her?" Hanson asked. "Valerie?"

"That's up to the Council," Martha said.

"What about her mom?"

"She was supposed to report in and she didn't. She had a job and we know that she did it, but she didn't report in, after that. She's AWOL, and they'll deal with it."

"Deal with it how?" Hanson asked.

"Don't ask questions you don't want to know the answers to," she said.

"Will they hurt her?" Hanson asked.

She glanced at him again.

"No one says," she said. "I don't think so, because... Well, if only because she's one of their strongest assets, I don't think that they'll hurt her, because they want to rehabilitate her and get her out at work again."

"What kind of people are you *working* for?" Hanson asked. "You aren't *certain* they wouldn't torture her?"

"I'm working for the people who are going to win the war," Martha answered. "Would you rather I be working for the ones who are going to lose?"

"I'd rather you be working for the ones who are *right*," Hanson said.

"Did I really not teach you this?" Martha asked. "I thought I had. There's no such thing as right and wrong, when it comes to people. The situations are always way more complicated than that. No one is *actually* right or *actually* wrong. I wouldn't be working for the Council if they were evil. They aren't. And they're truly *more* right, to boot. But these are the people who are going to go out and make it possible for us to *win*, to stop the Superiors from taking over and *enslaving* people. I think that counts as the good guys, right?"

"And what about Valerie?" Hanson asked. "Do you not care what happens to her? You were like a mom to her."

"I was around a lot as she was growing up," Martha said. "It doesn't make me *like* her mom. And it was part of the job. I needed to be able to track *her*, too, if Susan ran again. All this time, no one but me knew where she was, just waiting for the moment that the Council needed her again…"

Hanson looked at his mother, horrified.

"You're the one who told them where to find her," he said.

"They needed her," Martha said. "And once you've picked your horse, you stick with it. The Council are our only hope of beating the Superiors once and for all, and when they told me that Susan Blake was key to that - was always *going* to be key to it - I volunteered to follow her and keep track of her, so that they didn't lose their best weapon. I trust that they are the best chance we have, so when they contacted me and told me it was time… No, I didn't hesitate."

"Ma," Hanson said. "You're the bad guy. You ruined both their lives."

Martha looked over at him, then shook her head.

"You have no idea what I'm willing to do to make sure the right side wins this war," she said. "It's worth that much. You have no idea."

They took a room at a roadside motel, not taking anything out of the car. Grant had said something about swapping it for a new one, but Susan had told him that they would burn through their supply of cars too quickly, if they did that.

Valerie could remember a time when Susan had told her that they couldn't afford a bicycle for Valerie, because she wouldn't get enough use out of it. They'd never owned a car.

"All right," Susan had said as she came out of the bathroom, rubbing her hands and arms like she had lotioned, though Valerie could sense that there was more going on. "Let's send your mom and update to let her know you're doing okay."

Sasha sat up.

"Thank you, Mrs. Blake," she said, and Susan nodded, motioning to the end of the bed.

"Come sit."

Sasha sat down at the end of the bed, facing Susan Blake in a more trusting posture than Valerie could have imagined herself having, in that moment, and Susan put her hands to either side of Sasha's face.

"Put your hands around my wrists and focus," Susan said. "What this is going to do is send a pulse of energy to your mom. She'll recognize you and she'll recognize me, and she'll know we're together."

"How will she know that you're not in trouble?" Valerie asked, and the corner of Susan's mouth had twitched.

"Because it's me," she said simply. Sasha nodded and Susan closed her eyes.

"Focus on your mom," she said.

Sasha nodded again and Susan drew a breath.

There was a moment.

Valerie didn't know what it was, even how she'd known it had happened - was it expectation and a guess, or had she actually *noticed* something - and then Susan dropped her hands.

"I owe her at least that much," Susan had said, and then Grant had come back with a delivery menu for dinner.

"We have prep work to do tonight, so you two are on your own for entertainment."

"There are no rats to eat my eyebrows tonight," Valerie said, pushing her shoes off and going to lay on the bed. "I'm happy."

"Don't get used to this," Susan had warned. "It never lasts long."

"Why not?" Valerie asked, and Grant had looked over at her.

"Someone is always chasing us," he said. "One or the other of us. And now there are four of us to come after. Someone will come, and we'll hide. It always happens. Don't get comfortable."

Valerie had given him a glum look, then shrugged and picked up the remote.

"Television," she said to Sasha. "I can't tell you how much I have missed television."

Once, Sasha had helped Valerie to sneak out of their room and to the library in the middle of the night at Survival School.

She'd had thirty- or forty-odd instructions from Sasha, each one a cast that she had to get exactly right, just to get from her room to the library and back.

Breaking into Von Lauv Academy was comparably complicated, foot for foot.

They spent two hours at the motel getting ready, then Susan had spent the entire time casting.

She cast on the car, she cast on Valerie and Sasha, she cast on herself and Grant.

They got to an abandoned lot outside of yet another city that Valerie had managed to miss which one it was, and Susan and Grant sat together for a good five minutes, putting together a cast.

Valerie had questions, but she knew the rules of verbal casting well enough to wait until it was done.

Finally, a blue light went out from the car in all directions, and Grant started the engine again.

"I don't understand what's going on," Valerie said.

"We made ourselves uninteresting enough to escape attention," Susan said, sitting straight and marking the window next to her head, almost as a nervous habit. "We have to get past all of their defenses one at a time, and if they saw us coming in, inch by inch... Obviously we would attract attention."

"But the cast had to be specific enough to avoid the defenses detecting it," Grant said. "There are a lot of layers of work going on here."

"You're wasting it," Sasha said, and Valerie looked over at her.

"No we're not," Susan said. "We agree that this is the right thing to do with the knowledge."

"No," Sasha said. "If they're going to attack Survival School, you can't throw away the knowledge of how to get *in* at the Superior school on just sneaking us in for a day."

"I've underestimated you, if you think that either of us would turn this knowledge over to the Council to let them run an attack on the school," Susan said.

"Well," Sasha started, then shook her head. "No, the Council *wouldn't* attack the school. They wouldn't. But maybe if we let the Superiors know that we could get in at their school..."

"They'd alter the defenses and then we wouldn't be able to," Grant said. "It's a one-shot thing, it has to be secret, and we aren't giving it to the idiots on the Council, because they'd tie themselves in knots, justifying an attack on teenagers."

Sasha balked at this, then shook her head.

"You shouldn't be keeping this kind of knowledge away from the Council," she said. "This could be tactically helpful in the war."

Grant looked back at her.

"We can send Valerie in on her own, if you're uncomfortable with this, but the point isn't to gain advantage at the war, at all. The point is to understand how the war that the Council has sold you isn't even happening."

Sasha fell silent, and Susan started a new cast.

Foot by foot, they fought their way up a gravel driveway, creeping through the abandoned lot.

And then.

They crossed a line of some kind, and what had been an

abandoned lot, Valerie now saw to be an enormous campus of some kind. The grass was well-kept, even here in the middle of the winter, and the bare oak trees were regal all around the school, promising a gorgeous spring.

"Wow," Valerie breathed.

"This place is huge," Sasha said.

"It is," Susan said. "And you aren't going to be able to ask directions if you get lost. You'll want to sit together at lunch and try to avoid drawing attention to yourselves. You can pick the classes you want to go to, but they should be in the lecture halls. No classrooms, and certainly no focus sessions."

"Focus sessions?" Valerie asked.

"One teacher, five students," Grant said. "For specific skills, niche stuff. Mostly high-level, but some of it would be a good fit for you now."

Valerie boggled, and Sasha leaned her face against the window. "It's beautiful," she said.

"Last we knew, it was a student population of five-thousand," Grant said. "And we're early enough in the spring semester that you ought to be able to blend in. Just… try to avoid conversations with any of the teachers. Okay?"

Sasha nodded, and Valerie shifted forward in her seat, watching as students wandered outside of the building, talking and laughing and…

"This place isn't evil," she said.

"Nope," Susan said. "Almost everyone is happy to be here. They teach all three magics and while they'll talk about the risks that go along with using dark magic, they don't look down on people who have it."

"People with all three disciplines are celebrated here," Grant said. "I almost wish your mom had sent you here."

"They would have held her," Susan said. "You know that."

"You still can't prove that the Council *won't*," Grant answered.

"Lady Harrington wouldn't let them," Susan said. "You know that."

"If she could stop them. Merck is still gaining power with the fear play."

"What are you guys talking about?" Valerie asked.

"You walk from here," Grant said. "Just don't move wrong. You belong here."

"We don't have backpacks," Sasha said.

"Avoid labs," Susan said, handing back a pair of notebooks and a selection of pens. Sasha sighed.

"I'm going to have a hard time leaving, aren't I?" she asked, and Susan nodded.

"I'm jealous, myself," she said. "This isn't *about* the secrets, but you may learn some while you're here, all the same."

Sasha set her mouth and opened her door.

Valerie got out and walked around the car to stand on the sidewalk.

It was cold out.

She needed to get inside.

She waited for Sasha, then set off toward the front doors.

It was still early, and she was exhausted from odd sleep and getting up too early this morning, but at the same time, she was excited to the point that she had a hard time not bouncing on her toes.

She was *doing it*.

She was magic-ing her way into an enemy building. She was going to spy on them, and they were never going to know she'd been there.

This was what her mom *did*. This was what her parents did.

Sasha tucked in against Valerie's elbow, head down, just following.

Valerie went up the broad front steps and pushed open one of the sets of doors, walking into a long front hallway that echoed with a cacophony of voices.

The place was huge, but it was also *packed*.

She and Sasha waded through, picking up bits of this conversation and that. Some of the students were talking about classes, but most of them were talking about people. Relationships. Events. Things that were going on within the school. Gossip and teasing.

Valerie felt at home completely.

This was how her *regular* school had felt every morning.

They walked through, finding the end of the clot of students and going on, looking at doors and walls, trying to figure out how the place was laid out.

"Lecture halls," Sasha murmured, and Valerie nodded.

They had to be *big*. So she was looking for hallways that were widely-spaced or had very few doors.

She almost passed the first one, mistaking it for a theater. She widened her eyes at Sasha, indicating, and Sasha went to read the schedule on the back of the door.

"Forest survival and gleaned potions," Sasha said when she came back. "I want to do that."

"I feel like I'm cheating on Mrs. Reynolds," Valerie answered.

"Gleaned potions?" Sasha asked. "I mean… There are some of us who have done it because our parents have done it, but… I want to do that, Valerie."

Valerie nodded, looking back.

The front hall was emptying and students were making their way toward the rooms. The day was about to start.

"Cool," she said. "Just… Come over here with me."

She went to lean against the opposite wall, holding her notebook against her chest.

"What are we doing?" Sasha asked, mirroring her.

"Not being the first people to show up to class," Valerie said. "We want to get in there before the back is all the way full and there aren't seats together, but we don't want to be too early."

Sasha nodded, looking like she was trying to do complex calculus in her head.

"Don't worry about it," Valerie said. "I've got this."

Sasha swallowed.

"Do you know what they'll do if they catch us?" she asked.

"That's the last time you use those words today," Valerie said, raising her head as though she was watching for a friend to come down the hallway. Sasha looked over her shoulder, trying to see what Valerie saw, which would have been the wrong thing except for how natural it felt.

Just waiting on their third friend who would sit with them.

"Okay," Valerie said a minute later. She followed a group of students in through the double doors and she found a pair of seats halfway down a row about three from the back.

Perfect.

She and Sasha settled in, getting their notebooks ready, and Valerie listened to the conversations going on around them.

It was more related to the class, now, but it still all felt so *normal* compared to Survival School.

The teacher was a good one. She could tell that from the way the students were talking about the last lecture, and from the fact that the front of the auditorium was filling faster than the back.

A minute later a man in his late twenties came out onto the stage and the lights in the room dimmed slightly. He pointed at the screen behind him, and it lit up with vibrant images that Valerie was actually beginning to recognize.

"All right," he said. "We left off last week talking about the relationship between the wet light magics and the dry dark magics, and how you can make them work together if you've got the right intermediary. So let's pick back up there."

Valerie blinked and Sasha began scribbling madly.

It was...

It was without a doubt cheating on Mrs. Reynolds, but it was one of the best lectures on magic Valerie had ever heard.

It *made sense*.

There wasn't any percentage light and dark or funny scales for grouping things. For once, the way that the ingredients went together felt like he understood it, like *Valerie* could understand it, and she found herself taking notes just as fast as Sasha was. The teacher moved fast - he was brutally quick with how he moved from statement to statement, image to image - but it was intuitive. The problem was that she wasn't going to remember every *word* of it, and her hand hurt by the end of the lecture with her attempt to capture it all.

She rubbed her wrist as they walked out at the bell, giving Sasha a hard look.

"More," Sasha breathed. "I don't ever want to leave."

Valerie looked up and down the hall.

"All right. Let's find another one."

They skipped lunch.

They just went to another class.

There were too many students for Valerie to recognize any of them, but she caught a few whiffs of cliques going by, of hierarchy happening. It was *there*. The students weren't suddenly un-petty and fully-matured simply because their school was *awesome*.

They were just... down to business, for the most part.

The school ran them hard, the same long hours as at Survival School, and the number of them was so *huge* that no one stood out the way Valerie had, and still did.

It was a *good* place to be.

Valerie listened hard when she heard students talk about the war, but for the most part they seemed too concerned with the social aspect of the school and with their classes to be talking about the war.

It struck her that it didn't *matter* here, the way it did at Survival School.

Granted, there weren't any *demons* running around trying to kill everyone, either. So. That made a difference.

They made it to the end of the day - Sasha was running out of notebook - and they went outside, wandering with other students around them, ranging further away from the building. Valerie wondered if her parents shouldn't have been more clear about what was supposed to happen *after* classes let out, but she and Sasha spotted the car and made their way over.

Sasha was remarkably cool about it, the whole time.

Valerie was proud of her.

They got in and Susan lit a pile of stuff on the dashboard that filled the car with purple smoke for several seconds, and then the smoke was gone, as if it had never existed.

"So?" Susan asked as Grant turned the car around.

"I don't understand," Valerie said, putting on her seatbelt and slouching in her seat.

"What don't you understand?" Grant asked.

"How are they the bad guys?" Valerie asked. "They were cool."

"And really *good*," Sasha added.

"You didn't *meet* anyone, right?" Susan asked, and Valerie shook her head.

"No. We kept to ourselves, and no one cared."

"For the record, if you set *foot* in that school without the prep work we did this morning, they would have pounced on you and no one would have ever seen you again," Grant said.

"Still," Sasha said, sounding dreamy. "To be able to go there every day…?"

"It's a good school," Susan said. "So is Survival School and so is Light School, but they put together the best of the best…"

"And their fundamental understanding of magic is better aligned with how it actually works," Grant interrupted.

Susan sighed.

"I was going to avoid politics," she said.

"Why?" Grant asked. "It's all politics, if the definitions of the alignment of magics are politics."

Susan sighed harder and nodded.

"Light, natural, dark," Sasha said. "It makes so much more sense. Everything just… it just *works*."

"Tannis knows, too," Grant said. "So does your herbology teacher. Reynolds."

"Yes," Susan said, resigned.

"She knows. Too smart not to. But the Council says that it's apologizing for dark magic users, trying to create another category, so they don't tolerate anyone to teach it."

"But they're handicapping us," Sasha said. "Everything I've ever known about magic… Why didn't my mom tell me?"

"Don't know if she knows," Susan said, starting another cast. "Some people just make do with the Council-endorsed paradigm, and others don't teach it because it's impossible to go back."

Valerie looked out through the back window as they pulled away from the school and onto the road again. Abruptly it went from a gorgeous campus to a chain-link fence around a gravel lot. She shook her head.

She would have never guessed.

"So we saw it," she said. "I still don't get it, though. Why are we here?"

"Know thy enemy," Grant said, and Susan looked back at her.

"I gave you up to keep you safe, and Lady Harrington has done her best, but you are *involved* in all of this now. I need to make sure that you know what's true and what isn't, at least with the important stuff, so that you don't let people lie to you and change who you are."

"Then why am *I* here?" Sasha asked. "I'm never going to be a warrior."

"Because they'd have leaned on you to make you tell them where she was," Grant said. "And anything else you knew. We both assumed she'd told you things that we didn't want the Council knowing."

"What about Ethan?" Sasha asked.

There was a pause.

"Who is *Ethan*?" Susan asked.

"Ethan Trent," Valerie said, wishing Sasha hadn't said anything.

"Would that be Merck Trent's son?" Grant asked, and Valerie nodded.

"Yes," Susan said. "Older than you, or your grade?"

"Our grade."

"One of the cursed," Susan said softly. "When is his birthday, do you know?"

"Um," Valerie said. "Why does that matter?"

Susan looked over at Grant, who shrugged.

"Up to you," he said. "I didn't know."

Susan nodded, then turned in her seat.

"I was there, when Lan died. The head of the Pure. His death disrupted The Pure enough that the Council could get an upper hand and they ended the war. Didn't do it *right*, if you ask me, but they ended it."

"No politics, huh?" Grant asked, and Susan grinned.

"Sore spot. *Anyway*. I probably know more about the curse that is on the Council kids than anyone else living."

"Why do they keep dying?" Sasha asked, and Susan turned her attention to Sasha once more.

"Who?"

"The Council brat pack," Sasha said. "They keep dying."

"Do they, now?" Grant asked. "Well, that's interesting."

"Hush," Susan said. "Who died?"

"Patrick, Conrad, and Yasmine," Sasha said.

"Surnames?" Susan asked.

"Colt, Rose, and Smith," Sasha said.

Valerie had never known Yasmine's last name.

"When were they born?" Susan asked quickly, and Sasha shook her head.

"I don't know."

"Why does it matter?" Valerie asked again.

"Because you were the first," Susan said, looking at Valerie once more. I didn't figure it out until... It was a day, between when I figured it out and when I ran. I just looked around and saw all of these women with their toddler children and the talk about what the kids were going to *do* when they grew up and started taking over the world, and... I figured it out. You were the first, the oldest, of the Cursed, and the *next four*... They are the rest of the five."

Valerie blinked.

"What do you mean, I was the first?"

Susan licked her lips, then nodded.

"The curse was directed at me," she said. "My daughter was destined to bear the weight of it, though I didn't *realize* it was you until... then. I thought it was talking about *my future*. But *you* are my future. It hit me, and it bounced and it reverberated to the Council, and while everyone *knew* that the Council had been cursed, and their children had been cursed, no one figured out that it *started* with me. That you were *the first* among the cursed, and that the rest of the five were *chronological*. And I don't know how they would have, without having heard the curse in the first place."

"That's why you ran off," Grant said. "Without saying anything."

Susan nodded.

"I thought I could get away from it. If I never let magic *touch* her... maybe the curse couldn't take root and maybe I could just... If I pretended hard enough, maybe I could imagine that you guys would figure it out without her ever having to be involved."

Grant looked at Susan for a long time, the car idling at a stop light, and he finally nodded.

"You did the right thing," he said. "I'm sorry I doubted you."

Susan licked her lips again, then looked around the headrest at Valerie once more.

"Tell me about the Trent boy," she said. "Why is he important?"

Valerie shrugged.

"I *like* him," she said.

"Did you *tell* him?" Sasha asked, remembering the point and pressing it. Valerie glared at her, and Sasha ducked her head.

"Some of it," Valerie allowed. "A lot of it."

"*What* did you tell him, specifically?" Grant pressed with a tone of urgency.

"That you were alive," Valerie said. "That you taught me a bunch of stuff. That the Pure are trying to strip everyone's magic, that I spent two weeks with you where I was *also* at school... Not a lot more, I think... I didn't tell him about natural magic."

"Oh, that helps a lot," Grant said, exasperated. "I would have snagged him, too, if I'd known that you'd spill those kinds of secrets to one of the Council kids. The *head* of the Council, no less."

"She doesn't know," Susan said. "She doesn't know how the secrets work."

"I trust him," Valerie said. "He told me that he was spying on me to his dad, but he was going to stop..."

"He *told* you that he was spying?" Grant said. "And you told him that I was alive and that you'd seen me? You know that you are virtually guaranteed to be the person who costs Gemma her life, don't you? After all these years, I make contact with you *once* and you get my sister killed?"

"Grant," Susan said sternly.

"Tell me I'm wrong," Grant said, and Susan looked over at him.

"I'm telling you that you are a *parent*, and that you have to do better than that," she said. "We'll discuss it later."

"I had to tell *someone*," Valerie said. "It was all too jumbled up in my head, and I needed to talk it through, and Mr. Jamison

Chloe Garner

wouldn't talk to me about it…"

"Alan Jamison raises his ugly head again," Grant said, and Valerie frowned, shocked.

"He said that you were his friend," she said.

"Your father is a bad friend when he's angry," Susan said, and Grant glanced at her again.

"You put her there because Alan was there," Grant said. "My own daughter didn't go to Light School because your ex was at Survival School."

Susan shot Valerie a look that was somewhere between alarm and anger, then pointed at Grant.

"I was *never* with Alan," she said. "I was just closer with him than *you* for a while there, you remember?"

"Oh, I remember," Grant said. "I remember us being in for two whole weeks, and you spending the *entire* time with him."

"Because you were behaving like a jackass," Susan said. "I trust him with my life, and I trusted him with our *daughter's* life. I'm not going to apologize to you for that."

Valerie and Sasha exchanged glances and tried not to squirm.

Grant pulled the car over.

"Do you not care about Gemma's life at all, anymore?"

"I do," Susan said, her voice even. "I never stopped caring about her. But there's nothing we can do about it. And maybe she's right to trust him. I think our daughter has considerable discernment, which isn't something you would know."

"I wouldn't know because you stole her away when she was barely even *talking*," Grant thundered.

"I think that Ethan would do anything for Valerie," Sasha said, and the car fell dangerously silent.

"We're forming a Council of our own," Valerie said after a very, very long pause. "They've agreed to stop reporting anything about each other to their parents."

"They," Grant said, his voice thin.

"Shack, Ethan, Valerie, and Ann," Sasha said. "Milton wants to join them, but he's still torn. I think Ethan will talk him into it."

Valerie wasn't sure that *this* wasn't spying and reporting to her parents, but she let it go. It had frozen the fight, and right now that was all she cared about.

"It's the curse," Susan said quietly. "They sense it and they're reacting to it, even without knowing about it."

"You can't know that," Grant said.

"When is Ethan's birthday?" Susan asked, her voice gentle again. "Do you know?"

"December," Valerie said. She'd missed it, being angry at him.

"And any of the others?"

Valerie looked at Sasha, and they both shook their heads.

"December has got to be early enough," Susan said.

"It doesn't mean she can trust him," Grant said, and Susan shrugged.

"What's done is done. How many times did we say that? We can't take back our mistakes. We just have to move on."

"I need to get Gemma out of there, if there's still time," Grant said, and Susan nodded.

"I'll back your play, if you need me to. I can be very diverting."

"I know you can," Grant said. "What about them?"

"I can show them how field work really looks," Susan said. "I don't have to make a direct attack or go after something sensitive. I just have to make a big enough splash that everyone is looking the wrong way."

"Who is Gemma, again?" Sasha asked.

"My aunt," Valerie said quickly. "And high up in the ranks with The Pure."

"Aunt," Sasha said, and Valerie nodded.

"Privy to *everything*," Grant said with a moment of hesitation. "If I pull her out all at once, without warning, she'll never get back in."

"Probably not," Susan said.

"And we've upset three attempts at testing new casts in the last three weeks," Grant said.

"She's easily the most tactically viable player in the entire war," Susan said. "But it was always a matter of time."

Grant turned in his seat to look at Valerie.

"How much do you trust him?" he asked. "Your boyfriend?"

Valerie paused.

Thought hard.

Looked her father in the eye.

"I don't think he is going to tell anyone anything," she said. "He knows the politics, better than anyone else I know."

"You think he can avoid telling them that you've seen me before?" he asked, and Valerie considered again.

"I think so."

"You're staking your aunt's life on this," Grant said. "I know that you didn't much *like* her, but…"

"I know," Valerie said. "She's one of the good guys."

"She would want you to leave her in place, if there was any chance," Susan said, and Grant nodded, grim.

"I know," he said, starting the car and pulling away from the curb again. "All the same, I think we ought to put up a big distraction, in case she gets wind of a rumor that she needs to get out."

Susan grinned.

"Oh, I'm game for that."

Valerie looked at Sasha, excited again, and Sasha looked back at her, eyes wide.

"I don't think I like the sound of that."

Pursuit

They changed cars.

There was some significant reason about why, but Valerie hadn't understood any of the conversation as her parents had discussed it, and then she'd given up any hope of catching what they were talking about.

Grant pulled up to a dilapidated park, where a handful of vendors stood under tents, looking more like drug dealers than farmers, to Valerie's eye.

"You guys understand what your job is?" he asked.

"Stay close to Valerie," Sasha said, and Susan pointed.

"And look just like that. They aren't going to be able to resist."

They were bait.

And somehow neither of Valerie's parents were that concerned by this.

Nor was Valerie, when it came down to it.

If either Grant or Susan had voiced hesitation, she would have been worried, but Grant said that none of the merchants at the park were going to be prepared to defend themselves against her, if she had to keep them back, so long as they were outside of their booths when it happened.

So.

All she had to do was either draw their attention from inside of their booths *or* get their attention enough to draw them out of their booths before they did anything to her.

So long as all eyes were on her and Sasha, Susan and Grant would have free rein to do whatever it was the two of them were plotting.

Which didn't sound good, from the way they were talking.

They were too happy.

They'd done this kind of thing before - that much was obvious - but they hadn't done it in a *while*, and they were goofy excited about all of the things they both knew how to do, and all of the new ideas they'd each had since the last time they'd done it.

Sasha was kind of losing her mind.

"It'll be okay," Valerie said, putting her hand on the door handle. "Just walk behind me and stay close. I've got this."

"You don't know what they might do," Sasha hissed. "And you haven't planned or prepared a defense."

"Has, too," Grant objected. "She trained with me for two weeks, last semester."

"And I've been training with Mr. Finn all *this* semester," Valerie said. She saw the way resentment hit her father, and she kind of liked it.

If he'd wanted to be the one who trained her, he should have stuck around.

"So?" Sasha asked. "Mr. Finn gives you everything you're going to need to work through one of his puzzles."

"But I never do it *right*," Valerie argued, and Sasha gave her a desperate look.

"*Exactly.*"

"Do we need a different plan, ladies?" Susan asked, and Valerie shook her head.

"Sasha could just stay in the car, if she wanted."

Sasha jumped out.

"No. You aren't leaving me by myself."

Valerie grinned and got out, knocking on her mom's window on the way past.

Sasha scrambled around the car to walk next to her, and Valerie shifted, keeping her head up and looking around.

Just like walking home from school.

If someone put their hands on her, she would make them regret it.

She just had more weapons now than she ever had before.

The vendors noticed her quickly, giving the two girls dark looks as they went past, eyes turning, feet shifting. Valerie looked over her shoulder, but the men weren't following.

She stopped.

Sasha went on a full two steps before she accepted that Valerie wasn't going any further, then she scrambled back.

Valerie turned to look at one of the stalls, sniffing the air and looking at everything the man had, sitting in baskets, hanging from under the roof of the temporary booth.

The colors.

She knew better than to group magical ingredients by color to represent lightness or darkness, but everything that Sasha carried was gold or tan or white. These were deep teal and redblack and slate gray.

It was beautiful, if you let yourself think it, but it was so *different* from the selection of stuff she'd been using in the dorm room, even different from the stuff she'd been maintaining for Mr. Tannis.

Dark.

It *radiated* dark, and she could feel it.

This surprised her perhaps more than anything.

She could feel it.

"What do you want?" the man asked, a suggestion that she keep moving.

"The beads," Valerie said, taking a step forward and reaching up toward them where they hung. "What are they?"

He sneered.

"If you have to ask, you don't want them."

Valerie smiled, her fingers *itching* to touch the pearlescent greenblue surface. They weren't organic, and she didn't think they were glass...

"Valerie," Sasha said quietly. "Please?"

"How much are they?" Valerie asked.

He shook his head.

"Not for sale. Not to you."

She shrugged, seeing the way the rest of the men were repositioning, closing in around them from behind.

Valerie shrugged.

"Oh, well. They're pretty."

The seller sneered again, and Valerie set off once more, swinging her arms. Sasha skittered alongside, continuously looking back.

There were voices, languages Valerie couldn't make sense of. It was reminiscent of the way the demons had spoken in the hallway when they'd attacked the school the first time, but Valerie didn't think it was the same.

"They're following us," Sasha whispered, anxious to the point of hysteria. "Valerie, they're following us."

"So?" Valerie asked. "You could take every one of them out, if you actually chose to."

"No I couldn't," Sasha said. "I didn't bring any of my *stuff*."

"You have your hands," Valerie said, turning to look at the vendors. "And you have your voice."

She walked backwards for several more steps, then stopped.

The men were making up ground on her, walking faster, pairing and grouping in threes.

She'd expected them to look *hungry*, the way the boys on the streets did, but this was much more pragmatic. More transactional.

Dead.

They were all but dead.

There was a flicker of motion, like a bit of cloth caught in a sudden breeze, and Valerie straightened.

"What's going on?" she asked.

"You shouldn't be here," one of the men said. "It's a dangerous place."

"I like those," Valerie answered. "They're the most interesting."

There was a jostling as one of the men who might have just been warning her got elbowed out of the way by a man who had a knife out in his hand.

Sasha's fingers dug into Valerie's elbow hard enough that they were going to leave bruises.

The explosion was... well, it might have been the coolest thing Valerie had ever seen.

There was a shock wave of electric blue that tore through all of the tents like a blade, and then a rolling pink fire that followed it out. After that, she was pretty sure that all of the smaller explosions and fireworks were the ingredients there in the market burning, but it was spectacular.

The men turned back, and Valerie jerked her elbow to get Sasha's attention.

They started running.

Half the men, more, took off toward the market, hoping to rescue some portion of their wares, but a few of the men turned back again, then ran after Valerie and Sasha.

Sasha screamed and sped up - the girl was actually faster than Valerie by a good margin - but Valerie slowed, looking back at them.

And then slowing more, planting her feet and putting out both hands.

The first two men slowed, waiting, but the third of them kept running, his teeth bared and a knife poised over his head.

Valerie didn't think.

She didn't have time.

She just spoke three words, formed a fist, and punched.

He was still two strides away; she was punching air, but there was a direct line of force from her fist to his throat, and he grabbed his neck, dropping the knife and staggering back.

The rest of the men hesitated further, then one of them began to cast back.

Valerie waited, listening to make sure that Sasha's footsteps were getting further and further away, and when the man cast at her, she held her hands out, wrist to wrist, and she bounced the cast back at the man.

There was nothing visual about it - not like the fireballs her father had had her practicing with - but he was unprepared and didn't get a defense up fast enough.

The men's eyes moved, and then they ran.

Valerie watched them for a moment longer, then turned her head to find her mother standing just down the path from her.

"Are you showing off or stretching your legs?" Susan Blake asked, and Valerie shrugged.

"They weren't following us at first," she said. "Do they know you?"

"A couple of them," Susan said. "Good enough that they didn't see your father, but I want to be gone before anyone important finds out that I was here."

"The explosion," Valerie said, and Susan smiled.

"Thing of art, isn't it? I'd forgotten how much I like working with your dad on that kind of thing. He's so *creative*."

Susan put out an arm, and Valerie walked under it, letting her mom's arm settle across her shoulders as they walked.

"Is this what it's like, doing what you do?" Valerie asked, and Susan shook her head with a laugh.

"No, it's nowhere near this much fun," she answered. "Mostly it's boring, biding your time until it's time to move another inch or two. But it makes great stories, doesn't it?"

"Is Gemma going to be okay?" Valerie asked, and Susan shrugged, looking back at the men once more.

"This is a market that the Pure use a lot. It traffics in a lot of stuff you can't really get anywhere else. I expect there'll be a lot of activity today, trying to figure out who attacked the market and why... If she needs to slip away, we gave her her best shot."

"Should I have done something different, to keep them from seeing you?" Valerie asked. "Is she going to be in trouble because they knew you were here?"

Susan scoffed.

"They've known I'm around and active from the day you left me. That's not going to tell them anything useful at all. That I've got you *with* me? If they don't already know about it - which I expect they do know you're missing - now they know. So what? No plan ever goes simply. You have to trust that everyone involved is good enough to hold up their piece, no matter how things turn out."

"But you took Sasha so that no one would know where you went," Valerie said, and Susan shook her head.

"That would be their excuse, without a doubt, but they'd be asking a lot of other questions. We just didn't want anyone who knew *anything* alone in a room with Merck Trent when he's got an idea that they might know something interesting. Lady Harrington will keep her students *out* of that, mostly, but with you missing? She has to let them come look for you, on the off chance that something *bad* happened. It's a lot about a pretext to interrogate a student."

"Ethan grew up with that," Valerie said after a moment, and Susan nodded somberly.

"He did."

"And he's a nice guy, Mom. He is. I like him a lot."

Susan smiled.

"I'm glad. And I believe in you. I know if he screws up, you won't hesitate to walk away. If it turns out you're wrong, you won't have so much emotion and ego tied up in it that you can't break it off. So I hope nothing but the best for you."

"Oh," Valerie said. She'd been meaning to tell her mom, but she hadn't had a moment to do it. "Hanson."

"Yes?" Susan asked.

"He was spying on me for his mom."

"I thought as much."

"And then when he went home, his mom wasn't there. The Council called her back up again and… she just left him. *Abandoned* him. Lady Harrington took him in at Survival School, so he's… there now. And he and Sasha are kind of… a thing."

"What?" Susan asked. "He's… and she's…"

She put one hand up over her head and another at chest height, and Valerie nodded.

"Hasn't escaped us that she's a convenient elbow rest to him."

"I'm sorry," Susan said, and Valerie nodded.

"I hated him for like a minute," she said. "But he's my best friend."

"I know," Susan said. "You still have to be careful of him, though. You know that. Anything you say to him or do *around* him, she could take back… The Council, you said?"

Valerie nodded.

"How do you know that?" Susan asked. "I couldn't be certain she hadn't changed sides after school. Thought she might have been spying for The Pure, though why they would have held off coming after us, I couldn't figure."

"Yeah, Lady Harrington said that she could confirm that Mrs. Cox had been called up for Council work."

Susan nodded slowly.

"Well, she wouldn't get that wrong," she said. "Does explain how they found us. I thought my magic was pretty sound, keeping us hidden."

"Mom…" Valerie said, then stopped. She didn't know what she intended to say. Susan nodded.

"I wish we could go back," her mother said. "I wish it every day. I… It was a good time, as much as I missed your father and as much as I missed *magic*… But the idea that you were going to get to graduate high school and just go on to have a *normal* life? It was the best thing I could have imagined for you."

Valerie nodded.

"I wouldn't give up magic, either, but… I don't like the politics. Everyone spying on everyone else and everyone lying all the time, and everyone's lives being in danger all the time…"

"I don't mind the danger," Susan said. "I just wish it was more straightforward."

Valerie nodded, unable to contain a smile.

Sasha was already back in the car, and Grant was behind the wheel.

"You were really good, back there," Susan said. "I'm proud of you."

"Thanks, mom," Valerie answered, and Susan winked.

"You're my daughter. Wouldn't have expected anything else. But it doesn't stop me from being proud."

Valerie walked around to the far side of the car and got in.

Happy.

They'd just destroyed a market and men had come after her for reasons she shuddered to even imagine, and yet.

She was quite, quite happy.

She was good at this, like finding a glove that fit her to the skin.

She was happy.

Valerie had been here.

That's what his mom said.

Hanson wandered around the inside of the abandoned warehouse, standing in the dim blue of dusk, beams of light pouring down through thick dust and barely reaching the floor.

It was a gross place, full of the remnants of human industry and human despair, but Martha Cox was certain, and Hanson didn't question his mom when she was certain.

"There's magic here," the woman said, coming out of one of

the offices, just over that way. "There's magic here that I don't know. They cleaned it up well, so I'm not getting a lot of it, but Susan Blake was here, and I guarantee you that if Susan was here, her daughter was with her."

"Mom, what if someone *took* Valerie, and her mom is looking for her, too? Shouldn't we be looking for *Valerie*, not chasing around after Susan?"

Martha shook her head, going to pick up something that looked like a burnt flier, but that could have been any number of other things. Hanson had stopped picking things up several minutes ago.

"Susan Blake is not the type to lose track of her daughter. And the Council doesn't care about Valerie. They need to get Susan back on the leash again, and that's the only reason I'm here."

"She loved you, Mom," Hanson said. Martha looked over at him.

"I know," she said, her voice softer. "And I really was affectionate to her, as well. It was a long time, just living our lives. I'd forgotten how important the Council's work is, in that time. It wasn't until they called me in that I remembered. We have to find Susan and the Council has to find a way to put her back to work where she isn't going to just run off again the minute she gets out of sight. Hanson, the longer she's *out* here, the worse it's going to be, trying to earn back the Council's trust. They have to *know* that she's going to work for them or else…"

"Or else what?" Hanson asked.

"Or else they can't risk letting her out again," Martha said.

"You're talking about caging a woman who was your *friend*," Hanson said.

"No, I'm not," Martha said. It took several moments for Hanson to figure out what she meant by that.

"They'd kill her," he said.

"If they think she's not working in their interests," Martha said. "War is always won by narrow margins, here and there, where people made hard decisions. And Susan Blake is *key* to all of this. We need her."

"You're still talking about them *killing* her," Hanson said.

Martha nodded, picking up something else and putting her

tongue to it. He looked away.

"Without Susan Blake, we will almost certainly lose this war," Martha said. "With Susan Blake *against* us? We already *have* lost this war."

"How can one woman be so important?" Hanson asked. "I mean… Just… I just came from an entire school full of people who are really *good* at magic. Is she so important?"

"Yes," Martha said. "Because no one sees *conflict* the way that she does, and no one sees solutions to conflict the way that she does. I was a housewife the entire time you were growing up. Do you remember?"

"Of course I do, Mom," Hanson answered, looking up at the blue light forming beams through the dust over his head.

"And what do you think I did with my time, once you started going to school?"

"Um," Hanson said. He wanted to say 'clean the apartment', but it was glaringly untrue. Cluttered had been a kind way of describing their home, and while he'd never felt like the place was *unclean*, it hadn't ever really had a thorough straightening done to it.

"I studied Susan Blake," Martha supplied before he could get himself into trouble. "The Council gave me her war records when they sent me after her, and I spent your entire life studying her. I am the best known expert on that woman. I got to see what she was like *outside* of war, when she didn't think that everyone was spying on her or trying to kill her. I went to lunch with her once a week and we talked about your school and the neighborhood. I *know* how unusual her way of coming at things *is*. And what she does, when she's out of touch, off on a mission? It's *art*. I can't emphasize strongly enough how *talented* she is."

"Then why are you hunting her?" Hanson asked. "Why not let her do whatever she thinks is right?"

"Because if she's working against the Council, the Council is going to lose this war, son. And if they lose this war, the entire human population of the planet - every civilian man, woman, and child you have ever known - is going to *die*."

"You think she would actually work *against* a group that was trying to rescue the world's population?" Hanson asked, and Martha laughed.

"I think she *always* works against *everyone*. She never sees anything but her own agenda, and she thinks that her perspective is the only one that could possibly be true. She is *talented*, but she has an ego the size of this room, and, yes, she would absolutely gamble the population of the planet on her being right."

Hanson crossed his arms, watching his mother work.

He didn't have anything to argue against that.

It was possible that his mom was right.

He was just having a hard time giving her the benefit of the doubt, after the last few months.

Susan Blake hadn't abandoned her daughter.

"They were here," Martha said again. "I'm regretting not teaching you any magic, because I need you to check and see if Sasha Mills is still with them, or if this magic is from someone else."

"You think Sasha might have been here, too?" Hanson asked, and Martha looked up at him.

"Where else would she be? From everything you've told me, the two girls are inseparable."

She was actually betting that he was *right*.

That felt strange.

He'd only been around them a few days, in all...

It had only been a few *days* that he'd spent with Sasha.

And still.

And still, he felt funny thinking about her, like he had to make sure he didn't start smiling, like if he didn't watch close, his feet might drift up off the floor.

"We need to keep moving," Martha said. "This was a good find, but they're ahead of us. It's been days since they stopped here. If they keep moving, I'm never going to catch up."

She started for the door, and Hanson looked up at the ceiling again.

He hoped they kept moving.

They were in a cottage on a beach.

It didn't matter to Valerie that the cottage didn't have power and that it looked an awful lot like it had been mostly formed by the last major storm.

The waves were audible from inside the house.

She and Sasha were sharing a room again, but they'd spent an entire day out sitting on the sand, talking and watching the waves. Inside, Susan and Grant were up to *stuff*, but neither of Valerie's parents were interested in giving a tutorial on what they were doing, and frankly Sasha had had as much as she could take of the war effort, at just that moment, so Valerie let her friend talk her into going out and avoiding the casting from the early morning on through to the sunset.

Grant had come out with lunch, and Susan had brought them dinner, and it had been easy and nice and… Valerie was shocked that Sasha hadn't wanted to be sitting at the table, watching every move her parents made, but she wasn't going to question it.

Sasha had gone through a lot, these last couple of days, and the market had been the end of it.

Finally, as the sun went down and the air began to cool, Sasha stood.

"When do we go back to school, Valerie?" Sasha asked.

"I don't know," Valerie said. "I'd just been thinking we were along for the ride, right now."

"I don't know why we're here," Sasha said. "Is it so that we can see things how they actually are or because the Council is spying on you or because The Pure are hunting you, or because your teachers aren't good enough to teach you *actual* magic…? It feels like it's all of them and none of them, and like your parents don't even really *want* us here…"

She sighed, dropping her hands, and Valerie stood.

"I'm sorry," Valerie said. "I know this is hard. And you were excited for a second about seeing how things actually *were*, and… Yesterday was hard. I know it was."

"No you don't," Sasha said. "You don't. You had a great time. You punched a guy in the throat with *magic*."

"You saw that?" Valerie asked, and Sasha sighed, her shoulders falling.

"I was feeling wretched that I'd run off and left you to defend yourself on your own from all those *men*, and then I saw it, and I saw how they looked at you."

"They were looking at my mom," Valerie said. "She's the scary one."

"You're scary," Sasha said. "They don't have any idea, back at school. They still call you The Remedial."

"They do," Valerie said. That had stopped stinging about a month ago.

"Ethan…" Sasha said, then shook her head.

"What about him?" Valerie asked.

"He thinks he's going to be head of the new Council. He just assumes it, and so does Shack. But it's you. You're going to be more powerful than he is."

Valerie blinked.

"Um. No. I would rather hang myself with a poisonous snake."

Sasha looked out at the water.

"I'm not saying it's a meritocracy," the redhead said. "I'm not saying that. It's just… I don't think he's going to take it well, when he finds out who you really *are*."

"He knows who I *am*," Valerie said dismissively. "I mean. We just met a few months ago, so… it's not like Hanson. But he *knows* me. It isn't going to matter."

"Your parents are really neat," Sasha said.

"Okay," Valerie answered. She was still unnerved by how *close* Susan and Grant were. She could handle how much *unknown* they had to them, as individuals, but you put them together and it was like she'd never met either one of them *at all*.

"You ever wonder how your dad puts up with your mom being the important one all the time?"

"I don't see that he's putting up with *anything*," Valerie said. "She's not *that* important, and it's not like she's *more* important than he is. He was just dead this whole time."

"Everyone talks about what she did in the war, last time," Sasha said. "I knew who she was."

"Everyone knows who he is, too," Valerie said, feeling awkward. Her parents were rock stars, and she'd never had an inkling. "And no one *knows* what she did. They keep going on about… I don't know, *her*… but no one can say what she *did*."

Sasha sighed again.

"I think your dad is really cool for how he doesn't care that your mom is Susan Blake."

Valerie remembered something, tipping her head.

"No one knows *what they did*," she said. "It's all rumors and speculation and hype."

"I'm not saying…" Sasha said, but Valerie was already walking.

She went into the kitchen of the tiny little hut and she sat down on one of the chairs.

"The Shadows," Valerie said. "Real or not?"

"What?" Susan asked, looking at her.

"Real or not?" Valerie asked.

"Real," Grant said without looking up.

"Grant," Susan scolded, and he shrugged.

"I won't lie to her."

"I will," Susan said. "If it means not talking about the deep dark secrets."

"Who were they?" Valerie asked. Sasha slipped in and went to sit down against a wall, listening but trying to stay invisible.

"I *can't* tell you that," Susan said. "It would put lives in danger."

"Are they still active?" Valerie asked.

"Is your mother dead?" Grant answered. Susan gave him another sharp look.

"Did you kill the scientist who was making progress at taking away people's magic abilities?" Valerie asked.

Grant lifted his head, interested in this.

Susan gave him an extremely exasperated look, then turned her face to Valerie.

"If you know these things, you are in danger," she said. "I'm still trying to keep you safe from my past."

"Am I in any *more* danger than I already am?" Valerie asked, and Grant chuckled.

"She's got you there."

"Yes," Susan said. "Some of the people involved would kill you, just to keep the secrets from getting out. Even if we were all on the same side, back then."

"You think some of the Shadows have changed sides?" Valerie asked. "What *are* they?"

Grant raised his eyebrows.

"If you don't tell her, I will, and I doubt you're going to like the details I throw in."

Susan put her hands down flat on the table, glaring one more time at Grant, then closed her eyes.

"The Shadows," she said. "It was the result of a long night of drinking after a longer night of fighting. It was stupid and it was cool, and the cool overpowered the stupid."

"That's not how I remember it, but as I recall, I was *blackout* drunk that night."

"Oh, you were decidedly on the side of stupid that night," Susan said.

Grant laughed.

"Sounds like me."

Susan shook her head.

"The Shadows were a group of *covert* fighters. We all had our favorite tactics, and some of them had nothing to do with each other, but for reasons I am *not* going to go into tonight, we were all in the same bar after having been in the same fight. We'd won, but it was one of those moments where we realized that we were the only ones who *could* have won. The strike forces and the fighters and every last blessed graduate of Light School would have walked into a wall and *died* that night. It was just us..."

"The *Shadows*," Grant said dramatically, derailing Susan for just a moment.

"We had the knowledge and the information and the skills, among us, to do some really remarkable things. Gemma was there that night, actually."

"Was she?" Grant asked. "I didn't remember that."

Susan nodded.

"She won the bet on how many drinks you'd put down before you threw up. Guessed it on the nose."

"She was good at things like that, back then," Grant said. Susan shook her head.

"Anyway, we started talking and everyone was half drunk... it was one of those kinds of fights. I don't…" Susan licked her lips, sliding her hand along the table toward Valerie. "I ran away because I never wanted you to *experience* the kind of fight that drives you to drink and laugh too loud afterward. I wanted you to graduate with honors and go to college and study something just boring enough to pay well for the rest of your life. Not that. I really, *really* didn't want *that* for you."

"I didn't either," Grant muttered, then shook his head.

"It was one of those kinds of nights, though, and everyone was laughing too loud and we were talking about how we were the ones who hid in the shadows and saw everything and actually *got* it… And then someone said that we *were* the shadows, and we started calling ourselves that…"

She glanced at Grant, and he shrugged.

"You tell her what you want," he said. Susan nodded, then glanced back at Sasha.

"I'm about to say something that, if you were *ever* to repeat it to someone who cared and had power, they would absolutely end up killing people who don't deserve it. So if you don't want to be burdened with that kind of knowledge…"

Sasha hugged her knees to her chest.

"I think I accepted it the minute I walked out of the room," Valerie said and Susan shrugged.

"That fight went sideways," she said. "There were a lot of just plain magic warriors on both sides, killing each other for no reason but that they were on opposite sides, and… something changed that night. We all kind of saw each other, realized that the sides weren't nearly as clean-cut as either of us wanted to believe… The people at the table were on both sides of the war. The Council thinks that it's some jockish way that their people in the field refer to themselves, and boy did they latch hold of it and start shipping some *whoppers*, after they caught the name, but they don't know. The Shadows know that if you're working whole-heartedly for *either* side, you're supporting the *wrong*. And we came to realize that the *right* was going to need a new direction."

Valerie realized she had stopped breathing.

"You're rebels," she said.

Susan nodded.

"We are. And there aren't *that* many of us. We can't go up against our leadership directly…"

She paused.

"Susan," Grant said slowly. "I never asked because I assumed if you wanted to tell me, you would, but it's time. What happened when Lan died?"

Susan looked over at him, then pressed her lips.

"I would have told you, if I'd known that it was going to hit her. I'm sorry."

He nodded, glancing at Valerie, then settling back in his chair a fraction. Susan nodded.

"There's another of the Shadows, a man that your dad knows, but who I won't name. It's that dangerous. He was in Lan's inner circle, and Lan… Well, it doesn't matter now what he did that finally set the final fuse, but the Shadows came to the decision that if Lan continued to head The Pure, they were going to make a mistake and kill everyone. Lan just wasn't *worried* about it enough, and he was pushing his people so hard… I was there. It's true I was there. I was fighting Lan's people - including the other Shadow - and trying to *stop* this thing that was happening, and the Shadow killed him.

"It was a knife in the back event, but Lan was strong enough to send a final curse at me that reverberated through to the Council. I don't know if that was how he aimed it, but that's what happened. The Shadow heard the curse and figured out what it was, and while Lan was still casting it, the Shadow cast magic over top of it. Strong aligning magic. Magic that… when you mix what Lan was casting, I still don't know what to expect out of it. But it all hit me at once and I blacked out, and when I came to, Lan was dead and the room was empty. I ran away and… I found out I was pregnant a few weeks later."

"How did the story get out?" Sasha asked. "If you were the only one to tell it?"

Susan nodded, glancing back at Valerie's friend.

"I had to tell the Council that they'd been cursed. So I did, but I never did tell them the rest of the story. I went back out again and disappeared, and... They've never liked how easily I do that. They've always wanted to find a way to force me to do things their way. It's just a long history of me not going along, and I don't think that anyone has guessed how big a secret is hiding there."

Susan turned her attention back to Valerie once more.

"The Shadow who cast the aligning magic that settled on you... He knows about you. I told him. So if you are ever in a corner, you have at least one ally up high within the Pure who isn't your aunt."

"She hates me," Valerie said, and Susan shrugged.

"It's not personal. It's because you're my daughter."

"What happened?" Valerie asked, and Susan shook her head.

"That's a story for another day. We need to get cleaned up and packed up and ready to head out at first light."

"Why?" Valerie asked. "Why can't we stay here a couple days?"

"Because this isn't a vacation," Grant said. "There's work to do, and if we don't do it, no one will."

"You spent two weeks training me," Valerie said. "Wasn't there work to do, then?"

"I made sacrifices to do that," Grant said. "And things weren't as high-pitch as they are now. You've seen the two schools, and that was the real goal. Now..." Susan looked at him, and he shrugged. "There's so much for her to learn."

"I know," Susan said. "I let my hope get the best of me."

"It doesn't matter," Grant said. "She has to know it, so she will. There's no other way."

"What about the curse, though?" Sasha asked.

"What about it?" Susan replied.

"What does it *mean*? What are we supposed to do about it?"

"We?" Susan asked. "No. Grant and I will keep going at them the way we always have, you two will absorb everything you hear, everything you see, and everything you learn, and with any luck at all, by the time you graduate, you'll be ready to come at this war with the perspective that we need for you to *finish* it. There is no *winning* for the Council. Just knocking back the most belligerent of The Pure, for them to grow right back up again. We have to fight a different fight and go after different goals."

"But the Council brats," Sasha said. "They're *important*, right?"

Susan sighed, sitting back in her chair.

"Honestly? I'd rather forget about the whole thing. I'm grateful that Lan didn't manage to get a full, hard cast on every one of the Council's kids, because the civil war that would happen at the transition of leadership would *wreck* the magic community, but... I'd rather just leave it there. It's not worth my time or energy trying to convince someone else's kids that the world isn't the way everyone has made it out to be all this time. Especially not when they've grown up knowing, more than anyone else, that the Council is the end-all, be-all of truth arbitration. Hard enough to get my own kid straight on what's going on out here."

"Mom," Valerie said. "Ethan will listen to me."

Susan gave her a tight-lipped smile and nodded.

"I hope so. Maybe you do have an ally and I'm underestimating both of you. But... Just be careful, okay? It's so easy for it to look simpler than it is, and when you dig in, you realize that nothing was what you thought it was."

"You mean like both my best friend from childhood and the first person to be nice to me at school, outside of Sasha, both spying on me to the same leadership group?" Valerie asked. "Yeah, I'm getting that. I hate it."

"So do I," Susan sighed, and Grant shook his head.

"If you guys want to see cloak and dagger, try hanging out with The Pure for a while. I hate the Council as much as the next guy, but The Pure have got subterfuge down to an art."

"I'm not going to have the whose-leaders-are-worse fight with you again," Susan said.

"They aren't his leaders," Valerie said. "They *aren't*. Why do you guys keep acting like it wouldn't be a big deal if they *were*?"

Susan looked at her, and then at Grant.

"You have to tell her," she said. "It's going to come out eventually, and you're going to wish she'd heard it from you."

"You're not one of them, are you?" Valerie asked her father. He narrowed his eyes at Susan, then shook his head and sighed.

"Lan," he said after a moment. "He was a tight-fisted leader, and The Pure were a cult of personality. Passions run deep, over there, but he was the one who started it."

"Okay," Valerie said.

"When he died, there was a huge fight over who was going to take over. A lot of power factions rose up and fought each other for the soul of The Pure, but in the end, it was his first lieutenant who managed to take over. His name is Fact Alexander."

"That's made up, right?" Valerie asked.

"He took Fact as his first name a long time ago, but Alexander is his given last name," Grant said.

Grant looked at Susan once more, then shook his head.

"I had a teacher at school, Mr. Blake, who was really kind to me and encouraged me to think about things however I wanted to. It was just civilian public school, but he knew that I didn't like my parents' politics - he thought they were hippies - and he was really supportive. I used to sit with him at lunch a couple of times a month and just talk about... I don't know. Philosophy, I guess. He was a math teacher, but I really liked the way he thought, and he challenged me to look hard at how I came to my decisions about what I believed... Anyway, when I applied at Light School, I changed my name to Blake."

Valerie put her hands over her mouth.

"I'm named for your math teacher?" she asked, and he closed his eyes, laughing.

"Yes, daughter. You are named for my math teacher."

"You're the son of the head of the Superiors," Sasha said, standing.

"Thank you, Miss Mills," Susan said.

Valerie looked hard at Grant.

"That's why Gemma is the way she is," she said, and he shrugged.

"Everyone knows that she's an Alexander, but no one really points it out. It would be insulting to her to imply that she doesn't *deserve* every bit of confidence she gets, but it would also make Fact very angry if someone mistreated her. And he has a legendary temper."

"You're fighting him," Sasha said.

"I'm fighting everyone," Grant said, testy. He stood and started clearing off the table. "And we need to move again. I've got irons in the fire that I need to check on. Had enough problems the last time I went off grid for more than a day or two."

"But we're working together now," Susan answered. "We've got this."

He looked at her, then softened, nodding.

"I know. But people are going to die."

"People are always going to die," Susan said. "It's war."

He frowned, then returned his attention to the table. Valerie stood, grabbing Sasha.

"We'll go get packed up."

"Get *what* packed up?" Sasha asked.

They'd stopped at a thrift shop after Ground School and bought a few sets of clothes, but everything Valerie had to her name just now fit into a grocery store bag.

"Valerie," Sasha hissed as they got back to the room the two of them were sharing. "Are you *sure* he's on our side?"

Valerie went to get her bag of clothes, wishing again that she had a decent hairbrush as she pulled her fingers through her hair.

"You heard them," Valerie said, looking at herself in the tiny mirror on one wall. "We aren't on a *side*. We're on our own side."

The car rolled to a stop, and Hanson looked out his window at a large brick building with grid-spaced windows.

"What are you doing here, Susie?" Martha asked rhetorically.

"What is it?" Hanson asked.

"Ground School," Martha said. "Entry level. Even you wouldn't end up here. It's below you."

"Don't know. That sounds about right," Hanson said.

"It's below you," Martha said more emphatically.

"Ma, I don't do any magic," Hanson told her.

"No, but you could," Martha said vaguely, putting the car back into drive.

"How do you know?" Hanson demanded.

"Because you're my son, and because your father is your father, and because I sacrificed too much for you to be completely lacking in talent."

"Val is a natural," Hanson said. "Did you know that?"

"Do you even know what that means?" Martha retorted.

"It means she makes up magic and it just *works*," Hanson said. He knew precious little else, but he wasn't going to admit that.

"I don't see why it matters," Martha said, driving away from the school. "You belong at that school as much as anyone else does."

"No," Hanson said. "They took me in because you abandoned me. I don't *deserve* to be there."

"I went there and your father went there, and all you need is someone to teach you."

"They aren't going to, ma," Hanson said, slouching. "I'm too far behind, and no one is interested in it. They're teaching Val, but that's because she's so good and because she's important. I'm not important. They don't care if I can do magic or not."

Martha looked over at him and frowned.

"You can't defend yourself from the dark elements if you can't do magic," she said. "Letting a boy know that magic exists and then not teaching him so much as the basics of self defense? It's like chumming. Lady Harrington wouldn't do that."

"You did that," Hanson said, raising his voice again. "You failed to teach me *anything*, but you used me in a spy in your war the whole time."

"You never complained," Martha said, and he tipped his head back against the headrest.

"I thought it was just for things like making the dishwasher work again and cleaning stains out of the carpet. I never realized how… big it was."

"Yes, well, you know now, and what's done is done," Martha said. "Why would she have gone to the lowest of the low schools?"

"Val wouldn't care that it was below her," Hanson said. "She just would have worked as hard as she could."

Martha paused, looking over at Hanson.

"Susan wouldn't have cared, either. She would have expected to go to that school and come out being the best of the best anyway, and she would have *thought* that it was because she worked so much *harder* than everyone else."

"Ma, jealous isn't a good color on you," Hanson said.

"Don't talk like that to me," Martha said. "You have no idea. The golden girl that everyone thought was going to save us all. She just ran off, and thought that she could turn her back on everyone. Everything always has to be on her terms, her way."

Hanson sighed.

"Can you just take me back to school?" he asked. "I don't know what I'm doing here."

"I'll do no such thing," Martha said. "You're going to help me. If it's just the one tiniest thing that you happen to know that I don't, and it makes the difference, you will change the course of human life. Do you understand me? It's *that* important."

Hanson nodded, closing his eyes.

"Wake me up when the tiny detail shows up," he said, shifting once more lower into his seat.

They abandoned the car.

Susan and Grant were each carrying large backpacking backpacks, while Valerie and Sasha carried one plastic bag each full of clothes.

It was the strangest thing to see, except for all of the other weird stuff Valerie had ever seen, wandering around after school.

It was just city life.

"Are they going to kill someone?" Sasha asked at one point as they walked.

"We're hoping to prevent something," Susan said over her shoulder. "But prevention doesn't rule out killing someone, if that's what has to happen."

Sasha shuddered.

"Can I *not* be there when it happens?" she asked.

"We're not putting you two in the middle of a fight," Grant said. "We're headed to one of my apartments. You can order pizza and watch movies or whatever, then we'll spend the night there and move again in the morning."

Valerie sighed.

"It's no wonder no one can ever find you," she said. "I thought that being out in the middle of nowhere was hard to find."

"Never sleep in the same place twice in a row," Susan said. "It really does make it harder to find you."

"Does anyone ever just kind of wait around for you to show up someplace, because you're bound to end up there eventually?" Sasha asked.

"Yes, actually," Susan said lightly. "Survival School. Other than that, no one has any *idea* where I'm going to be, least of all me."

"That sounds exhausting," Sasha asked, and Susan laughed.

"I thought that I was looking forward to having a single home where I spent all of my time. It was the most maddening thing I ever did in my entire life."

Valerie smiled at this and shook her head.

"But the apartment was always spotless," she said.

"I know," Susan said. "Some days all I did was get angry and clean everything."

"I've seen those moods," Grant said. "I can't imagine what you would have been like, without the ability to sit and cast magic."

"Don't get me started," Susan said.

"What *are* you doing tonight?" Valerie asked, and Susan glanced at her once more.

"Best if you don't know."

"But they're gearing up for another big attack?" Valerie asked, and Grant nodded.

"How did you find out?" Sasha asked.

"I got a tip," Grant said.

"But you haven't talked to anyone since you came to get us," Sasha said. "Or have you been sneaking away?"

"I have an e-mail account," Grant said. "I go to cafes and check it every day, no matter what."

"Isn't that dangerous?" Valerie asked. "Doesn't that make you traceable?"

"It does," Grant said. "But I use public computers that aren't attached to me, which means it's actually easier to track me digitally than magically. The Council has guys who do that, but The Pure prefer to hack everything magically. If it requires a digital expert, an internet expert, they hire it out, and they won't hire out things that are as sensitive as the spy games."

Susan nodded.

"I don't like it, and I won't touch a computer, but he's been doing it a long time. I have to assume it works."

They turned into a building and started upstairs.

Six flights, and Grant went to a door, pressing his palm to the wood and waiting a moment. At first there was silence, but then there was a slow grating noise, one that Valerie instinctively associated with a deadbolt sliding out of its slot.

Grant opened the door and turned on the lights.

There were lights.

It wasn't a *nice* apartment, not even compared to the one that Valerie and Susan had lived in all those years, as Susan was pretending they had difficulty making ends meet, but it had lights and presumably it had running water, and there in the corner there was a television.

It was a massive CRT, but *still*. It had a cable plugged into the side and everything.

They had TV.

Valerie threw herself down onto the couch, stretching and closing her eyes.

"I'm going to go take a shower, if no one minds," Sasha said.

"There are towels in the closet," Grant called after her. "I think."

Susan went to sit on the floor near Valerie.

"I'll leave you money for pizza," Susan said. "The land-line here is warded pretty hard, so as long as you aren't on the phone for a long time, you ought to be fine. Hang up if they put you on hold and just call back. Okay?"

Valerie nodded.

"Civilization," she murmured. "Television and phone and internet… Oh, how I have missed you."

She thought abruptly of her phone.

"I haven't had a cell phone in months," she said.

"Good to break that habit," Grant said. "Takes way too much strength to be untraceable when you've got one in your pocket."

"But what if something went wrong and someone needed to tell you?" Valerie asked. "I mean, is it *really* that bad, or are you being paranoid?"

"Until you're actually responsible for your own life, you're going to have to trust my judgment," Susan answered. "No cell phones."

Valerie sighed.

"Not like there's anyone I'd call, anyway. No one at school has one."

"What are the rules for cell phones on campus, these days?" Susan asked.

"Upperclassmen can have them," Grant said. "Last I heard. So long as they leave them in the cottages."

Susan shifted, and something about the tension of the motion drew Valerie's attention.

"What is it?" Valerie asked.

"You've had too much activity at school," Susan said. "Just… a puzzle I've been piecing at for a while. I haven't figured anything out yet."

"Someone is trying to kill me," Valerie said, turning her head, and Susan nodded.

"Yes. That. I don't believe they're trying to *kill* you, because that would… that would end badly for them, but I do think that they're trying to *obtain* you."

"If they weren't trying to kill me, they wouldn't have left a bomb in the hallway," Valerie said, and Susan frowned, squeezing her hand.

"You know, I don't have an argument for that. I wish I knew what kind of bomb it was…"

"There were triggers all over the place. Dr. Finn helped me disable all of them, but… It was scary."

"Demons set it?" Susan asked.

"Yeah, they left it and teleported out," Valerie answered.

"Glitched," Grant said from the kitchen. "The word is 'glitch'."

"Whatever," Valerie said. "One second they were there and the next they weren't, and there were bomb triggers attached to everything."

"There are too many factions running around with demonic connections at this point," Susan said. "I used to be able to keep

144

them straight."

"It's like going nuclear," Grant said. "As soon as one of the rival factions makes an alliance, all of the rest of them feel like they have to, to keep even footing."

"When they go after Light School, they're never going to see it coming," Susan lamented. "Grant, I don't know if I can send her back."

"We'll talk about it," he answered. "But you know we don't have a choice. You need to be able to defend yourself, and you can't, while you're worried about her."

"Don't I get a say?" Valerie asked.

"What do you want?" Susan asked, turning to lean her back against the couch.

"I need to go back," Valerie said, and Susan tipped her head.

"I'm surprised," she said. "I would have thought that you would hate it there."

"Oh, I do," Valerie said. "They're authoritarian and backwards and they keep locking us in our rooms for days at a time when something goes wrong, but... If I hadn't been there, I wouldn't have been able to disarm the bomb before someone opened a door and set it off. They would have all died."

"If you hadn't been there, odds are good there wouldn't have *been* a bomb," Grant said.

"Yeah, I know," Valerie said. "But there's *going* to be, isn't there?"

Both adults were silent for a moment, then Susan shifted.

"Tell me what the teachers are doing," she said.

"What do you mean?" Valerie asked.

"She wants to know how involved they are with the war effort," Grant said.

"You said you were working for Mr. Tannis," Susan said. "Is he the only one working for the Council?"

"No," Valerie said. "They all are."

Susan nodded, looking over at Grant.

"There's a reason they're supposed to keep the wars out of the schools," Susan said. "It makes them less of a target for the Pure. So long as the Council is routing work through the schools, they're going to be tactical targets."

"And there will be another bomb," Valerie said.

"How are they getting in?" Grant asked, coming over with a plate of food. Everything had come out of a can, but it didn't look half bad, anyway.

He sat down on an armchair, and Valerie reached over, taking a slice of pear.

"I told you," she said. "They set something on fire in the hallway and it grew a silverthorn, and it put a hole in the defenses. I killed it back some more after I came back from training with you, but there's still a hole."

"And they haven't figured out how to ward it yet?" Susan asked, and Valerie shook her head.

"Apparently not."

"Is Alan involved in that?" Susan asked, and Valerie nodded.

"He and Mr. Tannis have worked on it a bunch."

"That's not a standard cast, then," Susan said, looking at Grant. Valerie's father sighed.

"We can't get in, Susan. Your mother won't let us past. We *can't* help them."

"They think you're with the Pure. The Superiors," Valerie said to her father. "Ethan told me to be careful."

"They knew I was alive?" Grant asked, and Valerie nodded.

"Well, okay, I don't *know* know that they knew you were alive, but he wasn't surprised when I told him I'd seen you."

"Interesting," Grant said.

"I put down a good cover story for you," Susan said. "And The Pure know you haven't been working *with* them."

"But if we can make them think that I'm working with one of the separatist groups," Grant said. "Without being clear about which one, we could get some distance between The Pure and the separatists."

"I can get some mileage out of that," Susan said, and Grant nodded, handing the plate across to Valerie again.

"So can I."

"What's going on out here?" Sasha asked, and Susan and Grant looked over. Valerie sighed.

"Apparently we're all *still* just spying for our parents," she said, and Susan grinned.

"It's for the greater good, honey."

Her parents left.

It was kind of strange, watching them go out the door of the strange apartment and looking over at Sasha.

"We're unsupervised," Valerie said, and Sasha shrugged.

"So?"

"This is the first time I've been unsupervised since I went to Survival School in the first place," Valerie said.

"You *left*," Sasha said. "I've been on campus the entire time."

Valerie nodded.

"Still, I was supervised the whole time. We should do something rebellious, just to have done it."

"I'm not sure I know how," Sasha said slowly, and Valerie shrugged.

"It's overrated. Pizza?"

They went through the delivery brochures her father had left on the counter and chose their pizza, then Valerie called to order it.

She was wholly prepared to hang up if they put her on hold, but the girl on the other end of the phone took her order promptly and promised the pizza would be there in thirty minutes or less.

Valerie went to sit with Sasha as the redhead scrolled through television channels.

"I don't know what to watch," Sasha admitted as she kept looking.

"Everything I was following was either streaming or I'm way behind now," Valerie said. "Just pick a movie or something."

Sasha found a rom-com that Valerie had wanted to see, before, and they settled in.

"Your parents are neat," Sasha said, sitting with her chin on her palms.

"Don't sugar coat it," Valerie said. "They stress you out."

"They do fight a lot," Sasha said. "And... Did they ever say exactly what they were doing tonight?"

"Nope," Valerie confirmed. "Pretty much on purpose."

"But what if something *happened*?" Sasha asked. "We don't know how to get in touch with them, and all they do is hide. We'd never find them again."

"They'd find us," Valerie said with complete faith.

"But what if we had to *run*?" Sasha asked. "What if someone came for us?"

"You think they planted a phony phone number on the flier?" Valerie asked. "Who would come here?"

"You said it," Sasha said. "If you want to catch your parents, you just go someplace they're likely to end up and wait there. Chasing them is pointless."

"It is pointless," Valerie said. "That's why they have so many hideouts. They wouldn't have left us here if there was any serious chance someone could find us."

"I know," Sasha said. "But your mom wouldn't have sent you to school if there was any serious chance of a bomb blowing you up, either, and yet…"

Valerie shrugged.

Sasha had a point.

"What do you suggest we do about it?" she asked, and Sasha looked around.

"I bet your dad has a cache of spellcasting stuff hidden around here somewhere."

"You want to search the apartment and put up our own wards?" Valerie asked, and Sasha shrugged.

"Maybe. It'd make me feel much better, if I had forewarning if something was coming."

Valerie looked over at the TV again, torn.

She didn't get opportunities like this very often, anymore.

On the other hand.

"Why not?" she asked, standing.

They had fifteen minutes until the pizza was supposed to show up.

"You start in the kitchen; I'll go through the main bedroom," Valerie said, and Sasha nodded.

"Leave everything like it was," Sasha said. "I'd be embarrassed

148

if they knew we'd gone through it all."

"I don't expect anything I do to be secret anymore," Valerie said, only half-joking. "Everyone is spying on me full-time. I may as well do something interesting to watch."

"Are you going to burn handprints into the back of the door again?" Sasha asked. "Between your magic and your dad's, I don't think I'd be able to get in at all."

"Maybe just to our door," Valerie answered, mostly kidding.

Valerie looked under the bed in the master suite, then went into the bathroom, going through the two drawers and the cabinet there. She turned up some basic stuff, in the bottom drawer in the bathroom, but nothing that deserved to be called a 'cache'. For all Valerie knew, it might have been used for personal grooming and nothing more.

"Here," Sasha called, and Valerie carried the little basket back into the main room.

Sasha had a giant popcorn tin in her arms, but she was carrying it like it weighed a lot more.

"Top shelf in the pantry," the redhead said, grinning, and Valerie grinned back.

"Let's see what they've got in here," she said, going to sit on the floor in front of the movie again.

Sasha opened the tin and started to unpack it. Valerie picked something up and Sasha gave her a sharp look.

"Can I… just… Please?"

"What?" Valerie asked.

"There's an art to taking something apart so that you can put it back together exactly the way it was," Sasha said. "And you're messing with it."

Valerie smiled, putting her hands in the air and simply watching as Sasha continued to unpack the tin.

There was an art to it, and Valerie was starting to get the hang of it by the time the pizza arrived. Valerie looked though the peephole, then opened the door and quickly exchanged the food for money and closed the door again, going to sit on the carpet once more.

"This thing is *packed*," Sasha said, still working.

"I'm just gonna eat, so long as I'm sitting here not doing anything," Valerie said, and Sasha waved at her.

"There's stuff I don't even know what it is," she said.

"Shocker," Valerie said, settling in to watch the movie.

If she watched Sasha work anymore, she was going to give in to the temptation to start touching stuff.

"Oh, cool," Sasha said. "I didn't know you could still get these."

"I'm watching, here," Valerie answered.

"Uh huh," Sasha said. "You're over there secretly plotting what you're going to do with all of this stuff. I know you."

"I don't know what any of it is any better than you do," Valerie said. "I'm just going to pick it up and throw it together and hope it doesn't blow up."

"Are not," Sasha said dismissively. "Three months ago, maybe, but you've got your stuff under control, now. You could do anything you want to do."

Valerie looked over her shoulder at the floor and shrugged.

It wasn't *untrue*, but it wasn't anywhere near as consistent a magic as Sasha liked to believe.

"Mrs. Reynolds says that magic is a constant learning process," Valerie said.

"And you need to know what all of these things are," Sasha said. "Just not to *use* them, apparently."

Valerie shook her head and went back to eating.

Finally, Sasha finished, putting the tin up on the arm chair and scooting back.

Valerie only in that moment realized the volume and diversity of *stuff* her father had there.

And some of it was *really* dark.

She knew that the three-branches theory of magic didn't really hold with the 'very dark' and 'very light' characterizations she'd been learning in school, but it was still *really* dark, if she was able to sense it.

"All right," Valerie said, handing the box of pizza over and sitting up. "What do you want me to make?"

"An alarm system," Sasha said without hesitation. "One that

warns us if someone is using magic as they come up the stairs. And aren't your parents."

"Aren't you choosey," Valerie said, putting her hands out over the ingredients. "You know that that probably isn't possible at all, not to mention with the stuff they've got here."

"It's possible," Sasha said. "I think. I think Lady Harrington has that kind of stuff all over the school."

Valerie sighed.

Of course it was possible.

She just didn't have a clue how to do it.

Thing was, her hands did.

She started picking things up and setting them to the side. Sasha abandoned her pizza and came to sort the ingredients so that she could put them back where they came from after Valerie was done with them, but Valerie was in her cool, mechanical operating state, just working by touch and instinct.

"What do you need from me?" Sasha asked.

"A knife from the kitchen," Valerie said. "Actually, an entire prep kit, as close as you can get to it."

"My mom carries a really nice one," Sasha said. "I think most magic users have one that they prefer, but they tend to keep it on them…"

Valerie glanced up.

She and Sasha didn't talk about Ivory Mills very often, but it wasn't because Sasha wasn't forthcoming or interested. Valerie just failed to ask much.

"Tell me what your mom does, again," she said. "Now that I at least have *some* clue what magic is and what it does."

Sasha nodded, starting to pull knives out of a block and put them on a plate.

"Right. So, she goes into hospitals and stuff like that, clinics sometimes, and she'll either tell people she's a counselor or a holistic healer or a social worker… You know that she actually has a degree from a civilian university in counseling?"

"I didn't," Valerie said. "When did she do that?"

"After the war," Sasha said. "After I was born. I remember a little bit of it, at the very end, but Bradley remembers all of it. She worked really hard, making sure that she put as much time into us as she could and didn't give up on going to hospitals and stuff, still. It was all local, back then. Here in the last year, I was only going to school a couple of days a week, and I was traveling with her the rest of the time."

"And your school let you do it?" Valerie asked.

"My mom didn't really ask," Sasha said. "She just told them that I was going to be traveling with her for work and that the exposure was worth skipping the days at school. I made up everything from the road."

"Huh," Valerie said. "Did you like it?"

Sasha shrugged, coming to sit on the armchair after she moved the popcorn tin to the floor and watching Valerie work some more.

"I think I did," she finally said. "I missed my friends, and everyone thought I was really weird, but I got to see my mom do a *lot* of magic, and that's helped me a lot with school. And I knew I was leaving after last year, anyway, so the fact that everyone thought I was super weird... Well, they mostly thought it before, too, but it didn't bother me as much because I knew that they wouldn't matter this year."

"Okay," Valerie said. "So what kind of stuff does your mom do?"

"She specializes in trauma," Sasha said. "She helps people heal faster and helps keep the complications from developing. She has potions that will keep most infections from happening, and ones that prevent clots..."

"Those are usually called *medicines*," Valerie said, and Sasha shook her head.

"It's only a medicine if it works when someone else does it," Sasha said. "My mom had to administer everything herself."

"Did she ever have you help?" Valerie asked, and Sasha shrugged.

"Minor prep work, sometimes. Not anything important. If it went wrong, she could hurt someone, and if it just didn't work... She would move on the next day, and if something didn't work, she lost her chance to help someone."

"What did she do for money?" Valerie asked.

"She got paid as part of the war," Sasha said. "And my dad has a construction business that he runs. His buildings are stronger and lighter and cheaper than anyone else's, because they're using magic to get them built and to make everything work... It's a really niche set of magic spells and potions that he uses, but he works on really *big* buildings, now. Anyway... I never hear my parents even talk about money.

"That's so weird," Valerie said. "To just not even have to think about it? I can't imagine."

"Did your mom talk about money a lot?" Sasha asked, and Valerie tipped her head back and laughed.

"I left my window open one night when it got cold outside, and she made me pay the heating bill out of my babysitting money."

"Huh," Sasha said. "And she had all that money the whole time."

Valerie shook her head.

"Do you think she gave up something *big*, running away? Like, a life of luxury?"

"Valerie," Sasha said, a tone of concern in her voice. "Have you *seen* your parents together?"

"Um," Valerie said. "I've been trying not to."

"Shut up. That's not what I mean. I mean they're *happy*. They get along and they like each other. They *love* each other. She gave up being with your *dad* to run away."

Valerie frowned, looking at the mostly-built cast, then nodded.

"You're right. I'm just so used to it just being the two of us, and my dad is so *weird*."

"He's smart," Sasha said. "And to the point. And, yeah, he scares me sometimes, but he's *good* at what he does."

"Is there anyone you *don't* see the best in?" Valerie asked.

"Elvis Trent," Sasha said without pause. Valerie laughed.

"Fair enough."

She held her hands out to the side.

"So. I think I've got this, actually, but I need you to open the door so it can see the hallway as it finishes setting."

Sasha sprang out of her chair and went to open the door, leaning against the doorway and waiting.

Valerie would have been watching for some kind of purple swirly smoke to go by, but Sasha seemed to be too seasoned to expect something like that.

It was still a bit disappointing. Valerie finished the spell and, while she could *feel* it doing a thing, she couldn't see anything. She liked the casts that came with pretty colors and explosions.

She looked over, the sense of the spell expanding and beginning to send her information about the room and the magic inside of it making her nervous for just a moment.

She didn't *want* to have that information coming back to her for the rest of her life. It would have been like having a radio on her shoulder that she couldn't turn off.

And then she realized that she *controlled* that signal, and she could turn it down, turn it off, even dismantle it at a thought.

And that.

That was remarkable.

The cast filled the outside hallway, and Valerie nodded.

"You can close it."

Sasha came back and started to clean up, and Valerie went to get the pizza, starting a new slice when she sat up.

"What is it?" Sash asked her from the floor, and Valerie shook her head.

"I screwed up the cast," she said. "It doesn't…"

But she hadn't.

She *hadn't*.

She'd done it exactly right.

She put her hands over her face, then turned the television off and looked at Sasha.

"Go get your stuff. Anything you need to have with you. We need to go."

"What?" Sasha demanded, and Valerie nodded, looking at the door.

"They're coming."

"No," Sasha said from the floor. "No. It was supposed to just be because I was paranoid."

Valerie shook her head.

"Go fast. I'm going to figure out how to get us out of here."

Sasha stood, looking around the room once with a sense of despair, then walked away, headed for the bedroom. Valerie could hear her stuffing things into the plastic bag, and Valerie slid off of the couch to look at what she had to work with, again.

Weapon?

Or diversion?

Her mother had killed the last two men that Valerie had attacked. Valerie hadn't had the stomach for killing them, and she still remembered how she'd felt when she'd thought she'd been the one who had taken their lives.

She couldn't do that again.

She couldn't.

She wouldn't.

So she needed something to distract them or convince them that she and Sasha weren't where they were.

How did she do that?

How had her *father* done it, when he'd come to rescue her?

She couldn't do that.

Whatever it was he'd done, she couldn't do that.

It was dangerous and it was hard, and…

No.

She needed a different plan.

Sasha was packing fast, and the magic outside of the doorway indicated that there were people casting… Scouting magic. It was the only word for it. It was like a giant hound was snuffling up Valerie's magic and figuring out what it was, and for a moment Valerie worried that she'd *attracted* them by casting outside of the apartment, but - no - they'd gotten here too quickly. They'd already been on their way and it was only Sasha's fear that had saved them from being surprised and ambushed.

Valerie needed to respect that more.

Her hands were working.

She wasn't sure yet what they were up to, but they were

working, and that was calming.

She was assembling magic... volatile magic. Smoke and confusion and noise and... violence. There was violence in there.

Heat.

She liked heat magic, it turned out.

Explosion.

Not enough to cook someone - the variety of casting ingredients that were here wasn't *quite* broad enough to do *that* - but enough power to knock them back.

Sound.

Sound-deadening.

She was going to make them deaf.

Not permanently, she didn't think, but...

For a few minutes.

At least.

They would have defenses.

It was possible it wouldn't work at *all*, though Valerie had never seen one of her casts fail...

She actually paused, sitting back on her heels to reflect on that. She'd *never* failed a cast. Mr. Jamison was right - there were kids in her class who were still trying to get casts to *work* consistently, and she whined about how far behind she was.

And here she was, building a defense bomb that was going to get them out of the apartment safe and alive.

While the bomb was setting and cooking and becoming as potent as it was going to be in the time she was going to get, she set to work on a pair of poultices. She knew intuitively what they were, but she didn't know *specifically* until they were almost done and Sasha was sitting on the floor in front of her again.

"Don't touch that one," Valerie said. "Don't you wish my parents had a cell phone now?"

"What?" Sasha asked, and Valerie frowned.

"Oh, you were in the shower. Sorry. Never mind."

"I do wish they had a cell phone," Sasha said. "How did they find us?"

"My parents are scary," Valerie said. "So they lay in wait on the apartment and waited for my parents to leave. They don't want to go head-to-head with the Blakes; they just want to manipulate them through me."

"You're awfully certain," Sasha said hesitantly and Valerie grinned.

"I'm thinking too hard about this cast to have room for doubt. It could be anything else. Maybe the neighbors are just cracked and decided to come abduct us for funsies. What do I know?"

Sasha rocked on her toes.

"What do you need me to do?" she asked, and Valerie nodded to the second poultice that she was just finishing.

"Do what I do," she said, dipping her fingers into the green-ish cream and spreading it from her nose back to her ears, then sliding her finger through the top curl of her ear to form a ring around the outside of her ear.

Sasha did it without question.

"That's going to go off when the door opens," Valerie said, indicating the bomb. "We can open the door or they can, but when it goes off, we need to be running."

"What happens then?" Sasha asked. Valerie shook her head.

"We keep moving. No matter what."

"And how do your parents find us?" Sasha asked. Valerie shrugged, looking at the ingredients still sitting there on the floor. She needed... Those.

She started stuffing things into her pockets and handing other things to Sasha.

"We have to trust that they're good enough to do it," Valerie said. "If we stay here, a lot of people are going to die, and we might be some of them."

She looked at Sasha, realizing quite suddenly that no one had any reason to keep Sasha alive. Her friend's mom was not tactically relevant. All they needed was Valerie.

"If they catch you, they'll kill you," she said quietly. "But maybe I could hide you...?"

"I'm coming with you," Sasha said. "We're not talking about this."

"Okay," Valerie said. "Okay. We're not talking about it." She finished putting things into her pockets and stood, looking at the door. "So… This is going to be loud."

"How loud?" Sasha asked.

The door opened.

Flying Solo

They were moving.

In retrospect...

Nothing.

No.

She couldn't remember what had happened clearly enough to have an idea what she would have done differently, though she was sure she'd *done* things differently than she would have if she'd been able to know what she knew after...

The world was made of bewilderment and fog and noise.

And then they were downstairs.

There had been two more people in the building, but the stun-bomb had hit them and for some reason they hadn't been wholly defended from it - heck, Valerie and Sasha weren't fully defended, and that was with Valerie's own cast protecting them - and Valerie and Sasha had been able to slip past them.

Or something.

It was a bit foggy exactly what had happened.

"Are you okay?" Valerie asked as she and Sasha leaned against the side of the building. The streetlights were beginning to come on and it was cold out. Sasha pulled a sweater out of her bag and handed the other bag to Valerie. There was a jacket in there, and Valerie paused long enough to put it on before she straightened and started walking again.

"There's a car around her somewhere," she said. "They didn't walk here."

"How do you *know*?" Sasha asked. "How do you know *any* of this?"

"It's guesses," Valerie said. Based on movies, if she was being honest. "If you've got better ones, I'm glad to hear them."

Sasha shuddered, looking back at the building.

They needed to make it to the corner before they figured out what had happened, inside.

"Should we run?" Sasha asked.

Valerie shook her head.

"I don't think so. I think they could follow that."

She could follow that, she realized, stunned.

"No, we need to walk, and we need to find a safe place to hide."

"And then your parents will come back and they'll…" Sasha started, then shook her head, wiping at her eyes. "What's going to happen?"

"I don't know," Valerie said. "I don't know, but… My mom said they could find us anywhere. We have to keep moving, or else they're going to catch us, and we lose our chance to decide…"

"Did your mom teach you all of this?" Sasha asked, and Valerie frowned.

Her mother hadn't taught her any magic, but they'd been talking about self defense and tactics and… They'd watched all of her mom's favorite movies over and over again, and her mom had talked about what was realistic and what wasn't…

"She did," Valerie said. "I didn't see it before now."

Sasha nodded, looking back once more.

"That makes me feel better."

"Come on," Valerie said, putting an arm around Sasha's shoulders. "I don't know what's going to happen, but this is the best we can do."

They stopped the car alongside a busy road, looking at chain link fence and a vast abandoned lot.

"What is this?" Hanson asked.

"I don't know," Martha answered. "It's warded. Heavily. I can't get past here, even on foot. There's something hidden out there on that lot."

"And they were here?" he asked. She nodded.

"They were here for a long time," she said. "Maybe they were digging, I don't know. They got past the wards, though. Susan's magic disappears in there."

Hanson couldn't imagine what his mom was tracking based off of, and he didn't like being in the car with her, though he had to admit that he was torn between wanting Valerie to get away and hoping that he would get to see her again soon.

He'd missed her badly while she'd been at school, and he was just getting used to being around her again when this had happened.

"Could you get in if you wanted to?" he asked, and Martha shook her head.

"No. I... maybe. But I'm out of practice, and Susie is the covert operative. I'm just tracking her."

Hanson looked out at the lot, squinting to try to see what Valerie might have been up to, then Martha put the car into drive again and pulled away from the curb.

"It's not ours," she said after a moment, looking over her shoulder. "I'm not *certain*, but it doesn't feel right. I think it's Superior-held."

"She took Valerie into an enemy property?" Hanson asked, and Martha shrugged.

"I don't have any idea what the two of them are doing," Martha said. "You shouldn't assume that Susan Blake is going to take care of that girl the way you expect her to, based on who you always thought she was. She's at war now, and she's brutal."

Hanson sighed.

"Seems like everyone changes," he muttered, and Martha looked over at him.

"Do you want me to teach you magic?" she asked and he turned sharply to look at her.

"Yes."

"We need to find a place to stay for the night. They came back out, but we're getting further behind. I need to report back what I've found and see if we can't come up with a way to get ahead of them."

"How would you do that?" Hanson asked. "Why would you be following them if you knew where they were going to be?"

"Look who's so smart," Martha said. "This is our opportunity to *matter*. Where would she take Valerie to reward her? To calm her down after something went wrong? What kind of thing is going to get Valerie back into a mindset where her mother can use her to work again?"

"Is Sasha still with them?" Hanson asked.

"How would I know?" Martha asked. "I've never met her. I'm following a magic trail, not using a crystal ball."

"Fine," Hanson said. "I'm just worried about her. No one seems to care what happens to her."

"Certainly not me," Martha said, then glanced over at him to catch his disgusted look. "Look out that window."

He turned his face away.

"Tell me what you see," his mother instructed, and he sighed.

"Sidewalk, buildings, cars... dude having an argument with a lamp post..."

"People, son," Martha said. "The world is full of *people*. People who matter to the people around them. Sasha Mills is just one of them. One among billions. I get that you care about her personally, but the minute you let that happen, you lose your ability to fight the war to save the rest of them. It's going to be the thing that hamstrings Susan Blake."

"Thought it was the leash you were going to use to control her," Hanson said.

"It cuts both ways," Martha said.

"So you don't care about me?" Hanson asked, not turning around.

"Look out that window and tell me that I should take care of you over all of them," Martha said.

Hanson rested his head against the glass.

He loved his mother.

He'd had a good childhood, he thought.

Happy.

He'd always been happy.

Even when they'd been yelling at each other, he'd always known that his mother was his staunchest - and most emphatic - ally.

This.

This was foreign in much the same way coming home to an empty apartment had been.

He didn't know what to think.

"When we get to the hotel for the night, we can start walking through the basics. I need to think about where I would start, teaching you, but everyone else does it, so it can't be so hard, can it?"

"So it would seem," Hanson said. "Mom?"

"Yes, Hanson."

"Did you ever think about just not coming back?" he asked. "Pretending like it was someone else's problem, keep going with the lives we had? We were happy."

"No," she said. "Possible that Susan Blake could walk away and forget about all of this, but it's been a part of my life the whole time. If we lose this war, I guarantee your dad will end up dead. He isn't going to walk away until we win it once and for all."

Hanson hadn't thought of that.

"Where *is* Dad?" he asked.

"Don't know," Martha answered. "They don't tell me that kind of stuff. Secrets are easier to keep when fewer people know them."

Hanson leaned his head against the glass, closing his eyes.

His life was a wreck, and it wasn't ever going to get better.

Yes.

He'd known *about* magic his entire life, but his mom hadn't told him anything about *any* of this world... And that she was some different person, now... Driven. She'd always been a force of nature, but this - *this* - this was what motivated her. He'd found it. And it was like she'd forgotten him.

"Where would they go, son?" Martha asked. "That's the one thing I need from you. Something special for Valerie to help her get her mind back together after something hard happened? We need to jump ahead. And you're the one who knows how that's going to go."

"Why not you?" Hanson asked. "You were Mrs. Blake's friend."

"I was, but she isn't going to be predictable on her on behalf," Martha said. "She knows how to not follow patterns. She'll break her rules for Valerie, though."

"I'll think about it," Hanson said.

"I want you to take a good long look out that window," Martha said. "You think about letting every single one of those people die because you want to keep me from finding your friend. I don't want to hurt her, and I don't want anything bad to happen to her mom. I just need to get her back on the right side of this fight. If you have the key to that and you keep it from me, you are complicit in the deaths of every single person we pass. You live with that."

"Mom," he said, but she shrugged and turned her attention forward again.

"You live with that," she said again.

"Mr. Trent, Mr. MacMillan, you have someone to see you," Mr. Benson said through the door after he knocked. Shack sat up and looked over at Ethan.

"You think they know something?" he asked.

"Everyone knows more than we do at this point," Ethan said, hopping down off of his bed and waiting for Shack.

There *was* a ladder.

Shack just declined to use it.

Ethan felt bad for the girls downstairs. They'd said something about it at lunch the other day, and Shack had been unrepentant.

So.

Ethan opened the door and went out into the hallway, where Mr. Benson was waiting for them.

"I swear, I've never done so much message delivery work," Mr. Benson said as they set off. "It's like they've forgotten what it means, that I'm the head of academics."

Ethan had several things he might have said to that, before he'd started at the school, but today he was a more mature, seventeen year old version of himself, and he kept his mouth shut.

They followed Mr. Benson down the hallway to the office, where he let them into the large conference room, where both Ethan's dad and Shack's mom sat.

Ethan looked over at Shack and stretched his eyes. Shack just shrugged, settling down into a chair the same way he would have anywhere else.

"Ethan," Mr. Trent said. "Shack."

"Mr. Trent," Shack answered. "Mom."

"Dad," Ethan said, still standing.

"Your reports have been unsatisfactory," Mrs. MacMillan said.

"Don't know what you expect us to do, ma," Shack said. "They've got us in lockdown while they try to fix up security."

Still.

Ethan couldn't imagine what was taking that long.

Merck Trent looked at Ethan with his eyebrows up.

"I understand that you are still eating meals with the full population of the school," he said, and Ethan nodded.

"Minus the interesting ones," he said.

"Milton Maury says that you boys are planning on starting a coup," Merck said.

Well.

He'd held off like a whole week before turning that one in.

Ethan was proud of him.

"It's not a coup," Ethan said. "We just don't trust you to have our best interests at heart."

"Never did," Shack said.

"Oswald," Mrs. MacMillan said sharply. Ethan tried not to smile.

Failed.

"Smug child," Merck said. "It isn't about your best interests because we are a part of *the Council*. We must balance *everyone's* best interests."

"No," Ethan said, short. This *attitude*, the one that had permanently eradicated any idea from his father's mind that Ethan might be the right one to succeed him at Council, it was like taking a step back in time and finding something he'd really liked about himself. "No," he said again. "You don't care about *everyone's* best interests. You care about maintaining power."

"Which is in everyone's best interests," Merck said, his tone dark.

Ethan pursed his lips, resting his arm across the back of the next chair over.

"Nope," he said. "That's just you. If we *elected* the dude who ran the Council, maybe the Council self-perpetuating would be in everyone's best interests…"

"If we *voted*, who would get the vote? Fact Alexander would take over the Council by manipulating an election, and then the only resistance to his genocide would go away. Is that what you want?" Merck asked.

"Maybe if the magic community *really* thought that the human race deserved to die for being inferior to us, sure. I'd be okay with it," Ethan said.

"Ignorant, short-sighted boy," Mrs. MacMillan said.

She was a cool lady, outside of the Council. She was a better basketball player than Shack, and there wasn't a single card game Ethan had ever tried where she didn't win every hand.

Sitting next to Merck, though, she was a ruthless ice queen, and Ethan had a hard time meeting her eye, even as he mocked his own father.

"We aren't here for you to tell us how much you dislike our politics," Merck said. "We are here because Martha Cox just reported back what Susan and Valerie Blake have been up to…"

"They're together?" Ethan interrupted. "It wasn't the Superiors who took her?"

He'd been afraid it was her dad, and that she'd gone along without a fight - he would have *heard* a fight, right? - because she'd wrongly trusted him.

He'd been deep-in-his-stomach afraid of that.

"That's what Martha says," Merck said slowly.

"You can't trust her," Mrs. MacMillan said. "She's too invested in currying favor. She's going to *lie* to us to try to convince us she's on the right path."

"If she's *found* Susan, am I *concerned* where the girl is?" Merck answered. Ethan gritted his teeth.

"Valerie matters because her mother loves her," Shack said. "In case you've lost sight of that."

"Yes," Merck said. "I remember, thank you. She called in tonight to tell us what they've been *doing*…"

"Do you know if Sasha is with them?" Shack asked. Mr. Merck straightened, pursing his lips, then went on as though Shack hadn't spoken.

"… and it is your responsibility as representatives of the council here at this school to consult on what it means."

Ethan sat forward.

They didn't know what Susan was up to.

That was a very good sign.

Not because he had some specific outcome that he was rooting for, but because he loved to see his father frustrated.

"I'm listening," he said.

"First," Merck said. "I need to know what interests Valerie has that her mother would be unable to avoid attending to."

Ethan raised an eyebrow.

"I have no idea what you're talking about. She goes to the bathroom like the rest of us."

Mrs. MacMillan gave him a cold look, and Ethan looked over at Shack, just to not have to see it.

"Mrs. Cox can't keep up," Shack said. "They're looking for a short-circuit to catch up with Mrs. Blake, and trying to use Valerie to do it."

Ethan narrowed his eyes and nodded.

"You're right. Mrs. Blake is too good for their spy, so they're trying to pile on *more* spies to tip the odds."

Shack gave him a phantom of a sideways smile.

Ethan looked directly at his father again.

"You gave me a mission," Ethan said after a moment. "Told me to get close to her."

"Didn't know that," Shack breathed, and Ethan dipped his chin, a nod.

"That's right. He held me back from my freshman year at magic school so that I could spy on an asset's daughter."

"And yet I find that even that was too complex for you. You've lost her, haven't you son?"

"Oh, no," Ethan said, lifting his chin and rolling his tongue in his cheek for a moment. "No. I could find her if I wanted to. I haven't lost her. *You* lost *me*."

Ethan stood, and Shack began to rise as well.

"*Oswald*," Mrs. MacMillan said, the strongest form of a command Ethan had ever heard.

"Yeah, ma," Shack said.

"Where are they?"

Shack shook his head.

"Val's cool," he said. "Knocks back demons, defuses bombs, likes this guy, I mean, seriously. But I don't know her like he does. I'm just hoping she comes back, because the rest of the year's gonna feel awfully flat if she doesn't. But that's between her and him and not you. Ma'am."

"You think that we have no power here," Merck said, sounding tired. "That you serve at your own leisure. You are mistaken."

"Are you going to pull me out of magic school, Dad?" Ethan asked. "Have your own son be a flunky who can't cast? Make me a target for the Superiors, because I can't defend myself for the rest of my life? There's a war on. Thought you needed every soldier you could get your hands on."

"Oh, no," Merck said. "I wouldn't take you *out* of school. But I could force you to drop out after next year and join the front lines."

"That's assassination," Shack said. "You wouldn't do that to your own kid."

"Oswald," Mrs. Macmillan said. "You watch your friend, and you watch him break. And then know that Merck is nowhere near as ruthless as I am."

Shack set his mouth and looked at Ethan, raising an eyebrow.

"You want me dead, Dad?" Ethan asked. He sighed. He *liked* magic. He also liked being *alive*.

"No, but I want you to think about it," Merck said. "Really *think* about it. That fear of being out where someone else is willing to kill you, no one to defend you, no one to save you. Your job to kill or be killed. Somewhere out in the dark, knowing that that other guy is *better* than you, that he's going to get you and it's only a matter of time…"

Ethan did think about it.

But every time he did, Valerie came out of nowhere raining fireballs on everything and dragged him back to safety.

He wasn't defenseless. But Valerie…

"She's good, dad," he said. "I know they all tell you, but I've *seen* it and you haven't. It's not right for you to own her."

Mrs. MacMillan looked at Merck.

"I can't tell which one he's talking about."

Merck was watching him with cool eyes.

"Ethan has never met Susan Blake," he said. "He thinks that the girl is going to be important in her own right."

"Damned straight," Shack said, going to lean his back against the wall.

"Mom won't let you pull me," Ethan said. "You can withdraw your support, but she'll pay my tuition, because she doesn't want to see me dead, I don't care how much tension it makes at dinner over break. And Lady Harrington won't bounce me, because you never *did* own her. You can threaten me with a draft, you can threaten to stuff me at the front lines, but let's face it, that's where I'd choose to be, because it's as far away from you as I can get. It isn't a coup. It's a revolution. We're declaring our independence, and what's more important is that we're declaring our allegiance. We're loyal to each other."

"Isn't the first rebellion I've squashed and won't be the last," Merck said. "And Lady Harrington may think that this school rides on her coattails, but I have more influence here than you'd think."

Ethan looked his dad in the eye, then shook his head.

"If she's in danger, you tell me how to find her and I'll go help her. But I'm not going to help you lock her up or use her. And we both know that she's really the path to her mom. So I guess you don't get *her*, either, as far as I'm concerned."

"Her father is alive," Merck said. Ethan frowned.

"So?"

"He's an agent for Fact. Always has been."

"Maybe that's who she's running from," Ethan said. "Trying to keep Valerie away from her dad. And maybe you've got so many spies in the Council that, helping you find her, it would help *him* find her, and be worse for all of us. Maybe, you think?, maybe her mom knows what's best for both of them."

"I don't *care* what's best for both of them," Merck said. "Better that the girl *die* and catalyze Susan to action than this nonsense."

"And there it is," Ethan said. "The legendary Council concern for the common man. Yes. I recognize that anywhere. I have studying to do."

"You don't have *class*," Merck said. "I can keep you as long as I like."

"Have to *keep* me," Ethan said, starting for the door. Shack shoved himself off the wall and started to follow, when Mrs. MacMillan stood.

"That will be enough," she said, making a motion with her hand. The door clicked, and Ethan didn't have to check to know that it was locked, though he did anyway.

Ethan turned to face her, and Mrs. MacMillan raised her chin, spreading her fingertips across the smooth surface of the desk.

"Oswald," she said. "Do you intend to rebel from under the authority of the Council?"

Merck looked up at her, and Ethan could see how badly he wanted to put Mrs. MacMillan back into her place, but apparently he was more interested in what Ethan could tell him about Valerie than he was in keeping his lieutenant in line.

"Ma'am," Shack said, turning to face his mom. "I've been spying on my friends to you my entire life. So have all of them. Got a third guy living in my room this semester whose mom used him the same way. Then this girl turns up and she's shocked and angry that we treat her like that, and it makes me think. Maybe the way we are isn't the only way it could be. So if you're willing to stop asking me about my friends, only ask me stuff that might actually be important to the Council's work defending magic users and civilians, maybe I stay. But if you're going to keep asking me to talk to you about things that only matter for power and politics? With respect, ma'am, I'm not going to do it anymore, because Valerie's right."

"You know what happens if I disown you, son?" Mrs. MacMillan asked.

"I do," Shack said, his voice still soft. Gentle. Ethan had only seen him properly angry a couple of times, and he feared his friend, in those moments.

"Do you understand that I will disown you if you rebel from under the Council that I represent?" she asked. "I cannot have a son who does not respect my authority, and that of the Council."

"I respect your authority," Shack said. "I just won't answer questions simply because you want to know the answers. You don't *have* that authority."

"We do," Merck said.

There.

Right there.

That was a threat, and Ethan heard it just as clearly as Shack.

Ethan didn't actually know what would happen if Shack's mom disowned him. It sounded personal. But Ethan's dad was threatening them with prison.

Magic prison wasn't like civilian prison. The threats came from the jailers, not the other inmates. There were lots of levels of prison, depending on how much of a threat you were and how much trouble you'd gotten yourself into...

"You suggesting you're going to put political opponents into the darkness?" Ethan asked. "You said you wouldn't do that ever again, when you took over."

"War has special rules," Mrs. MacMillan said. "People understand that."

"Do they?" Ethan asked. "When you put your teenage son into that? They're going to stand behind you? You might make it through the war, because people are afraid of changing leadership in the middle of it, but you'd never stay on after."

The Council might not be elected, but the power they held represented the people behind them. Ethan knew it was true enough that he was right.

"We won't be making the mistake we did last time," Merck said. "Declaring a simple victory after the Superiors lost their ability to wage open war. We have lots of time to talk. By the time the conversation is over, your stand will be meaningless, and you will regret losing our good graces."

"You're going to keep the war going to stay in power," Ethan said, then whistled. "You know, that's good. I wouldn't have even thought of that one."

"Don't make this mistake," Mrs. MacMillan said. "Don't make an enemy of me."

"I love you, Mom," Shack answered, then turned to the door and, without twisting the knob, put his shoulder into it once, twice, three times, then walked through, out into the office. Ethan looked back at his dad, trying not to look *too* elated - that would have sparked a fit of temper that he didn't *really* want to experience - then followed his friend back toward their room.

They huddled against a wall three blocks away, sitting behind a dumpster that, while it *reeked*, was blocking the stiff breeze that had kicked up since they'd been out.

"They'll find us," Sasha whispered, and Valerie nodded. Sasha hadn't stopped saying it since they'd found the spot, and Valerie knew from context that she was talking about Valerie's parents, not the people who had come for them at the apartment.

Valerie had an instinct that they needed to get further away, but she didn't want to be *so* far away that her parents wouldn't be able to do whatever it was they did to track her down. Just in case it was distance-based.

That might be real.

It seemed realistic.

She closed her eyes and tucked her face against her shoulder, trying not to think about how cold she was or how stunned she was.

An hour ago - less - she'd been sitting with a box of pizza in her lap watching a silly movie.

Comfortable.

Happy.

Had it been the phone call? Had she stayed on the line too long?

Her mom hadn't seemed to think that it was too big a risk, given how casually she'd given her instructions...

What had she done wrong?

She wanted to put up a defense of some kind, in case she actually managed to fall asleep, but she didn't know how, with what she had in her pockets. It wasn't that she was missing anything specific, and more that she didn't know how to *do* anything with what she had in her pockets on a wet and dirty ground. Any spell she tried to cast would be compromised by that ground, and just that moment, it was a hurdle she couldn't get over.

So they shuddered and tucked in tighter and tighter against each other, just hoping for dawn.

She'd been as good as her word.

Martha had sat with him and tried to teach him magic.

Hanson got the impression that it really wasn't his skills that were lacking, so much as her ability to focus, because she kept getting up and going to get papers or to pace around the room, pointing at the walls as she worked out something in her head.

Those habits, at least, were comforting to him. He knew what his mom was like when she was agitated, and she preferred to be moving.

So did he.

He didn't learn much, but just the idea that his hands, his words, his mind were capable of the things he'd been watching her do his entire life, the things that Valerie and Shack and Ethan *talked* about… It was mesmerizing, and it was almost enough.

It really was.

Almost.

The problem was it *wasn't* enough.

She'd left him.

And it wasn't about forgiving her or punishing her.

It was about trusting her.

The past five days had done *nothing* to give him the impression that leaving him had been a last resort, an act of desperation.

No.

She'd been defiant about it, proud. She would have done it again, for the right opportunity. All she cared about was the war and Susan Blake, and she thought that that was all that mattered.

He did not.

And he loved Valerie too much to just dog her around with this woman that he failed to recognize.

He didn't know what he was going to do.

He was six hours away from the School of Magic Survival, at least, and he had no money.

No friends.

Maybe he could have called one of his friends from his civilian school and they could have borrowed a car to come get him. Maybe from there he could have hitchhiked his way back out to Survival School again, but then it would just start over, wouldn't it?

His mom would just come get him again, try to talk him into helping her.

He knew about how stubborn she was.

He was just as stubborn.

Maybe he would have tried to get in touch with his dad, look for another path there, but he'd *never* known how to get in touch with his dad.

He wanted to go back to school.

Survival School.

The thought of not seeing any of them again, not seeing Sasha again, not seeing Valerie Blake again... It was painful.

But he couldn't just go wandering around the country with his mom hoping to trap his best friend as the best possible outcome.

He couldn't do it.

He went to get her purse off of the dresser as she was in the shower and he took out her wallet, emptying it of cash.

She had credit cards, of course, but she'd long mistrusted them and she preferred to do all of her transactions in cash, so she had a not-insubstantial stack of bills that he folded over and put into his back pocket.

He zipped up his bag, pulling it up onto his shoulder, then looked at the back of the room, toward the bathroom, once more and shook his head.

It was all broken.

He didn't know what to expect.

What to hope for, even.

But it wasn't this.

He left.

They got up the next morning, stiff and terrified and freezing.

They were alive.

No one had found them.

But no one had found them.

Valerie looked at Sasha and evaluated her friend for a moment.

"I need to know what you want to do next," she said finally, and Sasha nodded.

"I want to go back to school," she said.

Valerie nodded, pressing her mouth.

"If I had a way to do that, I would," Valerie said. "We can either keep running and hope that my parents catch up with us or we can go back and hope that no one is watching for us."

"Oh," Sasha said. "Where... They have to find us, Valerie. I don't know how else to be."

Valerie nodded.

"I know. But... We have to plan like they aren't going to."

"We don't have *anything*," Sasha said. "No food, no money, no place to go... We have to go *back*."

"If they catch us," Valerie said slowly, hating the words she was about to say. "I'm afraid they'll just kill you, Sasha. I'm really worried. I think we should have left you at school. You would have been so much safer there."

Sasha nodded, shaking.

"But..." she said, then shook her head. "I never imagined this is what it would be like. But this is your mom's whole life. And your dad's. And maybe it was *my* mom's, once, too. I don't know. I don't ever want to do this again, but... I needed to, once. I needed to see it. I think. I don't know. I'm so cold."

"I don't know what to do," Valerie whispered.

The problem was that she knew what she was *going* to do.

She couldn't go back.

Not unless she was *certain* that her mom and dad were there and that they would be able to keep Sasha safe.

And there wasn't any way to know that...

Maybe the attack had scared off her parents. Maybe. Though she doubted it.

More likely, her parents were at or around the apartment, waiting for Valerie and Sasha to come back. Just like the people who had come to the apartment were waiting for Valerie and Sasha to show up. And it was, what, a dice roll?, who was going to find them first.

Could she get there *fast* enough that her parents would at least be able to fight for them?

Did she *want* that?

At this point, she was certain that her mom didn't have the resources to find her. Susan Blake would have been here hours ago, if she knew where Valerie was.

They needed to move *on*.

And what maybe upset her even more was that she knew what was going to happen from there.

"Come on," she said, to Sasha, putting an arm around the girl's shoulders and walking toward the mouth of the alley.

"What are we going to do?" Sasha asked, and Valerie nodded.

All night she'd been thinking about it.

Doing the what-ifs.

All night.

She knew the answer.

Knew it cold.

She just couldn't believe that she was the one who was about to do it.

They walked.

And walked.

And walked.

There had been boys at one point, proving that it was a weekend or a *really* bad part of town, but Valerie had given them a look over her shoulder and somehow that had been enough. She'd wondered for two blocks what they'd seen on her face that they'd all just turned back around.

Sasha leaned against her long after the sun's presence warmed the air enough to be comfortable in their coats. The girl shuddered from time to time, and eventually Valerie had to ask.

"You were so much better, the last two times someone threatened your life," she said. "What's going on?"

"My mom doesn't know where I am," Sasha said after a moment. "And I haven't got a door that's mine."

Valerie nodded, not entirely understanding, but having some intuitive sense of what Sasha meant anyway.

"We'll go as fast as we can," she said. "Okay? As fast as we can."

"Where are we going to go?" Sasha asked, and Valerie shook her head.

"You remember the bar my parents were talking about, back at the beach?"

"The one where your dad was too drunk to remember it?" Sasha asked, and Valerie nodded.

"We're not legal to drink, but I'm about to go find that bar again."

"They never said where it was," Sasha said, and Valerie nodded.

Ahead.

There.

It was a bank.

She could work with that.

They went through the doors, and Sasha sat down on a chair, seeming like a huge weight came off of her.

Valerie looked around, trying not to look suspicious, then took a selection of things out of her pocket - her fingers found them by touch - and she crushed them together, spreading the powder across her lips and licking it off.

Two, maybe three minutes.

She went to sit behind an empty desk and looked at the phone.

Lady Harrington had done it for her, last time. This time it was up to her.

She picked up the phone and breathed words as they occurred to her, licking her finger and putting it above the buttons.

She dialed.

The phone rang twice and then stopped.

Valerie waited.

"Who is this?" a voice asked.

"Lady Harrington, this is Valerie Blake," Valerie said.

There was a very, very long silence.

"Valerie, where are you?"

"I need you to not ask me that," Valerie said. "People are

looking for me, and… If I come back to the school, they're just going to know where I am. You know that and I know that. The kids there are in danger, if I come back."

"Who took you?" Lady Harrington asked.

Valerie considered that.

"I was with my mom until last night, and then something happened," Valerie said. "I'm on my own, now."

"Where is Miss Mills?" Lady Harrington asked.

"She's with me," Valerie said. "Honestly, she's not taking it very well, but she's okay."

"Tell me where you are," Lady Harrington said. "I will come for you myself."

"No," Valerie said. "No, that's not what happens next. I'm not going to be the reason that everyone at school dies. I can't live with that."

There was another very long pause.

"Then why are you calling me, young lady?" the woman asked.

"I need you to get Ethan Trent," Valerie said. "I need to talk to him."

"You can't be on the phone that long," Lady Harrington said, and Valerie shook her head.

"No. I can't. But I can call back in about fifteen minutes."

"You know who his father is?" Lady Harrington asked, and Valerie nodded.

"I do."

"They've been here several times this week, leaning on him for information to help find you," Lady Harrington said.

"He doesn't have anything useful to tell them," Valerie said.

"Don't be so sure," Lady Harrington said. "Again, if you will tell me where you are, I will come get you personally. I don't like the idea of you out on your own like this."

"I need to talk to Ethan," Valerie said. "Please."

Lady Harrington sighed.

"All right. He will be here when you call back. But I hope you reconsider."

Valerie nodded.

"Thank you."

She hung up the phone and went to sit next to Sasha.

"You okay?" Valerie asked, and Sasha nodded.

"There are guards with guns," she said. "I know in my head that that isn't going to stop a magic user from coming in here and... I can't even imagine what they would do, because it scares me so much, but just seeing them..."

"Does your mom have a phone?" Valerie asked.

"Yes," Sasha answered. "Why?"

"Do you have the number?" Valerie asked. Sasha nodded. "It's memorized."

"Do you want to call her to come get you?" Valerie asked. Sasha paused.

Licked her lips.

"What's going on Valerie?" she asked.

"I'm going to call Ethan Trent back in about fifteen minutes and I'm going to convince him to bring Shack, Ann, and Milton out here. The five of us."

"And then what?" Sasha asked. Valerie shook her head.

"That isn't your problem. You can go, if you want to. I won't tell anyone where you went, so no one should come try to get you to tell them where I am. We'll just let them all believe that you're still with me. That I'm hiding you away for a bit. But... You'd be safer with her and you'd be happier with her."

"What would happen to you?" Sasha asked.

"It isn't your problem," Valerie said. "You have been... amazing to me. I mean, beyond what I could have ever hoped for, if I had even known what to hope for. You're smart and you're fun and you have kept me not just sane but *alive*. And I owe it to you to return the favor. You need to stay alive, and I am not the person to *keep* you alive. If my parents had turned up by now... It would be different."

"If I call her, they can trace it," Sasha said. "This isn't a warded phone, and hers will only cover *where* she is and what we talked about. They could be hoping that I'll call her and they'll know where we are immediately."

Valerie nodded.

"So we'd tell her where to find us and then we'd run. And she would come and get you and... And it would be over, Sasha. I know you're being brave, talking about *needing* to do this, but I actually *do* need to do it. No one else can. You don't have to. You can go."

"Do you want me to go?" Sasha asked.

"No, and yes," Valerie said. "I don't know. I don't want you to be unhappy and I don't want you to *die*. I mean... I don't think I could live the rest of my life knowing that you died because I kept you with me. It's *dangerous* out here, and you should be someplace safe. That's why you went to Survival School. I remember. Because you wanted to be the one who *helped* people, not the one who fought the wars."

"But I don't want to leave you," Sasha said. "I..." The girl straightened. "Do you think that I could just run off with my mom and pretend like that was okay? Knowing that there are people *out* here who are trying to find you, that you might end up dying? Maybe I could help. I know more about magic than you do, when it comes to books, and I want to help. I just..." She looked around. "I'm so scared."

"You're allowed to be scared," Valerie said. "I know you are. I am, too. But... This is your moment. After this, I don't think I can find a way to get you out of it. Not until we find my parents again or something. Even then... I don't know the *rules* well enough. I don't actually *know* how they found us last night. Until... You aren't going to be safe again, Sasha. I don't know *when* you would be safe again."

"I'm staying," Sasha said, setting her chin and nodding. "I'm staying as long as you are. I'm not leaving you alone."

Valerie blinked, finding that she had sprung tears of relief, and she sat back in her own chair.

Sasha wasn't leaving her.

She could do this.

Sasha wasn't leaving her.

A man came over.

"Can I help you ladies?" he asked.

"My dad is back in one of the offices with... someone," Valerie said. "We're just waiting for him."

The man nodded.

"Can I get you anything?"

"Do you have a water?" Valerie asked. "Or two?"

"Sure," he said, leaving and returning with two bottles of water. He gave them a quick nod and went back to his desk.

"How do you do that?" Sasha asked.

"Do what?" Valerie answered, opening her water. She hadn't realized how thirsty she was until it was in her hand.

"Just make up a story. I would have stuttered and blushed and they would have thought we were here to rob the bank."

"I don't know," Valerie said. "It was just… the story that came to me as we walked in the door."

She shrugged and slouched in her chair, drinking her water and thinking about what she was going to say to Ethan.

It wasn't unlikely that the *hard* part was yet to come.

Fifteen minutes passed and Valerie sat up again, taking out the same three ingredients and crushing them in her fingers.

She had enough for one more call, but that was it. After that, this trick wouldn't work anymore. And she was saving it for in case Sasha changed her mind and Valerie could find a phone again.

She sat down at the empty desk again, picking up the phone.

She wasn't bad at numbers; it was possible she could have memorized the school's phone number, but she was using magic to dial it again. She suspected that *knowing* the school's number was a burden she didn't want to carry, and she was shocked to find that the number had changed. She was *certain* it hadn't had three threes in a row the first time.

"Hello?" Lady Harrington asked.

"Ethan," Valerie said.

"You haven't changed your mind," Lady Harrington said, and Valerie shook her head.

"No."

"All right."

"Valerie," Ethan said. She put her hand to her forehead, blinking fast.

"Ethan."

"Where are you?" he asked. "How are you? Is everything

okay?"

"I need you to listen," Valerie said. "The cast I'm using to keep them from noticing that I'm using the phone doesn't last very long. I need you to get Shack, Ann, and Milton and find a way to come to me. You can't involve anyone else. No drivers. I assume one of you has a license."

"Why?" he asked.

"Because we need to talk. The five of us. There's stuff going on that I know about that you don't, and... Secrets. There are secrets that you guys need to know."

"Milton went to his dad and told him about us," Ethan said. "I won't bring him."

Valerie paused.

What did that *mean*?

That only left four.

There had to be five of them.

Didn't there?

"Are you sure?" Valerie asked.

"Certain," Ethan said.

"But you'll come?" Valerie asked.

"All you have to do is tell me where, and I'll be there," Ethan said. "No one will stop me."

She closed her eyes.

"Okay. How long will it take you to get organized?"

"I can leave as soon as I get Shack and Ann," Ethan said.

"How?"

"Shack has a car," Ethan said.

"On campus?" Valerie asked.

"Yeah. In the parking lot."

There was a parking lot.

She seriously needed to take out the campus map and look at it at some point.

"Okay," she said. "Don't write it down and don't tell Lady Harrington or anyone else. Don't even tell Shack and Ann."

"Why is it so secret?" Ethan asked. "Are you okay?"

"There are people trying to catch me," she said. "They want to use me as leverage on my mom, I think, but it's possible some of them just want to kill me. I can't tell anymore."

He took a slow breath.

"Okay," he said. "Tell me."

Checking one of the business cards on the desk to find the city, she gave him the address of one of the buildings she'd passed that day. It had looked empty. She hoped it was empty.

"Tell me again," he said.

She said it once more.

"I'm running out of time," she said.

"I'll be there..." He paused. "I'll be there at normal speed."

He wasn't giving Lady Harrington a clue about how far away it was.

"You should leave the car at least a half mile away," Valerie said. "They can track it. Maybe. I don't even know."

"I know a lot of the Council's tricks," Ethan said. "We'll do our best to be there without anyone following. Is Sasha okay?"

"She's freaking out, but she's going to make it," Valerie said. She hoped.

"Okay," he said. "I'll be there."

"I... See you," Valerie said, hanging up. She stood and quickly walked away from the desk as her spell dropped off. Sasha stood and Valerie nodded, heading for the door. Sasha followed.

It was obvious her roommate didn't want to go out again, but there wasn't an option.

They had to keep moving.

Shadows

The building wasn't entirely empty, and it was locked up better than Valerie had expected, but Sasha had a spell that she could cast that would get her past a rudimentary lock - her brother had taught it to her in preparation for school, because breaking into each others' dorm rooms and playing pranks was a part of the experience, apparently.

The door never stood a chance.

Valerie went in, finding herself in a two-story building with a lot more rooms than it had looked like outside. There were four of them off of a single hallway - three of which appeared to be occupied at least some of the time.

It had to be the weekend.

Beyond the rooms, there was a two-story open space with crates stacked up to the ceiling along most of the walls, and a metal staircase that led up to more rooms. None of these were in use, and Sasha broke them into the one at the end of the hallway.

They closed the door behind them and re-locked it, then went to sit on the floor.

Valerie was beginning to get hungry, having missed her breakfast, but it was warm and out of sight of the street, and that was a win in her book.

"So talk to me about how you track someone," she said quietly after several minutes.

"I'm not sure," Sasha said. "I mean, it's not something my mom taught me, and it isn't something you need for Survival School…"

"So just… talk it through with me," Valerie said. "Do you track… who they *are*? Do you track something about their *magic*? Do you track something they're wearing or something they're carrying? I had a moment where I was pretty sure I could track you by your fear, if I wanted to."

Sasha stared at her in the dim light through the square of glass

184

in the door.

"You could?" she asked, and Valerie nodded.

"I don't know how to do it anymore, but there was just a minute. You know?"

Sasha shook her head.

"I don't."

"I'm trying to make sure that it was dumb luck that they found us. If they're tracking us, then I'm bringing our friends into an ambush."

"If any of those things were possible, shouldn't they have found us days ago?" Sasha asked.

That was a good point.

"What if they just found out that we were out here?" Valerie asked.

"The Council has known for days," Sasha said. "I bet The Pure know, too."

"Maybe my parents were warding things so that they *couldn't* track us, and the wards wore off or broke or something."

Sasha narrowed her eyes.

"Maybe. But we were outside on our own at the market. Warding is typically attached to something solid and stationary."

"We weren't outside for *long*," Valerie said. "Maybe they couldn't get there that fast."

"Okay. Maybe. But why haven't they come for us yet? We sat outside all night last night, and no one found us. Why haven't your *parents* come for us? They could have even walked in at the bank and it wouldn't have been a big deal."

That.

That was a *very* good point.

"There's barely *anything* that The Pure could do that my parents can't, right?" Valerie asked.

Sasha nodded.

"I think so."

"So if my parents haven't found us, The Pure, or whoever is looking for us, shouldn't be able to, either, right?" Valerie asked.

Sasha nodded, encouraged.

"Yeah, I think that's right."

"And no one is going to be looking for us *harder*," Valerie said. "So it isn't like they've just stopped paying attention."

Sasha nodded once more.

"Right."

Valerie sighed, leaning back against the wall.

"Lady Harrington wanted to come get us," she said. "I said no."

"Because you don't want to go back to school and put everyone at risk," Sasha said.

"I could have let her just come get you, but if I had, they would have come and tried to make you tell them where I am," Valerie said, then put her hand over her eyes. "It's all so *much*. I don't know how my mom does this. I mean, to be thinking like this *all the time*?"

"Yeah," Sasha agreed. "I just want to cry, and it isn't even because I'm scared or whatever. I'm just... it's so overwhelming. And scary. You know. That, too."

"You just wanted to go to school," Valerie said. "And my mom pulled strings for you to be in my room. You would have been better off with *anyone* else."

"No," Sasha said after a minute. "I would have been *safer*, a little bit, and I probably would have pitied whoever *did* room with you, but... no. This is... You can't say I would have been *better* with anything else happening. This is meaningful. People are killing each other and you and your parents are trying to do the right things to make it stop."

"But you could have..." Valerie said, and Sasha shook her head.

"Please don't tempt me. All I can think about is how bad I wish I was in my bed. But I *want* to be here. I'm glad that it gets to be me. I *get* to be the one who sees how the end of the war is going to start. That's... Just knowing how much of it is lies, and then getting to be here to actually *witness* something like this, so that it isn't just *knowing* the truth, but *seeing* the truth? No. And you're my friend, so shut up and stop feeling sorry for both of us. It's... It's fine."

Valerie bit her lips between her teeth and nodded.

"Okay."

She rested her head against the wall, then she sat up and started emptying her pockets.

"I just want to see what we have," she said. "It was all moving so fast when it happened…"

Sasha emptied out the spellcasting ingredients that she'd carried, and Valerie sat on the floor looking at them, picking up one and then another, as if they were going to speak to her.

"Anything?" Sasha asked, and Valerie shook her head.

"I don't want to cast anything," she said. "I'm afraid that opening the door to cast the alarm spell into the hallway is what made them come, last time."

"You know it isn't, right?" Sasha asked. "They *had* to have already been there, as fast as they came."

"Still," Valerie said. "It felt like I caused it. And all of this."

"I told you to shut up," Sasha said. "I think I'm going to take a nap. I didn't sleep at all last night."

"You can sleep?" Valerie asked her, and Sasha smiled.

"Traveling with my mom, I got used to sneaking sleep whenever I could. If I just let myself get sleepy… I think I can, yeah."

Valerie nodded, scooting back over to sit next to Sasha.

"You won't sleep, will you?" Sasha asked.

"Not without waking you up first," Valerie promised. Sasha nodded, and leaned over to lay on the floor.

The carpet, while it was dense and flat and cheap, at least didn't smell dirty. They'd sat on the ground all night, the night before. It was hard to say that this could be *worse* than that.

Valerie tipped her head back against the wall once more and just breathed.

Things were happening.

Things she could control and things she couldn't.

All she could do now was wait.

At three and a half hours, Valerie went back downstairs.

She hadn't heard anything the entire time she'd been upstairs, but she wanted to check to be sure no one had come in to work while they'd been hiding. It was mid-afternoon by now, and the light from outside was turning golden as the sun began to set.

Short days, these days.

She sat against the wall, reviewing all of the self-defense spells she'd figured out or learned while she was staying with her dad in the caves, then the doorknob twisted.

Valerie stood and went to unlock the door, closing her eyes for just a moment and pulling it open, ready to run, to fight, to do… she had no idea what.

"Valerie," Ethan said, shoving his way through the door to hug her.

She hugged him back, hard.

"I… It's so good to see you," she said as Ethan stepped both of them out of the way so that Shack could come in. "Where's Ann?"

"She wouldn't come," Shack said. Ethan shook his head.

"She said that you're cursed worse than she is," Ethan said. "I'm sorry. I know… I get why it was important, but we couldn't talk her into it. Especially not without telling her more than I was willing to."

"It's just the two of you," Valerie whispered. She shook her head.

It wasn't something she could change. Not anymore.

"Come on upstairs," she said. "How is Hanson? I half expected him to show up with you."

Ethan looked over at Shack, then he put his arm around Valerie's waist and shook his head.

"His mom showed up the day after you left and took him. They're supposed to be out looking for you."

"Looking for… Why?"

"Because you disappeared and no one knew who took you," Ethan said. "I mean… We were afraid the Superiors had done it."

Valerie turned her face into his shoulder, then sighed.

"My *dad* took me," she said.

"I told you to be careful," Ethan said. "How did you get away?"

"I didn't," she said. "He went out to do work, and someone came to the apartment where we were to get us. We only just got away."

"Did they attack you?" Ethan asked. Valerie paused.

"Well, no."

"How do you know they weren't there to rescue you? Maybe the Council sent them."

Valerie snorted.

"Rescue me? He's working with my mom *for* the Council."

"Your mom is AWOL," Ethan said. "No one is talking about her turning, yet, but… She needs to be careful."

Valerie put her hand over her face, then shook her head.

"I should have known," she said. "Everyone wants to use me to control my mom. Both sides. It's because she's on a side of her own."

"What does that mean?" Ethan asked as Valerie opened the door to the little office. Sasha sat up.

"What?" the redhead asked.

"They're here," Valerie said softly. "Well, Ethan and Shack, anyway."

"Where's Ann?" Sasha asked. "She *has* to be here."

"Apparently her highness had other pressing matters today," Valerie said. "It is what it is."

"But… There's only three of you," Sasha said. "There have to be five. I mean… I thought Milton might come around, that they could go back and tell him, but…"

Valerie shook her head.

"It is what it is."

There was a thud downstairs and Valerie straightened. Sasha staggered against the wall.

"They're here," Valerie whispered. "They followed you."

"Nobody followed us," Shack said. "I can't *tell* you how careful we were. No one even knew we were coming but Ann and Lady Harrington, and Ann is locked in her room."

"Then how did they find us?" Valerie hissed.

They were trapped.

There were two windows out of the office, but they were two stories high.

Shack went to go stand by the door, and Sasha slowly slid down to the floor against the wall.

Moments passed, and then minutes.

189

Valerie frowned.

"Maybe it was just someone coming in to work late," she whispered.

"I'll go look," Ethan said, and Valerie shook her head.

"I'm coming with you."

"We've played this game before," he said. "You should stay here."

"Not arguing this with you again," Valerie said. "I'm coming."

Shack opened the door quietly and Valerie and Ethan went out into the hallway. They walked very slowly to the railing that looked down into the storage space…

… and Hanson Cox looked up at her.

"Hanson?" she asked. "What are *you* doing here?"

Ethan put his arm across Valerie.

"You didn't see her," he said. "Shack and I came here to goof off and play hooky. Valerie wasn't here."

"I ditched my mom this morning," Hanson said, still staring up at Valerie. "I've been wandering all day today, and I just… I kind of ended up here."

The next moment, Valerie was running.

She went down the stairs three at a time, a miracle she didn't trip over her own feet, and she hit Hanson at speed, sobbing against his chest. He held her tight for a long time.

"Are you okay?" he finally asked.

"I'm so happy to see you," she said.

"Better greeting than I got," Elton said from upstairs.

She ignored him.

"You were tracking me?" she asked. He shrugged.

"My mom is obsessed with finding your mom and bringing her back before the Council. She was just using me to try to find you faster."

She hugged him again.

"Where is she?" Ethan asked.

"Don't know," Hanson answered. "I stole her money and I walked out the door before the sun came up this morning.

"Are you guys killing each other out there or what?" Shack called.

"Shack's here?" Hanson asked. "What are you guys *doing* here?"

Valerie looked up to find Shack and Sasha looking down over the railing at them. Hanson let her go almost abruptly enough for her to fall, running up the stairs to hug Sasha.

"I was worried about you," Valerie heard him say, as she followed him back up.

"I was so scared," Sasha answered. "I'm so glad you're here."

"No, seriously, wait a minute," Shack said. "How did he *get* here?"

"Cabs. Hitchhiking. Walking a lot," Hanson said. "Why are *you* guys out here? Shouldn't you be at school?"

"She called and asked us to come," Ethan said, putting out an arm as Valerie got close again. It felt good to step near him, even if she did need to separate herself once they got into the back room. She had things she needed to say, and it was too serious to do it from hip-to-hip with Ethan.

"Valerie," Sasha said softly from somewhere beside Hanson. "There are five of us."

Valerie blinked.

"There are," she said.

"Is this about the curse?" Ethan asked, and she shook herself, going to stand against the wall to face the other four.

"Some," she said. "A lot not, but some. So. Sasha and I have been learning a lot of interesting things, here this last week. My parents have been showing us a lot about how magic *actually* works, how the Council works, and how the politics on the other side of the war work. And we have so much to tell you about what we saw. Nothing... just *nothing* is the way they told us."

"Nothing," Sasha echoed.

"Okay," Ethan said.

"Magic... it works differently than they've taught us, and there is no such *thing* as the Superiors - the Council is fighting a bunch of different groups who basically only agree that the Council is bad. And the big bads, the ones who actually show up to *fight* with the Council... they're called The Pure, and they aren't even *trying* to kill civilians. They're trying to eliminate their ability to develop magic powers."

"That doesn't make sense," Shack said.

"I know," Valerie said. "It's really hard to believe that everything we know about the war isn't *true*…"

"Are you sure?" Shack asked. "I mean… they're your parents, and I get that, but… They've been off on their own for a while, and… I mean… *Everyone* knows about the war. How could your parents…"

"I saw it," Sasha said. "We went to a Separatist school where they taught that there are three branches of magic, and everything just suddenly made *sense*."

"You went to… To a *what* school?" Ethan asked.

"Separatist," Valerie said. "They just want the Council to leave them alone. The Pure are involved with the school, and they use it for recruiting, my mom says…"

"Why were you at Ground School?" Hanson asked. "My mom couldn't figure it out."

Valerie felt her eyes go wide.

"How do you know that?" she asked.

"We were tracking you," Hanson said. "What were you doing there?"

"You went to *Ground* School?" Ethan asked.

"It was part of the point," Valerie said, feeling like this was slipping away from her. "Look, we can talk through all of the *things* that aren't the way we thought they were, and Sasha and I can do our best to prove it to you, but…" She closed her eyes, regathering her thoughts. There was a point. *This* was the point. "A long time ago, before any of us were born, a bunch of spies got together. From both sides of the war. And they started talking. And they realized that both of the sides were *crazy*. That they didn't want either side to win. And they agreed that they were going to try to work toward ending the war, but that they weren't working for one side or the other, anymore."

"The Shadows," Ethan murmured, and Valerie nodded.

"They were right. My parents were both Shadows, and they are both Shadows now. They are *trying* to stop the war, but if the Council wins…"

"They're going to make everyone register and they get to decide who goes where for school and…" Ethan started, then nodded. "No, the word Separatist may be new to me, but I'm a sympathizer there."

Valerie nodded.

"The Pure think they can separate civilians from their ability to use magic, but every time they try, it kills everyone. I think my mom is afraid that at some point they're accidentally going to kill a *whole lot* of people, or that they'll figure out how to get rid of people's magic ability and they'll turn it against Council fighters."

"Of course they will," Shack said. "That's obvious."

Valerie nodded.

"So. Both wrong. Both *crazy* wrong. And someone has to *do* something about it, not just keep going along and hoping that it turns out okay."

"You're talking about a second generation of Shadows," Ethan said, and Valerie nodded.

"I had thought that it would be the cursed kids, but… I mean, I guess not. Maybe… Maybe this is who it's supposed to be."

"I'm not sure *supposed*…" Ethan started, then Hanson held up a hand.

"I have no training in magic," he said. "I *don't* belong here. Every one of you can see it. But. I'm here. And I had no idea where I was going all day. I just… I ended up here. That has to *mean* something, right?"

"Does it?" Shack asked.

"It does," Sasha said. "I'm not supposed to be one of you, either, but… I couldn't leave, when Valerie gave me a chance. I had to stay. I'm *supposed* to be here."

Valerie had a sudden thought.

"Hanson's birthday is January second," she said. "And Sasha's is the fifth."

The two of them looked at each other with more than saccharine happiness, and Valerie shook her head.

"Mine is October sixteenth, and Ethan's is December…"

"Third," he supplied.

"Mine is November twenty-eighth," Shack said.

"Do you know Ann's or Milton's?" Valerie asked.

"They're still sixteen," Shack said. "We were teasing them at dinner a few weeks back."

Valerie closed her eyes.

"Sasha... You might actually be one of us."

"No," Sasha said. "That's not possible. Not me and not Hanson. It was a curse directed at *the Council*."

"It was a curse directed at my *mom*," Valerie answered. "It had backsplash to the Council, yes, but it hit her friend Ivory, too. And I bet Hanson's mom has been spying on my mom for a long time. Maybe long enough that it got her, too."

Valerie put her hand through her hair, looking at the five of them.

"The ones who showed up when I called," she said. "The new Shadows. This is us, guys. This is who we are and this is what we were *literally* bred to do. We're going to stop all of it, take down the Pure, take down the Council at the same time, put it right."

"We can't do that," Sasha breathed. "We're just kids."

Valerie looked at her friend and nodded.

"I'm not saying it's going to happen fast. But... Can't you guys feel it? Hanson *wandered* here. Sasha wouldn't leave, even when I all but pushed her out the door. We all *live* together. I mean... None of this is *coincidence*."

"So what are you suggesting we do?" Ethan asked. She nodded.

"We trust each other," she said. "Just us. I'm not saying if my mom walked in here and told us to run that I'd give her a side-eye, but... This is *our* team."

"What about... everything?" Shack asked. "I mean, it's great to have a neat club where I like everyone so much, but what are we supposed to *do*?"

"Yeah," Valerie said. "I can't go back. I don't think Ethan or Sasha can, either."

"My dad threatened to throw us into the darkness for not helping him find you," Ethan said.

"Technically, my mom threatened that," Shack said.

"Pretty sure it was my dad's idea first," Ethan challenged and Shack grinned.

"No, your *dad* threatened to put you on the front line and then have everyone else take a step back."

Ethan shook his head.

"Anyway. That's what they'd do to their own kids. If there's any *hint* of a chance that the Council thinks that Sasha or Hanson knows things that would help find you... They can't come back. I'm sorry. You're right, but you're *really* right."

"Yeah," Shack said. "We can give my mom lip and live, but anyone else...?"

"Valerie," Sasha said softly, desperation, and Valerie nodded.

"We're going to keep looking for opportunities to hook back up with my parents. They're teaching us a lot about how things *are*, and I think we need to know that if we're going to pull this off."

"So, still with you and stuff, but why not leave it to *them*?" Shack asked. "I mean, there's a reason everyone is all afraid of them. They seem a lot more likely to be able to pull it off."

"I don't know," Valerie admitted. "And if they can do it while we're still trying to figure it out, that's great, and I'll... I don't know, I'll make a public apology for being such a drama queen. It's just... I'm out here. I can't go back. Hanson and Sasha... They have to come with me."

"Have to," Ethan cut in, and Valerie nodded.

"And... I just was kind of realizing that *this*... This is what we were talking about at lunch that day. This is us picking up and making a stand all on our own because the two sides are *wrong*. The Shadows are right, and... And we have to keep going. We have to *do* something."

Shack gave her another apologetic look.

"I just wish you could tell me what that *is*."

"I guess let's start by simply understanding what this war *is*," Valerie said. "Because it isn't what Mr. Jamison told me."

"I mean..." Shack said. "He *fought* it."

"Just listen to her," Sasha said, sitting down. "Nothing is what they made it out to be, and people need to know it."

"The Pure, the only way to stop them is to actually fight them," Valerie said, nodding. "Yeah. But you stop the Council by taking away their control, and you take away their control by getting the truth out there."

"At school," Sasha said. "Where maybe you're the only ones who can say anything, because of who your parents are."

"If we push this too far, my mom will put us in the darkness," Shack said. "She loves me, but she takes her role on the Council more seriously than anything."

"I'm not sure my dad loves me," Ethan said. "But... Look, you tell us what you've figured out, and we'll go be subversive. I'm good at that."

Valerie nodded, sitting down on the floor and looking at Sasha.

"I need you to help me. You understand a lot of the magic stuff better than I do."

"Yeah," Sasha said. "I can do that."

Valerie took a breath and started.

"So. There are three branches of magic..."

They spent the rest of the evening talking.

Valerie told them everything she could think of that she'd learned, either directly from her parents or from going to one of the schools.

The risks to new magic users and how the two sides treated them.

The way that magic was taught between the two sides.

The coalition building against the Council because of how they treated magic users.

The Shadows and how they'd come into being.

Sasha told them about the apartment and Valerie's cast there, and she told Shack and Ethan about the specifics of several of the classes at the Separatist high school.

"They're going to be so much better prepared than we are," Sasha said as she finished. "They understand *magic* so much better."

"Mage," Shack said, trying the word out.

"I'm still dark," Ethan said. "It doesn't change anything about that."

"But you're probably a mage," Sasha said. "Because you aren't *only* dark."

"That makes me feel so much better," Ethan said. "Does it

make the tests invalid?"

Sasha considered, then shook her head, and he shrugged.

"Then I'm still dark and it doesn't matter."

"I'm still not understanding what we're *doing*," Hanson said from where he sat against a wall. "After they go back to school and start *spreading the word* that there are three branches of magic rather than a continuum… Where's the giant blow against evil? Is it them, for spilling some modestly big secret? Is that it? The three of us just kind of hide out and hope the right side finds us first?"

"I don't know," Valerie said. "I'm just making this up as I go along. I didn't plan anything other than getting Ethan and Shack *here*, and even that, I'm kind of fuzzy on why. My parents did something *important*, figuring out that the two sides are both wrong. I felt like… Like I needed to do the same thing."

"You did," Shack said, shifting and looking over at Ethan. "I know I gave you a hard time, but everyone at school, at *all* the schools, feels like there are only two paths, and they both head straight to war. Maybe the right answer is that we need to be fighting both sides…"

"How?" Ethan asked. "I'm with you, but Hanson's right. We don't have any opportunity, we don't have any leverage…"

"When you throw a party, who shows up?" Shack asked.

Ethan frowned.

"Everyone. But it's because my dad is on the Council."

"So don't cut ties," Shack said. "Just start talking about the Shadows again, tell them that they're spreading rumors about the way the Council structures teaching on magic, how they keep saying that there's a better way to understand it… That the war isn't about killing civilians, it's about people being allowed to use magic how they want to…"

"That's *good*," Hanson said.

"It's not true," Sasha said. "No one is arguing that everyone ought to be able to use magic however they want."

"Maybe the Shadows are," Shack said. "Maybe they aren't. The point is to get people to talk about the rules. To actually see them."

"The teachers know that the structure they're teaching is wrong," Valerie said.

"How?" Ethan asked, and she shrugged.

"They didn't say. I guess they know people who know."

"Then why are they still teaching this way?" Shack asked.

"Because light and dark is simple," Ethan said, shifting to lean his shoulder against Valerie's. He wove his fingers through hers and looked out at their feet, thinking. "Light is good, dark is bad. It means that anyone who doesn't fit into the standards that my dad and the rest of the Council are pushing, they are all *trying*. They're chasing after approval. You can't get *in* at Light School if you have too much dark. They're all trying to prove they're worthy. If it was three and none of them had moral weighting to them…"

"I didn't say that," Valerie said. "Dark magic is still *dark*. I just…"

"We don't know what that means," Sasha said.

"My dad uses dark magic. He told me that much. But he said it was a personal choice, and that I was lucky because I have a choice."

"Not everyone does," Ethan said quietly.

"I know," she answered. She sighed. "I don't know what I'm doing, guys. I don't want to be in charge. I was supposed to eat pizza until I fell asleep on the couch last night, but… That didn't happen, and now…"

"We're out here on our own," Sasha said.

"Not anymore," Hanson said, and Shack shook his head.

"Not anymore."

Ethan squeezed her hand, and she nodded.

"Right. So. I don't *know* what we should be doing. If we even *should* do something. I just… This is our team. We needed to look each other in the eye and know it."

"And you needed to hold still long enough for Hanson to catch up," Shack said. "Still not over that."

"I can't do magic," Hanson said. "I have no idea what I'm doing here."

"Doesn't matter," Valerie said. "Sasha's a good teacher, and… You belong here. Same as the rest of us."

"We need a way to find you again," Ethan said, and she shook her head.

"If we need you, I'll find a way to call you," Valerie said. "If you know how to find us…"

"Not a good idea," Shack agreed. "We have to walk away and they need to run."

"We don't have any money," Sasha said.

"I have some," Hanson said. "I stole it from my mom this morning."

"They're magic users," Ethan said. "They don't need money."

"Maybe you don't," Valerie said, mock-indignant. "Or maybe you've just never had to go without."

"No, you just…" Ethan said, frowning. "People with magic never need money. They don't."

"How do they *get* it?" Valerie asked. "I'm all ears."

Ethan looked at Shack, and Shack shrugged.

"Council," he said.

"How does the Council get its money?" Valerie asked. "I mean, apparently they paid both my parents a whole bunch, but where do they get it? Is it from the schools?"

"No," Sasha said. "The schools don't begin to cover the budget that the Council has."

"Taxes?" Valerie asked, looking at Ethan. "Do they collect taxes?"

"Access," Shack said after a minute. "I can't prove it, and I'm probably mostly wrong, but I bet at least some of it is for political access."

"And draft dodging," Ethan said. "The Council's friends don't have kids who go off to war the minute they graduate."

"No, they get in at Survival School for upperclass studies," Shack said, and Ethan nodded.

"Yeah."

"That doesn't help me," Valerie said. "Though… Seriously, who thinks it's okay for a group of unelected men and women to have so much power that they can extort enough money from people *voluntarily* to be able to fund a war? I mean…"

"I don't think that's all of it," Ethan said. "Though I've never thought about it. Possible they're selling stuff, same as everyone else."

"Selling *what*?" Valerie asked.

"Healing," Sasha said quietly. "Among other things."

"Does your mom sell healing?" Valerie asked, and Sasha shook her head.

"No. My dad's business brings in enough money. My mom just does it because that's who she is. But… I know there are people who do."

"Well, I don't have any marketable skills, so that's out," Valerie said. "How are we supposed to feed ourselves?"

"I've got… a thousand dollars," Hanson said, counting through a stack of bills.

"You've what?" Valerie asked. He shrugged.

"I told you I stole it from my mom's purse when I left this morning."

"You *never* had money," Valerie said. "What is she doing with all of that?"

"Apparently we did have money," Hanson said. "We just had to act like we didn't as long as we were stalking you. Now that we're out in the open about it, she can stay at nice hotels and carry a thousand dollars in her wallet."

"Does everyone have money but me?" Valerie asked, and Shack nodded enthusiastically, then grinned.

"We need to meet again," he said. "Here's hoping you catch up with your parents, but color me skeptical. The Council can't find them with all of their resources; I don't know what chance you've got with nothing."

"Our one advantage is that my parents will be *looking* for us," Valerie said, and he shrugged.

"We need to do this again. Take some time, make some plans. You guys need to figure out what you're going to *do* with yourselves. I mean, you can't stay out here forever."

"I can until they get rid of whoever is trying to help the Pure abduct or kill me," Valerie said. "Are they making any progress on it?"

"No one says," Ethan told her. "But we're still locked in our rooms. I think the Council is behind it, anymore, but what do I know?"

"Someone is trying to kill you," Hanson said. "You think it's someone on campus. And no one is looking for them?"

"There we go," Shack said. "There's a project."

"You think that we can make progress on that where Mr. Tannis, Mr. Benson, and Lady Harrington didn't?" Ethan asked, and Shack nodded, then grinned.

"And you know why?"

"No, why?" Ethan asked dryly, and Shack grinned wider.

"Because people talk to us."

Ethan paused, apparently looking for a rebuttal and finding none.

"All right. So we… stir the pot. Spread some rumors about the Shadows being back, get people asking questions, and in the meantime, we figure out who would want Valerie dead. Or at least who is willing to betray her to get rid of her."

"What about us?" Hanson asked.

"We move," Valerie said. "Maybe… I mean, it's a terrible season for it, but if we go south, maybe we can scout some naturally-occurring magic ingredients and start stocking up…"

"I know some about that," Sasha said.

"I don't," Hanson said. "I don't know what I'm *doing* here, Val."

"Bankrolling us, for one," Valerie said. "Shack is right. This is all completely un-thought-out. We need to take a beat and work through what we want to *do* and then start forming plans. You think Lady Harrington will let you break out again?"

"I'm shocked she let us do it once, frankly," Ethan said, and she nodded.

"Can you sneak out?" Valerie asked, and he shook his head.

"I don't know. Not if you're going to have to call us and tell us where you are."

Valerie nodded slowly, an idea coming to her like a seed germinating.

"So if you could find us on your own, is there any way for you to get out of there?" she asked, and he looked at Shack.

"It's not a prison. We could just… walk out."

"Could get us suspended," Shack said, "but, yeah, that would work."

"So we just walk out," Ethan said. "I'm willing to have that fight when we get back."

Shack nodded.

"But we don't know how to find them."

Valerie stood, pulling three strands of hair from her head one after the other. She went to Sasha and pulled three long red strands from her friend's head - one at each temple and one from the crown of her head - then she went to Hanson and did the same. She sat down on the floor, reaching into her pocket to find… things… and then she tied the nine strands in a knot. It wasn't a good knot, and Hanson's hair was very much on the verge of falling out of it, but she mixed a bit of this and some of that together, forming a paste in her palm. She closed her hand around the knotted hair, waiting for it to set. Her skin was clean when she opened her hand again, and she handed the tangle of hair and globby stuff to Ethan.

"Set it on fire…" she said, then looked at Sasha. "Bright pink fire?"

"Strontium chloride," Sasha said, nodding quickly. "They can get it in the lab."

"See," Valerie said, shaking her head. "Burn it in that stuff, and breathe the smoke. It will bring you to us exactly once."

"Breathe the smoke," Ethan said. "You know, if it was anybody but you, I'd give that one a hard pass."

"It will work," Valerie said. "But just once."

"Good design," Shack said.

They sat for a moment longer, then Valerie shook her head.

"I feel like something started today," she said. "I don't know what it is, and I don't feel like I'm in *charge* of it…"

"This is crazy," Sasha breathed.

"Look, I'm sorry, but this is *awesome*," Shack said. "We're *doing* something. Everybody goes to magic school with these big ideas of all of the exciting things they're going to do, and it's just more school. We're actually *doing* something."

"I'd rather just be at school," Sasha said quietly, and Hanson nodded.

"I'd like to learn magic, as it turns out," Valerie's best friend said.

"Shame Shack and I can't stay with you out here and the two of them go back," Ethan said. "I'd rather be here, too."

Valerie shook her head, looking around the room.

"We're going to be scavenging for everything. No place to go, no allies… This is going to be *hard*."

"I'm up for hard," Ethan said. "I just can't do pointless anymore."

Valerie nodded slowly, then looked around the room.

"Then let's not be pointless."

"To the Shadows," Shack said. "Let's get it done, this time."

He stood and, after a long hesitation, so did Ethan.

"Give you a minute," Shack said. "Then we need to get going. I want a huge dinner on the way home, and then we'll turn up sometime after midnight so no one can tell how far we went."

Ethan nodded, and Hanson scrambled to his feet, pulling Sasha up and following Shack out into the hallway.

Ethan took both of Valerie's hands and rested his forehead against hers for a full minute.

"Don't die," he said. "And don't disappear."

"Take good care of them, if anything happens to me," Valerie said. He shook his head.

"I just told you not to disappear. If you disappear, I'm giving Mr. Tannis that bundle of hair and letting *him* come find you. You know he's angry you aren't there to clean up his classroom anymore."

"You don't know that," Valerie said, smiling. "And the cast only works if the three of us are together. It's part of why it's okay to give it to you. If you lose it, we can split up for a while and still stay secret."

"I miss you," he said. "I was so happy when I heard your voice."

"You're being dramatic," she said. "We haven't been together that long, especially if you don't count the part in the middle where I wasn't speaking to you."

"You're the first real thing in my life," he said. "I've been playing politics for all of the rest of it. Don't tell me that you're not allowed to mean that much to me."

She sighed.

Wrapped her arms around his waist and put her head down on his shoulder.

"I miss you, too," she said. "Feels like we should be doing this together."

"Sasha is not your wingman," he said. "I'm a damned fine wingman."

She snorted, turning her forehead down against his collarbone, then straightening and stepping away.

"I don't know what's going to happen," she said. "But I'll see you again."

"I don't like the idea that you might *not*," he said. "I mean war is war and stuff, but... we're freshmen at Survival School. This stuff is supposed to be *years* off. We're just *kids*."

"I know," she said. "But... You figure out who's letting them in, who's trying to get rid of me, and I can come back. And we can just do classes and lunch and dinner and studying at the library and pretend all of this isn't happening. I'll do it if you will. But right now, I'm endangering everyone, being there, and I won't do that. So I may as well do something else, out here. Just as soon as I figure out what."

"Just run," he whispered. "I'll find them and Lady Harrington will turn them into a mound of cockroaches, and then you can come back."

"Can she do that?" Valerie asked, quiet, and he shook his head.

"If I got to choose, she could."

"No," Valerie said. "I won't just run. This *matters*. And you know it. We have to do better than our parents did."

"Your parents did pretty well," he said. "And they still are."

"You believe that?" Valerie asked. "That my dad isn't one of the bad guys?"

"I believe that Hanson Cox just walked in the door downstairs, of all of the places in the world, and if you told me that your dad was leading a battalion of *green* magic users, I'd believe you. I'd have questions, but I'd believe you."

She closed her eyes tight and just breathed.

"All right," she said. "This isn't getting any easier. Go. Just go. You have things you have to do, and… and we have to run. We can't stay here tonight, and I don't even know where we *will* stay."

"It's cold out," he said, and she nodded.

"Believe me, I know. But you were here with us. By the time you get back to school, we won't be here anymore."

"You could stay tonight," he said. "I'm not going to tell anyone where you are, and neither is Shack."

She nodded.

"I trust you." She paused, remembering something Mr. Jamison had said to her, about picking a middle path on trust, because she couldn't trust everyone and being alone would make her crazy. "I trust Shack. I just don't know everything that's possible, with magic, so until I'm a lot more sure what *can't* happen…"

"You're going to be extra careful," he said, nodding. He hugged her close again, then nodded.

"Okay. Okay. Just be safe and try not to freeze to death."

"It's not *that* cold," Valerie said. "I'll see you soon."

He nodded, then let her go, looking back once as he opened the door, but not saying anything. Valerie covered her face with her hands and went to sit against the wall.

She didn't want to be doing this.

She wanted to be back in her regular life doing regular things.

Only that wasn't how she met Ethan, was it?

No.

She had to be *in* magic, and if she was involved in magic, this… this was her world.

She put her head back against the wall as Sasha and Hanson came in.

Neither of them seemed to know what to say, so they sat quietly for a few minutes, then finally Valerie stood.

"Well, Sasha and I haven't eaten since last night," she said. "Let's go get food and figure out what happens next."

New Targets

It was amazing how much clearer Valerie's mind was with food in her belly.

"Okay," she said around a mouthful of burger. "Here's how I see it. We can hide. We can look for my parents. We can fight."

"Who would we fight?" Sasha asked. "And how? And why?"

"See, that was the first one I eliminated, too," Valerie said, nodding as she swallowed. "Right. So, we don't know where the fights are going on, or who's on what side, and they'd probably all stomp us anyway."

"So why even put it on the list?" Sasha asked.

"Completionism," Hanson said with a grin. "You have to find *all* of the options before you can be sure you're eliminating the right ones."

"Well, we could go to the moon, too, just to see what's there," Sasha said.

"File under 'hiding'," Valerie said, and Hanson grinned wider. "Unless you think it's possible that's where my parents are."

"Not funny," Sasha said, and Valerie shook her head.

"I know it's not, but I'm not hungry anymore, and that's enough for me, right now."

"Not me," Sasha said. "I just signed on to the stupidest, most dangerous thing I've ever *heard* of, and we don't have a plan. Or even a place to sleep tonight."

"You can open doors," Valerie said. It wasn't intended to be dismissive, but it came out that way. "We'll find someplace that isn't populated at night and we'll sleep there. I'm not sleeping in an alley again tonight."

"You slept in an *alley* last night?" Hanson asked, looking down at Sasha. He had his arm around her and it was disgusting how cute they were, even with everything.

"Didn't sleep," Sasha muttered, and Valerie nodded.

"We… They were chasing us and we just got away. I think.

Whole thing is kind of blurry and afraid. But. We aren't doing that again."

"My mom can track magic," Hanson said. "If she's close enough."

"Okay," Valerie said. "Explain that to me. Mr. Jamison could tell that my dad had been the one to cast on my door, at one point…"

"When did your dad cast on our door?" Sasha asked, and Valerie shook her head.

Too much for one night.

"Doesn't matter. And Lady Harrington scanned all of us to see if we'd been involved with the silverthorn thingy. Does that mean that you have to *know* someone's magic to track it?"

Sasha paused for almost a full minute, considering.

"If you really knew specifically what *kind* of magic they were casting, or if you had an alarm net set up in the area already, I think you could do it without, but I think that, if we're just off somewhere that they don't already have magic set up, and if they weren't aware of really precisely what kind of unlocking spell I was using… Yeah. I think we should be safe."

Valerie nodded.

"Good. Then that's what we do."

"But it's *illegal,*" Sasha said.

Valerie stared at her.

"You *want* to sleep outside?" she asked. "We don't have the money to get a hotel. Not for long. And we don't have any friends we can go stay with… We don't even *know* anyone around here. So we can turn ourselves into child services and go into foster homes or something… I can't even imagine how that would work. But I bet that they could find Hanson's mom, and then… Yeah. None of that makes sense. We won't make a mess. We'll just sleep there and leave in the morning."

"And what about brushing my teeth?" Sasha asked. "What about showers?"

"You're freaking out, aren't you?" Valerie asked, and Sasha frowned.

"Maybe."

"We'll find a convenience store and buy toothbrushes," Hanson said. "And soap."

Valerie glanced at him and he gave her a half a smile.

He wasn't afraid.

Maybe he *should* have been, but he wasn't.

"Are we running, or are we trying to find my parents?" Valerie asked.

Sasha looked up at Hanson, and he shrugged.

"I'm not sure those are separate options," he said. "Why wouldn't we do both?"

"Because if we're looking for my parents, we go back to the beach hut," Valerie said. Sasha gasped, and Valerie nodded. "It's risky, because if Hanson's mom keeps following us from Von Lauv, she'll end up there eventually, but I can actually *find* it, it was comfortable enough for what it is, and maybe my parents come looking for us. The other place we stayed that I might be able to get back to is that warehouse…" She shuddered. "My mom said she cleaned it out for us. I can't imagine what it would have been like, normally."

"I'd rather sleep outside," Sasha agreed.

"If we run, we just pick a direction and we run," Valerie said. "But nothing changes until Ethan and Shack come up with something. We won't do anyone any good."

"No," Sasha said. "That's not true. We'll have time to talk about what we saw with your parents and what it means, and I can teach Hanson at least a little bit about magic."

"I shouldn't be here," Hanson said. "I'm used to being the bodyguard type, hit things hard when they need hit, but you guys are both better fighters than I am. And I'm not as smart as either one of you."

"Shut up," Valerie said. "I'm not having the 'who's smarter' fight with you again."

"You think you're smarter than he is?" Sasha asked, and Valerie shook her head.

"Nope."

Sasha blinked.

"I don't get it."

"She's smarter than I am," Hanson said. "Without a doubt."

"He's smarter than me," Valerie said. "And I can back it up with numbers."

He stuck his tongue out at her and she smirked back.

"What?" Sasha asked, then shook her head. "Okay, never mind. None of us are *warriors*. We're not *healers*. We aren't *leaders*. We're *kids*. We're at magic school to *learn* magic. Right now… Honestly, we're just trying to out-wait someone at Survival School figuring out how everyone got in for the attacks, and then we'll go *back*. Right, Valerie? That's all it is?"

Valerie chewed on her cheek.

"I think so," she said. "If they were able to figure out *exactly* what allowed all three attacks…"

"Two," Sasha said firmly. "Your mom was the one who triggered the second one."

"All right, fine, both attacks… Yeah. I think we could go back and do the rest of this from there. But… Sasha, they treat us like prisoners. There's no guarantee they'd let us even *see* them, and I don't think they plan on teaching Hanson."

Sasha raised her eyebrows.

"You'd rather I sleep in the streets?" she asked. "We're in *danger* out here. As soon as it's safe at school, we have to go back."

Valerie let her attention drift out the window, watching all of the *normal* going on out there. She'd missed it, and she had to admit that she didn't like the idea of going back to campus, where everything was so blocked off and it was just her and her four-hundred closest critics.

"Valerie?" Sasha warned.

"Give her a minute," Hanson said. "I know that look."

"What look is it?" Sasha asked.

"It's her better judgment having a good long talk with her impulse generator."

"Okay," Sasha said slowly.

Valerie was her mother's daughter.

"My mom never comes in, either," Valerie said after another moment. "I get it now. I thought… You know, she was out here fighting all these fights and just so *busy* that she couldn't, but…

Coming in means giving up being free."

"Doesn't have to," Hanson said.

"Doesn't it?" Valerie asked, turning to look at him. "If we go back, how do we get *out* again? My dad had to come *break* us out in the middle of the night."

"Why don't we just *leave*?" Hanson asked.

"I don't have a car and neither do either of you," Valerie said.

"My parents were going to get me one, but I didn't want to take care of it," Sasha said, ducking her head. Valerie tipped her head to the side to look at her roommate, and Hanson shrugged.

"All three of us have money, apparently. And Shack *does* have a car. And I *live* with him, you know."

"They won't stand for it," Valerie said. "They want to tell us when we can go and where, they want to know who we're with. They'll follow us if they don't think we're telling them the truth. Out here, now? No one knows anything and no one can control us."

"Valerie," Sasha said. "We're *kids*."

"They expect us to fight their war," Valerie said. "And they don't even tell us the truth about what it's about."

"We have to go back," Sasha said. "I won't stay with you after they figure it out."

"If you go back and I don't, they'll put you… wherever Ethan said, the bad place, for not telling them how to find me."

"You won't stay out here by yourself," Hanson said. "And… Val. Please. Let the better judgment win. You're just fighting with us because your impulse doesn't like losing."

"I know," she said softly. "I know. I just can't stand it. Every minute, they get to say where I am and what I'm doing. Because *magic*."

"It ends," Sasha said, and Hanson shook his head.

"No it doesn't. It's the same thing the Council is doing to the adults. And that's what she sees."

"And what I'm fighting. I'm not saying that The Pure should be allowed to keep killing people in the name of keeping magic in the *right* hands, and I'll get to that, someday, if my mom doesn't first, but… The Council are just right *there*. Pushing against me, asking for the fight."

"Val," Hanson said. "If we can find your parents, that's great, but if we can't... We can feed ourselves for a long time on this money if we're careful, but we have to think about *everything*. Coats and toothbrushes and bags and transportation. Unless you can come up with a way to make *more* money, this is going to run out. We need a plan for when it does."

She nodded, folding her hands and looking down at her wrists.

"I know. And I'll go back. Dr. Finn has been helping me figure out how to control my powers, and Mr. Tannis was working with me on how to structure my classes to get the most out of the school as a natural. Lady Harrington actually conspired with me to get Shack and Ethan out of there unnoticed, and Mrs. Reynolds is the coolest teacher I've ever had. Mr. Jamison... he's just great. All the time. I don't *hate* everyone there. I just..."

"Not yet, Val," Hanson said. "You can't be out here on your own yet."

"You're going to, though, aren't you?" Sasha asked. "The first opportunity, you're going to ghost us and we'll never see you again."

"I don't know," Valerie said. "Maybe."

Yes.

"We won't let her," Hanson said quietly. "We'll figure it out."

Sasha didn't look entirely convinced, but she nodded. Hanson shoved her with his ribs.

"I showed up here out of nowhere, didn't I? I think it's looking like she can't wander off without us, no matter what she wants to do."

Valerie gave him a look of mock-dismay, and Hanson grinned.

"I don't *want* to ditch anyone," Valerie said. "That's not what it's about. I *liked* my life before this. My friends, my school, my home. I just..."

"I know," Sasha said. "It's just... I don't know. You've got a new look in your eye, and it's scaring me."

"So?" Valerie asked, changing the subject. "Are we running or are we taking a risk in hopes of meeting up with my parents again?"

"I want to meet your dad," Hanson said. "I can't believe he's still alive."

Sasha nodded.

"I... I don't want to think about what happens if they catch up to us again, but I really want to not be on our own anymore."

"I think what's most likely to happen is that my mom catches us," Hanson said. "And, yeah, that's *bad*, but it's not bad like the other side finding us. She's just going to take us back to school."

Sasha nodded and leaned against him.

"Yeah. Okay. Let's do that."

"All right," Valerie said. "Do you remember what city we were in?"

Lady Harrington had shown them back to their room wordlessly. As far as Ethan could tell, no one even knew they'd left the building. If Franky Frank was in on it, he didn't say anything.

"So," he said to Shack the next morning after breakfast. "How do we find out who's working against us?"

Shack shrugged, leaning so that he could hang his elbows off the side of the bed.

"When the teachers haven't managed it," he said, and Ethan nodded.

"When the teachers haven't figured it out. They *are* busy."

"Yeah, but at the same time," Ethan said. "They've locked everyone in the dorms for *days* now, and they haven't managed to do anything."

"How do you know?" Shack asked.

Ethan frowned.

"That's a good point," he said thoughtfully.

"Uh oh," Shack said, grinning. "The last time I saw you make that face, I ended up grounded for two months."

"Oh, that's only if they catch us," Ethan said, wiggling an eyebrow at him. "You up for making another escape brew?"

Shack sighed dramatically and swung his legs over the edge of the bunk.

"You know eventually they're going to plug all the holes and keep you locked down in here, right?" his friend asked, and Ethan grinned.

"That's why we make hay while the sun shines, man," he answered, going to his desk and starting to dig out ingredients.

They could have stolen a car.

Valerie couldn't stop thinking that maybe that would have been the easier way to do this, but *no*, they'd walked for six hours to get to a bus station, where they'd slept in the lost-luggage room and caught a bus the next morning that was headed to the right city.

The trip via bus was fine; Valerie had ridden on one before, but on the other end they were left on foot once more, with just a tourist brochure for a map on how to get to the coast.

They could have stolen a car, but they walked. They stopped for lunch and then again for dinner, and Valerie marveled at the number of vehicles they'd ridden around in, while her parents were in charge, the number of places she'd stayed with them. The work it must have taken to set all of that up, the money, the energy to maintain that.

Being a spy was a serious investment.

She wasn't sure she was really interested in that level of focus and attention to detail.

She just liked being the recipient of the benefits of all that work.

Meanwhile, as she worried over whether her shoes were going to make it long enough to make it back to school, Hanson and Sasha talked.

They talked about their personal stories. They talked about the things they saw. They talked about politics and their parents. They talked about magic.

Hanson couldn't get enough of listening to Sasha talk about magic, deep in the dopey early-on stages of attraction, and Sasha couldn't find enough air to pour out all the words she wanted to say.

Early on, Ivory Mills had said that Sasha was quiet until you got to know her, but Valerie had never found that to be the case. Now, she felt like she understood what the contrasting option was.

It was actually possible that Hanson was retaining some of what he was hearing, based on the questions he was asking; it was possible that he was going to learn how magic worked just based on the torrent of information Sasha was giving him.

"Do you even know if you can *do* magic?" Valerie asked at one point.

"Ethan measured me," he said, and Sasha's eyes went wide.

"What was your result?" she asked.

"Strong light magic, really weak dark magic," Hanson said. "Not as strong on the light magic or as weak on the dark magic as Shack, though."

"I'm not strong on either," Sasha said. "I can do both, but I think I've got capabilities that the testing doesn't capture."

"Yeah, you do *natural* magic," Valerie said over her shoulder, and she heard Sasha gasp. Valerie turned to walk backwards. "What?"

"I do natural magic," Sasha said. "That's why I don't test strongly on either light or dark."

Valerie spread her fingers without raising her hands.

"Thought we knew that," she said. Sasha shook her head.

"I hadn't put it together yet."

"Okay," Valerie said. "Were you worried that you weren't good at anything? Because literally no one else was."

"Maybe," Sasha said. "I could do enough light magic to get in at Light School, I think, and I test really well, but I thought that maybe I had too much dark on my light-dark balance…"

"Nope," Valerie said. "Every single person has always asked you why you were slumming at Survival School. Every one of them."

"I do natural magic," Sasha said. "You know, I can live with that, knowing that it isn't just dark-tainted light magic."

Valerie turned to walk forwards again, shaking her head at Sasha's constant insecurities. She actually had an ego the size of the city, Sasha did, but it was really, really specific. If you asked her was she *sure* that those two ingredients would do what she said…? Oh, the wrath of Sasha was intense. The rest of the time, it was like she was never really sure if she measured up to anyone's standards for anything.

"So your result was strong?" Sasha asked. "What test did Ethan use?"

Valerie listened to Hanson describing the details he could remember from the event, with Sasha filling in the blanks, and Valerie realized quite abruptly that Hanson had had experiences that she - Valerie - hadn't. Experiences with *magic*.

"No one's ever told me how I test," Valerie said, not intending to sound sullen, but coming across that way anyway.

"I expect you're off the charts," Sasha said, not covering the jealous tone in her voice. "You certainly *cast* like you're off the charts."

"But I don't *know*," Valerie said. "And I never know what I'm *doing*."

"The tests aren't there to capture your *knowledge*," Sasha said. "Obviously. They're there to capture your capability. And you've got so much capability packed into you that it just explodes out any time it gets a chance."

Valerie frowned.

She *knew* she was good at magic. She did things no one else she'd met at school could do, save Dr. Finn. She worked almost the same way her mother did, if she understood the clues right, and her mother was one of the best of the best. She didn't *doubt* that she would test high.

She just wanted to see it happen.

"So what does it mean if he tested strong light?" Valerie asked.

"If he's got weak dark, but more dark than Shack, it probably means he'd have a hard time getting in at Light School. They just... all they want is pure light users, if they can get them."

"But they'd take you," Valerie said. Sasha ducked her head.

"I don't know. They wanted me to take their entrance exam. Maybe they would have let me in. I don't know. I just... My skills were always only what I could *prove*. I'm just really good at proving them, I think. My mom was a really good teacher."

"I bet," Hanson said. Valerie rolled her eyes.

"You smell that?" Sasha asked. "That's the ocean."

Valerie nodded. The air had been changing for blocks, now, and they just had to get far enough out of town that the property values dropped and the houses began to shrink.

They were actually close.

"We should keep our eyes open for a grocery store," Sasha said. "It's going to be a lot safer and a lot cheaper if we buy our own food rather than going to restaurants to eat."

"Do you cook?" Hanson asked, an honest question.

"Some," Sasha said.

"Valerie's a good cook," Hanson said. "She and her mom used to cook dinner together a lot."

Boy, that thought, that memory hurt a lot more than Valerie would have expected.

"I can do stuff that you boil out of a box and then put stuff on it," Valerie said. "And I can chop vegetables and fruit and put them in a bowl. Other than that, I need a recipe, and we got all of our recipes off of our phones."

"Now there's irony," Sasha said, and Valerie frowned.

"Why is that?" Hanson asked.

"She can't cook without a spellbook," Sasha said. Valerie shook her head. She'd seen that coming.

"Come on," she said. "There ought to be a strip mall along here somewhere with a grocery store in it. We need to get enough food to last us maybe a week. Keep in mind that the cottage doesn't have power. No fridge, no stove."

They did find one, and they loaded up with more groceries than were likely going to fit in the tiny beach hut's kitchen, but Hanson was more than willing to carry the bulk of them, and they went on.

Maybe an hour later, they found it. Tucked in between two untended lots, with greenery threatening to engulf it at any moment, Valerie hadn't ever seen anything more beautiful.

All the same, they waited another hour, until after the sun had set, to go in, trying to figure out if anyone might be watching it.

Sasha let them in and they put the groceries down on the table, then went to watch out the front window, kneeling in a row on the threadbare carpet.

Nothing happened.

Nothing happened.

A car went past without slowing, but all three of them watched it until it was out of sight.

"Do we go to bed?" Sasha asked.

"I think we have one of us stay up," Valerie said. "If someone comes, it would be better if they didn't catch all three of us asleep."

"Do you have anything to cast on the house or around it or anything to help defend it?" Sasha asked, and Valerie emptied what was left of the spellcasting ingredients onto the unstable kitchen table.

She looked at them, running her fingers across them, then shook her head.

"I don't think so."

"That's tell weed, isn't it?" Sasha asked, and Valerie nodded.

"I think so."

Sasha smiled and picked it up.

"Let me see what I can do," she said, and Valerie frowned, taking a step back.

"Be my guest."

She and Hanson leaned against the kitchen counters to watch as Sasha worked. She was using a lot of spoken casting and a lot of patterns, and at one point she went outside to get a handful of sand - which made Valerie cringe, because that stuff was gonna get *everywhere* - but Valerie could feel the subtle power of the cast as Sasha worked on it. She glanced at Hanson and nodded.

"You getting this?" she asked, and he shook his head.

"What language is she speaking?" he asked.

"Don't know," Valerie said. "I've only learned a little bit of a few languages, so I'm a bad person to ask. I do most of my casting in English, which she says is really hard." She paused as Sasha shot her a look. "Oh, and we aren't supposed to talk while she's working."

"Sorry," Hanson whispered, and Sasha shot him another look.

He put his hand over his mouth.

The entire cast took maybe twenty minutes, then Sasha threw the majority of the sand back outside, coming back in to brush her hands over the sink.

There wasn't some giant aha moment, like when Valerie had put up the red protection bubble in class, but she suspected that that was the point. No one driving past the house would notice anything about it.

"Who wants to stay up?" Valerie asked. "Four hours, then come and get one of the others."

"I assume that means you want to sleep?" Hanson asked. She smiled.

"You'll recall we missed a night, three nights back."

"But we all slept in the luggage locker at the bus station," Sasha said. "And on the floor at the clothing store. I'll go first. I need to think about where we can go to get some more spellcasting ingredients that will do us any good, anyway."

"I'll do it," Hanson said. "I was just teasing. Val loves to sleep."

"I know," Sasha said. "But I'm not. I need to think. We have *nothing* left, so we need to figure out how to get more, without access to the lab."

"How does everyone *not* at school get their stuff?" Hanson asked.

"Markets," Sasha said. "And dealers. Neither of which we have access to, either. Which means we're stuck with natural collection and dual-use civilian goods."

"Look, you two can duke it out for who's most willing to make the sacrifice. I'm going to go fall face-first into my pillow, and you can either wake me up midway through the night or you can not. With any luck, we'll have a little bit of time here to see if my parents come to find us, but we need to rest up while we can, because if they don't turn up, we need to keep moving."

Hanson nodded and waved.

"Sleep well, Val," he said. She gave him a tight smile and turned her attention to Sasha.

"I feel better," her friend said. "We'll talk in the morning, if I come up with anything clever."

Valerie nodded, turning to walk down the short hallway that lead to the two bedrooms and the bathroom.

"We could just both stay up," she heard Hanson say, and she shook her head.

They were going to do it, and they were going to spend the entire night talking and grinning and feeling happy and alive because they were together.

She'd never seen Hanson act like such a puppy dog.

It would have made her happy - it *did* make her happy - except that she'd just sent Ethan back to school, and she was genuinely afraid that she was going to wake up to people who were there to kill anyone in the house who *wasn't* Valerie, and to take Valerie prisoner.

She should have had the hardest time going to sleep, knowing that. And yet. She laid her head down on the pillow and her mind turned off gratefully and easily.

"So, the question is," Ethan said as they finished the last of the breakout brew potions, "who has access to external communication and how do we prove it?"

"Opportunity," Shack said. "I was going to go looking for motive. Who would want to let demons into Survival School?"

"Means, not opportunity," Ethan said. "Anyone could have opportunity, because we're all alone at some point around here. It's the question of *how*. And everyone could have motive. One of the students could decide that Valerie *really* doesn't belong here and cast that first seed cast, and then have completely lost control of it for the second attack. A teacher could think the same thing. Or it could be someone who is actually working for The Pure and trying to help them get leverage on Valerie's mom. Or it could be about *not* her, entirely. Actually. I don't even care. I just care about how they got the information *out*."

"Anyone with a car could leave after school is out," Shack said. "Just go drive out until they hit cell phone reception again and send a text."

"So we look at people's phones," Ethan said. "Next?"

"I've heard that some of the cottages have spotty reception where the upperclassmen have been picking at the warding for years and years."

"Still a cell phone," Ethan said. "But now anyone with a car and anyone who can get into a cottage."

"Just the upperclassmen cottages though," Shack said. "I think the visitor cottages are still locked down." He paused, lining up the potions. "Tell me again why we're breaking out?"

"Because no one is going to consent to let us hack into their phones, especially not someone with incriminating texts there. So we're going to go break into the *office* and see what the files there have to say."

Shack pursed his lips, nodding.

"I thought that the explosion there was looking like overkill, but if you're breaking into the office, too, that might not even make it."

"I've got a redundant breaking spell, over here," Ethan indicated. "I'm worried about the damping spell."

"And the tracking spell," Shack said. "You know she's going to have that buried under *everything* else."

"I'm hoping the damping spell will hold her off," Ethan said. "If we can get it situated just right, her spell won't report back strong enough to wake her up, and maybe we can get in and out without them noticing."

"You know the first time we did this was the night of the first attack," Shack said. "You have to at least *think* about that."

"What, consider that maybe we were the ones who let in the let in the demons? Sure. Thought about it."

"And?" Shack asked.

"There's still someone who planted the seed, who got past everyone to get in and to get out, with everyone awake, *and* there's no reason to think that someone would have chosen that specific night, when we had the defenses down, to come try their attack. I didn't *tell* anyone we were going to do it, unless you found a way to let them know."

"This wasn't supposed to be me telling you to treat me like I might have done it," Shack said, and Ethan shrugged, grinning.

"Just proving I *thought* about it. I know you wouldn't bring demons in here any more than you would your own house."

"I just feel bad," Shack said. "If we're doing the right thing, we shouldn't have to be defeating the defenses to do it. I mean, we *are* creating risk, doing this."

"And if Valerie's right, it won't matter, because she isn't even here."

Shack sat back to lean against Hanson's bed.

"I don't buy it, actually," he said. "I didn't want to say it in front of her, because it obviously bothers her so much, but I think they're after the Council kids."

Ethan tipped his head.

Something about that tickled.

"Keep going."

"Right, so, they killed Yasmine in the first attack. They were all over the place, down there, if you listen to what the girls say, dragging them up and down the hallway, trying to get them all in one place, and Valerie was there, pulling them off into her room so that the demons couldn't get to them, good for her, but… Yasmine was *dead* before they left. Like… Are we sure that that *wasn't* who they were looking for, and once they killed her, they bailed? Why *else* would they leave?"

Ethan had an answer to that, but also a promise to keep it a secret. He just nodded.

"Where was Ann?" he asked.

Shack shook his head.

"I don't know. She wasn't in the room that Valerie was guarding, I know that, but I asked her about it and… She doesn't like to talk about it. She and Yasmine were close. I'm not sure she remembers a lot from that night. I know she *saw* Yasmine…"

Ethan shuddered, shaking his head.

"Okay, so they killed Patrick and Conrad in the second attack, but they also injured Kit…"

"Kit was with them in the bathroom when the demons teleported in. They were… Well, you remember."

"I was with Valerie," Ethan said. "Down out of the building. I wasn't up here at all."

Shack frowned.

"I thought I could have sworn you were here when it happened. Weird. Okay, so… They were blowing up doors and pulling people out into the hallway, a lot like what the girls say, throwing people against walls… People were fighting back, people were trying to *hide*… But then two of them went into the bathroom and there was this big… *noise*. I don't know how to describe it. And Kit survived because he was in a shower and didn't hear it, so whatever it was… it just didn't hit him as hard as it did Patrick and Conrad."

Ethan closed his eyes, remembering that night.

"They put a *bomb* in the girls' hallway," he said. "I can't imagine it was an assassination, with as close as we came to the entire school blowing up."

"I know," Shack said. "The details don't all add up. But, as you say it, maybe we can rule out everyone who lives in the dorms? I mean, would you sign up to be a spy when they're going to try to bomb the place out from under you?"

Was anyone *not* here when it happened?" Ethan asked. "Other than Valerie and me?"

"Tell you what, you're looking better and better as a suspect, actually," Shack said, scratching his head. "I don't know. I thought you were here. We were talking, and then there was all of this yelling and the first door blowing off the hinges…"

"Hanson was here," Ethan said. "Are you thinking of that? Valerie came up here to talk to us, give him her blessing with Sasha, right?"

Shack frowned.

"Maybe that is what I'm remembering. Anyway, I don't know who else was here and who wasn't. We were just hanging out, you know? Not paying attention to what was going on in the hallway, especially not enough to count."

"Yeah," Ethan said. "I just… Maybe you're willing to burn your own spy and just blow up the whole building. Maybe they didn't know. I just… If I *knew* they were capable of that, and I was helping them pick a day, that would have been a good time to be out looking at the stars."

"Is *that* what you were doing?" Shack teased.

"Where was Ann the second time?" Ethan asked. "Were they looking for *you*, too?"

"Dude, the wards on that door are ones my mom taught me herself," Shack said. "They couldn't get it open."

Ethan nodded.

"Is Ann a part of this?" he asked, and Shack shook his head.

"I know she rubs everyone the wrong way, sometimes, but she would have come with us, if she was trying to help them. She's just got her own agenda, and it isn't about getting along."

Ethan nodded.

"What about Milton?" he asked. "Where was *he*?"

"Again, don't know," Shack asked.

"You didn't ask him?" Ethan asked. "Everyone wanted to talk to *everyone* about where they were when it happened."

"Milton keeps his own counsel," Shack said with a shrug. "I don't think I've ever known him to volunteer anything."

Ethan nodded.

"So it could be him."

"Are we seriously looking at Council kids as potential spies who are working with the Superiors to try to kill the rest of us..." He paused. "That actually does sound in character for us, in general."

Ethan nodded.

"And then there's the theory that Valerie is still at the center of this, because of her mom."

"I know," Shack said. "Does it have to be one or the other? Kill off some of the Council kids, try to grab her and run?"

"No," Ethan said, shaking his head. "No, it could be both. Probably *would* be both, if they were hunting us. No reason not to go after Susan Blake's daughter, while you've got her cornered."

"Well, there *is* good reason not to go after her," Shack said with a sideways smile. "But they didn't know that at the time."

Ethan grinned.

"No kidding."

Shack smiled, then shook his head.

"I'm down for this," he said. "I *do* think someone is helping them get in. And I think that you're right that it wasn't us, the one time, though I can't prove it and I don't like it. I just had the thought, and didn't want to let it wander off without talking about it."

"I think that going after Valerie is *great* cover for killing off the Council kids," Ethan said. "And if you add in the curse..."

Shack frowned.

"I hadn't thought about the curse."

"If they think that *we* are the ones who are going to take down The Pure... Wouldn't you come after us?"

"Why wait until now?" Shack asked.

"Dude, would *you* want to try to figure out how to break into your parents' house? Or Yasmine's? Or Milton's? They're all fortresses. Maybe they didn't know how old we were or when we were starting school. Maybe it was just that they didn't want to make a move until the war was already going again..."

"They were getting other things ready," Shack muttered. "We were so flat-footed..."

"Can't change it now," Ethan said. "Regardless, we're all grouped up in one place, now, and they've got someone on the inside casting holes for them that are apparently *really* hard to close..."

"Means," Shack said. "Who *could* cast that?"

"A silverthorn?" Ethan asked, then shook his head. "I don't know. Maybe that will be in the files?"

"I just want to know what we're looking for before we risk getting suspended over it," Shack said. "I mean, surely none of the underclassmen could do it, right?"

"None of the ones in *my* classes," Ethan said. "Unless you count Valerie."

Shack nodded.

"She could, couldn't she? No. It's got to be... an upperclassman. Someone who doesn't live in the dorms... or a teacher."

"Or Franky Frank," Ethan said. He didn't mean it literally, but Shack nodded.

"Franky Frank wouldn't do that," he said. "But I get it."

Ethan stared at the line of potions.

"Are we really talking about an upperclassman student helping *demons* try to kill *the entire school*?"

Shack stood.

"Don't get cold feet now," he said. "That's exactly what we're talking about."

Sasha and Hanson never did come wake her.

Valerie got up the next morning - okay, afternoon, if she was being honest - and she found them asleep on the couch in the front room, every bit of the magic casting material Valerie had left on a cutting board in between them.

Valerie picked it up and moved it to the kitchen, then went to look out the front window.

It was a beautiful location.

She was just altogether too aware of the creeping greenery on each side, how *close* someone could get to the house before she'd know anything about it, in ways that hadn't even occurred to her when she'd been here with her parents.

She was responsible, now.

"We just fell asleep a few minutes ago," Sasha said quietly. "I swear."

"No harm done," Valerie answered just as quietly. "You should go sleep in the bed, though. Get some real rest. You're going to need it."

She heard Sasha get up and leave on soft feet, and Valerie went to sit across from Hanson.

He stirred and opened his eyes, not moving as he looked at her.

"You're not Sasha," he said, his voice hoarse.

"You've been talking all night," Valerie answered, and he smiled.

"She's sweet."

"You need real sleep," Valerie said. "And then we're going to go get groceries and make a plan to get raw magic ingredients."

"She taught me some stuff," he said, nestling his head deeper into his elbow again. "She's nice."

"There are two rooms off of the hallway," Valerie said. "The one on the right is where you're sleeping."

"I'm fine here," he murmured, and Valerie shook her head.

"I don't want you out here," she said. "Go lay down and sleep. I'll come wake you up in a few hours."

"Life is weird," he said, yawning and stretching as he forced himself to his feet. "I miss basketball practice."

She frowned, not sure where that had come from, but he was

shuffling off down the very short hallway, and that was enough.

She went to sit in the front window again, watching, then switched to look out the kitchen window for a few minutes before going to get a piece of paper.

Which she didn't have.

Anywhere.

She could have sworn her mom had had paper around here, somewhere, that she and Valerie's dad had been working on, but the cabinets were bare. There was no place to put it that Valerie hadn't looked, after about five minutes, other than the bedrooms.

There was one pencil, sitting in a cupboard above her head.

And that was it.

Valerie took it, going to sit on the couch and tapping her knees with it.

She was hungry again.

Strange, this awareness that she needed to eat more meals than she skipped. When there was food around all the time, she didn't even think about it.

They'd seen a strip mall down a side street that had looked promising, so they needed to get back there today to buy groceries, so that she could eat when she woke up in the morning.

Food was important.

Her parents.

It was after noon.

If they'd had an alarm on the house - whatever shape that might have taken - that was going to tell them that Valerie and Sasha were here, they ought to have been here by now.

She knew this.

And yet.

She was going to stay on for a couple more days, just to be *really* sure, even if she knew that Hanson's mom could turn up at any point.

Or worse.

People who wouldn't hesitate to kill Hanson and Sasha.

For a moment, Valerie considered setting off on her own, hoping that her parents would come and find Hanson and Sasha and give them shelter, and let Valerie take all of that heat and all of that risk onto herself, but even if she'd been willing to do it, it was Hanson and Sasha who needed to leave, not Valerie. Leaving would have made her safer, not them.

She needed a better map, if she was going to find a park that would have real plants, not just grass and swing sets. She just felt inadequate at the idea of going and looking for magic ingredients, because she didn't know what *anything* was. She would be relying on her gift to point out the plants that were worth picking and what to do with them after, and she wasn't sure that that was how it worked.

She wasn't sure how any of it actually *worked*.

So she finally got up, putting the pencil away, and went to the side door, opening it and letting the cool breeze coming off of the ocean fill the kitchen for a moment. It wasn't comfortably cool, out there just now, and she would need a sweatshirt, but she made up her mind that if she was going to find useful things, it was at least as likely at the ocean as anywhere else, and if she searched the beach, she could stay close to the house without just sitting around all afternoon waiting for it to be time to wake up Sasha and Hanson.

She left her shoes by the door, walking out across the sand in her sweatshirt and her jeans, wrapping her arms around her as the wind grew gusty and impatient.

Sand skittered across everything, and Valerie walked slowly along, realizing how everything in front of her was either a part of the long tangle of plant rolling ashore with the waves or it was the crushed-up and destroyed body of a deceased sea creature. Seashells dominated the bits and pieces, but there were other bits of crustaceans and the like, as she fingered through everything.

She picked up a leaf from the seaweed, rubbing it between her fingers and watching the horizon.

Something Mrs. Reynolds had said in lecture came back to her as she crushed the greenleaf plant between her fingers, the goo inside mixing and evening out.

Everything has magical properties, if you know how to coax them out, the woman had said. *We used the ones that are easiest, because you are beginners, but as you get better at recognizing where those properties come from and how to harness them, your palette of tools is going to expand beyond your wildest imagination.*

Natural magic.

Mrs. Reynolds was good at natural magic. Valerie could sense that intuitively, the way she looked at the world and the way she worked. It was possible she had no skill at all with either light or dark, and yet she worked in a construct that required her to pass as halfway decent at either, or none.

Very much like Sasha.

And stupid.

Natural magic came from the natural *world*. There was no reason that it shouldn't come from seaweed and seashells, should it? And sand and seawater? Sasha had used the sand the night before, though Valerie had had the impression that it had been tying the protection magic *to* the sand, rather than consuming some power *from* it.

She looked at the green on her fingers, then nodded with a hard frown.

She wasn't *getting* something from it. Not like the inescapable magic she'd been doing all along, like someone had a string attached to her nose and she was just following along rather than fight it. If she was going to make this work, she was going to have to *work* at it.

Which was what every single other person in the world had to do.

She was willing.

She would stay away from bombs.

Probably.

Because while she trusted her instincts at this point, she didn't trust her decisions when she was working off of *knowledge* rather than *instinct*. She was going to have to be careful, because Ethan hadn't been wrong when he'd scolded her for using magic casually: it was dangerous, and it could kill people, including her, if she wasn't cautious.

But.

There was magic here, if she was willing to understand it and coax it out. Her body didn't *feel* it the way that it often did, but her mind *knew* it with a conviction that was well beyond what Valerie ever argued with.

There was no bringing sense to things she *knew* like that.

She knelt, picking out the pieces of shell and exoskeleton and such that were the largest and the least worn, the most complete, then she picked up feet of tangled seaweed and slung it over her shoulder, shivering at the wet but ignoring it. She walked up the beach a few dozen feet, collecting bits of this and that that called to her, then she walked back to the house, laying all of her bounty on the floor in the kitchen and going back out for a soup bowl full of sand. She brought that in and she sat down cross-legged in front of it, closing her eyes to think quietly.

It was here.

She just had to find it.

The damping spell had done its job. Shack and Ethan had managed to take down all of the defenses between the dorms and the office, and no one knew it had happened.

Which was kind of scary, that that sort of thing was even *possible*, but they'd had to have been *inside* the cast to do it, and Ethan had seen the schematics for the defensive magic when his father had approved them for the school year. Lady Harrington - and all of the heads of schools - re-did the top layer of defense every year, so that it didn't get old and worn from too many students casting too much stuff, and so that no one could figure out what it was and work around it.

And it was a good plan.

Right up until someone like Ethan had been left *alone* with the plans and copied them down for his own mischief.

At the time, it had *felt* like it was just for mischief, because the war had just been a titillating whisper at the time, something everyone was atingle over, because of how much *power* and *glory* you got from being involved in a war.

The last war was far enough behind them that no one in Ethan's circles had had any *clue* what it might mean for it to come back.

It wasn't like it was in stories.

Or how anyone had imagined it.

There had been bodies. His friends were dead.

And the girl he suddenly cared more about than anyone in the world was the subject of a multi-party manhunt, with easily half of them trying to kill her and *all* of them interested in capturing her and manipulating her.

It wasn't like it was in stories.

They got to the office and Shack forced the door - there was a mechanical lock on it that they didn't have a spell for, so... they did what they had to.

The records room they managed to open without breaking the door, and then they paused, looking at the long row of filing cabinets, the shelves of books, the tiny desk in the corner.

"Wow," Shack said.

"There ought to be a roster for this year around here somewhere," Ethan said. "And then we can start pulling files for the students."

"I'll go see if Mrs. Young has one at her desk somewhere," Shack said, and Ethan nodded, going to open the drawers. They were full of manila folders, all in alphabetical order, the age showing on most of them.

"Digital era didn't make it here," Ethan murmured, going to find Ann's and Milton's folders first. He put them down on the little desk in the corner, then went back, going through who he could remember was living out in the cottages, and then looking for the folders for the staff.

The bulk of the filing cabinets were dedicated to students, but he was able to find a number of the staff who had attended Survival School as students, and he pulled those folders as well, going to sit and page through Ann's folder.

Her test with Mr. Tannis hadn't been spectacular, apparently. There had been three different test objectives and three impediments, and Mr. Tannis had mixed them at random for the students. Ann had gotten the healing ward for impact injury and the distraction cast.

Apparently she'd spent the second half of her entrance test sitting and talking to him about how she did her hair before a dance that her parents had hosted the month before.

Her healing ward had been going the right direction when she'd succumbed to the distraction cast, though, and... well, they didn't really have the *option* to turn her away, given who she was. It wasn't written down in the folder, but it was all over the place, anyway. Her *potential*.

She'd been assigned to live with a girl named Meg that Ethan knew, but she'd gotten herself switched to room with Yasmine instead. She had a few discipline infractions noted, but they were simple insubordinance, not anything particularly significant.

Milton's folder was thicker. He'd killed his entrance exam, partially because he had noticed the drain cast on Mr. Tannis' desk from the moment he'd walked into the room, and he'd gone and destroyed it before Mr. Tannis had even given him his prompt.

Which sounded like Milton.

He had a lot of reprimands, though. Ethan went through them, all of them written out by hand from his teachers, fights he'd gotten into during class, students whose work he had disrupted by critiquing it, times that he'd been out of his room and out of the dorm wing without permission...

Ethan whistled, low.

He hadn't realized Milton had such a rebellious streak.

Shack came back with the list and Ethan handed him Milton's folder, going on to the upperclassmen.

"Wow," Shack said after a minute. "Would someone who was here as a spy act out *this* much?"

"If he's got no impulse control," Ethan answered. He was sorting folders into two piles: the ones that were interesting and the ones that weren't. Most of them had very little information at all after the entrance exam and background work. Who their family was, their magical history and any notable skills, interviews, that kind of thing. Particularly among the upperclassmen out in the cottages, it seemed that the school took very little interest in what they were up to.

"He gets good grades, though," Shack said, handing Milton's file back. "You really think we're going to find something like this?"

"If you've got a better idea..." Ethan said. He handed the list of students back to Shack. "Meantime, you want to pull these?"

Shack checked his watch.

"How long are you intending to be here?" he asked, looking at the door. The lights were out, and the records room wasn't visible from the front of the office, so the teachers on their patrols wouldn't notice them, but Ethan knew that Shack wanted to be out of here *long* before anyone was up and working. They had a few hours at the most.

"We're going to cut it as close as we dare," Ethan said. "This is to keep Valerie and Sasha and Hanson safe."

Shack nodded, opening one of the folders and looking at it.

"Wow, they keep a lot of records," he murmured, and Ethan nodded.

"Lady Harrington has a reputation for writing *everything* down."

"And never touching a computer," Shack said, looking around the room once more. "You think she wrote *all* of these?"

"Could be," Ethan said. "I don't know for sure how far they go back, but some of the folders are pretty worn."

"This is crazy," Shack said softly. "Did you know that Dominic turned down a scholarship at a civilian college to play soccer, in order to come here?"

Ethan shook his head.

"Do you think he's got a history that looks like maybe he knows people from The Pure?"

"Not specifically," Shack said.

"Then keep moving," Ethan told him. "There are a lot of students here, and we're looking for the ones that we need to stalk. Not who's actually a lot cooler than we give him credit for."

"But he is, right?" Shack asked, and Ethan grinned.

"Yeah, that is pretty cool."

He tossed the folder he was holding into the uninteresting pile and he picked up the next one, rubbing his eyes and forcing himself to focus.

He could do this.

It was just going to be a long night.

Valerie went outside with the compound she'd formed, pouring it into the sand at the front corner of the house.

It wasn't as satisfying as the giant red bubble of protection, but it would keep the house cloaked from a lot of detection magics, and it made her feel a lot calmer.

She went in and sat on the couch for maybe five minutes before she got too bored for that and went in to wake up Sasha.

"What time is it?" Sasha asked.

"Four," Valerie said. "You've been asleep almost three hours."

Sasha groaned and rolled over, pulling her pillow onto her head. Valerie poked her again.

"We need to go get food, and I don't want us to split up. So you have to come."

The redhead groaned again.

"Couldn't we just go later?" she asked.

"My mom said everything around here closes early, and we have a long walk ahead of us."

Sasha sighed and pulled her feet over the edge of the bed, pressing her eyes with the heels of her hands.

"Is Hanson up?" she asked, and Valerie shook her head.

"No. I don't expect he'll wake up until we're about halfway there," Valerie said. Sasha frowned, confused and sleepy.

"I thought you said you didn't want us to split up," she said, and Valerie nodded, standing.

"Exactly."

She left as Sasha staggered out of her bed to get dressed and she went across the hallway, poking Hanson in the back with her foot.

"Get up, man," she said. "We're going to get food."

"I'm hungry," Hanson muttered, not moving.

"I know," Valerie coached. "That's why we're getting up and going shopping for groceries. Because I'd like to eat, too. None of us have had anything to eat since dinner last night?"

"What time is it?" he asked, still not moving. She told him, and he rolled onto his stomach.

"Five more minutes."

"Up," Valerie said. "Or I'll pour water on your head."

It had been a long time, but she'd done it before.

He sat up, bleary, and nodded.

"I'm up."

"Good. Get dressed and meet us out in the living room."

He nodded.

"Don't go back to sleep," she told him.

He nodded.

He was going to go back to sleep.

"Get up," she said again, pulling him by his arm out of the bed. "Go wash your face or something."

"I'm awake," he said, his eyes closed. She got him up onto his feet and waited for a moment. He didn't sit back down again.

This was the best she was going to do.

She left him, going back out into the small front room.

Frowned.

Looked into the kitchen again.

Yes.

There was a stooped old woman in there in a black blouse and a green skirt, washing her hands at the sink.

"Are you here to kill us?" Valerie asked.

"No," the woman answered without turning around. "I'm here because you called me. You've been sending up signals for days, but you finally sent out the beacon I needed to find you."

"I'm capable of defending myself," Valerie said, and the woman chuckled softly.

"I should say you are. This place is a fortress."

"Who are you?" Valerie asked. "What do you want?"

The woman turned off the water and shuffled around to look at Valerie.

"I need to tell you some things."

"Okay," Valerie said slowly, and the woman shook her head.

"I thought you'd be older," she said. "But you're just a child."

"Am not," Valerie said, knowing she sounded insolent.

"You are up against things you don't understand," the woman said. "Things *I* barely understand. And I need to tell you some things, because you may be the only one who can beat them."

"Who are you?" Valerie asked. "Why are you following me?"

"I'm following you because you called me," the woman

answered. "We're tied together, you and I, and you called me here. I came because I've already lost everything at home. If I can help you salvage some of your life and your world, maybe it won't all be for nothing."

"I didn't call you," Valerie said.

"You called me the moment you killed the silverthorn," the woman said. "I knew that you were the one I had to find."

"What about it?" Valerie asked. "How do you know that?"

"You called me," the woman said, brushing past Valerie to go sit on the couch.

Valerie...

... was at a loss.

"What do you want?" she asked.

"I am Daphne Leblanc," the woman said. "I am among those who spoke with Merck Trent over the past summer, and had pledged my support to help turn back the tide of interest in segregating magic from non-magic."

"You're on our side?" Valerie asked. The woman shook her head.

"Oh, no, child, you aren't on anyone's side any more than I am. Which is why I've come to you. You have the skills to destroy the powers that each side is using, and they both fear and covet you. I hope I've come early enough to give you what you need to resist such things."

"You want to help *me*?" Valerie asked. The woman nodded.

"I thought that I could throw my weight behind Merck's coalition and keep the worst of the killings from happening, but they came to me, to my own halls, and they killed my people. It was only by luck and wit that I survived."

"You're the one with the other... Ethan saw the mark on the wall at your house," Valerie said, and the woman nodded.

"I didn't find any way to close that door, and that was the opening that they walked through to come to me."

Valerie licked her lips.

Daphne seemed to be remembering things that were far, far away, and it made Valerie feel cold. That she could have felt that way about school... There was something kindred to it, in a way she couldn't have expressed if she'd tried.

"What do I do?" she asked. "I won't go back to the school until I know that everyone is going to be safe."

"There is a cast that I can teach you now that will purge the dark magic that mars the defenses," the woman said. Valerie shook her head.

"No. Thank you, but that's not enough. Someone there is helping them. Getting rid of it once doesn't keep it from happening again."

The woman nodded slowly.

"You are so young," she said. Valerie frowned. There was so *much* in Daphne's voice.

"What happened, when they came?" she asked.

"A bomb," the woman answered after a moment, her face turned away. "It tore through my home and laid waste to every life and all magic within. I have nothing left but a shell where once lived five-hundred years of history and everyone I cared about."

"I know that bomb," Valerie said. "They tried to set it off at school."

The woman nodded.

"Your *Council* hunts you, does it not?"

"Yes," Valerie said. The woman nodded.

"They are as bad as the villains who want to kill us. I sensed a magic stronger than my own, one that went against the very casts that destroyed me, and I have been searching for you ever since my life ended. I did not think you would be so young."

"I don't understand why you keep saying that," Valerie said. The woman sighed.

"Because I am torn, putting such knowledge and responsibility on such a child. I had a granddaughter your age."

Valerie gritted her teeth, refusing to let that hit her.

"Then tell me," she said. "Let me go after them *because* of your granddaughter."

The woman nodded, looking around the house.

"The magic here isn't yours," she said. "But it is deceptively similar. Whose is it?"

"My mother's," Valerie said.

"And where is she?" Daphne asked.

"I don't know," Valerie said. "We got separated and I was hoping she would look for me here."

"I see," she said. "Perhaps it is not one, but two that I seek. Your mother shares your spirit?"

Valerie nodded.

"She doesn't think either side is right, either."

Daphne nodded, looking at her hands and then licking her lips.

"There is a woman. In North Carolina. She is called Samantha Angelsword, and while her existence is not something that any of us know, for reasons that escape me, she is among the strongest of the magic users and one who might help your cause."

"Why?" Valerie asked.

"Because she cares about justice and freedom and the lives of the civilians. Explain to her what is going on and ask her plainly for help, and I believe she will give it to you, though I will warn you that you will never see our ways the same again."

"I don't understand," Valerie said. "Who *is* she? Why don't you go?"

"You should not rush into it," Daphne said. "You are so young and so... green. If you can find another path, you should take it. But when you find yourself without another option, she may be the one who can help you end this war."

"Why would I take another path, if I could end the war?" Valerie asked, and Daphne shook her head, then lifted her eyes.

"Because it may very well kill you instead, and... I don't want another death on my conscience. Even now, I hesitate."

"They're killing people," Valerie said. "Trying to kill people I care about, and might be coming to try to kill me."

"Oh, they're coming," Daphne said, nodding slowly. "They're coming and they have big plans for what they intend to do with you. If I read them right, they'll just kill the two standing back there in the hallway."

Valerie spun on the couch. She'd forgotten Sasha and Hanson, who were hiding in plain sight; the hallway wasn't that long.

"They shouldn't know I was here," Daphne said, standing. "I need to go."

"Help us," Sasha said, stepping forward. "Please."

Daphne sighed.

"The roots of my magic were in my home. You wouldn't understand, with your new country and your flying around from place to place. I have nothing to offer you but my knowledge, and that knowledge will only help you if they don't know you have it."

Valerie closed her eyes.

"All right," she said. Daphne went to the table and produced a roll of paper in the same way that Valerie had seen Roger do it in her apartment, back before all of this had started. She still didn't know how to do that.

She wrote for about a minute, then turned the paper to Valerie.

"Can you do this?" she asked.

"I think all of those are words," Valerie answered. Sasha edged around the table, nodding quickly as she ran her finger down the page.

"Yes. I can help her do all of that," she said. Daphne looked at Valerie quizzically.

"Was it you or not who called me this morning?" she asked. Sasha looked at Valerie, confused, and Valerie shrugged.

"I put up a protection spell," she said. "If that's what you're talking about."

"You could put up a protection spell that was *that* delicate, but you cannot so much as *read* this?" Daphne asked.

Valerie nodded.

"Seems to be the size of it, yeah."

Daphne shook her head, then produced a second piece of paper.

"This is the address," she said. "For the Angelsword. Do not go to her unless you are prepared to lose your life in this war. It isn't for children to fight adults' battles. I don't like even giving you her name. But you… They fear you, for what you can do. If it comes to it…"

Valerie nodded.

"I want to stop the war," she said, and Daphne shook her head.

"This will do much more," she said. "I can't even predict what. If it's possible there's another way, you should use it."

She lifted her head again, like she could hear something Valerie couldn't.

"You aren't safe here much longer," she said. "I need to go. I wish you the best of luck."

"That's it?" Sasha asked. "One spell and a name?"

"That's all I have that's worth anything to you," Daphne said, then set her mouth. "I hope for you that you never have to use it."

Valerie took a step back as Daphne started for the door. The woman looked back at them once but she didn't speak, and then she was gone.

Valerie rolled up the cast and handed it to Sasha and then the address and gave it to Hanson.

"We need to move," she said.

"Where?" Hanson asked.

"Doesn't matter," Valerie said. "I don't care that she said that she didn't have magic, she knows something we don't. And she tracked us down. Someone is coming, and we need to be gone by the time they get here."

"What if it's your parents?" Sasha asked, and Valerie shook her head.

"No. They wouldn't be using magic to find us." She looked out the window. "I don't know what kept them from finding us the first time, but my hope was that they would *know* we were here and just… come get us. They shouldn't be *tracking* us down." She nodded, feeling chilled. "This is something else."

The sun would come up soon.

Ethan knew it.

He could see it on Shack that his friend knew it, too.

Shack hadn't looked up from a folder in the last hour, though, going from one to the next like a machine, putting the ones that he thought were interesting in front of Ethan and Ethan doing the same.

At this point, Ethan was resigned to having to do it all over again, breaking out, and only using this trip as simple reconnaissance, but he hated the idea of leaving the work half-done.

Also, they were going to have to put the folders all back again, or they were going to get busted for having been here, even if they *did* make it back to their room.

Lady Harrington knew Ethan's magic.

He was getting blurry eyed, when Shack suddenly sat forward.

"Listen," he said. "Expressed resentment at being tested, that he should have to compete with people with lesser magic pedigrees. Frequently absent during class. Absence. Absence. Absence. Reprimanded for stealing a student's books and turning them into hay. *Suspended* for locking a student to a wall and practicing explosions casts. Both times, he said that he chose the student because he was first generation at a magic school. That he didn't belong here."

"Who is that?" Ethan asked, and Shack gave him a grim look, turning the folder to face Ethan.

Elvis Trent

Ethan felt his shoulders drop, and he took the folder from Shack to read it for himself.

There was more.

Elvis was popular. Everyone liked him, everyone wanted to be in his good graces, in much the same way that they liked Ethan. Elvis might have been more attractive, but he had a girlfriend at Light School, a senior, who he'd recently gotten back together with, so Elvis might have flirted a lot, but he didn't have a casual flock of girlfriends at Survival School. Although, neither did Ethan.

He shook his head.

"It couldn't be my brother," he said. "Elvis is a jerk, but he'd never go against the Council."

Shack shrugged.

"I know. I know. It's just, we both kept skipping his folder, and…"

Ethan looked at it again.

"I see it."

He closed the folder then stood, looking at what was left.

They'd gotten through almost the whole school.

"If they were any *good* at being a spy, they wouldn't draw attention," he said after a moment, and Shack nodded.

"We were both hoping we'd see something Lady Harrington didn't, but there isn't anything here that just screams 'I let the demons in'. I don't know what we do next."

"We need to clean up," Ethan said. "I don't want them to know we were here."

Shack nodded and started sorting through folders, handing them to Ethan in something that was more-or-less alphabetical order. Ethan started shoving them back into the drawers, knowing he had to have been making mistakes in his haste, but knowing it was better for the folders to be back and not where they went than not back at all.

They were late.

They were *so* late.

He put the last folder into a drawer and pushed it closed, then froze.

There were voices outside.

Lady Harrington talking to Mrs. Young.

He closed his eyes.

This was going to take the biggest bluff of his entire life, waiting for the right moment for both him and Shack to walk out of here like nothing was happening.

The door opened.

Ethan straightened, though Shack reclined deeper against the wall. No telling which was the better play, because neither of them were likely to work.

"I'm always amazed at how much the students at my school think they can get away with without me noticing," Lady Harrington said. "I hope you found some interesting things, because I hardly think it will have been worth it."

She stepped to the side, and Ethan reached down to help Shack up to his feet, walking past the headmistress. She pointed.

The conference room.

Well.

Nope, he had nothing redeeming at all about that.

They were in *trouble*.

Lady Harrington sat down at the conference table and lifted her chin.

"I think you should start with what you were doing in there, gentlemen," she said.

It was just her.

Ethan didn't know what to think of that.

He was used to balancing out whole committees asking him questions, trying to work one interest against another to weaken the resolve of the group.

Lady Harrington... Well, she was just flat-out *tough*.

"Looking for the person who is sabotaging the school and trying to get Valerie captured," Shack said.

Truth.

When all else failed, lead with the truth.

"And you think that you are more qualified to do that investigation than myself and the rest of the staff?" Lady Harrington. "You jump to sabotage awfully quickly."

"We think we might know things that you don't," Shack said. "And that we might be more motivated."

"More motivated?" Lady Harrington asked, raising her eyebrows. "You have been locked in your rooms for days on end, losing out on precious instruction time, as we have been hunting down answers to what has gone wrong with the school's defenses. And then the two of you come trampling in on them and shut them down entirely, in the name of solving the mystery. I am... I am beyond words."

"Valerie won't come back until she knows that the school is safe," Ethan said.

"She think she's safer *out there* than here?" Lady Harrington asked, and he shook his head.

"No. She thinks *we're* safer with her out there," he answered.

Lady Harrington folded her hands on the table, watching the two of them.

"I see," she said after a moment. "And did you find anything incriminating, pawing through my students' personal files?"

"Nothing useful," Ethan said, and Shack shook his head.

"People at this school are messed up," he said, and she tipped her head at Shack.

"They are indeed a handful to manage, always presuming that they know best and that the things they *can* do are simultaneously things they *may* do."

"You haven't made any progress," Ethan said. "Have you?"

The corner of her mouth twitched, and she resettled her shoulders.

"We are working on a great many important things," she said. "Right now, everything says that it is life or death and that we should work on it first."

"But you haven't, have you?" Ethan asked.

"Not nearly so much as I would have liked," Lady Harrington said. "No."

"Do you have anyone you *think* it might be?" Shack asked, and Lady Harrington gave him a cold look.

"You insult me, asking," she said. Ethan shook his head.

"We couldn't get files on the staff," he said.

"My school was *attacked*," Lady Harrington said. "It is a great black mark on my record. And yet, it has happened not once but *three* times in the space of a single year. Under normal circumstances, I would be outraged that you would suggest that one of my faculty or staff might be disloyal, but I am in a position that should not be possible."

"How would you do it, if you were us?" Ethan asked after a moment. "If you could break the rules and if you could talk to students without *being* Lady Harrington?"

She lifted her chin.

"I would start with the cottages," she said. "I would sweep them to find which of them have cellular access. As soon as they see me coming, they put up patches to keep me from finding out they've poked holes in the shielding, but you could get close without them putting up the temporary patches. It is my best estimation that the person involved in the first blackroot cast was perfectly permitted to be in the school, and that they had to inform the outside world somehow that the cast was ready and in place."

"We were thinking cottages, too," Shack said. "We were just thinking about trying to get people's text history."

She shook her head.

"Find the cottages with holes in the cellular shielding, then look at who was in the building the night that the silverthorn was cast."

Ethan hesitated.

"You *know* that?" he asked, and she gave him a wan smile.

"Of course. My office recognizes every legitimate person on this campus."

Ethan hadn't accounted for anything *like* that in his breakout potions.

"You knew we were here," he said, and she nodded.

"I know that you sometimes go to the library to study late at night, presumably because of Mr. MacMillan's study music selections."

Ethan nodded slowly.

"And because I like to think that I'm sneaking around," he said.

"This is my *job*, young man," she said. "You underestimate me *entirely* if you think I am unaware of the more trivial things going on at my school, simply because I do not react to them. I would rather *know* that they are happening than drive my students' attempts to disguise their activities further underground."

"You're a smart lady," Shack said.

"That means so much, coming from you, Mr. MacMillan," Lady Harrington answered.

"So we'll go find out who's got access to the outside world," Ethan said. "And then we'll compare that against your records…"

"Oh, no," Lady Harrington said. "No. You misunderstand me. That is what *I* would do. With the information on whose attempts to elude the warding have been successful, *I* will check *my own* records, and I will take appropriate action to inspect the resulting students who meet both requirements."

"You don't want to do that," Ethan said, not sure why not yet, but also not wanting to let control completely go.

"Is that so?" Lady Harrington asked.

"Yeah," Shack said. "If you talk to the students who were in the building when the cast was set, they might figure out that you've got more security on the building than you told the Council about…"

"What do you know about the plans I submitted to the council?" Lady Harrington asked, and Shack fell silent.

"I've seen them," Ethan said. "And I bet the saboteur has, too. They've managed to avoid you knowing about them all this time, is it really possible that it's luck and skill and not inside information? I mean, you're talking about someone who *already* agreed to be the insider for the Superiors. They *know* how valuable it is to have inside information."

She pursed her lips.

"And what would you suggest?" she asked.

"Let us talk to them," Ethan said. "Everyone knows I'm feuding with my dad right now. We could put out the word that Mrs. MacMillan threatened to send Shack into the darkness because she thinks he's hiding information about my girlfriend…"

"Girlfriend," Lady Harrington said dryly, and he shrugged.

"I asked, she said yes. Is it more complicated than that? Anyway, they also know that Mrs. Blake isn't on good terms with the Council, either. If I played dumb the right way, they could think that I'm sympathetic to the Superiors, and try to use me."

"Quite a dangerous game you two play," Lady Harrington said quietly. "Being children of the Council has rubbed off on you."

"That's another thing," Ethan said. "Shack has a theory that they're hunting Council kids."

She nodded.

"We've noticed, and the Council agrees."

Ethan dropped his chin.

"My ma *knows* that there might be a group of people literally trying to kill me, and she left me here?" Shack asked.

"They agreed that withdrawing their students would generate the appearance of a lack of faith, and they chose not to do that."

"We're their second-string kids, anyway," Ethan said.

"That's quite a cold view of it," Lady Harrington said, and Ethan shrugged.

"My brother is the heir apparent at Council," he said. "It was in this very room that my father threatened to put me out on the front lines without support, because I wouldn't help him find Valerie Blake."

"I assure you with great confidence that neither of your parents would carry out the threats they were making over Miss Blake," Lady Harrington said. "Now. If you do not get moving, you are going to be late for breakfast, and that absence will be noted."

"What is my brother doing, all those times that he's not in class?" Ethan asked, and she shook her head.

"The upperclassmen have a certain amount of liberty that we go to some lengths to protect," she said. "I know that he is not generally in the building, and I know that it does not appear that he is spending that time studying for other classes."

Ethan drew his head back.

"My brother isn't doing well in his classes?" he asked, and Lady Harrington raised her eyebrows.

"Those words never left my mouth, now did they, young man?"

"I never heard about him getting suspended," Ethan said.

"It was largely overturned," Lady Harrington said. "He was allowed to stay at his cottage and do his work, turning it in at leisure during the week, or the week after. It had no material impact on his academics, though it was allowed to remain in his file."

"Horrors," Shack muttered.

"Please go on, now," she said. "You should appear at breakfast in the same way that you always do, and it would be best if you unwound your casting on the defenses from the same location where you first cast it."

Ethan nodded, then looked at Shack.

This had *not* happened the way he'd expected it.

His friend stood.

"We'll be in touch," he said and Ethan shook his head.

Shack had *nerve*.

Lady Harrington watched them coolly, and Ethan stood, going to the door and opening it. Shack went past him and Ethan glanced back at Lady Harrington. She shook her head at him, unimpressed, and he shrugged.

He couldn't do better.

He was already doing the best he could.

"Um," Hanson said from the front window as Valerie finished packing up what she thought was worth taking from the kitchen. "Val, you should come see this."

Valerie left Sasha with the bags and went to stand next to Hanson at the window.

There was a car parked against the curb, there in front of the house, and Hanson's mom was getting out of it.

"You think we can outrun her?" Valerie asked, and he shook his head.

"She goes out running with my dad when he's in town, and he runs six miles a day."

"What about stealing the car?" Valerie asked.

"Do you know how to drive?" Hanson asked, and she shrugged.

"How hard could it be?" she asked.

"She will have taken the keys with her," Hanson said, and Valerie shrugged, looking over her shoulder.

"Sasha is good with locks, right?" she asked.

"I could unlock the doors," Sasha answered. "But not start the ignition."

"If we split up, she couldn't catch all of us," Valerie said.

"She would only go after you," Hanson said. "I'm sorry. I don't know what to tell you."

It had been a bad bet.

She'd been kind of elated, after talking to Daphne. It had felt like she'd unlocked something important and now all she had to do was open it.

But it had been a bad bet.

She'd wagered that her parents would find her, or that no one would find her, and instead Martha Cox had found her, and that meant she was going to have to fight the woman over going back to Survival School or - worse - just going to see the Council.

Some safehouse somewhere, with just Ethan's dad to talk to.

Valerie shuddered.

"I assume you don't like the idea of me hurting your mom," she said as Martha walked across the front yard.

"We've got bigger problems than that," Sasha said, running

from the kitchen and peering out the front window. She moved around from side to side, like a cat watching a bird. "Do you see them?"

"What are you talking about?" Valerie answered.

"The Pure," Sasha said. "Or someone with some *really* strong magic. They're trying to blow up the detection spell I put on the house."

"But not the protection spell *I* did?" Valerie asked.

"I can't even tell it's there," Sasha admitted. "I've been taking your word, especially since Daphne was so aware of it."

"Okay," Valerie said. "Maybe it's just Hanson's mom."

The woman had gotten to the side door, by now, and was out of sight.

Valerie looked at Hanson. He pressed his lips, then shook his head.

"I wish I knew what to tell you," he finally said, when there was a knock on the door.

"I can defend myself, if it comes to that," she said softly. "What's the worst thing she's going to do to me?"

"Drag you back to school, I think, or in front of the Council," Hanson said. "I know she doesn't want you dead, and she won't hurt me. I don't think she'd do anything to Sasha unless she got in the way."

Valerie straightened, letting her shoulders fall away from her ears and she went to the door as the knock repeated itself.

"So don't get in the way," she said, opening the door.

"So," Shack said at breakfast. "One thing we didn't talk about with Lady Harrington."

"How we're supposed to casually get out to the cottages when the entire school is on lockdown?" Ethan answered, and Shack nodded.

"Yup."

"What's up, guys?" Milton asked, setting a tray down next to them. Ethan looked over at his long-time acquaintance with knew eyes.

Milton was an insurrectionist.

He just didn't *talk* like one very much.

He was too thoughtful for the big speeches.

Could be he was the brains and that someone else was the access to the outside world, still.

"Just wish we could figure out how to get everything back to normal," Ethan said, shaking his head. "Everyone missing and the school shut down... Stupid to just be hanging out here waiting for the other shoe to drop."

"Are you considering calling your dad and asking him to pull you out?" Milton asked. "Because according to the handbook, if you leave for more than three continuous weeks or you announce you're withdrawing before the final exams, you don't get credit for the year, and they're very hesitant to take freshmen who are older than the rest of them, even by a year."

"No, I'm not threatening to bail," Ethan said. "I just wish they'd get *on* with it, you know? It's like... they aren't even changing anything at this point. Are we really that much safer in our rooms than in class?"

"First time I've ever heard you moan about not having classes," Shack said passively, looking around the room. Ann was sitting with a table of girls, and seemed to have no use for the Council brats table today.

It had been a few days since she'd sat with them.

"You don't have to tell *me* it's strange," Ethan said. "It's just so *boring* being locked in our rooms all day."

"They have to correct the fault in the defenses," Milton said, turning to his breakfast. "Otherwise the parents are going to shut the place down. Two attacks with casualties? Lady Harrington is lucky she hasn't been executed by the Council for dereliction."

"That's not fair," Ethan said. "Someone *attacked* us. From the inside, it looks like. How is she supposed to keep *all* the spells from working, when someone on the inside is casting them? At a *magic* school?"

Milton shrugged.

"Her problem, not ours. At least they probably won't attack us again, so long as Valerie is gone. She finally did something right, by us."

"You do remember that she and Ethan made up, right?" Shack asked, and Milton raised his eyes.

"I'm sorry, am I not allowed to point out that three of us are *dead* because she was here? She's a military asset, and she should be held at a military-grade establishment. If we held to Geneva conventions, we'd be breaking them, hiding her in with *children*."

"She isn't an asset," Ethan growled. "She's the same age as the rest of us, and she isn't legally allowed to be considered part of the war."

Milton snorted.

"Right up until the Council needs her, right?"

Ethan looked over at Shack.

He couldn't argue with that.

"Where do you think she is?" Milton asked. "You think she's still alive?"

"Dude," Shack said. "Too far."

"I bet Sasha Mills didn't make it," Milton went on, chewing thoughtfully. "Valerie is basically defenseless in the face of *real* magic, but Sasha? She's just *soft*. She's supposed to be behind lines, taking in survivors and trying to keep them alive."

"When did you get so dark, man?" Ethan asked.

Ethan shrugged.

"They called up my sister," he said.

"Hadn't heard," Shack said, and Milton nodded.

"Yeah. My mom fought it, but they said that they have to make an example and prove that Council kids aren't immune."

Shack and Ethan glanced at each other.

Certain kids were definitely still immune, but Milton's mom was far enough down the food chain, and part of a different power sect, and it wasn't all that surprising that Merck and Mrs. MacMillan would be willing to sacrifice Milton's sister.

"She isn't out fighting, is she?" Ethan asked, and Milton shook his head.

"No, she's tactical support, actually, and she's having a great time. Gets to boss around everyone, and where she landed, everyone *cares* that she's a Council kid. So. She landed on her feet well enough, but she's still a target."

"We're all targets until this war ends," Shack said.

Milton nodded.

"That's why it's better for the really *juicy* targets to not be *here*. It just gives them an excuse."

"But them attacking here is still *bad*," Ethan said, and Milton frowned hard.

"Why would you even ask that? They *killed* Patrick and Conrad."

Ethan nodded.

"Just, you could make a case that forcing the Council to treat this like the real war that it is, and to get serious about it rather than playing politics, that it could be better for everyone."

"Are you questioning how your parents are running the war?" Milton asked. "Because *clearly* my mom is out of power."

Ethan shrugged.

"Everyone knows there are politics," he said. "There are people out there who are actually working against *both* sides, I heard."

"Suicide squad?" Milton asked. "The Superiors are enough to crush anyone without the Council to back them."

"What does your mom say about the last war?" Ethan asked, and Milton scrunched his face to the side.

"I don't know. What do you mean?"

"Like," Ethan said, feeling out how he wanted to pitch this. "Just. They're these rabid fanatic genocidalists, right?"

Milton shrugged.

"So?"

"How did we not *know* that, at the end of the last war? How did we let them get away?"

"We didn't want to interrogate everyone. The war was over, and we won," Milton said. "You know this story. I don't want to talk about the peace divide with you. There's no point."

"No, just hear me out," Ethan said. "If they're all completely crazy, why would we have *had* to interrogate them to figure out who was crazy?"

Milton set his mouth for a moment, then shook his head.

"I give up. Why?"

"I'm not sure they were," Ethan said.

"Are you *humanizing* the Superiors?" Milton asked. "You do need something better to do with your time."

"No, that's not... Okay, so maybe I am. Why not?" Ethan asked. "If we're going to run this war, you know, one day, we need to understand *why* they're doing it, and I'm not convinced they were all just bonkers."

Milton shook his head.

"You're adorable," he said. "We are never going to run this war, the three of us. My sister is going to hot-foot it up the chain of command, with my mother quietly running interference for her, and my sister is going to be *on* the Council before we even *graduate*. And you know they don't let two people on the council with the same last name."

"Then get her to marry someone," Ethan said dismissively. "You see my point."

"No," Milton said. "I don't."

"The point is that I'm not sure they're all crazy," Ethan said, trying one more time. "But they're still all fighting against us. What does that *say*?"

"That they're afraid of the crazy ones?" Milton said, finishing his breakfast. "You're getting cabin fever, Ethan. Pull it together."

Ethan frowned after him as Milton went to throw his trash away and took up with another table.

It had once been that the Council brats took up most of a central table, within the lunch hall, very exclusive. Now, it was just Ethan and Shack and Ethan was feeling ostracized from the rest of the school.

They had to get out of the building.

"You need to work on your pitch," Shack said, still eating happily enough.

"I know," Ethan answered. "But Milton is going to be the *last* person I convince to change his mind."

"You don't even know what his mind *is*," Shack said, and Ethan nodded.

"Exactly."

Martha Cox brushed through the door and closed it behind her, leaning her back against the hollow wood like it was much more significant.

"What do you have for defenses, here?" she asked.

"What?" Valerie asked. Sasha was still looking out the window like a wound-up cat.

"I told you, they're coming," Sasha said, and Martha looked over.

"Exactly," the woman said. "The Superiors are coming, and if we don't defend ourselves, they're going to kill us and take you, and the war will be over before it even really starts."

Valerie looked over at Sasha.

"Sasha," she said. "Sasha I need you to focus."

"*What do you have?*" Martha asked again, her voice much louder and angrier.

"Almost nothing," Sasha said. "We used it getting here and setting a defense around the house, but they just finished picking off my anti-detection spell, and they're starting to target the house."

"Almost…" Martha said, then shook her head. "Almost none. What kind of… Never mind. I'm going to start making weapons. You three go back into the back and get under something."

"No," Valerie said, and Martha stopped moving.

"What did you say to me?" she asked, her voice even louder. "What did… Hanson, you need to tell your friend that I'm not just here on a social call. All of our lives are on the line here, and I don't have time for her teenage rebellion…"

"Ma, she's one of the best there is," Hanson said. "You need to let her help you if she thinks she can."

"Oh, she thinks she can help," Martha said. "No. All three of you back in the back."

Valerie looked at Sasha, who looked like she was moments away from complying.

"I need you to go through the house," Valerie said. "Get creative. I cast a protection spell with seaweed and seashells. Anything that might help, bring it to me."

There was an odd sensation, of someone pulling her hair or tugging at her heel, as though those were the same thing, and she went to stand at the window.

"What *is* that?" she asked.

"What is what?" Sasha asked, coming to stand next to her.

"Are they hard of hearing?" Martha demanded of Hanson.

"Something… pulling," Valerie said. "I can *feel* it, but I don't understand."

"I don't know," Sasha said. "Does it have to do with your protection spell, do you think?"

Valerie nodded slowly, feeling it out.

"Yes, I think so."

"They've got a hold of it," Martha said. "It was an amateur cast and they're going to funnel magic into you through it. You need to scuttle it before they knock you out."

"It's what's keeping them out," Sasha said. "I've seen her hold a door closed against *demons*."

"They've got a link to it. Who are you? Why do you keep talking back to me?" Martha demanded

"Ma, this is Sasha, my girlfriend."

Sasha ducked her head - Valerie suspected they hadn't gotten all the way to agreeing to call each other boyfriend and girlfriend - and Valerie held her hand out just enough to get Sasha's attention again.

"Anything you can find. I think I can work with it. You know what you're doing."

"Seaweed?" Sasha whispered, and Valerie nodded.

"You need to let go of your cast," Martha said, coming to stand next to Valerie. Her tone was different now, more conciliatory. "They're going to get through it, and when they do, it may be too late to protect you. I… I can't make you any promises. I don't know how many of them there are, but I'm going to try. You are *key* to this war, and I'm not going to let you go without a fight."

"Neither am I," Valerie answered. "Hanson, you should probably go sit in the tub, though. That's where the protection warding will be the strongest."

"You're saying I can't fight this," he said.

"Not unless Sasha has taught you an awful lot of magic in the last two days," Valerie answered.

"Get under the bed in the back," Martha said. "And don't come out until I tell you."

Valerie looked over at Hanson, who mouthed *sorry* at her, and went back into the bedroom he'd slept in.

"The warding is stronger at the tub," Valerie said. "I tied a lot of the protection cast to water, so…"

"Your cast is misshapen and it's going to bring their attacks straight at you," Martha said. "And if I'm outnumbered by more than two or three to one, we're all dead, anyway, regardless what happens to you. I'm just hoping, if they do manage it, that they are happy *just* killing you."

"There, we agree," Valerie said. Sasha came back into the room with a stack of blankets.

Only Susan Blake would stock a linen closet in a tiny beach hut with blankets. She was always cold.

Valerie picked one of them up and put it to her nose as Sasha looked out the window again.

"There isn't much else," she said, and Valerie nodded. The blanket smelled like her mom.

"I can work with this," she said, going to sit on the floor.

Martha went to get her own bag of spellcasting ingredients, taking up residence at the table.

Whoever it was, they were out there. Right now. It was just a question of how long Valerie could hold them off and whether she and Martha Cox could be prepared for what came next.

They were in *big* trouble.

Lady Harrington entered the cafeteria.

Looked around the room in anticipation of the voices there dropping off, which they did little by little and then all at once. She lifted her chin with the faintest of nods, then took one more step forward.

"I know that many of you have been highly dissatisfied with the events of the last few weeks," she said, her voice stern. "You say that you came here to learn and be around other magic students, and I understand that. At the same time, we cannot take shortcuts with your safety, and we will not. I expect the student body to accept this gracefully and cooperatively, regardless of how much disappointment you may feel over it."

Ethan glanced at Shack, but Shack was paying attention to the room in the casual way that he did, his elbows back on the table and his feet way out in front of him, not looking at anything in specific.

Ethan didn't know if Shack had learned that from his mom or if he'd come by it naturally, but it was one of the greatest intel-gathering tactics Ethan had ever witnessed.

"You will all return to your rooms for not more than fifteen minutes and find the things that you must have for the evening, and then we are going to ask that all of the dormitory students exit the building. The visitor cottages will be open for sheltering in during the next three hours, while the faculty are taking actions that would not be possible with students *in* the building. It is our hope that these exercises will be enough to return us to our normal activities, but no one should rely on that. At the end of three hours' time, you will all be counted back into your dorm rooms. I expect promptness and compliance. Is that clear?"

Ethan looked over at Shack.

"Lady Harrington isn't a bad wingman to have," Shack murmured as voices around them picked up in comparable conversation.

"Your fifteen minutes begin now," Lady Harrington said. "Please clean up after yourselves as you normally would, then proceed to your rooms."

Ethan frowned.

"Well," he said, equally quietly. "That solves that."

Ethan and Shack were among the first out on the front lawn, milling around and talking to people. Sure, they ate their meals together every day, but this was the first time they'd been able to just hang out and *talk* in weeks. Everyone was eager, despite the cold, and after a while, they started down toward the visitor cottages, just the weight of the crowd drawing them forward.

"Hey," Ethan said as people were starting to move. "Why go

down to the visitor cottages? The upperclassmen have been living it up while we've been on lockdown, and they've got food and movies and all of that. You know? I'm going to go knock on Elvis' door and tell him that we're going to go stay there while the teachers are exorcising the school."

Shack laughed.

"I want to be there to see his face."

"I mean," Ethan said, putting out his arms and walking backwards, "they owe us that much, don't they? School spirit and camaraderie and we're all in this together, right?"

"Party," Shack said quietly, and the word spread like wildfire. Ethan grinned with a nod.

"Party at the upperclass cottages," he yelled, putting a fist in the air and charging the other direction.

People followed him, as they generally did when he set off to do something visibly, and he jogged back up the hill and along the ridge to where the upperclass cottages were tucked in against the tree line.

Ethan looked over at Shack.

"Divide and conquer?" he asked, and Shack nodded.

"I'll start at that end, you start at the other end. Meet you in the middle."

Ethan shook his head.

"I'll start at the other end after I put in an appearance with Elvis."

Shack nodded, looking behind them.

"I probably should, too."

Three hours really wasn't going to be much, to go through all forty-odd cottages that the upperclassmen resided in, and they would have to move quickly, but he thought they could do it.

He strode up to Elvis' door and knocked, looking over his shoulder at the wedge of underclassmen coming along the ridge behind him, trailing and taking and laughing, the word 'party' rolling along and through the crowd with a predictable potency.

Elvis came to answer the door looking like he'd just gotten out of bed.

"Ethan," he said, frowning hard and scratching his head.

"What are you doing here?"

"Lady Harrington kicked us out of the school so that they could work," Ethan told him with a grin. "So we came here for some place to be and for something to do."

"Is that... is that the whole school?" Elvis asked, straightening and walking around past Ethan.

"Every last one of us," Ethan said. "Open up the cottages; we're here to hang out until the teachers are done at school, and it's the first time we've been out in weeks."

Elvis held up his hands, but the next words out of his mouth were lost as Ethan slipped past him and Shack after that, and a dozen more kids besides. The others split up; Ethan could hear the conversations as they talked about which upperclassmen they wanted to crash with. Some of them it was a sense of friendship, while others had revenge on the mind, but it sounded like if they waited the right amount of time, most of the cottages would be open for them.

This just might actually work.

Ethan threw himself onto a couch next to one of his brother's friends, crossing his legs on the coffee table and draping his arms across the couch to either side.

"What's on?" he asked.

"We don't get a TV signal out here," the young man told him, and Ethan shrugged.

"But you've got a DVD player," he said.

"Why are you *here*?" Elvis' roommate asked, and Ethan gave him the short answer that avoided mentioning the visitor cottages.

Ethan heard the refrigerator open and close several times, and the roommate stood to go defend his food. Ethan snagged the remote and slid across to lean on the arm of the couch as he went to go see what DVDs were loaded.

"Ethan," Shack said, sitting down next to him.

"Seriously?" Ethan called after the roommate. "Who here watches rom-coms?"

"Ethan," Shack said again, his voice serious. Ethan picked a movie and gave Shack his attention.

Shack pulled his phone out of his pocket and showed it to

258

Ethan.

Mercifully, they both had charged phones, just now, so all they'd had to do was get them out of their room before they went outside.

It had signal.

Ethan froze.

Shack shook his head.

"Doesn't mean it's one of the people in this cottage," Shack said softly, putting the phone away again. "Just means we need to keep looking. Could be it's a *huge* hole."

Ethan nodded, numb, then nodded again.

Of course.

Of course Shack was right.

He stood.

"Nothing here to watch," he announced to no one in particular. "I'm going to go see what everyone else has got going on."

"Don't make a scene," Shack muttered as he walked past, and Ethan gave his friend's back a dark look.

He wasn't making a *scene*. He was just letting everyone know…

Right.

He wouldn't have done that, normally.

The cell signal here had thrown him off.

He nodded and headed out.

More cottages to run down.

Not enough time.

Two more.

Ethan found two more cottages with cell service.

But they weren't right next to Elvis'. They were at random up and down the woodline; Elvis' cell service was something he had carved out for himself. Or, at least, one of his roommates had.

Ethan met up with Shack as everyone was starting back toward the building at the end of the three hours, and Shack shoved his hands into his pockets, shrugging his shoulders against the cold.

"One more," Shack said. "Down by the end."

"Two," Ethan said.

"Four total," Shack said. "How sure are we?"

Ethan shook his head, but one of the girls went running past him, grabbing his elbow and tugging at it with laughter.

She hopped and talked for several minutes about absolutely nothing, and then they were back at the school. Lady Harrington was watching everyone as they went by with a cool expression, and she crooked her finger at Ethan as she saw him.

"I need a word with you and Mr. MacMillan, please," she said, uncrossing her arms and going into the office. Ethan ducked his head and whispers went up around him - probably about the cottage swap as much as anything; it was a good scapegoat - and he and Shack followed Lady Harrington into her office.

"Well?" the woman asked as she seated herself behind her desk.

Ethan had never been in Lady Harrington's office before. All of his conversations with her had happened in the conference room.

"Four," he said, looking over at Shack. "We found four cottages with cell phone signal."

"Which?" Lady Harrington asked.

"My brother's," Ethan said, and she gave him a tight frown.

"And the rest?" she asked.

Ethan gave her his two, and Shack told her which one he had found, and Lady Harrington gave them a brief nod.

"I will follow up with this, thank you," she said.

"No," Ethan said. "No, we want to still be involved. My *brother* is on the list of suspects, now."

She gave him another tight frown, then nodded, getting out a list.

"This is the list of people who were in the building the night of the silverthorn cast," she said.

She took out another piece of paper and started making a list.

"And this is the list of upperclassmen who live in those four cottages."

"What about the night of the demon attack?" Shack asked. "If I knew it was coming, I'd want to be out of the building."

"Mr. MacMillan, your insight is useful and I appreciate it, but I intend to scan the magic of every person on this list, regardless of when they were in the building. I've reduced it by enough that I will not hesitate to do so, even if I do invade the privacy of students who have done nothing wrong. I am beyond my tolerance of patience with this situation."

"I thought most of the upperclassmen knew how to ward their magic to keep you from scanning it," Ethan said, watching as she went down the list and circled names.

"Yes, but not the magic in their actual casts," she said. "And upperclassmen are well known for using copious magic around their cottages. I will know which cottage contains the saboteur, if it is one of them, and then I *will* know whose magic it was that cast the original seed."

Lady Harrington was *scary*.

Ethan had known that his entire life, but he hadn't actually been *afraid* of her until just now.

"I simply do this to put Mr. Trent's mind at ease," she said. "Because... Oh."

"You've been waiting out of decorum?" Shack asked.

"Politics, Mr. MacMillan," she answered.

"What is it?" Ethan asked.

"The elder Mr. Trent was in the building for dinner that day," she said. "It doesn't prove anything, one way or another, but I had hoped that he had missed his entire day that day, as he often does, and would rule himself out."

"It doesn't make any sense," Ethan said, shaking his head. "My brother wouldn't have any reason to cooperate with the Superiors. He lives for taking on my dad's role someday. He basically believes he is *on* the Council, now."

"You aren't wrong," Lady Harrington said, rolling up the two lists and putting them away. "I'd just hoped to rule him out preemptively. You appeared worried."

"I'm not," Ethan said.

"No, you look worried," Shack said. "Have since I told you that I got signal at your brother's cottage."

Lady Harrington frowned.

"What is it?" she asked.

"Nothing," Ethan said. It was. It was *nothing*.

"Speak," Lady Harrington said, and Ethan shook his head.

"It's just that Elvis really hated Valerie. From the very first. He was... Anyway, I know he was supposed to get on her good side, and he wouldn't do it, because he... He just hated her too much."

"By that logic, anyone in the school might merit suspicion," Lady Harrington said. "They all dislike her presence."

Ethan hadn't been sure how aware of that Lady Harrington might have been.

"Yeah," he said. "Maybe."

She frowned, then stood.

"Come with me," she said, walking around her desk.

"Where are we going?" Shack asked.

"A young man who suspects his brother of such treason, sincerely or otherwise, realistically or otherwise, deserves to know, if only to heap coals on his own head for his misjudgment of his sibling's character," she said, opening the office door. "I told you to go down to the visitor cottages," she said more loudly, and Mrs. Young looked over, then shook her head.

"You invaded your brother's living space without invitation, and I expect you to apologize to him personally," Lady Harrington said. Ethan sighed.

"Seriously? You didn't even have the heat turned on at the visitor cottages, did you? We were just supposed to sit down there and shiver while the upperclassmen did whatever they feel like, like always?"

"It is not for you to question my authority," Lady Harrington said, opening the door to the office and leading the way down the hallway.

If it weren't for, like, *everything*, Ethan would have been having the time of his life.

Shack followed along behind, hands in his pockets, unconcerned as he ever was when Ethan was about to get in big trouble. It didn't matter how many times Shack got in trouble *with* him, Ethan always took the brunt of everything because no one could actually *believe* that someone who acted as not-guilty as Shack did had any *real* hand in what had happened to merit punishment.

Which meant that Shack was - almost - always on the loose to spring Ethan when he got himself grounded or sent away or whatever.

Ethan had been a hard kid on his parents, as he looked at it. Not that they hadn't been hard parents on him.

They walked across the lawns, the chill in the air tolerable now with the sun overhead. Ethan realized he'd missed lunch in the intensity of searching for cottages with cellular service.

Lady Harrington glanced at Ethan, and he pointed at Elvis' cottage.

"It's not him," Shack murmured. "We both know he wouldn't do that."

Ethan nodded.

He did know.

He knew.

But Merck has given Elvis a *mission*. An honest-to-goodness Council-mandated mission to spy on Valerie Blake. And Elvis had blown it because he couldn't stand that Valerie had been allowed in at Survival School.

Ethan had never known his brother to pass up an opportunity like that.

Lady Harrington knocked, and one of the other roommates opened the door. She took a step back and raised an eyebrow at Ethan.

So.

The cover story was actually the one they were running with.

"Um," he said. "We were…"

"No," she said sternly. "You need to assemble all of the roommates from this building to apologize to them."

Elvis' roommate grinned and stepped back.

"Guys," he called. "Guys, Lady Harrington is frog-marching him."

Ethan rubbed the side of his face, and the rest of the cottage emerged.

"Um," he said again. "I'm supposed to…"

"No," Lady Harrington said again. "Do it right."

He looked back at her and she raised her eyebrows.

She was *good*.

"Right," he said. "I'm sorry I talked everyone into coming up here instead of going down to the visitor cottages like we were supposed to. If you want help cleaning up or anything…"

"Kitchen needs cleaning," Elvis said. "And the bathroom."

Ethan dropped his shoulders.

That was real, for what it was worth.

He was going to have to go clean his brother's bathroom.

Probably for real.

He sighed, then looked back at Lady Harrington, who raised her eyebrows higher at him.

He dropped his head and shuffled through the group of young men, looking back once.

"Where do you keep your cleaning stuff?" he asked.

Shack and Lady Harrington followed, and Shack rolled his jaw to the side then went in with Ethan to get a basket of cleaning supplies from under the sink where Elvis showed them. Lady Harrington crossed her arms, and Ethan tipped his head to the side.

Was she *really* going to make him do this?

Couldn't she just do her magic check-'em thing and let him off the hook?

She tipped her head the other direction.

Did he deserve this?

For suspecting his brother of sabotage? Of being willing to let students - Ethan's friends - *die*?

He was being ridiculous.

Elvis *wouldn't* do that.

No matter how much he loathed Valerie.

He nodded and turned, going back to the bathroom and setting to work.

Thing was, he'd never *cleaned* a bathroom before, and he spent the next fifteen minutes staring at the bottles and glancing at the words printed on them like they were going to tell him what he needed to do without actually *reading* them.

"Mr. Trent," Lady Harrington said, and Ethan stuck his head out of the bathroom.

"Yes, Headmistress?" he asked.

That was laying it on thick, and felt wrong even as he said it, but she shook her head.

"The Elder Mr. Trent," she said. Elvis shoved himself off of the table where he'd been watching Shack clean up drinks from off of the counter.

"Yeah?" Elvis answered.

"This is your room, is it not?" Lady Harrington asked. He walked quickly past her to close the door.

"Yeah," he said. "Sorry. I didn't... I would have cleaned if I'd known you were going to be here today."

"The warding on the door is quite... unusual," Lady Harrington said. "Especially for a Light School graduate."

He shrugged.

"My dad has been teaching me how to ward a door since I was a kid."

"No one helped you with it?" Lady Harrington asked, and he shook his head.

"No. That's all my casting."

Ethan felt his stomach start to sink.

"I see," Lady Harrington said. "You need to come with me, I'm afraid."

Elvis started to say something off-putting, jovial even, and then Ethan saw his brother realize it.

Realize what he'd just admitted.

To Lady Harrington.

He shook his head and bolted past her, making for the front door.

He made it three steps before Shack flattened him.

Fallout

As long as they sat very, very still, no one asked them to go back to their room.

So Shack and Ethan scarcely breathed, sitting there in the office as an ever-quickening stream of the who's-who of the Council-controlled magic community arrived at the school and went into the main conference room.

They should have moved to the cafeteria or one of the classrooms by now, but the shouting coming out of the conference room suggested that no one was really thinking about pragmatic things like that.

Mr. Tannis and Mr. Benson had shown up early, but things had been loud on the other side of that door - reframed, since Shack had broken it down - ever since Merck Trent had shown up with half the council. Apparently they'd been in session.

It was dark outside by now, and Ethan was occasionally aware of just how hungry he was after two skipped meals, but he wasn't moving.

He wasn't moving until someone told him what his brother had done and *why*.

And who was after Valerie.

And what the Council was going to *do* about it.

He kept his fingernails clipped short, but he still had fingernail marks in his palms from how tight his fists had sat, clenched, all afternoon and all evening.

He was seething, and he couldn't even *speak* for fear that Mrs. Young would look over and shoo them away.

The door opened once more, and Mr. Benson lifted his chin at Ethan and Shack.

"We need to speak with you," he said, taking a step back against the door and putting out an arm. It was the motion of invitation, but nothing about the way he moved suggested this was voluntary. Ethan looked over at Shack, and Shack nodded.

"You might have to hold me back," Ethan said under his breath, and Shack snorted.

"He's only got a problem if someone has to hold *me* back," Shack answered. "He killed my friends."

Ethan nodded, and they walked past Mr. Benson and into the packed-out conference room.

Elvis sat at one end of the table, haughty as ever.

"Why?" Ethan asked.

He hadn't planned on speaking, but the word was out the same way his foot was going to catch him on the next stride forward. His body compelled it just to keep him from falling.

Elvis looked over at him dismissively.

Exactly the way Elvis had looked at him any other given day.

"You aren't here to discuss any of that," Lady Harrington started, but Ethan was still falling.

"Like *hell*," he said. "He got our friends killed, and he's got people out there *hunting* Valerie. She would *be here* if it weren't for him."

"We are all concerned for Miss Blake's safety, as well as Miss Mills," Mr. Tannis said. "It's why you are allowed to be a part of this conversation at all."

Ethan looked hard at Lady Harrington, trying to figure out how much she might have told the Council.

She still thought that he was on the Council's side, after all, didn't she? What other side would there be?

Before he found his next words, Shack answered Mr. Tannis.

"You may be concerned about them, but we aren't going to help you until we get some answers. We aren't chesspieces."

"You have no right," Yasmine's mom said. "I lost my daughter to this animal. You have lost *nothing*. You make no demands here."

Ethan looked at Shack and they agreed wordlessly, turning back toward the door.

Mr. Benson was standing there with his arms crossed.

Mr. Benson was a tall guy, stout in an in-the-classroom-all-day kind of way, but sturdy if by force of will alone. Shack could go through him, but it wasn't going to be neat.

"Do better," Mr. Benson said. "This isn't the time for

ultimatums."

"Sure it is," Shack said, once more before Ethan could speak. "You've been going around behind closed doors, behind *locked* doors, keeping everything away from us about the war, about how it was going on right in our own school, because we're just *students*. We aren't real people who deserve to know what's going on because this is our *lives* you people are talking about. We graduate, and you're going to toss us into the wood chipper right along behind all the rest of them, and you're hoping if we don't find out about how *bad* it is, we'll get caught up in the *glory* and the potential for power plays and we'll go right along with it. I'm done with their brand of evil, and you just go along."

Ethan didn't turn to stare at his friend.

In his head, he certainly did, but he kept his eyes forward.

Shack.

Dude had passion.

He just didn't bring it out very often.

"That's *enough*, Oswald," Mrs. MacMillan said. Shack turned his attention to his mother.

"No," he said. "We're just starting. Last time you were here, you threatened to send us into the darkness for not being willing to help you *find* Valerie. You turn up that one of the Council brats - the heir apparent, no less - is behind multiple *deaths*, and you expect us to just fall back in line? No."

"Hell no," Ethan echoed.

"I expect you to behave like the soldiers and like the proper children of Council leaders that you were raised to be," Merck said. Ethan gave his father a cold look, and Lady Harrington stood.

"I expect you to put others' lives ahead of your own anger," she said coolly.

The room went still.

She nodded.

"You are *right* that there are people trying to find Miss Blake, and that none of us like to consider what would happen to her if the Superiors managed to catch up with her. If she is with her mother, she will likely die, both of them will. Her mother is compromised so long as Valerie is not somewhere *safe*, and that place should be *here*."

"She should be in a safehouse," Yasmine's mom said. Most of the Council members nodded agreement.

"No," Ethan started to argue, but Lady Harrington held up a hand that felt particularly intended for him.

"You are being short-sighted," Lady Harrington said. "You believe that you can make the most out of her by keeping her nearby and under your direct influence, and I certainly understand the environment that has evolved those thoughts. You think much the same of Susan Blake. But I have spent more time around either of them than anyone else in this room, save the two young men, and I believe I have ample authority to tell you that that is the *wrong* way to handle either of them. You don't tell them what to do. You don't try to *contain* them. You feed them information - coherent and good faith information - and you hope like hell that they see things like you do, at the end of it. You lie to them *once*, you put your own interests ahead of theirs, ahead of your responsibility to consider theirs, they will walk away and they will not look back."

"Easy thing for a schoolteacher to say," Ann's dad said.

"Watch your mouth," Mr. Benson answered, and Ethan clenched his jaw to control a smile.

"If you want Susan to work in your interests, giving her compelling cause. If you want Valerie to join your efforts, give her *compelling cause*. But freely, and with all the knowledge you can safely offer her. Anything else is destined to blow up in your faces, much as it already has."

"You're laying the blame for *this* at *our* feet?" Yasmine's mom asked, outraged.

"You had a student working with our enemies under your nose for almost six months," Merck said. She looked at him with a chilling lack of defensiveness.

"Would you like to have a conversation about *how* and *why* he came to be enrolled at my school?" she asked.

"I deserved to be here more than she does," Elvis said.

"She is a hundred times the magic user you will ever be," Lady Harrington said without looking at him. "And that is not without significant respect for the work that you are capable of doing."

"I put a hole in your defenses that you are never going to repair," Elvis said casually. "There's no way to do it. I watched Mr. Tannis and Mr. Jamison work at it for *months* now, and neither of them made a dent in it. Even your precious Valerie couldn't eliminate it. You may as well just close down the school. It isn't like you're teaching anyone anything, anymore."

Shack shifted, and Ethan put his hand on his friend's elbow.

Yes.

That.

That deserved to be punched in the mouth over it.

But.

Ethan was watching Lady Harrington's face, and she didn't look beat.

"A school is not a building," she said. "It is a collection of knowledge and those with the interest to seek it."

"Only if you can keep everyone inside from getting dead," Elvis said.

Ethan looked at his brother.

Elvis had always had an *ego*. And he'd been a lot more motivated by power than idealism. But Ethan had identified with both of those. It had been unquestioned in Ethan's mind that he would have been *exactly* like Elvis if he had had the combination of his brother's superior looks and his superior birth order.

"Is this what you are, when the hope of running the Council slips away from you?" Ethan asked. "Because I've never been *that*, whatever it is."

Elvis sighed.

"Do you know why Dad picked me over you?" Ethan's brother asked.

"You got here first," Ethan answered, and Elvis shook his head.

"He didn't tell me that I was going to take his spot on the Council until I was a teenager. He picked me over you because you were a whiny brat and you weren't ever going to do anything but whine and rebel. But he couldn't have *ever* picked you because you and your dark magic weren't ever going to get within a *mile* of the Council. The Council is the *best* magic, and it isn't you and it isn't *her*."

"It's funny how the Council is packed out with a bunch of purists," Shack said. The temperature in the room went ice cold, and Ethan had a half a second where he wasn't sure who he was supposed to be looking at to not give away that he knew *exactly* why.

Lady Harrington.

Better than anyone else in his range of vision, or the table.

"You took lives, and you will answer for it," Lady Harrington said. "You coordinated with the Superiors, and you will answer for it. This conversation, I remind *all* sitting at this table, is not about Elvis Trent. Or Ethan Trent. Or the Council. It is about getting Miss Blake and Miss Mills someplace safe."

"Into protective custody," Yasmine's mom said again.

"We will discuss what happens to her after we have her," Merck answered, looking at Ethan.

It was supposed to - *supposed* to - signal to Ethan that there was wiggle room to *maybe* leave her at Survival School instead.

It was a ploy.

It didn't matter how right Lady Harrington was - and Ethan knew she was dead on the money - the Council wasn't going to give her up. They were going to try to get in her ear and get her to play whatever games were going on, on their side of the closed doors.

"I'm not going to help you," Ethan said. "I told you that."

"You'd rather she be *out there*?" Mr. Tannis asked.

Ethan scratched the back of his head.

"If it were in my power - and it isn't - but if it were, I would go get Sasha and bring her back here. She deserves to be here. But Valerie? I'm not going to try to help the Council find or control her. No way."

"Cold, for you to rather she *die* than work with us," Mrs. MacMillan said.

He needed leverage.

He *wanted* Valerie back.

Wanted her back *now*.

But they would use everything that had happened as a pretense to go against her mom's stated intentions for her, to usurp guardianship and award it to the Council, and whisk her away.

He licked his lips.

"She's a natural," he said. "You can't hold her. She'll get out. And if she has to escape *from* you, she won't come back here. She won't come back anywhere."

Lady Harrington nodded.

"I can't imagine trying to contain that young woman."

"It would be for her own safety," Mrs. MacMillan said. "We are all concerned about keeping her *safe*. The things that the Superiors *won't* do to get ahold of her and try to neutralize Susan? She is in *danger*."

"She held the demons out of her room," Ethan said. "She defused a bomb. It seems like she's the only one *not* in danger, and then only because of *him*."

"There is a hole in the defenses here," Merck said. "We are going to have to discuss shutting the school down."

The room went very cold again, and Lady Harrington shook her head.

"This is not the time nor the place for *that* conversation. Within the confines of her room, Valerie is safe until we determine the correct plan to move forward. I believe that we can mount a significant defense against and surrounding the magic that Elvis Trent planted in the girls' dorm wing, and that we could make it through to the end of the semester before ripping everything out down to the foundations to remedy it."

"Won't work," Elvis muttered.

"Who taught you to do that cast?" Ethan asked, looking at his brother. Elvis turned the corners of his mouth down, smug, and Lady Harrington held up a hand once more.

"*Not* this conversation, Mr. Trent," she said. "Please refrain."

Ethan glanced at her, then turned his head away.

"You're suggesting that you take responsibility for her until we figure out what to do about the school and the hole in your defenses that can't be closed," Merck Trent said.

"I'm suggesting that she would be much more willing to return here, knowing that we have found the source of the attacks and are working toward a plan to amply ward the known issue with the defenses. More importantly, I'm suggesting that your son would be more willing to aid in our search for her."

"Martha Cox is going to find her eventually," Ann's dad said. "Just let her work. We don't need help from anyone here, at all."

Ethan sighed.

"I can find her faster than Mrs. Cox can," he said. "And I don't like her being out there. I will help Lady Harrington find her, but only under the condition that she stays here."

"I can't promise that, regardless," Merck said. "If we have to shut down the school…"

Would he really shut down the entire school just to justify taking Valerie?

It was possible.

But.

This had been *her* condition, not his.

If they tried to box her up… Well, he could find her again, so long as she gave him another cast to do it, and he'd come break her out, if she hadn't already done it for herself.

"I'll do it if you promise to let her stay here as long as you keep the school open," Ethan said.

And what was his father's promise worth?

They both knew.

Just as much as it had in it for him.

How was he going to sell this as not a complete push-over?

"Can Lady Harrington guarantee her adequate supervision, so long as she is here, to keep her safe?"

"Oh, she won't like that," Lady Harrington murmured. "I will have one of the teachers posted at the end of the dorm wing at all times. Mrs. Gold is already there, and you already know what she's capable of."

"Not enough," Merck said. "Two teachers posted on the hall and one at each classroom."

Ethan closed his eyes, wondering if he was even going to *tell* Valerie about the terms, if he wanted her to come back at all.

"Very well," Lady Harrington said. "But you should not underestimate the capabilities of this faculty. We've made steady progress even as we've been trying to purge the original cast, itself."

"Won't work…" Elvis murmured.

No one even looked at him this time.

"All right," Merck said, looking at Ethan. "Tell me how you would find her."

Ethan shook his head.

"No. You leave. You take him with you and you throw him down in the Darkness where he belongs for what he did. Lady Harrington can help us figure out how to track down Valerie."

Merck looked at Mrs. MacMillan.

"Are you happy with that?" he asked. She took a very long moment, then nodded.

"It will put this very unhappy chapter behind us and allow us to refocus our energies where they belong," she said. "I am quite disappointed, though, in both boys for not stepping forward that they had important knowledge. They should not expect to go unpunished for withholding it from the Council."

"A conversation for another day," Lady Harrington said, standing. "If that will be all."

There was a general shuffling and untangling as all of the adults made their way out of the room. Merck and Mrs. MacMillan went to stand on either side of Elvis' chair.

"Don't make this more of a scene than it already is," Merck said, and Elvis shrugged, standing.

"You're making too big a deal out of her. She's a nothing. Doesn't know any magic, and way too dark. She isn't one of us."

"She is a tool to be utilized by the Council at our discretion," Merck said, a low growl. Ethan wasn't sure if he was supposed to be able to hear it or not, but it hardly came as a surprise. That was how Merck always talked about the war, at home.

Always.

Finally, it was just Mr. Tannis, Mr. Benson, Lady Harrington, and Ethan and Shack in the room.

"Mrs. Young, you can retire for the evening," Lady Harrington said, going to stand at the open door. "Mr. Benson, Mr. Tannis, will you do final rounds, please? I expect we are going to have to endure shenanigans tonight after letting everyone loose today."

"Are you sure you don't want us here?" Mr. Tannis asked. "If this is going to be complex magic…"

"I will resummon you, if I have need of your talents," Lady

Harrington said, waiting for both men to leave, then closing the door and going to sit at the table again.

It was possible, just possible, that she looked a shade tired.

"I certainly hope, after that display, that you have a *promising* lead on Valerie?" she asked, rubbing her temples with her fingers.

"I can find her," Ethan said. "She gave me something and she told me what to do with it, and… Apparently I'll just go straight *to* her."

"She handed you a tracking spell?" Lady Harrington asked. "How intriguing."

Ethan checked his watch.

It was almost eleven.

"I don't know where she is," he said. "Or how far away it is. And once I use the cast, I don't know how long it will last."

She nodded.

"We could leave now, but it has been a very trying day, and driving through the night is not something I would choose without compelling reason."

"I don't like her being out there," Ethan said.

"We should go now," Shack said. "Everyone is looking for her. We need to be the first ones to get there."

Lady Harrington nodded, then roused herself and nodded again.

"Very well. You are correct, and I am simply overtired. I will regain myself in the car."

"Oh," Ethan said. "I wasn't going to… It was just going to be us."

The woman looked at him with clever eyes and shook her head.

"No. Not on the trip when we intend to bring her back. I will not let you meander off on your own once more from under my nose."

"No one meandered," Ethan said.

"Though I was thinking maybe we could stop and get some food," Shack said. Ethan twisted his mouth and nodded.

"Yeah. We should do that."

Lady Harrington sighed and rose.

"Then, gentlemen, shall we go?"

Valerie looked out the window, then went back to weaving strands of the curtains together with bits of throw pillow.

Her mother had lived in this little shack on the beach a lot of times. Valerie could feel it, the way the magic in the place curled around itself tightly, woven into the very fibers of the limited permanent fixtures.

It was something, and she was weaving it into more.

Just not *fast* enough.

Martha Cox was in the kitchen, working with a much more ample supply of ingredients, and while Sasha had tried to go take things from Martha's supply, Hanson's mom had rebuffed her aggressively, telling her that Sasha and Valerie should have been in a back room, and that there wasn't any way that Martha was going to hold off the Superiors on her own, either way.

"I don't care what art project she's got going on up there," Martha had said, and Sasha had relented.

Valerie might not have, but her hands were busy.

"What next?" Sasha asked.

"Are there any hangers in the closet?" Valerie asked.

"Let me check."

Valerie nodded, counting weaves.

She'd never been the arts-and-crafts type of kid. She preferred being out and exploring, but it wasn't entirely unlike some of the things she and Hanson had built as kids, fortresses and castles and swords. It was just a matter of getting the pieces to lie right.

Only, now, there was *magic* involved, not just gravity, and everything got ten times more complicated.

She could do this.

She *had* to do this.

She tugged at the curtain once more, then opened the window a fraction, tucking the end of the long braid under the window and closing it again. The tail of curtain threads now formed an X across the window, one from each side, woven in with fabrics from all over the house that were touched routinely.

It was like the seaweed, but *not* like it, and Valerie was moving too fast to think about it more than that.

"People," Sasha said. "I see people."

Valerie nodded.

"Let your cast down," Martha said from the kitchen. "Or else they're going to just blow us all up through it and not have to do anything but watch from outside."

"Don't know if you've heard, but they *do* want me alive," Valerie said, tying bits of this and that to the coat hanger and hanging it from the curtain rod.

Something twanged and clicked, a loop of magic she hadn't even been planning on creating springing into being, and she looked up at the hanger.

A coat hanger.

"They want a *rumor* that you're still alive," Martha called. "Even if they *don't* manage to save your life from the cast, your mom *thinking* you might still be alive would be enough."

"Ma," Hanson yelled from the bedroom. "Would you... just..."

"Just telling them like it is," Martha yelled back.

"They can *hear* you," Sasha hissed, ducking below the window.

True enough, there were four adults out there in the front yard, hidden in among the trees and creeping toward the house. They were dragging something along between them, sort of sweeping up the magic from the house and pushing it in tighter and tighter. Valerie could feel it like a physical pressure, though she didn't know what they intended to do about it. The force it was going to take to keep going forward would build and eventually one of the... Oh, yup, that was it. Eventually, one of the magics would break, and they were betting it was hers.

Well.

That just wasn't going to happen.

Valerie ran back to the kitchen, looking at what Martha had laid out on the table.

"That's all defensive," she said.

"I went to the School of Magic Survival and I spent the rest of my adult life following around your mom," Martha said. "It's not like I have a lot of experience with anything else."

Valerie twisted her mouth to the side, coming to look at one of the casts.

They had a dry, textbook feel to her for reasons she couldn't have explained.

"If you..." she started, and Martha slapped her hand.

"We are outgunned in every way possible," the woman said. "They are going to come through that door, and if you want *any* hope of turning back the first *volley* of attacks on us, you will *leave those alone.*"

It occurred to Valerie for the first time that this might not have just been temper.

Martha Cox was afraid.

"We don't die here," Valerie said, and Martha looked up at her, giving Valerie her full attention for just that moment.

"Oh? Is that so? How would you know? What could you *possibly* have up your sleeve to prevent it?"

"If you knew that we were in that much trouble, why did you even come?" Valerie asked.

"Hanson was in here," she said. "I knew it the minute I stopped the car. This is where he *would* be, isn't it?"

"Of course," Valerie said. "You left him, though."

"He was safe," Martha said. "He was safe until the *minute* he decided he was going to come try to beg for your forgiveness, for betraying you. You're the one who got him killed. He could have gotten a scholarship. Baseball? Basketball? Maybe even football."

"Ma, I'm not *that* good," Hanson called.

"Yes, you are," Martha yelled back. "And you could have gone to *college*. Lived a *normal* life."

Valerie looked at the door.

She needed sand from the threshold.

"He isn't going to die, and neither are any of us," Valerie said. "That isn't how this ends."

"You don't know anything," Martha muttered. "People just *fail* to come home all the time. Your own mom could be dead by now, and you wouldn't even know it."

"This is how I work," Valerie said. "I don't know what it means, but this is how I *work*. They aren't coming through that door."

Martha put her hands down on the table.

"So I should just sit back and let the master work then?" she asked.

"Would have been more helpful if you'd given me your stuff ten minutes ago," Valerie said, then opened the door and took a handful of sand from just outside of it, closing it again quickly as the power of her casts whooshed out the door like a balloon.

Worth it.

She went back to the front window, pouring the sand across the sill in a solid line, then running her hand across it to flatten it.

Sasha stood at her elbow as Valerie started drawing symbols in the sand.

She used her little finger to do it as intricately and as small as she could, glad of the wide windowsill to work on.

The symbols from the door at the apartment.

The one over the window in her room.

The ones carved into the bottom of Susan Blake's shoes.

The one Susan had drawn on Valerie's backpack her first day of first grade.

A dozen symbols, and there were more.

"More sand," Valerie said, all but a whisper, going to the window in the kitchen and brushing the dust off of it as Sasha ran for the door.

More sand, more symbols, more pressure.

The men with the rope out front were trying to crush her, but Valerie... Valerie wasn't the type to crush like that, and her mother had trained her.

She didn't even know how, but Susan had trained her exactly how to do this. Every symbol hidden all over the house came back to her and she stepped back, looking at them.

"Don't breathe on them," she said, going to the side door and beginning to trace out the main protection symbol there.

"What *is* that?" Martha asked as the door began to scorch under the potency of the magic. "Is that *dark* magic?"

"No," Sasha said. "It's fire magic, and it's one of Valerie's strengths."

Valerie didn't look over, but she wanted to.

Sasha said it with such matter-of-factness, like she'd known for some time.

Valerie was shocked at it as a simple revelation.

She was good at fire magic.

Yes.

That was true.

She felt the symbol click into place and she started drawing the next one.

"How far away are they?" she asked, and Sasha went to look. Valerie heard the girl squeal as she ducked back behind the window, but Valerie only hoped that Sasha had managed not to disturb the sand.

They were close.

Close enough for Sasha to see their faces, and for them to see hers.

Valerie focused on the second symbol, letting her hand work over it and over it and over it as the door smoldered and smoked, leaving a char in the painted wood.

They fit like lock and key, the two symbols.

"What *is* that?" Martha asked again.

"My mom taught me," Valerie answered, going back to look out the window.

"She didn't teach you anything, I thought," Martha called, and Valerie shrugged.

"I guess I was wrong."

The men were struggling against the rope, a great, long trawling thing with tendrils dragging along behind it in the yard, like a gutted-out fishing net.

Her magic was holding.

It was *strong*.

She saw the closest man, one who took a moment from yelling at the others to look at the window, and she met his eye.

He was an adult, maybe older than her parents. He had a grizzled chin and a scar down his face, and he had rough hands - he was close enough for her to see it from here.

He'd been in the last war.

And he was looking her in the eye through the window of the

beach house as he tried to break through the defenses and come… to take her? to kill her? It didn't matter.

She was going to stop him.

He took out a gun and pointed it at her, and she stepped out of sight, watching the men on the other end of the rope struggle.

Finally, they lay down the rope and started getting out other things, trying to attack her magic from other angles.

It wasn't perfect.

It had been hasty and it was literally cast in sand.

She was moving again, going through the house and looking for things to shore it up.

"We need to go after them," she called out to Martha. "If we don't, they're just going to keep trying."

"Don't know what you expect to do," Martha called.

Valerie went through the front room, checking the window there, but it wasn't ever opened, and it didn't have any sense that it would let someone *through* the way the front window and the kitchen window did. Not that *people* ever came through it, but just that it was a point of entrance or exit of any kind. She glanced at Hanson as he sat in the bathtub on her way past, and he frowned. She didn't remember hearing him move.

"I feel silly," he said.

"Stay in there," she answered, going into the bedroom where she and Sasha had slept and looking at that window.

The window faced the ocean, and it had that sense of coming and going, of sitting and watching the outside world, bringing it *in*.

"Sasha," she called over her shoulder. "Sand."

Sasha showed up a moment later with another handful of sand, and Valerie spread it, using a different set of markings. These were ones she'd seen her father use, though it shocked her that she could remember them.

They were… pointier.

They were going somewhere, but Valerie had no idea where.

She thought of going through the obstacle courses that Dr. Finn had set up, one step at a time, solve one problem at a time, look for the intuitive solution that got her to the goal by the most direct - if least obvious - path.

She needed to run them off.

The way to do that was to prove to them that they were more likely to die than capture her.

Right?

Or was there another way?

Was *undefeatable* possible?

Could she get them to give up by show of defensive force?

She smiled.

No.

Not by show of defensive force.

By making it impossible for them to beat her defenses.

She went back to the front room, looking at the array of casts the men were setting out, trying to break through her layered defense.

It took her almost no energy to hold her position, and they were exhausting serious resources trying to chip away at it.

Defense was easier.

Her dad had taught her that.

She could just hold, withstand, and let them exhaust their energy, and it would cost her almost nothing.

And then she could go after them, if she still had the resources.

That was the *core* tactic of the School of Magic Survival, even if no one had explicitly said it yet. That was what they were teaching her to do.

Except it wasn't.

Dr. Finn never told her to sit back and let the magic casts in a practicum room wind down or wear out or expire. He sent her in to go after them.

And Valerie didn't want to sit and watch and wait to see if they were going to succeed at breaking her defenses.

They were good.

They would hold.

Right up until they didn't.

No.

She wasn't going to wait.

She had a plan and she was going to *do* it, because she wasn't going to play to not lose.

She was going to play to win.

Her *mom* taught her that.

"I need those," Valerie said, going back into the kitchen.

"No, Martha answered.

"Ma," Hanson called. "Give her what she needs."

"No," Martha answered, louder, for Hanson's benefit. "I have my casts ready."

"That one isn't going to work," Valerie said, pointing. She didn't know why. Didn't even know what it was. She just knew that it was defective somehow.

Martha frowned and poked at it, pushing something back into alignment, and it popped in some way that Valerie didn't yet have the vocabulary to describe it.

She nodded.

"Okay, it will now. But they're draining. If my defenses hold up long enough, your casts are going to be done before they even get in the door. Let me use what you have."

Some of it was spent.

A *lot* of it was spent.

But there were things she could disassemble and use, still, if she worked quickly.

"Come look," Sasha said. "Look how hard they're working to get through what Valerie has up."

Martha looked down the hallway at Hanson.

"Ma," he called. "Please."

Finally, Hanson's mother stood, walking cautiously to the window.

"Careful," Valerie called. "At least one of them has a gun."

"And they wouldn't hesitate to shoot me," Martha murmured, going to stand next to the window and peeking out through the curtains.

She watched for almost a full minute, shaking her head.

"Those are serious casts going on out there," she said, looking back at Valerie. "They're leaving scorch marks on the grass already."

There wasn't *much* grass, and the short scrub grass that was growing out front wasn't exactly the kind to catch fire easily.

Valerie nodded.

"Let me go after them," she said.

"What are you planning?" Martha asked, coming back to the kitchen.

Valerie shook her head.

"That's not how I work. I just put my hands on things and they *do* things, and it works."

Martha frowned.

"Naturals are weird," she said. Valerie shrugged.

"You've met Dr. Finn, then," she said. Martha pursed her lips sarcastically.

"When I knew him, he was just Gregory," she said. "And he was all the way weird, even without magic."

"Still is," Valerie said. "But he's a really good teacher and a really, really good magic user. Probably better than anyone else at school, for what he does."

Martha shook her head, then threw up her hands.

"If we all die, I guess it doesn't change much," she said, and Valerie slid quickly into the chair, pulling things apart and reorganizing them, sorting them the way she'd done in class and in Mr. Tannis' room, letting her hands put things where she wanted them to be.

She didn't know where she was going until she got there.

Piece by piece, she started assembling things, then she frowned and sat up.

"Hanson," she called. "Is there a pair of nail clippers on there? In one of the drawers, maybe?"

Hanson scrambled out of the tub as the house shuddered, and Valerie looked up at the ceiling.

It was not *much* of a house.

Seriously, she wasn't sure how much there was holding down the roof. If it weren't for how beautiful the days were, day after day, it would have been a dreary little place, and it wasn't meant to hold up under that kind of physical force.

She'd wondered, once, how it survived that long against

hurricanes, but figured that was a Susan Blake trick and not something she needed to worry about.

"If you're planning on using fingernails, they tend to be more potent if you peel them rather than cut them," Martha said from the counter.

Valerie looked over her shoulder and nodded.

"Thank you," she said, realizing immediately that Martha was right.

She put her fingers into her mouth, one after the next, settling on her ring finger. She bit through the fingernail and tore it off, then dropped it on the table, continuing to work.

The cast came together in... seconds.

It was just sitting there, waiting for her.

She put it all together, then put her index finger back in her mouth and drew a circle around it in saliva.

Which was outright gross, truly, but...

That was what she was supposed to do.

She put her hands down on the table, to either side of the cast, and she looked up.

Sasha was watching her with an intentness that suggested she would have been taking notes if she'd had paper sitting out.

Hanson was leaning against the wall in the kitchen.

Should have been in the tub, but she wasn't going to remind him.

Besides, he deserved to be here. The tub was only going to save him if the roof collapsed, and even then...

Nevermind.

Martha was leaning against the sink with her arms crossed.

Skeptical, but not completely dismissive, just now.

Valerie nodded.

This had an all-or-nothing feel to it.

Between the ingredients that had already expired by the time she got to them and the ones that she was consuming for this cast, there wasn't much left.

If this failed, she could continue layering *some* defenses, with what she had for spoken casts and written casts, but the potions were exhausted.

And if the men outside had unlimited time and unlimited resources, they were going to make it through.

That much was… inescapable.

She could wait.

But it wasn't her instinct.

And so far, and everything that Dr. Finn had taught her, what she knew was to trust her instincts.

She spoke.

Six different languages, none of which she'd been able to speak or read before she'd come to school, diction like moving through a mechanical routine that simply allowed no other options, words that she would never be able to speak again unless she needed them for a cast.

It took thirty seconds, and then the walls popped and the whole house swayed. She closed her eyes and pressed down on the table, feeling the surge of power as the spell caught and rolled out, not a bubble like it had been in Mrs. Reynolds' room, but a flame front, burning and consuming any magic that wasn't hers, wasn't her mothers. She felt the tatters of Sasha's spellwork burn away, then the dark magic out front.

It had no hope.

No defense against the rage of magic coming at it.

Defensive magic that ate everything in front of it.

There were yells, and Sasha and Martha both ran to the front window to watch.

"There's a car," Sasha said. "Another one."

Valerie shook her head, still holding the spell, still consuming the casts that were set, the ones that were in progress, the ingredients themselves.

It was going to burn out.

Quickly.

The *instant* she let it go.

So she had to be sure she got it all.

She forced it out another foot and another, and Sasha yelled.

"It's Ethan," she said. "And Shack."

Valerie's head flew up.

Four men from The Pure, driven by Valerie's own magic,

straight at Shack and Ethan.

"We have to help them," she said, holding the spell for one more moment. "We have to get them in the house somehow."

"No," Sasha said, a smile in her voice. "No, Lady Harrington's with them…"

"Wow," Martha breathed. I didn't realize."

There was an awed pause, and Valerie let her cast go, standing.

"There's a reason she's headmistress," Sasha said. "I guess."

"Wow," Martha said again.

By the time Valerie got to the window, all she saw was Lady Harrington leading a very astonished-looking Shack and Ethan across the lawn, through the prone bodies of the four men.

"Are they…?" Valerie asked, and Sasha shrugged.

"Don't know."

"How did she *do* that?" Valerie asked. "She doesn't *have* anything."

"You…" Sasha said slowly. "You missed it."

Valerie went to the side door and opened it, going to stand out in the sand.

Ethan rushed up to hug her and she held on to him for a long time as Shack and Lady Harrington went inside.

"You're okay," he said.

"You're here," she answered.

"Would have been here earlier, but there was a crash on the interstate in Atlanta," he said, squeezing her hard.

"What was that cast we saw when we drove up?" Lady Harrington asked. "Was that yours, Mrs. Cox?"

"It was Valerie's," Martha answered.

"I thought as much," Lady Harrington said, and Valerie felt Ethan laugh silently.

"That woman is a *beast*," he said, just for her, and she sighed.

"You found the saboteur?" she asked, finally pulling away and taking his hand to go into the house.

"My brother," he said. She looked over at him, and he shrugged. "I didn't think he *could*, but he *did*."

She shook her head and tipped her temple to rest against his shoulder.

"I'm sorry," she said.

"We still have the issue of the cast that started all of this," Lady Harrington said as they closed the door behind them. "The school is compromised, and there is only so much I can do with that burr in our defenses."

"It's my job to take her to the Council," Martha said, stepping forward.

"No," Lady Harrington said. "I am taking her back to school."

"I have my job," Martha said. "And I found her."

"No," Lady Harrington said again. "I will not permit it."

There was something even stonier in her voice than Valerie recognized, and Ethan let go of Valerie's hand to put his arm around her in a motion that was somewhere between protective and supportive.

It had been a long day.

She let it go.

"She is the *path* to Susan Blake," Martha hissed. "And the Council needs Susan to *fall in line*. If we don't win this war, *everyone* could die."

"Frankly, I trust Susan and Grant more than the entire Council combined," Lady Harrington said, then pinched her mouth slightly. "Actually, I trust any *member* of the Council more than all of them combined, as I say it."

Valerie took a breath, then nodded.

"So everyone at school is safe if I go back?" she asked. "There isn't anyone there feeding information to the... the Superiors?"

"As far as I am aware, no," Lady Harrington said. "But we are going to increase our security on you, personally, until we get the cast settled out."

"Oh," Valerie said, just figuring out what Lady Harrington was talking about. "Oh, I can fix *that*."

Lady Harrington raised an eyebrow at her, and Valerie nodded.

"Yeah. Just. Can we go back, now? I'm tired."

"I expect you are," Lady Harrington said, collecting Sasha with a sweep of her arm and starting for the door again. Shack waited until the headmistress was past and then followed, like a rear guard of some sort.

Valerie was glad he was there.

"Are you coming, Mr. Cox?" Lady Harrington asked without looking back.

"Am I invited?" Hanson asked in return.

"You have a place at the school, if your mother chooses to send you there. As a student, not as a ward. I've heard a rumor that you have potential."

Valerie swallowed again as Ethan pivoted her around and opened the door.

"I will make a *full* report to Merck Trent," Martha called after them. "And you had better not lose her, in the meantime."

"Lock up when you leave," Valerie called over her shoulder as she went out once more into the cool air and the sunshine.

Headed back to the School of Magic Survival.

The mark on the wall just vanished.

Sasha had had to help her figure out all of the pieces that went into the spell, but sitting on the floor in the dorm hallway with all of the pieces - not just casting *elements*, but *tools* as well - with half the teaching staff gathered behind her and most every door on the hallway open despite Lady Harrington's repeated demands that the girls *close* their doors or face being sent away while Valerie worked, her hands knew what to do without Sasha needing to read out any more than the first instruction.

The mark had no chance any more than any of the casts at the beach had.

She turned her head to look back at Dr. Finn and Mr. Jamison, where they stood just off to the side behind her, and Dr. Finn nodded.

"Well cast, Miss Blake. We will resume our work on Monday."

He gave her a quick little smile and turned away, brushing through the crowd of teachers who were still trying to work out what Valerie had done. Mr. Jamison watched her for another minute, then nodded.

"You're just like her," he said quietly, then gave her a much more sincere smile and nodded again. Valerie pressed her lips and nodded back, turning back to the cast to dismantle it and make sure that it didn't go off again.

Strange thought, but she felt the potential in it just as the thought occurred to her, that the cast still had *way* too much power in it, and if she wanted to… she could take aim and use it on something else entirely.

What? She had no idea.

And that was why she was tearing it down.

But Daphne Leblanc had taught her a new tactic that she'd never used before, and a new method for employing the wand that Mr. Tannis had given her the previous semester.

Boy, what she wouldn't have given to have the *wand* with her in the beach shack…

She tucked the wand away in a pocket and stood, squatting to pick up the remains of the cast and brush the final bits onto a sheet of paper that she folded over and turned to Mr. Tannis to hand it to him.

"You can do whatever you want with that, but *I* would burn it," she said, and he nodded.

"We should have a conversation about what classes you want to take next semester," he said, looking at the impromptu envelope thoughtfully. "I think we may need to plan a curriculum around you, and now is the time to get started on that."

She wrinkled her nose.

"Do I have to be special?" she asked and he sighed at her.

"Don't underestimate how much everyone around you *wishes* they could do what you do. Not excluding myself."

She sighed.

"Tell me that when everyone's trying to kill you to get someone *else's* attention."

His brow creased just a fraction and the corner of his mouth came up.

"You think that I haven't been in the crosshairs, young lady?" he asked.

She frowned at him.

"You were in the war?"

Of course he was.

She *knew* that, even, if not factually, by circumstance. They'd come to him for support, first thing. He knew about how to fight.

"I narrowly avoided fatal casts more than once," he said. "I don't know what happened out there, but if you need to sit and talk it through with someone, my door is open. Can't imagine your faculty advisor *not* being available to you for such a thing."

He gave her a dry but genuine smile, then held up the envelope.

"I'm going to go analyze this," he said. "I will see you Monday."

"Monday," Valerie muttered, then turned to find Sasha once more.

"Monday?" Sasha asked, and Valerie shook her head.

"Everyone is all set for me to just pick back up where I was when I left off."

"Well," Sasha said quietly, then shook her head, glancing the length of the hallway where the teachers were still clustered and clumped, numbers of them going to poke at the wall where Valerie had just eradicated the spellwork there. "Come on."

Valerie followed Sasha back into their room and they each sat down on a bed.

It wasn't home.

Valerie still resented how she'd been *dumped* here and wouldn't *let* it be home.

But it was nice to be *back*.

Sasha looked at her bracingly, and Valerie went to lean against the wall, her feet out in front of her.

"Okay, what?" she asked.

"Are you going to do what the lady said? From this morning?" Sasha asked.

"Daphne?" Valerie asked. "What do you mean?"

"The woman," Sasha said. "In North Carolina. Are you going to go see her?"

Valerie shrugged.

"I don't know yet. I mean…" She chewed on the inside of her lip. "I want to talk to my mom."

"But you don't know when you'll *get* to," Sasha said.

"Do you think I should?" Valerie asked. "Go?"

"No," Sasha said emphatically. "I think we should stay here

and let the grown-ups do their jobs. Today…" She shook her head. "But we can't, can we? I mean, if the five of us… Hanson just *showed up*. That has to mean something, right?"

"Yeah," Valerie said. She wanted to challenge it, but there was no other explanation than that he *belonged* with them. "What did you guys talk about last night?"

Sasha blushed, looking away.

"Everything," she said. "Just… magic and school and you and Ethan and the Council and the beach and… Everything."

"He kissed you," Valerie said abruptly, and Sasha ducked her head. Valerie rolled her jaw to the side and nodded. "He did. He kissed you."

"Yes," Sasha said, blushing furiously.

"He's a student here, now," Valerie said with no small amount of astonishment. "He actually *goes* here."

"Yeah," Sasha said softly. "And you don't hate him or anything."

"Nope. I don't hate him or anything."

Sasha wound her arms together in front of her and twined her fingers, sitting with her knees against her shoulders and her chin on her arms.

"Can't we just… everything is perfect, now, right? Can't we just…?"

Valerie sighed.

"I don't know, Sasha," she said. "My parents are out there, *fighting* this, and maybe if I can help."

"Would your mom want you to go out there?" Sasha asked. "I mean… They came and took us. So. Yeah. They wanted us to *see*, but was there a lot more they wanted to show us, or was Von Lauv really kind of *if*? And then… you weren't safe here, and there was no way for us to come back, and so we kind of got… stuck?"

"I don't know," Valerie said again thoughtfully. "I want to *ask* her that. But… I mean, there's this whole *world* she never told me about, and when I did ask her, even when we were with her… Did she ever really *answer* anything directly? It's like, they're so tied up in their secrets that they can't ever give me a straight answer about anything, either of them."

"They did *tell* us a lot," Sasha said, tempering it, and Valerie nodded.

"And I'm grateful. I am. The Shadows…"

Sasha nodded.

"Yeah," the redhead said. "Yeah."

"Just. They had to show us, not tell us, and it was *complicated*. I just want a simple answer. Should I do this or shouldn't I?"

"I think if life were that simple, there wouldn't be wars," Sasha answered.

Valerie gave her a dour look and put her elbows on her knees.

"Wish you would stop sounding so smart," Valerie said. "You make me feel dumb."

There was a knock on the door and Valerie straightened. Sasha got up and went to open it.

"Let us in," Ethan hissed. "Before Mrs. Gold sees."

"Are you kidding me?" Sasha asked, moving out of the way as Ethan, Hanson, and Shack crept in. "We just got back and you three are willing to risk *suspension*? For what?"

Ethan threw himself onto the bed next to Valerie, who shifted away from him and gave him a sideways look.

"She has a point," she said. "You shouldn't be here. Say what you came to say and get out. I don't want to get in trouble today."

"Are you kidding?" Ethan asked with an easy smile. "You're the school's *hero*. Last *night*, my dad was threatening to shut the whole school down because of that cast, and you just got rid of it with the entire faculty watching. You're *untouchable*."

"But Hanson isn't," Sasha said, standing under Hanson's arm.

"They aren't going to catch us," Shack said. "We put up the right casts on our way down."

"Yeah, at midnight," Valerie said. "It's almost dinner time. *Everyone* is out."

"What did they say?" Ethan asked, sitting forward and putting his hand on Valerie's knee.

His eyes were earnest, so she didn't mock him.

Wanted to, but didn't.

"They said… see you Monday. Why? What?"

"Lady Harrington said she would post teachers at the end of

the dorm wing and outside of your classes," Shack said. "Only way she could get Ethan's dad to agree to let you come back here at all."

Valerie drew her head back.

"Oh, I'd like to see them try to make me go *anywhere* else," she said. Ethan grinned.

"That's what I told them," he said. "And Lady Harrington, too."

Valerie shook her head.

"No. If you guys are in danger, I'll do what I have to do, but…"

"No," Ethan interrupted. "No. Don't say that. It's a lever, and my dad *will* use it. Okay? He'll threaten to do all kinds of *terrible* things to me, and you know what, he may even be willing to go through with it, okay? But don't do it. Anything that he has to make a threat to *me* to make *you* do? I'd rather *I* go through it than you, because I *promise*, what he's asking you to do is worse. Okay?" He dodged his head to the side, trying to get directly into her eyeline. "I'm serious. Promise me."

Valerie shrugged.

"I don't…" she said slowly.

"Me, too," Shack cut in, easy enough. "Every word of it, me too."

She looked over at him, shaking her head.

"No. I won't *carry* that. I… I cast at someone and tried to *kill* him. And I… I still am not *over* it. I can't. Sometimes I can't even look at my hand because I can't believe I *did* that. I'm not going to be the thing that puts the two of you in danger. I don't care…"

"Promise," Sasha said softly. "You have to. You have to promise."

It was almost Valerie's mom's voice. Almost.

She had to promise.

"Because if I don't promise, it will work," Valerie said softly. Sasha nodded.

"If we all know, if we all *believe* that you wouldn't trade our safety for your cooperation, there's hope that they won't go through with it. It's the *only* hope."

"If what you have to do is worse, I don't want you to do it, Val," Hanson said.

"You don't have any *idea* what they could do to you," Valerie said, and Hanson shrugged, pulling Sasha closer against his side.

"Neither do you," he answered.

"But *they* do," Valerie said. "Especially Ethan and Shack."

"Exactly," Ethan said. "We know. And you *have* to promise. You *have* to."

Valerie shook her head, then moved back against the wall, putting her forehead against the knuckles of her closed fists. This time she didn't resent it when Ethan came to put his arm across her shoulders.

"It's war," he said softly, loud enough for the room to hear it. "You didn't ask to be a key player, but you *are*. What you decide *matters*. We don't want to be the reason that you make the wrong choice. None of us do. Promise. You'll do the right thing, and you won't let our parents push you around. We are something *else*, Valerie. You said it, and we all agreed. Don't let them own you."

She lifted her head, tears spilling down her face.

"Maybe I shouldn't have come back," she said. "This is a Council school. Maybe this is too close."

Ethan shook his head.

"The Council sponsors the school, but this is Lady Harrington's school. As long as she's here… She's more than I thought she was."

"She's my grandmother," Valerie said impulsively, and the room went quiet for a moment.

"That explains some things," Shack said after a minute.

"A lot of things," Ethan agreed.

Sasha was looking at Valerie with piercing eyes.

"What are you going to do?" her friend asked, and Valerie shook her head.

"Mr. Tannis wants to talk about my curriculum for next semester," she said. "That feels like a lifetime away."

"What do you mean?" Ethan asked Sasha, sensing that there was more to her question than the words indicated. Sasha intensified her look at Valerie, and Valerie sighed, giving Ethan and Shack the short version of what had happened with Daphne.

"She didn't *want* me to go," Valerie said. "And I don't want to go, either. I want to stay here and actually *learn* to do magic. The things my parents can do, guys... It's..."

"We grew up with it," Ethan said.

"We did," Sasha agreed, "but they're next level."

Valerie nodded.

"I thought they might be. I want to be like *that*."

"They're next level because they understand magic so much *better*," Sasha said. "Understanding the alignments and the configurations, I was learning stuff just in a few lectures in one *day* that might have taken me months to master, here or with my mom."

"Could you figure it out on your own, now?" Shack asked. "Knowing what you know now?"

Sasha shrugged.

"Maybe."

"Can you teach us?" Shack pressed, and Sasha stiffened, looking at the floor for a moment as she considered that.

"Yes," she said abruptly. "That's exactly what I have to do. I need to... my notes. I need to go through my notes..."

She went digging through her bag, getting out her binder and threw herself onto her bed, poring over it for a moment. Valerie looked at her roommate with great appreciation for a moment, then she nodded.

"So that's what I'm going to do," she said. "Unless anyone has any arguments, I'm going to stay put. For now. I'm going to learn, *you're* going to learn, we're going to get stronger and better, and... Truth? I'm going to go. Someday. I don't know when. But not tomorrow."

"Library," Sasha said, not looking up.

"Need more than that," Hanson said, and Sasha glanced up so quickly she couldn't have seen anything.

"Library on lab days, Wednesdays, we meet. I'll put together... stuff... curriculum. We'll go through our classes for the week and we'll... figure it out. Figure it out with natural magic and... It changes *everything*."

"Gonna take your word on that," Ethan said. "I'm not sure I can *use* natural magic. I'm too dark."

Sasha looked up at him with real exasperation.

"Don't you *get* it? They're *independent*. It isn't a balance that tells you how *good* or *bad* you are. They're families of magic, and we have *never* discussed how natural magic even *fits*. You could still be *strongest* in natural magic, Ethan."

Something about his posture changed, like a weight had come off of him, and Valerie looked at him, trying to read him.

He was blinking at Sasha, not even seeing Valerie.

Which didn't happen very often.

"All right," Shack said. "So. We're all staying. Nobody is leverage. We get to be the best of the best of the best, and then we go back out there and we own them all. All of them everywhere. Settled?"

"Yeah," Hanson said. "If I even can."

"Don't talk like that," Sasha said dismissively without looking up. "I'm in."

"Yeah," Ethan said softly. Valerie nodded.

"Me, too."

"You didn't promise yet," Shack said, and she frowned.

"Right," she said. She considered this with real weight, trying to figure out if she *could* ignore threats to any of them and keep doing her own thing. She had to. Susan Blake *said* she had to. Valerie nodded.

"Okay," she said finally. "Right. I promise."

"Good," Shack said with an easy smile. "Who's hungry?"

The End

More Fiction by Chloe Garner

Urban Fantasy

In the **Sam and Sam Series** an evasive Samantha joins Sam and Jason as they travel the country hunting that which would otherwise hunt people. As they work together and grow their skills they soon find they're players in a game they didn't even realize existed.

<u>Rangers</u>
<u>Shaman</u>
<u>Psychic</u>
<u>Warrior</u>
<u>Dragonsword</u>
<u>Child</u>
<u>Gorgon</u>
<u>Gone to Ground</u>
<u>Civil War</u>

To call Carter Samantha's mentor would be wrong. He wants nothing to do with her. He wants nothing to do with anybody. When she showed up at his apartment looking for answers about the death of her family, though, he turns her into the type of woman who can get her own justice.

<u>Book of Carter</u>

The Makkai lead a nomadic life, traveling as a tribe, going where they are needed and solving problems that only they can.

<u>Gypsy Becca: Death of a Gypsy Queen</u>
<u>Gypsy Dawn: Life of a Gypsy Queen</u>
<u>Gypsy Bella: Legacy of a Gypsy Queen</u>

Science Fiction

Monte and the crew of his ship The Kingfisher keep ending up in the middle of some of the galaxy's biggest problems.

Following Cassie, an analyst and former jumper at the Air Force's portal base in Kansas we chase foreign terrestrial (you know, space alien) Jessie to other planets. This is about as sci-fi as it gets, with a side helping of military politics.

Sarah Todd is the law in Lawrence, a mostly abandoned mining town at the end of the rail line. But when a new deposit of absenta is found trouble starts pouring into town. Mostly in the form of Jimmy Lawson, head of the Lawson clan and the former enforcement in town.

ABOUT THE AUTHOR

I'm Chloe and I am the conduit between my dreaming self and the paper (well, keyboard, since we live in the future). I write paranormal, sci-fi, fantasy, and whatever else goes bump in the night, I also write mystery/thriller as Mindy Saturn. When I'm not writing I steeplechase miniature horses and participate in ice cream eating contests. Not really, but I do tend to make things up for a living.

I have a newsletter that goes out about twice a month with promotions on my books and other authors' books, cover reveals, book releases, and freebies from me. It's a great way to discover a lot of new writers and find your next favorite series. Check out my website, for more info.

www.blenderfiction.wordpress.com

Printed in Great Britain
by Amazon

37635171R10175